The Iron Gate

Book Two of the Iron Soul Series

J.M. Briggs

J.M. Briggs

Contents

Dedication

For Aunt Janice and Uncle Hartwig.

I am so grateful for all your love and support over the years.
You have been an amazing part of my life, and I wish
I had the words to express how much you mean to me.

1

Magic Spark

—⚬—

Magic sparked in Alex's hand, tiny flickers of dark silver jumping between her fingers as she turned her palm upward slowly. She could feel her connection to the Earth pulsing deep in her chest, feeding her the energy of the realm and merging with her life force to power the sparks. After weeks of frustration and being unable to use magic, Alex felt awe as she forced more sparks of magic into being. Smiling, she ignored the fatigue that was beginning to creep through her system as she mentally commanded the sparks together, imagining an orb like the one she'd created in the dark tunnels of the Sídhe. In a rush of color as the sparks came together, an orb appeared in her hand, and Alex shivered at the thrum of energy against her skin.

She was fascinated by the pulse of the magic in her palm, remembering how only five days ago she had first used her magic to fight back the Sídhe. Alex had to contain a shudder at the memory of her capture by the Sídhe Riders and waking up in the underground tunnels that they used to enter Earth from their own world. It was nothing like the fairies that her five-year-old self ever would have imagined, but Alex was quickly learning that fairy tales had almost nothing to do with the reality she now found herself in.

"Good," Morgana's voice said, jarring Alex from her thoughts.

Alex looked up to find the dark-haired college professor Morgana Cornwall, also known as Morgana le Fey watching her with a small pleased smile. It was a rare expression on the usually stoic woman, but Alex saw genuine pleasure in Morgana's dark green eyes that boosted her confidence. They were both sitting on the floor in a small classroom in the Kittell building, just down the hall from the others and Merlin. So far, the private magic lesson and assessment of her magical powers seemed to be going well, and Morgana's praise allowed Alex to relax a little.

"Your control is remarkably good," Morgana said as Alex shifted out of the meditative position they'd settled into. "Especially given how difficult your form of magic is to visualize."

"What exactly is my form of magic?" Alex asked, her eyes dropping back to the orb resting in her palm.

Morgana raised an eyebrow in surprise, but answered the question calmly, "Energy, Alex, you are controlling your magic as pure energy rather than giving it an elemental form or just willing an effect. It is a bit unusual."

"But your magic looks a lot like this." Alex raised the orb in a gesture towards Morgana.

"I visualize my magic as light," Morgana explained. "Merlin and I can both use magic as raw energy, but we both started with a more... understandable form." Morgana smiled, and her eyes moved to the orb. "Judging from your description of the fight in the tunnels if sounds like you even can influence energy released by others. That is something I have not seen before, and it could be advantageous."

"Oh," Alex replied slowly, not fully understanding as her eyes dropped to the orb. It was becoming uncomfortable in her hand, the thrum giving her goosebumps up her right arm.

"Disperse the energy," Morgana instructed, "without unleashing it."

"What do you mean?"

"Allow it to seep back into the world," Morgana explained patiently. "Don't use it to attack, just let it go. It is important that you can not only gather the energy but also release it if you no longer need it."

Alex nodded her understanding and looked back to the orb. While she understood what Morgana was saying, she'd only ever thrown her magic at the Sídhe. Closing her eyes, Alex felt the tug of her magic and the sparks in the orb pulsing with power. She tried to imagine it seeping away like water, but the energy just seemed to become fluid. Opening her eyes, she found the orb melting into a pool of dark silver in her hand. In front of her, Morgana chuckled but said nothing. Alex closed her eyes and visualized the orb once again, trying to bring the energy back into a form she was familiar with. A strand of her long blonde hair escaped her braid and fell into her face, but Alex ignored the urge to push it back.

Alex was still as she pondered the problem. Nicki used water that was around her and didn't have to release it. Aiden simply had to will the fire to go out, and Bran just stopped moving whatever he'd been using his magic on. Looking down at the orb, Alex nibbled at her bottom lip and tried to ignore the gaze of Professor Cornwall as she considered the problem. She didn't want to risk doing the lightning bolt thing, as cool as it was to see, it could hurt anyone around her. Thinking of it like water had only turned the orb into fluid. Her mind went back to watching the Sídhe and Hounds die, the way they just dissolved. Focusing on the orb, Alex did her best to imagine it slowly falling apart and blowing away like a Síd. There was a moment of resistance as the magic pulsed, but slowly the orb began to dissolve in specks of dark silver that faded into the air.

Releasing a slow breath, Alex lowered her hand once the last of the orb had faded. She felt exhausted, and the muscles in her back were now tense despite the meditation at the beginning of the magic lesson. Her leg was beginning to ache from sitting on the floor and now that she wasn't so focused on using her magic, Alex had to resist the urge to scratch at the itchy stitches.

"Good," Morgana said. The professor stood up and held down a hand to help Alex to her feet. "You'll need to practice that; otherwise, there is too much of a risk of you harming your allies. Remember that offensive magic is not just a danger due to the form it takes, but the mere collision of one being's energy with another being."

"What about controlling other energy?" Alex asked as she leaned over to grab her bag from a nearby desk. "How did I do that in the tunnels?"

She had been wondering that for days. When the Sídhe attacked she'd been able to stop their magical blasts and turn them back on the casters. Alex had no doubt it was the reason she was still alive.

"I suspect that was largely survival instinct kicking in," Morgana told her. "Focus on controlling your energy first and dispersing it safely. Then we will start experimenting to see what limitations you have on controlling energy."

"So, it might just be Sídhe energy I can control?"

"I doubt that. I haven't seen magic take this form before, Alex, but I highly doubt that you are limited in that fashion."

That confession made Alex's stomach turn with nerves. She'd been afraid that Morgana would say something like that after the strange expression her first demonstration had gotten. Morgana said something else that Alex missed, and she blinked at the professor.

"I'm sorry what?" Alex asked sheepishly.

"I said sit down, and I'll check the stitches in your leg," Morgana repeated.

Nodding, Alex sat down on top of the nearby desk and shifted so she could pull up the leg of her jeans. She maneuvered it carefully, trying to avoid dragging the denim over the stitches. Looking away when the red curve of stitches came into view, Alex focused on the notes written on the room's whiteboard. Morgana set a hand on Alex's ankle and made a small sound of consideration. It had only been five days since she fought her way out of the tunnels and Morgana had tended to her injuries, but it already felt to Alex that she'd been hiding the injury from Jenny for weeks. She did her best to stay still and hoped for some good news.

"It's healing nicely," Morgana remarked with a nod. "On Saturday I want you to come to my house to have them removed." Giving Alex a small smile, Morgana told her, "I'll even use a little magic to help prevent a scar."

"I thought you said you only used it in the most desperate of situations?"

"Usually," Morgana confessed with a chuckle. "But the ebb of magic is high, and I used medicine to heal the worst of the damage. I can spare a little magical energy. Besides, you earned it." The older mage fiddled with her triskele pendant as she stepped away from Alex.

Nodding in relief, Alex pulled her jeans back down to cover the injury carefully. Morgana's tone rang with gratitude and relief. Alex knew that the professor was thinking of the children that she'd rescued from the tunnels during Imbolc. She'd saved them from becoming slaves to the Sídhe like Morgana had been during her youth almost three thousand years ago.

Morgana waited for her to climb off the desk before she turned and strode towards the door with Alex following. Walking in silence, they returned to the door of the primary classroom they used for magic lessons. Alex could barely believe that it had only been three months since she'd found out that magic was real and she was a part of a war across magical realms. When she'd started her freshman year of college, she'd expected some changes and new challenges, but nothing like this.

Morgana paused in front of the door and waved her hand, releasing the protective spell that Merlin had placed on it. The door swung open without Morgana touching it. Looking inside, Alex could see the others practicing their magic and Merlin watching with a smile as he sat on top of the teacher's desk. Morgana moved inside, but Alex paused to watch Aiden shape a small ball of fire in his hands into a rough looking horse. The fire highlighted his dark hair and his brown eyes were glowing with glee as he played with the flames. Nearby, Nicki was swaying with large bubbles of water floating around her and following the movements of her hands. Her friend's auburn braids were moist from where her twirling had crashed with the bubbles, but Nicki didn't seem concerned.

Sitting at a nearby desk with his wooden cane propped up next to him was Bran who was staring at dozens of small candies which were floating in the air and writing out an equation. Twitching his hand, he brought one of them towards him and into his mouth. At the front of the classroom, sitting on the edge of the large desk was Merlin also known as Professor Ambrose Yates. Merlin was humming softly to himself as he wrote in a small notebook. He was wearing his usual tweed jacket, and his triskele pin was gleaming in the light of the classroom.

Morgana moved over to Merlin, gaining his attention with a small cough. Nicki jumped at the sound but kept the fluid masses of water in the air. Aiden waved his hand, and the fire vanished in a small puff of smoke. Glancing over at them, Bran began to lower the candies in the air and held open a bag for them to slowly fly into.

"How did it go?" Merlin asked, looking past Morgana at Alex.

"Adequate," Morgana replied. "It will take time, but her power has great potential once she gains more control."

"It went fine," Alex answered.

"Excellent." Merlin winked at Alex.

He gestured to the row of desks where Bran was seated. Alex moved over to join the others, and they sat down. Morgana crossed her arms over her chest and watched them patiently. Nicki grinned at Alex and gave her a questioning look, but Morgana cleared her throat, cutting off anything else Nicki may have said.

"You've all made your connections to your magic and the power of Earth itself," Merlin said with a beaming smile. "I know that February 2nd was an intense day for you all, especially you, Alex, but you all performed beyond my expectations." A smile tugged at Alex's lips despite her exhaustion. "Many mages do not learn how to access their magic so quickly. Remember even when you are frustrated that you have already achieved a great feat."

Next to Alex, Nicki shifted in her desk and raised her hand. Merlin chuckled, and Aiden snorted, but Morgana nodded to Nicki.

"When will the Hounds return?" Nicki asked, lowering her hand.

"Merlin and I were able to sever the Sídhe's connection between the tunnel entrance and our realm, but most of the tunnel's magic is intact." Morgana didn't sound like she was talking about a magical invading army that had already enslaved whole worlds. "I estimate that they will repair the connection enough to send the Hounds through once again in late March. The Sídhe Riders will be able to pass through sometime in May, potentially Beltane if they devote their magic to the repairs."

"Beltane is May 1st," Merlin added quickly. "The next seasonal day when their powers on Earth are at their peak." He looked at Alex. "And remember that it starts at sundown, not at midnight."

Alex flushed and nodded. It had been her forgetting the sundown rule that had resulted in her being captured by the Sídhe. It wasn't a mistake she'd make again.

"Is there anything else we can do to slow them down?" Aiden asked from down the row of desks.

"I'm afraid not," Merlin replied with a sigh. "Once Morgana and I cut the connection we cannot affect the tunnels until the tunnel is reformed and stable. Remember that the Hounds do not need a completely stable doorway to pass through."

"Will it be in the same place?" Bran asked. "Can we guard the entrance on Beltane to keep the Riders from attacking any people or trying to kidnap children again?"

"The tunnel entrance will probably be close, but I doubt it will reappear in the same location," Morgana answered.

Alex frowned, barely containing a shiver at the memory of the dark stone tunnels that the Sídhe used to make the transition between their world and hers. When Morgana had told her that she and Merlin had severed the connection she'd thought that it might be over for a brief moment. And just yesterday, Merlin and Morgana had told her even more about the war in which she was now a warrior. Not only was Earth connected to twenty-eight other worlds via magical roads that bound them together, but there was a unique human soul that was the protector of Earth, the Iron Realm. Worse yet, it was the guy she had a crush on who was dating her roommate. She hadn't had time to wrap her head around that just yet and all the ramifications but knew she'd have to tell the others soon.

"I think that is enough for tonight," Merlin announced as his eyes settled on Alex who was pale from exhaustion. "Alex is still recovering from her battle in the tunnels." He looked at the others and added, "I trust that you aren't interrogating her. You will be told everything in due time. Morgana and I are planning to go back to the tunnel entrance and check the protections we put in place soon. When we're ready, we would like you four to accompany us."

Nodding in relief, Alex collected her coat from her desk and pulled it on without a word. She readjusted her bag and double checked that her dagger was accessible. Around her, the others were pulling on their coats and gathering their things with Nicki stealing some of Bran's candy. Aiden and Bran were both shooting Alex curious looks, and she barely contained a sigh. They'd been very patient with her telling them about what happened in the tunnels over the last five days, but there were always more questions. Alex forced a smile and said goodbye to Morgana and Merlin before starting out of the room. Nicki skipped to join her with the boys close behind.

Morgana remained silent, leaning against the large teacher's desk, as the four college students marched out of the room. She could hear voices echoing down the empty hallway as the questions began anew. Behind her, Merlin silently erased the notes he'd made on the board throughout the session. He sat down in the creaky chair behind the desk. They were both quiet for a long moment, gathering their thoughts before Merlin waved his hand towards the door. It closed with a soft click, and a soft blue field covered the doorway, sealing it.

"What do you think?" He asked Morgana softly, resting his elbows on the desk.

"Her powers are interesting, Ambrose," Morgana informed him without turning around as her hand moved to her triskele pendant. "They all have strong potential, one of the best groups we've ever had."

"I agree," Merlin replied with a cheerful tone that quickly faded. "But other issues need addressing."

"Indeed. At least the police have followed the trail you made for them out of town."

"That went in our favor." Merlin folded his hands in front of him. "If they continue to follow the trail then with any luck it will go cold near the Canadian border. I was careful to give the impression that while kidnapping attempts were made, there were no children actually in danger."

"The authorities may operate on the assumption that there are," Morgana reminded him with a sigh. "I regret the need to waste their resources."

"As do I," Merlin admitted. "But there is still a chance that someone will see something and accept it for what it really is. I still find it hard to believe that all the witnesses believed the Hounds were normal dogs. This age of cameras could be very dangerous for us. While most dismiss magic as primitive beliefs, there are always those with open minds."

They were both silent, lost in thought until Morgana spoke once again, "What have you observed recently with Arthur Pendred?"

"It goes well," Merlin replied. "He is... exactly what I've been hoping for. There is power in him that seems ready to manifest fully when the need arises. The fact that only Alex has formed a Connection with him thus far worries me a bit. I don't like the idea that something is interfering with or wrong with his magic, but otherwise, he strikes me as an intelligent young man, athletic, and good-tempered." Merlin looked over at Morgana's back, watching as she tensed. "Arthur reminds me of Arto when he was that age. His mannerism and easy charm are so much like..." Merlin trailed off and slumped back in the chair. "Although I am not certain how he will handle the revelation when the time comes."

"Alex is smitten with him," Morgana observed with a frown. "That could become an issue."

"Or it may be the saving grace," Merlin countered. "From what I've seen he is very fond of Alex in return. When his relationship with Jennifer comes to its conclusion, then Alex may be able to stabilize the situation. She is a link between the life he knows now and the truth."

"If he is still alive when the betrayal passes, Ambrose," Morgana reminded him sharply. She breathed in slowly and murmured, "But I worry about putting too much on the girl. She has not settled from her experience in the tunnels, and her magic has aspects that we aren't familiar with. Putting her into too many difficult situations may cause her harm or cause an accident with her magic."

"You've become very fond of her," Merlin observed with a soft smile. "It's been some time since you were so taken with a student."

"She reminds me of myself in a way."

"Really?" Merlin blinked and shook his head. "I don't see it, but I suppose you know yourself best, Morgana."

"Indeed." Morgana pushed herself off the desk. She turned to look at Merlin and added, "The others are gaining control faster than I expected. This group is certainly talented, but we must keep control of the situation."

"Agreed, we need to form some plans for dealing with the Sídhe. They will repair the tunnel soon enough."

"The students need more information," Morgana said. "I suspect that Alex will talk to them about the Iron Soul soon. Once she does, allowing them to ask their questions freely is the next step."

Merlin leaned back in his chair, giving Morgana a calculating look before saying, "I'm not sure I agree with your idea of having Alex tell them about the Iron Soul."

"Alex has the potential to be a great mage. Having her tell the others about the Iron Soul gives Alex a chance to assert herself. They need to trust each other and work together." Morgana frowned and shook her head. "You know that we can't always be there, Ambrose."

"Perhaps not," Merlin agreed sadly. "But a question session should be particularly interesting with Nicole. I wonder if she has a list of questions ready to ask."

"Even if she doesn't, I suspect that she will still manage," Morgana said with a raised eyebrow. Her fingers fiddled with her pendant and Merlin glanced at the triskele thoughtfully before reaching down to his satchel.

Merlin withdrew a thermos and two small cups, making Morgana smile. She turned and gestured to a chair at the side of the room. It floated off the ground and flew over to her, landing on the floor with a soft sound just before Morgana calmly sat down on it. Chuckling, Merlin poured her a cup of tea and handed it to her. They both raised their cups in a silent toast and took a sip, each lost in their thoughts.

2

Healing a Wound

A lex's blue car came to a slow halt in the driveway of a large gray Victorian house with white trim. Dark clouds churned overhead, threatening more snow as Alex climbed out of the car and looked up at the house. Even when she'd found out about magic and mages being the protectors of Earth against invaders from other worlds, she hadn't been to Professor Cornwall's house. Now in less than a week, this would be her third visit. Stepping onto the front porch, Alex adjusted her bag and rang the doorbell, trying not to squirm. The door opened after a few moments, and Professor Cornwall nodded to Alex, gesturing her inside.

"How is your leg feeling?" Morgana asked

"Itchy." Alex resisted the urge to scratch the long curve of stitches.

"It could have been much worse," Morgana reminded Alex as she started moving down a hallway towards the back of the house. "When a Hound gets ahold of a body part, they rarely let go."

"It didn't let go." Alex followed the professor. "It died after I stabbed it with a blood-covered sword." Alex paused and considered, "or was it the dagger?"

"It doesn't matter." Morgana chuckled as they stepped through a large archway and into the kitchen.

Alex paused at the doorway and took the room in. It was a large space with an island dominating the center and white counters and cabinets.

Old fashioned looking bottles filled one set of white shelves and herbs were hanging from the ceiling drying. Several potted plants filled the windowsill of the large window that looked out into the backyard and to the forest beyond.

"Alex," Morgana called, regaining her attention. "Sit down."

Morgana gestured to a chair that was sitting next to a long small table. Alex sat down and carefully pulled up the leg of the sweatpants she'd decided to wear today. At Morgana's request, she toed out of her sneaker and raised her leg. Morgana adjusted the table and Alex set her leg down, exposing the semicircle of stitches to Morgana.

Her professor vanished behind Alex for a moment before returning with a standing lamp which Morgana positioned to put more light on the stitches. Alex turned her attention back to studying the room, not wanting to see the wound in her leg. She could hear the professor moving around a bit more before another chair was pulled up to her and Morgana sat down.

"Just stay still, Alex," Morgana told her. "This won't take long. There will be a slight tug as I pull out the stitches. If you need me to stop, just let me know." The tone was gentler than how Morgana usually spoke, and for the first time since learning it, Alex wasn't surprised that Morgana had been a practicing medical doctor.

The Professor set a hand on her leg, holding it steady and waited as Alex took a deep breath. Closing her eyes, Alex heard the snip which echoed in the stillness of the kitchen. There was another snip and then another. Alex did her best to stay still and tried to ignore the sound, but her mother wasn't here to distract her like she had been last time Alex needed stitches. Breathing deeply, Alex used the meditation techniques that Morgana and Merlin had taught her to regain some control. The snipping stopped, and Alex tried to relax rather than tense up. There was a gentle tug in the skin of the leg which only lasted a few seconds. There was another tug and then another. Alex kept herself from counting and kept breathing slowly, curling her fingers around the seat of the chair to anchor herself.

"Stitches are out," Morgana announced a moment later, sounding pleased. "No signs of infection and the scarring can be cleared up with healing magic."

Alex nodded and took in another deep breath. She'd only experienced healing magic once after she'd sliced her hand during a fight with the Sídhe Hounds. At the time Merlin and Morgana had discouraged the use of healing magic but agreed to teach them in case of emergency. Nicki had healed her hand but had been left almost unconscious from the effort. Alex herself had been so drained by the conversion of Nicki's magical energy that she barely remembered anything. Aiden had even teased her about the strange things she'd said as he took her home that night.

"Relax," Morgana commanded. "I've done this before."

Exhaling, Alex stayed still and tried to relax her tense muscles as Morgana placed both her hands over the wound. She felt a small spark of magic hit her skin, feeling like an electric shock and fought the urge to flinch. Closing her eyes, Alex gripped the seat of the chair once again and breathed slowly as Morgana began to pour more magic into her leg. Alex's skin tingled softly as a sense of discomfort washed over her. Alex resisted the urge to shudder and scratch at her skin as it began to feel too tight. It almost tickled her, just at the level where she could feel it, but not yet causing laughter.

When Nicki had healed her, there had been a sense of exhaustion creeping up on her which was absent. Alex dismissed it as Morgana simply being better practiced in healing magic despite her and Merlin's instructions to use it only in the most desperate circumstances. Nicki's effort had been successful, but Alex had been forced to push away Nicki's magic herself when the redhead had lost control. Much of the process was a blurry memory as Alex had been left disoriented and exhausted when the cut in her hand had been healed.

Alex risked opening her eyes as the light began to shine through her eyelids. Barely holding in a gasp of awe, Alex studied Morgana whose entire attention was on Alex's leg. A bright silvery aura surrounded the professor, causing her triskele pendant to look like it was glowing. The light swirled tightly around the professor with small sparks around her head giving Alex the impression of a halo. A sudden need to scratch her leg made Alex grit her teeth and hiss. Morgana's grip on her leg kept Alex from managing more than a small movement, and she tightened her grasp on the seat of the chair, fighting the instinct to move. Closing her eyes again, Alex struggled to keep her breathing even as the itching became worse. After a few moments, Alex felt more in control and looked down towards the wound.

The long curve of pale pink and red across her thigh surrounded with purple bruises was shining under the light of the lamp as silver magic began to flow over it like a thick ointment. Morgana's swirling magic almost looked solid to Alex's eyes, glistening as the sparks caught the light. A sudden stinging sensation made Alex hiss again, but she kept her eyes focused on the wound as the magic seeped into her skin.

The raised bumps of flesh left by the stitches began to take on the silver color of Morgana's magic. Breathing deeply, Alex fought to stay still as the stinging sensation worsened, but noticed a moment later that the skin around the wound was beginning to smooth out. The vivid purple bruising faded slowly back to Alex's natural skin tone. Morgana exhaled slowly, and the small red marks of the stitches smoothed out and faded in color. More skin shifted and smoothed, the thin red line where the stitches had held her skin together fusing the rest of the way in a series of small sparks of silver and light.

Alex gasped painfully as the magic suddenly pulled back from her, feeling like she'd been on a rollercoaster that suddenly came to a stop. Morgana was panting, the sound filling the kitchen and Alex looked over to see the older mage's hands shaking. The flow of magic eased away from Alex more gently now, and Alex could see the light surrounding Morgana fading away. Slowly, her professor lifted her hands from Alex's leg and slumped back in her chair.

Leaning forward, Alex ran a hand over the smooth crescent patch of skin that was bare of hair or any sign of injury. She almost laughed as she felt her skin go from slightly hairy to silky smooth. Her eyes landed on the tools Morgana had used to remove the stitches and the small bits of black nylon. Pulling down her pants leg, Alex swung her leg off the table and turned her attention to Morgana.

Her professor was slumped in the chair, breathing slowly and deeply with her hands clasped together over her chest. Standing up, Alex pushed her chair back and carefully slid the table away from Morgana's chair. She looked through the far archway in the kitchen that led to the dining room and connected with the living room, trying to judge the distance.

"Professor Cornwall," Alex called. She reached out, placing a hand on the professor's shoulder. "Morgana?" Green eyes fluttered open to look at her and Alex gave Morgana a small smile. "Can I help you into the living room?"

Morgana groaned softly but managed a small nod. To Alex's relief, the Professor shifted slightly to the side and gave Alex room to maneuver her shoulder under Morgana's arm. Standing slowly, Alex helped Morgana to her feet and moved towards the living room with slow steps as the professor leaned on her. Alex resisted the urge to speed up the pace as the weight of the professor on her right side became uncomfortable halfway through the dining room. She carefully shifted their bodies so that when she released Morgana, the older mage slid down onto the long red sofa. Sighing, Morgana leaned her head on one of the red throw pillows placed by the armrest.

"Okay," Alex groaned, rolling her shoulder and stretching.

She moved forward and helped Morgana raise her legs onto the sofa, letting the woman stretch out. After a moment of hesitation, Alex tugged off Morgana's black loafers and set them next to the sofa. Moving through the room, Alex turned off two of the lamps and made sure that the blinds were closed, dimming the room significantly. She returned to the kitchen and after a few tries found where Morgana kept the glasses. Filling one with water, Alex set it on the small side table near Morgana's head.

"Alex?" Morgana called startling Alex, her eyes fluttering open. "How is your leg?"

"My leg is fine," Alex replied, trying to calm down from her surprise. "Thank you."

"Good," Morgana sighed, setting her head back onto the pillow. "That's good."

"Yeah." Alex watched her professor curl up on the sofa. "I'm meeting the others this afternoon to tell them about the Iron Soul."

"The Iron Soul," Morgana murmured, her eyes opening. "I miss Arto."

"I'm sorry," Alex replied slowly, feeling a knot in her stomach beginning to form. "It must have been hard to lose him."

"He was all I had left," Morgana sighed, staring off into space. "I know that Gwenyvar didn't mean to hurt him, but he felt so alone. Arto loved everyone around him so fiercely. He wanted to save them, wanted to protect them... The army was scattered by the general fleeing. The Queen pushed us so hard..." Tears welled up in Morgana's eyes, and the professor sniffed. "Feels like it was just yesterday sometimes. I feel like I could walk through the woods and I'd find a roundhouse with Arto inside. Airril would be there too, laughing."

"Who was Airril?" Alex asked before she thought better of it.

"My first husband," Morgana answered, her voice tight and pained. "He deserved better than me. I was never around after Arto and Merlin came. I wonder if he ever resented them for me leaving."

"I'm sorry," Alex whispered, standing up and looking around the room for a blanket or throw. It felt like she should leave, but Professor Cornwall seemed exhausted and not herself.

"My own fault," Morgana snapped, her voice taking on a harsh tone. "Yet, the Sídhe never paid for it, not really. All the things they did and we couldn't punish them." A snarl escaped her teacher. "I wanted them to. I liked how they suffered in the Norselands when they tried to return. I hoped that the corruption would spread into their realm and they'd understand even some of the pain they caused." A small muffled sob escaped Morgana and Alex pretended not to hear it.

Alex risked opening a large attractive wooden chest at the side of the room and sighed in relief when she found a stack of blankets inside. She grabbed the top one, a thick quilt with faded patches of embroidery and carried it over to Morgana. The professor was whispering under her breath, too softly for Alex to hear as she unfurled the blanket and laid it over the professor. Morgana's words faded as her eyes slid shut. Alex was still and waited for Morgana's breathing to even out.

Pulling out her phone, Alex scrolled through her contacts until she came to the number for Yates. She sighed softly, but hit the call button and waited for him to pick up the phone. A few moments later, Merlin's warm voice washed over Alex with a gentle. "Hello, Alex, what can I do for you?"

"Professor, I'm at Morgana's house," Alex explained. "She just removed my stitches."

"Indeed," Merlin replied. "That's good to hear. I hope that it doesn't scar too badly."

"Uh," Alex paused nervously. "She used healing magic to finish healing the wound. There's no scar at all."

"I see," Merlin said much more slowly, his tone irritated, but resigned. "She did not tell me she was planning to use healing magic."

Alex's nervousness only grew, and she felt like a snitch. It sounded like Morgana had broken the rules against using healing magic for her. "Well, she seems very tired," Alex informed him quickly. "I just wanted to make sure that she'll be okay on her own or do I need to stay with her?"

"She'll be fine," Merlin assured Alex. "Nicole recovered with no trouble once she had some rest. Just lock the house up, and Morgana will be alright."

"Are you sure?" Alex asked, glancing over at Morgana who was sound asleep and breathing deeply.

"The tunnel has been severed so nothing dangerous can come through," Merlin reminded Alex, his tone becoming more soothing. "Additionally, Morgana's home was constructed with iron in the doorframes and window frames. She is quite safe. If it makes you feel better, I will check on her this afternoon."

"Are you sure?" Alex asked. "Do you have a key?"

Merlin chuckled and replied, "Morgana and I have known each other for nearly three thousand years. It is very safe to say that we have spare keys to each other's homes."

"Okay then." Alex nibbled at her lower lip. "I'll leave her to rest then."

"Yes," Merlin agreed, "That's a good idea."

"I'll see you next week then."

"Alex," Merlin called before she could hang up. "One more thing, if Morgana said anything in her exhaustion... well, don't bring it up. I'm sure she didn't mean to..."

"She hasn't said anything," Alex lied as she moved towards the front door. Merlin knew it was a lie but calmly accepted her statement.

"Very well then," Merlin answered. "I will see you in class on Monday."

"Of course, Professor Yates," Alex agreed. "See you Monday."

The call ended, and Alex slipped her phone back into her pocket as she reached for her jacket. She glanced back into the living room one more time to make sure that Professor Cornwall was still sleeping comfortably. Alex stopped and looked at the professor for a long moment before she shook her head and opened the front door. As she pulled out her car keys, Alex made sure to lock the professor's door behind her.

3

Leaving Home

8 11 B.C.E. Somerset Levels

The tension in the roundhouse felt heavy as Morgana tightened the cord of the large bag she'd just finished packing with spare clothing and supplies. She'd left many of her personal items sitting on the shelves and was already wondering if she'd ever see them again. Taking a deep breath, Morgana swung the bag over her head, positioning the strap across her body and allowing the weight to settle comfortably in the small of her back. She turned towards the door of the roundhouse and swallowed when she found Airril still watching her silently. Morgana was grateful for his silence. Her explanation had been so short before she insisted that she was leaving with Merlin and Arto.

Morgana shifted uncertainly as Airril stepped closer to her and fought the urge to look away from his sad brown eyes. The only thing left to do was say goodbye to her husband. Calloused fingertips touched her cheek gently as Airril stepped right in front of her. She could feel his warmth and leaned into his touch, allowing herself a small sigh.

"I'm going to miss you, Morgana." Airril placed his other hand on her arm. Morgana could feel the warmth of his hand through the fabric of her sleeves. "I know that we were a trade alliance match," he said. "But we've made a good pair."

Nodding, Morgana swallowed as tears pricked at her eyes. That surprised her; she hadn't expected to feel so emotional about leaving. When Merlin had suggested she join him and Arto in their travels to fight against the Sídhe, she'd agreed that it was the rational choice. It would allow her to protect Arto and learn more about what her magic could do. She had no children and thus hadn't hesitated to accept the invitation. Now she was starting to feel the weight of leaving behind the village and people she'd known for years.

Throwing her arms around his neck, Morgana pulled herself tightly against Airril. Strong arms came up around her and held her close as Airril softly spoke to her, but Morgana didn't hear the words. She focused on memorizing his smell and listening to the beat of his heart under her ear. They stood like that, Airril running a hand down her back underneath her long dark braid and kissing the top of her head softly between gentle words of comfort.

"I'm going to miss you too," Morgana managed to say despite the tightness in her throat.

"I know," Airril assured her, speaking more loudly now. "What you are doing is important. If Merlin is right and you are a mage then learning to control your abilities is important."

Morgana nodded against his chest, her stomach twisting at the reminder of the edited truth they'd provided her husband with. There was a temptation to tell him everything, tell him about being raised by the Sídhe and her struggle with her loyalties, but Morgana couldn't bear the thought of how he might react. The arm around her tightened, and Airril kissed her temple before he released her. Morgana didn't resist the soft push he gave her to make her let go of her tight grip and stepped back. She brushed the tears away from her eyes quickly and coughed to clear her throat. Airril was smiling sadly at her, one of his dimples barely showing. Morgana's chest tightened; she was going to miss that smile.

"It will be alright, Morgana," Airril promised.

Morgana barely contained a huff at the words: her husband didn't fully understand what she would be facing. Instead, she forced a smile and nodded. "I'll try to visit." Morgana adjusted the bag over her shoulder. "Whenever we come back into the area. Please take care of yourself, Airril."

Airril nodded and stepped close to her once again, catching her chin in his hand. He tipped her face up and brushed their lips together in a soft caring kiss. The flap of the animal pelt that served as the door of their roundhouse alerted Morgana to the fact they were no longer alone. Pulling away from Airril, Morgana turned to see Merlin looking a bit sheepish with his gaze on the floor.

"Time to leave, I suppose." Morgana raised an eyebrow at the older mage who didn't meet her eyes.

"Indeed," Merlin replied. "Arto is waiting outside."

"I'll be just another moment," Morgana informed Merlin as she stepped closer to Airril.

Her husband chuckled and hugged her once again, kissing her forehead. His fingers brushed the cloak clasp that he'd given her and Morgana smiled, glad to have it as a memento.

"Take care, Morgana," Airril whispered into her hair before he took a step back from her.

Morgana took a slow breath and turned towards Merlin who was waiting near the doorway. Taking a step forward, she raised her chin and did her best to rein in her emotions. Merlin finally looked up from the floor as he heard her move. Her green eyes met his brown ones, and a rush of magic surged through her. Everything faded away as her knees felt weak and her body shuddered.

Morgana could smell a summer forest and feel the soft moisture of morning mist on her face. The wind blew through her hair, and she heard birds singing around her. She was overwhelmed by the smells, sounds, and sights, caught someplace other than where she was, but feeling peace and tranquility seeping into her bones.

"Morgana!" Airril's worried voice called, penetrating the fog of Morgana's vision.

Blinking, Morgana took in a deep breath, grateful for her husband's stabilizing arm around her waist. In front of her, Merlin blinked and shook his head before smiling warmly at her. Merlin moved his staff in front of his body and leaned forward on it, watching Morgana with a gentle expression.

"No need to fear, Airril," Merlin assured her husband. "It will pass in a moment."

Feeling more stable, Morgana gently pulled away from Airril's grasp and gave him a shaky smile before carefully looking back at Merlin. She braced herself, but the vision did not reoccur.

"Calm yourself, Morgana," Merlin told her cheerfully. Then he turned his attention to Airril who was struggling to stay still. "Morgana and I experienced a Connection," he explained calmly. "It occurs when two mages with similar magic look into each other's eyes. It only happens the first time, thankfully." He looked back to Morgana. "The power of the Iron Realm flows in you freely now with no conflicts," he added in a gentle voice.

Swallowing, Morgana nodded her understanding and tried not to smile. She took another step forward. When Airril set a hand on her shoulder, she dared not turn to look at him, but raised her hand and placed it over his for a moment.

"Morgana!" Arto's voice called from outside the roundhouse impatiently.

Shaking his head, Merlin gave Morgana an apologetic look. She nodded in understanding and squeezed Airril's hand before walking forward. His hand fell away, and she heard him make a small sound behind her. Against her better judgment, she paused at the doorway and looked back. Morgana forced a smile which he barely returned before she stepped out of their home.

Arto jumped to his feet with wide, excited brown eyes. His brown hair was a mess with twigs and grass in it from leaning against the roundhouse. Grinning at Morgana, he stepped towards her, and their eyes met. Morgana gasped softly and felt Merlin grip her arm as another vision rushed through her.

A strange dark metal orb gleamed in hot flames in front of her before its surface cracked. Molten orange spilled forth onto a smooth stone. She recognized it as similar to Arto's sword creation as she smelled the fire and charcoal before three heavy metallic clangs rang out.

Arto swayed on his feet in front of Morgana as she came back to herself. Her brother shook his head and then laughed with a wide smile. To her surprise, he didn't mention the strange vision, and Morgana distracted herself with turning her eyes towards the Sword strapped across his back. Morgana's eyes were drawn to the golden hilt which gleamed in the sunlight and her breath caught in her throat as she felt magic radiating from the blade. Arto grinned at her and reached back towards the blade.

"No, Arto," Merlin told him firmly, stepping up next to Morgana. "Do not draw that Sword lightly."

Morgana expected a protest from the young man, but instead, her brother nodded his understanding and glanced around at the villagers. Many were watching with interest, and Morgana swallowed thickly, suddenly uncomfortable.

"Come." Merlin's hand grasped Morgana's arm and gave it a light, comforting squeeze. "We need to be going."

"Where are we headed?" Morgana asked, her voice thinner and weaker than she liked.

"News came from the White Cliffs of Sídhe tunnels in the area," Arto told Morgana as they began walking towards the gates of the village.

"The White Cliffs," Morgana murmured. "That's on the other side of the isle."

"Indeed," Merlin agreed as he moved ahead of Morgana to lead the way. "But Arto and I are used to the travel: you will be soon. We're going south. From there we'll use a boat to travel around the shores."

"I've never traveled so far," Morgana admitted with a look at her brother who did not seem at all concerned about the distance.

"Oh, Morgana, I'd say that you have traveled further than most have," Merlin remarked with a chuckle. "And there is more ahead for you."

They passed through the gates, and Morgana's eyes swept the sturdy wooden walls, hoping that they would continue to protect her village. Looking over her shoulder, Morgana spotted Airril standing on the hill in front of their roundhouse watching her leave, with his long bronze sword grasped in one hand. She swallowed and turned her gaze forward again, ignoring the voices behind her growing stronger as the villagers spoke. Gradually the voices and sounds of the village faded as they moved further and further away. Ahead of them was the tor, rising out of the flat moors and Morgana shivered at the memory of the blood spell.

"The village will be safe," Merlin promised in front of Morgana, his eyes also on the tor. "Arto's spell will protect this area for many years."

"Really?" Arto asked, turning to look at Merlin and nearly tripping on a tuft of grass.

Smiling, Merlin nodded. "I cannot say for certain how long of course, but even now I can feel the magic here. The power of the Iron Realm is strong here, anchored by your power."

"So the Sídhe won't come here anymore?" Arto asked. Morgana looked hopefully at Merlin.

"My mother used the same spell as you and the Sídhe avoid my home village to this day." Merlin tilted his head and hummed softly. "That was twenty-three years ago," Merlin added before shaking his head. "I'm getting old."

"You don't look old," Arto informed his teacher.

Merlin laughed, patting the teenager on the shoulder. "Well, I'm not done with life just yet, my boy, too much to do." He looked over his shoulder at Morgana. "But you needn't worry about the village. The power of the tor will guard them against the Sídhe."

Morgana nodded and looked up at the tor as they began to ascend the hill. Stopping, Morgana turned and beheld the moor. The long, flooded valley stretched out before her with causeways linking small islands. She took in the scent of the distant ocean on the breeze. Her eyes found her village on one of the small rolling hills near the water's edge.

"I'm going to miss this place." Morgana breathed in the scent of the air.

"That is to be expected," Merlin told her, joining Morgana in looking over the valley. "This was your home."

"I missed my mother when I came here, but not the village," Morgana whispered. "I've never missed that place."

"All the memories made here were yours." Merlin placed a hand on her shoulder. "Nothing here was shared with the Changeling; no one here knew the Changeling that you once were. It is natural that it is harder to leave than your childhood home."

"Enough, Merlin." Morgana refused to look at him as she turned and began to walk, spotting Arto a ways ahead of them. Merlin said nothing and fell into step next to her. "I am fond of Airril," she told him a moment later. "And I will miss him."

"Ah love." Merlin grinned with another look towards Morgana.

She said nothing, tilting her head up to enjoy the warmth of the sunshine. Next to her, she heard Merlin chuckle again before he called to Arto to slow down and wait for them. The young man obeyed, coming to a stop and grinning at them as they walked towards him. Once they were all together, Arto slowed down to keep pace with Merlin and Morgana.

"Let's see," Merlin murmured. "I suppose I should tell you a bit more about magic. I don't imagine that the Queen shared many details of how the magic of the Iron Realm worked did she."

"No," Morgana agreed with a nod. "She did not."

"Well then, the magic of the Iron Realm is largely tied to the power of the world itself, although according to Cyrridven, it is possible to gain magical power in a few other ways, but we won't concern ourselves with that right now."

Morgana was tempted to hit the older man as he began to ramble about mages being born with the ability to connect with and control the powers of the Iron Realm. Sighing, Morgana rolled her shoulder and glanced towards Arto. The young man winked at her and nodded towards Merlin with a grin. Seeing that she wasn't alone in her boredom with the lecture, Morgana smiled in return. The siblings shared another look before turning their attention back to minding their footing, as they began to climb up a hillside, and listening to Merlin's words.

4

Truth and Myth

T he university's library was quiet with only a few students present, mostly graduate students judging from their ages and use of the rental storage desks. There were a couple of students shelving books that looked up as Alex passed them while she glanced into the different study rooms. She finally located the others in one of the small study rooms at the back of the third floor right beside the "B's" which housed the religion and mythology books.

The door was closed, but the large window allowed Alex to see the others hunched over several books and Nicki typing things into a propped-up tablet. Aiden and Nicki were on the side furthest from the door with Bran alone on the other side of the table, his cane propped up against him and the chair positioned to give his legs plenty of room allowing Alex to see his leg brace. She could just hear Nicki's voice as she read the book entry in front of her and allowed herself to focus on that for a moment while she gathered her courage.

"Brownies are small fairies that inhabit houses and do chores in the home. They don't like to be seen and work at night, traditionally in exchange for small gifts of food. These don't seem really dangerous, so I'll put them under other. Honestly, I'd sort of like to have one around."

"I'm imagining a dormitory with a Brownie," Aiden's voice was soft through the door. "I doubt it would consider only one room the territory to clean."

"And Gran's studio wouldn't work well either," Nicki joked in return. "She'd declare war on it for moving her tools and cleaning up her clay projects."

They lapsed into silence, and Alex reached for the door latch but didn't turn it. She was just out of view of the window now and kept staring at the latch, trying to figure out what to say when she still wasn't used to the truth that Merlin and Morgana had told her.

"I'm having a hard time figuring out what is ancient and what is medieval creation," Bran said. "That's when all the records are from."

"We'll have to confirm with the professors," Aiden replied. "I'm having the same issue. It's supposed to be Celtic, but that's a hundred years after the war, and then there are the changes from the oral tradition to the Christian monks who recorded all this."

Bran hummed in agreement. "Here's an entry on Redcaps. These are nasty, they murder people and dye their hats in the blood of their victims," Bran said before adding, "I don't think this is right. According to this, the Redcaps wield iron pikes; it also says that they will die if the red ever fades. The professors said that all the species of the Sídhe's empire were weak to iron."

"That might be a later mistake," Nicki said. "Maybe it was some kind of tradition non-Sídhe shock troops followed, or it could be a made-up creature or the red may have come from something else, but this is the story that developed."

Even a week ago, the conversation would have bothered Alex greatly, but after her experience in the tunnels, she understood the others' desire to know what they were up against. She was stalling, Alex chastised herself. They needed to know what was going on and standing outside out of view wasn't going to get that done. Taking a deep breath, Alex adjusted her bag and tried to force a smile before opening the door. Bran looked up at her first and nodded in greeting with Aiden giving her a small wave and a smile. Alex closed the door firmly behind her with a soft click and wished that there was a way to lock it.

Nicki kept frantically typing something. "Hi, Alex, just give me one second...and done." Nicki pulled her hands away from the tablet and looked up at Alex with a wide smile before she blinked and the smile turned to a frown. "What's wrong?"

Aiden moved to stand up from his position next to Nicki, but Alex headed towards the free chair next to Bran. Slipping off her bag and coat, Alex sank into the chair, uncomfortably aware of the others watching her.

"I've got something I have to tell you." Alex did her best to sound calm and in control. "Morgana and Merlin answered some questions for me on Wednesday and agreed that I should bring you up to speed." No one spoke, all three just watching and waiting. Alex's mouth felt dry, and she had to fight the urge to pull out her water bottle and drink it all down. Alex folded her hands in front of her, knowing that they wouldn't stay still for long, but wanting to seem calm. "The First War was tied to the creation of a special human soul; Morgana and Merlin called it the Iron Soul. It had the ability to draw power straight from the Earth and had power over iron. The first life was a man called Arto." Alex held up her hands as she talked, unsure of what to do with herself.

Nicki motioned for Bran and Aiden to be silent, a gesture that Alex caught in the corner of her eye and that bolstered her resolve. She took in a deep breath, licked her lips and forced herself to keep talking. "Merlin and Morgana didn't lie when they said there was no King Arthur, but what they didn't tell us at the start was that there was an ancient leader named Arto who led the first war against the Sídhe back in the Bronze Age. He had a special iron sword and everything."

Alex lowered her hands and waited for the others to take in her words. Next to her, Bran started to chuckle softly and shook his head. Across from him, Aiden snorted and began to laugh just before Nicki's nervous giggles started. Alex was irritated at first, but then a soft laugh escaped her chest, easing the twist of tension that had taken over her lungs.

"So, there is a King Arthur of sorts?" Aiden asked, wiping his eyes. "Are you serious?"

"Yeah," Alex answered with a firm nod before she giggled and shrugged. "He even had the special sword and united Britain against the Sídhe."

"Oh, so many Monty Python jokes so little time." Aiden sighed before shaking his head and turning serious. "It's Arthur Pendred, isn't it?"

"Right in one." Alex leaned onto her hand. "But, yes he's the latest incarnation of this magical soul that was created to save the world."

"And of course, he's a quarterback," Aiden huffed with a mock frown. "I don't know how I feel about that."

"I knew it," Nicki hissed, sounding triumphant and barely containing her excitement. "Having so many other mythological roots in their story, it just seemed too weird that they avoided the subject of Arthur." Now it was Aiden who calmed things down by reaching over and placing a firm hand on Nicki's shoulder to keep her from vibrating out of her seat.

"So, he can help us?" Bran toyed with his pen; his expression serious. "Are they going to train him to use his powers to fight as well, it sounds like he should be more powerful than us."

"Uh…" Alex hesitated. "Well, I think that long term they'll train him, but there's sort of a complication right now that has the professors worried."

"What is it?" Nicki asked, leaning forward eagerly.

"Jenny is Guinevere and Lance is Lancelot," Alex explained in a rush. "Those weren't their actual names. Hers was similar, but I don't remember his exactly," she rambled nervously at the stunned expressions she was getting. "According to the professors, they keep being reincarnated along with the Iron Soul but keep repeating the cycle of betrayal leading to the downfall of the Iron Soul whenever they are around. The professors are worried about it happening again now."

Taking a deep breath, Alex fell silent and clutched her hands together. The others were gaping at her, trying to determine if she was serious. Then Aiden gave a low whistle and sank back in his chair, shaking his head.

"That… is insane," he muttered, bringing a hand up to rub his face. "Every time?"

"That's what they said," Alex confirmed with a nod. "They aren't around in every life, but a lot of them, maybe a third of them."

"Reincarnation," Bran murmured, "I almost feel like I shouldn't be surprised by that entering this messy equation and yet I am." Bran paused and leaned on his hand with a thoughtful expression. "I suppose it confirms the notion of the soul, but it could also be proof of the Buddhist view of constant reincarnation and the inability to escape the sorrows of past lives." Bran's frown deepened, and he quietly added, "I wonder how that equates into the laws of physics… maybe some kind of energy that has events imprinted on it and is transferred. Or an undiscovered kind of particle."

"Something like that," Alex agreed to stop Bran's thought process and bring him back to the issue at hand. "At least the being unable to escape past sorrows bit." She swallowed thickly as the sinking feeling in her stomach returned.

Aiden's expression softened, and pity flashed over his face for a moment before he asked, "How are you coping with Jenny?"

"I'm not," Alex muttered, slumping back in her chair. "I've been avoiding her since Wednesday. I just..." Alex shrugged and huffed. "I don't know how to take the news. It's weird, she's just Jenny to me, but apparently, she's been all these other people, and for some reason, she keeps making the same mistake over and over again."

"Plus, your crush on Arthur," Bran observed with a deep frown earning him a harsh glare from Nicki that made him flinch back.

"God," Alex groaned, leaning over the table with her face in her hands. "Does everyone have to point that out?"

"Easy, Alex." Nicki reached across the table to squeeze her hand. "It's okay to be upset by this news; it's crazier than what we originally signed up for."

"And you haven't had an easy week," Aiden added gently. "Your friendship with Arthur, Lance, and Jenny can't make this easy."

"I'm sorry." Bran placed a hand on Alex's shoulder. "I didn't mean it as... coldly as it came out."

Alex brought her head up, swallowed quickly, and pushed a loose strand of blonde hair from her face with a nod. "I'm fine," she lied quickly. "You're right, they are my friends, and now I know something huge about them that they have no clue about. I'm not sure how to deal with it yet."

"Did Merlin and Morgana say anything about that?" Aiden asked.

"No," Alex replied with a shake of her head. "When they told me they were... fighting, I guess. There was some kind of disagreement between them, so I called our meeting short before it got too bad. Morgana did say that the cycle has happened twelve times, I guess this is the thirteenth time they've been reborn near the Iron Soul." Alex shifted uncomfortably, remembering the tense words between the professors, referencing things that she hadn't understood.

"Did the professors give you any indication of their personalities?" Bran asked her thoughtfully. "The original personalities, I mean?"

Shrugging, Alex turned her attention towards Bran. "Not really. I got the feeling that Morgana didn't like her, but Merlin said that was just her being Arto's big sister." Alex stumbled over the name Arto awkwardly, the instinct to say Arthur refusing to be shaken off.

"So, they might be different now or might be the same," Bran concluded, his frown deepening. Leaning on his elbows, he hummed thoughtfully. "Well, at least this explains the vision I had of the tunnels."

"You mean the hammering and heat?" Alex thought back on her conversation with Bran about the strange dreams they were having of dark stone tunnels. Her adventure in the tunnels had proven that Alex's dream had been a vision of her future, a warning of what was to come, but Bran's had been a little different.

"Which vision?" Aiden asked with a glance at Bran.

"I was in the tunnels, but they started to change and smelled more... natural I guess would be the word. Up ahead I heard this metallic hammering and saw the light and felt the heat of a fire." Bran shrugged slightly. "I looked it up and thought it might connect to blacksmithing, the forging of iron."

"Maybe," Alex agreed with a nod. "That could have been a magical vision of the Iron Soul, something being forged deep in the earth."

"And it is similar to the Connection you had with Arthur," Nicki added with an excited smile, her fingers playing with a wisp of her red hair.

Nodding in agreement, Alex thought about the strange vision she'd had the first time she met Arthur. There had been the smell of smoke; she'd seen fire and heard a strange metal hammering that Bran had agreed was similar to his vision. Everything seemed to be in agreement that Arthur Pendred was, in fact, the new incarnation of the Iron Soul. Except none of the others had formed a Connection with him, ever.

"So, what do we do about Jenny and Lance?" Aiden asked, and Alex's shoulders slumped.

"I don't know." Alex folded her arms on the table and lowered her head dejectedly.

"Well, Alex is already their friend so she can watch them," Bran said with an apologetic glance towards Alex.

"But that doesn't answer the question of what to do if they do... you know," Nicki pointed out uncomfortably. "I wonder how much control they have; I mean, they don't remember so why does it always happen? It isn't motivated by any sense of malice towards the Iron Soul."

"Their souls may be trying to help the Iron Soul," Bran suggested with a frown of his own, causing lines to appear between his green eyes. "Only they keep making the same mistakes. Religions that believe in reincarnation do acknowledge that souls may seek to redeem a mistake or grow beyond it in the next life."

"Maybe Jenny and Lance are soul mates," Nicki replied with a thoughtful tilt of her head. "But Jenny's soul keeps meeting Arthur's soul first. They become lovers, but once Lance enters the scene, she's always drawn towards him."

"Soul mates?" Bran repeated doubtfully.

Nicki stuck out her tongue at him. "With everything else can we rule it out?"

"But why would it always destroy him?" Aiden countered with a shake of his head. "Cheating is bad yeah, but why is it always a catalyst."

"Maybe they're just stuck," Nicki suggested. "Their instincts are playing out the same actions, and the timing is always bad. Cheating isn't the end of the world, but it can leave someone feeling depressed and vulnerable. And if the cheating cost you not only your significant other but your best friend that it could be really bad depending on what else is going on."

"Perhaps," Aiden agreed. "But yeah, you do have to wonder how much control they have. Is Jenny going to choose to betray Arthur with Lance or is it just going to be a compulsion that she has no control over?"

"That's a creepy idea," Nicki muttered as she shuddered. "That sounds like being hijacked by a former life. How do we deal with that?"

"Maybe there is some kind of spell..." Aiden muttered before shaking his head. "No, the professors would have used it already if there was."

"Not to mention the moral issues there," Nicki added with a shudder. "Maybe they can just be convinced to leave after this year is over. Just drift apart."

"Arthur and Jenny have been dating since sophomore year of high school," Alex informed them. "He was the one who picked this school; Jenny followed him here. Worse, it was through Arthur that Lance and Jenny met." Alex swallowed and played uneasily with her hands. "They may already be attracted to each other; I'm not sure. Lance isn't the easiest guy to read, and Jenny has seemed sort of depressed lately. She was sad when they got back from Christmas." Her frown deepened. "And she and Arthur were originally planning to live together this semester, but Jenny renewed in the dorm with me out of the blue. Arthur even asked me about it."

"That doesn't sound good," Bran observed. "But I don't know what we can do."

"Look, cheating is bad; yes," Nicki announced. "But if we're around to support Arthur when it happens then maybe we can lessen the negative impact when it does happen."

"It's his best friend and girlfriend," Aiden argued, earning him a sharp look from Nicki. "I'm just saying that he's not friends with anyone here but Alex, hell I'm sure he still hates my guts for making Alex cry." Aiden shifted nervously at the last part of his statement, and Alex gave him a small forced smile to assure him of her forgiveness for the incident back when she was still refusing to accept magic as real.

Everyone was silent for several minutes, playing with their hands and avoiding eye contact with each other. Across from Alex, Nicki made a small sigh before she thumped the book on faery mythology down and stood up. She walked to the door and was opening it as Aiden asked, "Where are you going?"

"I'm off to find some book on Arthurian mythology," Nicki announced, looking over her shoulder at them. "After all, if the French school of courtly love literature accidentally remade the correct story by adding in Lancelot, then who knows what else we might learn from the full scope of the older stories. I propose making a list of major characters and potential myths they come from to start separating what might be the fact or fiction around this Iron Soul."

A soft laugh escaped Alex, releasing some of the tension in her chest. "Only you would think like that, Nicki." Alex collapsed into giggles.

Nicki gave Alex a wide smile as the blonde wiped tears out of her eyes and took several deep breaths. "That's why you love me." Nicki winked, flipping her red hair over her shoulder.

"Maybe a little," Alex returned with a calmer smile.

"Oh, don't encourage her to flirt with you," Aiden warned. "That was how she got fixated on Sarah."

Chuckling, Alex ignored the wink between Nicki and Aiden before Nicki dramatically said, "You stole my one true love, Aiden, you're lucky I forgave you for that."

"I thought you had a thing for Maria Valdez in our mythology class now," Bran said.

"Well, she's hot." Nicki looked to Alex. "They're abusing me, you've noticed right?"

"I've abused you plenty of times before," Aiden teased. There was a real smile on his face now.

"Yes well, I got better," Nicki said before heading out of the room and into the mythology section.

5

Ill Thoughts

Stopping in front of her dorm room, Alex took a deep breath and braced herself in case Jenny was home. The research session had gone on for hours with Nicki grabbing every book with Arthurian legends or analyses of the legends from the shelves. Aiden had finally insisted that they were done and threatened to tell Nicki's grandmother that she was 'being obsessive' again if she didn't take a break. At the time Alex had been grateful to get away from the books, but now the dread of seeing Jenny, knowing the truth about her reincarnation status, hit Alex like a punch in her gut.

The door was unlocked, and Alex slowly stepped inside, hoping that Jenny would be taking a nap, but her roommate was painting her nails and texting on her phone with earbuds in. Jenny looked up as Alex shut the door behind her, giving her a wide smile and a wave. Forcing herself to smile, Alex returned the wave before busying herself with unpacking her bag. Behind her, Jenny stood up and began moving around, humming gently along with her music.

Turning her head slightly, Alex studied Jenny thoughtfully as her roommate moved around her side of their room, putting shoes away and tidying up the top of her dresser which served as a vanity. Jenny's long black hair was partially tied back in a bun with a few long strands hanging around her beautiful olive face. For a moment, Alex was struck by the easy grace with which Jenny moved and wondered if it was an echo of the queen she'd been so long ago. Shaking her head, Alex reminded herself that Arto had been a leader, but not a crowned king, so his wife hadn't been a queen.

Alex retreated to her desk, pulled out her Spanish workbook, and started filling in the blanks with conjugated verbs. She made a note to herself to recheck it later since her eyes kept glancing up towards Jenny and her mind wasn't on her homework. After straightening up her side of the dorm room, Jenny returned to her desk and began texting on her phone again. Soft giggles escaped Jenny and Alex glanced over curiously, but Jenny made a dismissive hand gesture. Alex went back to her work, trying not to wonder who Jenny was texting with.

"So?" Jenny asked as she pulled out her earbuds. "Can I assume you were at another study session or is there any chance you were out with a boy?"

Alex turned her chair around to find Jenny watching her with a mischievous smile. "Study session." Alex raised an eyebrow.

"Alex," Jenny whined softly. "Come on, I agreed to let you get through the first semester without nagging you, but come on! It's college, get a boyfriend!"

"That's not high on the priority list right now." Alex turned back to her Spanish book.

"You've had a boyfriend before, right?" Jenny asked, sounding remarkably worried.

"Yes," Alex replied, barely containing a smile.

"So, what was his name?" Jenny turned her chair around and stared at the back of Alex's head.

"Thomas Williamson," Alex answered with a shrug, refusing to look at Jenny.

"Why'd you break up?"

"We broke up just last March; we'd been accepted to different schools and were growing apart. He suggested we part as friends rather than risk dragging things on too long. Tom's at Northeastern University in Boston now."

"What about prom?" Jenny scooted her chair closer, almost bumping into the mini fridge between their desks. "You did go, right?"

Chuckling, Alex nodded. "Tom and I went as friends," she assured Jenny. "With a bunch of our friends as a group, we had fun. Only Michelle is still with her high school boyfriend, they both went to the University of Washington." Alex turned slowly to look at Jenny. "I suppose it's only natural to drift apart after such a big transition."

Her roommate flinched slightly, her smile fading only for a moment before it returned and she reached for her phone. Turning her attention back to the textbook in her lap, Alex took a slow deep breath to control her reaction. Arthur had indicated that he and Jenny were more distant and maybe Jenny felt weird about it, but her flinching didn't mean that anything had happened with Lance yet.

"Are you hungry?" Jenny asked a few minutes later, just when Alex had finally started to focus on her homework properly.

"Uh?" Alex asked, not having caught the question.

"Are you hungry? The boys are over at Michaels for dinner and wanted to see if we could join them."

Jenny was already putting on her shoes and reaching for a coat when Alex processed the question. Swallowing, Alex nodded and stood up. All the other mages seemed to have agreed that it was her job to watch Arthur, Lance, and Jenny, but her stomach turned at the notion of being around all three of them at once. She'd avoided the group ever since finding out the truth on Wednesday, and her hands began shaking with nerves.

Her roommate was a few steps ahead of her, already in the hallway and having turned the lock for the door when Alex joined her. Jenny studied Alex for a moment and frowned slightly.

"Are you okay, sweetie?" She reached towards Alex.

"I'm fine," Alex told her quickly only to get a suspicious look. "I'm a little run down," Alex said with a small shrug. "I'll probably go to bed early tonight."

"That's a good idea," Jenny agreed, closing the door and testing that it was locked before she led the way to the stairs. "Maybe your night owl habits are finally catching up with you," Jenny joked to lighten the mood.

"I can't help it that I'm most productive between ten at night and two in the morning." Alex followed Jenny down the stairs.

They settled into a calm silence as they left Hatfield Hall and crossed the lawn over to the large red brick building that was Michaels Hall. Despite the chill in the air, many students were standing in groups around the doorway talking with friends and even a few debating when they could use the volleyball pit again. Jenny shivered at the idea of playing in the cold and tugged open the door, holding it open for Alex with a soft smile.

"The boys should be waiting for us." Jenny stepped inside next to Alex and glanced around.

The boys in question were waiting near the door of Michaels Cafeteria, Arthur leaning against the brick wall with a wide smile. Even at a distance, Alex could see his blue eyes twinkling at something Lance had said. The other young man, Lance, was standing with his arms crossed with a wide smile on his face. He was a black man who was a little taller than Arthur and more strongly built. Skipping ahead of Alex, Jenny called to them both and slid up next to Arthur who grinned and planted a quick greeting kiss on her lips. Lance turned to face Alex and nodded to her as she joined them.

"Hi," Alex greeted, grateful that she managed to force the word out as she avoided staring at Arthur. "How are you guys?"

"Good," Lance replied, shrugging his broad shoulders and nodding his head towards the door. "Starving, though."

"Me too," Arthur agreed. "Weight training builds up an appetite."

"I still live in hope for a weekend that your life isn't controlled by football," Jenny sighed with a dramatic roll of her eyes.

The light-hearted banter continued between Jenny and Arthur as they led the way into the cafeteria with Alex and Lance trailing behind them. Despite not feeling hungry, Alex got herself some pizza and a salad, taking a few moments to calm down before joining the others at their table. Jenny was seated between Arthur and Lance with a broad smile on her face as Alex took the fourth seat across from her. As Jenny began telling Arthur about an upcoming project she had for her journalism class, Alex forced herself to take a few bites of her pizza.

Feeling lightheaded, Alex fell silent and let the others talk around her. Next to her, Lance was his usual quiet self, interjecting into the conversation only occasionally. Jenny switched topics easily with a smile, expressing her excitement for the upcoming Spirit Squad tryouts, asking Arthur if he wouldn't reconsider joining the Ballroom Dancing club with her and discussing classes. Arthur smiled gently at Jenny's rapid speech, and there was no sign of the concern for their relationship that there had been only a few weeks ago. Everything seemed fine with Arthur occasionally joking with Lance and allowing Jenny to talk his ear off.

She felt like an outsider. The knot in her chest tightened, and she clenched her fingers tightly around her fork. These three had known each other time and time again for three thousand years; it was no wonder that she felt like a fourth wheel. To outsiders, it probably seemed a nice balance, a group of friends, but Alex now felt certain that it wasn't the case.

There was a shadow over them now that couldn't be unseen. Jenny's bright smile was drawing looks from Lance out of the corner of his eye that Alex hadn't noticed before, but then he'd look at Arthur and drop his gaze back to his food. Arthur reached over and squeezed Jenny's hand only to have her eyes move quickly to Lance. Looking down at her food, Alex speared a piece of lettuce and forced herself to take a few more bites. Maybe she was just over thinking what she saw. Maybe there was nothing strange going on yet, but what if the betrayal was already happening?

"Alex?" Arthur called gently. "Alex!" Snapping her head up, Alex blinked at Arthur, meeting his worried blue eyes. He was frowning at her, a look of concern on his face. "Alex, are you okay?" he asked.

"I'm fine," Alex croaked out before clearing her throat and forcing a smile. "I'm just a little brain dead. We were working on a world mythology project earlier," she lied easily, suddenly grateful that she had a shared class with Aiden, Bran, and Nicki.

"Oh," Arthur replied with a nod. "What's the project about?"

"The project?" Alex blinked and shook her head to force herself to focus. "It's on King Arthur. We were looking at some of the Celtic myths that may have helped inspire the story."

"That's sounds interesting," Arthur said with a smile slowly appearing on his face. He ran a hand through his blond hair as he leaned back in his chair, his shoulders relaxing slightly. "I thought it was just a medieval story."

"Well in some ways it is." Alex glanced at Lance and Jenny in the corner of her eye only to find them listening. "It was updated greatly;

Camelot, for instance, is a medieval creation. Some of the earliest stories related to King Arthur may have their roots in warrior chiefs and the warfare that took place before the Romans arrived. It's hard to say since a lot of traditional stories were recorded by Christian monks and the oral tradition was lost."

"That's neat," Arthur agreed. "I bet that's an interesting project for you at least since you're a literature major."

"It's interesting," Alex confirmed. "But a lot of work. Nicki's the one who is good at the folklore research."

"Still, King Arthur, I love those stories," Arthur said with a wide grin. "There's a lot of different versions though so I bet you have your hands full trying to sort them out."

"Yeah," Alex agreed. "But we'll manage, we have some time to get it done." She added the word 'hopefully' in her mind.

The conversation shifted away from her with Arthur commenting on the online class discussion for International Politics he'd added to that morning. His energy for the subject was palpable, and Alex found herself smiling softly even though he was rambling on a bit. Then Lance asked Jenny about the homework they had coming up for their chemistry lab. Alex dropped her fork; she'd completely forgotten that Lance and Jenny had the same Chemistry class and Chemistry Lab. Blushing, Alex leaned down to pick her fork up from the floor and glance under the table. Jenny was sitting with her ankles crossed and her knee touching Arthur's, but one of her feet was touching Lance's left foot.

Sitting up, Alex set the fork to the side and swallowed thickly. She wasn't sure if she was overthinking things or not. Slowly she raised her eyes back to Jenny who was speaking with Lance about the upcoming lab. There was a soft, happy smile on her face and a matching one on Lance's.

Alex's stomach turned as she watched the interaction. It looked so innocent, just a smile between two friends. Arthur was smiling right along with them, but Alex couldn't help but wonder. Had the betrayal already started, was it too late to stop whatever romance was going to happen between Jenny and Lance? She couldn't help but think back to Halloween night. After Arthur had left to drive some drunk teammates home, Lance had driven Jenny home and promised to come back and pick her up. He never had. It was while walking home that Alex had been attacked by the Sídhe Hounds for the first time with the other mages and learned that magic was real after Professor Cornwall and Professor Yates had saved them. She'd holed up in Nicki's dorm with Aiden, Bran, and Nicki until sunrise ended Samhain and limited the Sídhe's ability to enter her world.

And yet... she'd still gotten home before Jenny. At the time Alex hadn't given it much thought, but now she wondered about why her roommate came stumbling into their dorm after sunrise when Lance was supposed to be taking her home hours earlier. Alex shivered as her limbs grew heavy and cold worry, anger, and guilt coursed through her veins.

"Alex," Arthur called. "You alright?"

Tearing her eyes away from Jenny and Lance, Alex met Arthur's concerned eyes and her stomach turned. She jumped up from her seat, covering her mouth and ran towards the restroom tucked away in the far corner. Knocking into several chairs, Alex barely reached the bathroom and didn't bother to lock the door before collapsing in front of the toilet. With painful heaves, she lost her dinner and felt hot tears running down her face. Her fingers clutched so tightly at the toilet bowl that her hands began to ache. Sobs mixed painfully with the heaves, leaving Alex with no control left.

Warm hands pulled her long hair out of her face and away from her neck, gathering her hair together in one hand. Another hand moved down to her back, rubbing gentle, comforting circles. Alex gasped for breath as the heaving eased and sniffed loudly.

"Easy," Jenny cooed to her, still rubbing her back. "Easy, Alex, it's okay, sweetie."

Alex's stomach rolled again, hearing the voice of the very person she now couldn't help but suspect of cheating on Arthur and potentially destroying the mages' chances of stopping the Sídhe. But the gentle rubbing forced her muscles to relax, and Alex sighed in defeat. Reaching around Alex, Jenny flushed the toilet before tucking the ponytail of hair she'd collected in the back of Alex's t-shirt.

Feeling Jenny pull away, Alex stayed on the floor and listened to her roommate's movements around the bathroom. The sink turned on a moment later, and she heard paper towels being ripped out of the dispenser. Jenny returned a few moments later, pulling at Alex's shoulder to get her to turn towards her. Closing her eyes, Alex allowed the movement but wasn't prepared to look at her roommate in the eyes just yet. The moist paper towels were gently applied to her face and some of her hair to clean her up in silence.

"Time to get you home." Jenny stood up and tugged at Alex's hand. Standing up slowly, Alex finally opened her eyes but kept them lowered. Jenny mistranslated the hesitance. "It's okay, sweetie," Jenny told her. "Everyone gets sick sometimes, and at least you made it to the bathroom."

They opened the bathroom door to find Lance and Arthur waiting outside, holding their coats and bags. Alex managed to give Arthur a small, grateful smile as he helped her into her coat and took her bag from him.

"Get some rest," Arthur said gently. "And try to feel better."

Not trusting herself to speak, Alex nodded quickly and allowed Jenny to take her hand and lead her towards the door. If other students were looking as they left Michaels Cafeteria, Alex didn't notice. She only noticed they were outside by the sudden drop in the temperature. Inhaling the chilly air, Alex felt her head clear a little and took several slow deep breaths to regain control.

She and Jenny made their way slowly across the large lawn between Michaels Cafeteria and their own dorm Hatfield Hall. Alex's eyes traced the darkness around them carefully. Morgana and Merlin had collapsed the Sídhe tunnel, at least for a while, but the paranoia of the dark of night that Alex had developed wasn't so easily shrugged off. Jenny moved ahead of her and pulled out her key card to unlock the front door, gesturing Alex to go ahead of her. They took the elevator to the third floor, something Alex didn't usually bother with, but Jenny didn't seem to trust her on her feet. Her roommate unlocked the door of room 321 with a practiced motion and pushed the door open. Flicking the light switch, Alex mumbled a quick thanks to Jenny before grabbing her pajamas and toiletries. She retreated to the floor's communal bathroom to wash her face properly and brush her teeth. Using the sink, Alex rinsed out part of her hair and considered calling the other mages before deciding against it.

When she returned to her dorm room ready for bed, the comforter and sheets of her bed were pulled back, a glass of water was set at the corner of her desk for easy reach, and their trashcan had been moved from its perch behind the microwave next to her bed. Jenny was at her desk, texting on her phone and looked up to give Alex a soft smile. Managing to return the smile, Alex crawled into her bed and grabbed the plush dog that had been her lifelong companion. Hugging Galahad to her chest, Alex tugged the blankets over her head and closed her eyes. She heard Jenny stand up from her desk and move around for a few moments before the dorm room door opened once again. The lights turned off and the door shut with the click of the lock, leaving Alex alone with her tumultuous thoughts.

6

Magic Protectors

8 09 B.C.E. The Dales, Cumbria

Long glinting teeth just missed Morgana's arm as she spun out of the Hound's reach, narrowing her eyes at the beast. It paused and snarled at her, curling back its lips and pressing its ears flat back on its head. Above Morgana's head pulsed a small orb of light which allowed her to see the long, lean Hound crouching for another lunge, its translucent fur almost glowing in the magical light, exposing the sharp angles of its body. Morgana could almost count the ribs of the beast as she slowly drew out her new dagger with her right hand. It felt strange in her hand; the wooden handle fastened to the dark gray metal unworn and unfamiliar. Holding her left hand forward, Morgana allowed the silvery sparks of her magic to gather in her palm, forming a small orb and braced herself for the Hound's attack.

It lunged, its body shooting forward towards her. Morgana released the sparkling orb with a soft huff. It collided with the Hound's upper chest, knocking it back in a flash of light. Tumbling to the ground, a sharp cry of pain escaped the Hound. Rushing forward, Morgana brought her dagger down at the beast's neck, driving the iron blade into the flesh. The cry of pain turned to a gurgle as the body began to dissolve.

"Morgana!" A male voice shouted behind her. "Another Hound to your right!"

She jumped back up and turned quickly to the right, gathering another orb of magic in her hand just as another Hound burst into the light surrounding her. Far in the distance, a horn sounded, echoing through the valley before it was joined by a long howl. Her green eyes locked on the Sídhe Hound, Morgana pushed her arm forward and released the crackling orb of magic into the air. The Hound tumbled to the ground, a gaping wound of silver blood on its side.

Out of the corner of her eye, Morgana saw Arto jump forward towards the Hound. Light flashed off of shining metal as a long blade swung down on the neck of the beast. There was a flash of magic as the Hound's form vanished. Without a word, Morgana turned away from the figure and scanned the area for any more enemies. After a moment of hesitation, she raised her hand towards the light orb floating above their heads. It's light intensified, spreading out further to reveal the grassy slopes of the dale with the occasional rocks.

"Looks like that's all of them here," Arto said.

Looking over her shoulder, Morgana gave a small nod to the tall teenager standing behind her. His brown hair was messier than usual from the fight with a sheen of sweat shining on his face.

"Indeed, Arto," Morgana agreed before glancing around again. "But I heard a horn and at least one other Hound."

"Then we should backtrack to Merlin," her brother replied.

"You should return to the village." Morgana took a few steps towards the nearest hill where she thought the horn might have come from.

"Honestly, Sister, I'm sixteen." Arto trekked after her, crunching down the brittle autumn grasses with each step.

"Merlin would want you safe," Morgana reminded him, not mentioning that she was far more concerned than Merlin would be. She glanced down at the muddy ground with distaste, noting the large patches of mud on her dress. "We're going back to the village."

Arto huffed again but said nothing else. However, he did not stop following his sister up the slope of the hill. Morgana dimmed the light quickly when another burst of a horn rang down the dale. Ahead of them, on the crest of the hill, another light appeared alongside two Riders on their tall shimmering steeds. For a moment no one moved, taking in the other side cautiously.

Morgana's eyes quickly scanned the golden armor worn by both of the tall and lean figures. It was elegant, but nothing suggested they were high ranking. One of them had longer horns with his long white hair twisted around them in an elaborate style, marking him as the older of the two Sídhe Riders. Each of them had a drawn sword clenched in their hands with the light glinting off the golden protectors that the Sídhe wore over their long claw-like fingernails.

The sharp violet eyes of the elder Rider narrowed on Morgana, assessing her as she had him. "The Traitor," he hissed slowly, his dark tone rumbling through the darkness along with the musical hint that all Sídhe voices had. "The Queen will reward us for your demise."

Giving the Rider a dark look, Morgana gathered more magical power in her hand and allowed the light to brighten, illuminating the sloped field of battle. "You are not the first Rider to say that," Morgana replied with a slow smile. "And you won't be the last."

Next to her, Arto chuckled, and she heard the slide of metal as her brother pulled out Cathanáil. In the corner of her eye, Morgana watched Arto step up next to her, holding the Sword out in front of him. She risked a glance towards Arto to check on him, but her brother was watching the Riders calmly, waiting for their move. Tiny white sparks of magic jumped over the blade as Arto's right hand began to glow.

She couldn't help the slight smile that was tugging at the corners of her mouth.

There was a moment of silence, and then the Riders spurred on their steeds. As the horses crashed down the hill towards them, Morgana focused on the Rider rushing towards her. Taking a quick breath, Morgana felt the tingle of magic up her arm and silently commanded it into another orb. She threw her hand forward, sending the silver orb flying through the air. The horse reared up and the Rider fell from the beast's back just as the silver orb crashed into the horse's chest. Magic sparked over the horse's torso like tiny lightning bolts as the creature began to dissolve like mist into the chilled air.

Ignoring the urge to turn and see how Arto was managing as the other Rider charged him, Morgana pulled her iron dagger and rushed up the hill. Up ahead, the Rider climbed quickly to his feet, recovering his long golden sword from where it had fallen. Morgana panted as she struggled against the chill sinking into her bones. Exhaustion was creeping over her, and she found herself wishing she'd used less magic against the Hounds.

The Sídhe Rider smirked as he raised the blade in front of him in one hand and magic began to swirl around his other. Eyes darting, Morgana quickly took in the gathering magic and lunged forward. Her sudden movement surprised the Rider causing him to jerk back just before the iron dagger clinked against his armor. The magical orb he'd created shot off into the distance, leaving a glittering trail of gold sparks behind it, but Morgana refused to be distracted from her target.

The sound of metal scraping against metal filled the air, sending shudders up Morgana's arms. She pulled back her arm as the Rider shifted his posture and swung the sword towards her. Gasping in alarm, Morgana stumbled back, her foot slipping on the thick mud of the slope. The sword barely missed her. Throwing her weight forward, Morgana caught herself with one hand as she hit the ground. The iron dagger fell from her grasp as Morgana pulled sharply on the connection to the Earth, letting its power race up her spine and into her hand.

Swinging his blade, the Rider brought it down towards Morgana just as a blast of magic escaped her hand and slammed into his torso. A panicked scream escaped the Sídhe Rider as he fell back against the moist earth of the hill. Standing up, Morgana watched for a moment as he tried to use his magic to save himself or at the least destroy her. His violet eyes glazed over and his mouth fell open just as his body began to dissolve. A moment later nothing remained save an imprint in the mud of the hill.

The sound of metal crashing into metal made Morgana's eyes widen as she remembered Arto. Spinning, she spotted Arto battling the remaining Rider with his sword. The steed was gone, and the Rider was lower on the hill with Arto using the added height given to him by the slope against the Síd. Cathanáil slammed into the Rider's long golden sword, nearly knocking the Rider to his knees. Growling at Arto, the Rider removed one hand from the hilt of his sword as magic began to swirl around him. Morgana bent over, grabbing her dagger and a fistful of mud from the ground.

Arto huffed, bringing Cathanáil down against the golden sword. With only one hand, the Rider wasn't able to defend against Arto's strong swing. Arm forced down, the Rider started to bring a magical orb towards Arto, but her brother thrust Cathanáil forward. Morgana flinched at the scraping sound of metal against metal as Cathanáil pierced the Síd's armor and slid into the Rider's chest. Arto was still for a moment, waiting as the Síd's magic and body dissolved like mist in front of him. When Cathanáil was freed, Arto lowered the Sword and took in a deep breath.

"Are you alright?" Morgana stepped closer to her brother with a small smile of relief.

"Yes," Arto agreed before he looked up towards the crest of the hill. "But I want to check something." Before his sister could stop him, the young man rushed up the slope to the crest of the hill. Once he reached the top, Arto created a small white orb of magic that cast light over the hill. "Look at these tracks," Arto called from the crest of the hill.

Dusting off her shoulder, Morgana tossed back her hair and started to climb up the rest of the way. Her right knee ached, and she grit her teeth together to keep in a cry when her leg caught on a rock, nearly tripping her. Finally, she reached Arto and glanced down at the remarkably clear tracks from the Rider's horses in the mud.

"We could track them back to the tunnel entrance," Arto suggested with determined eyes. "If we find the entrance, we could mount a better defense."

"The locals already said it was to the northwest," Morgana reminded him, her eyes darting between the tracks and her brother.

"That's just a general direction." Arto shook his head stubbornly. "Come on, Morgana, if we can find the entrance soon it lessens the opportunities that the Sídhe have to hurt these people."

Shoulders slumping in defeat, Morgana nodded and ignored the triumphant smile that lit up her brother's face. Instead, she took in a slow deep breath, focusing on finding the small spark warming her chest and tugged at it. The light above them began to glow more brightly, better illuminating the tracks. Arto led the way, keeping Cathanáil out and at the ready, glancing back at Morgana as she slowly followed him, mindful of her footing. They followed the gentle slope of the hills until the slight hints of daylight on the horizon warned that dawn was coming just as they entered another small valley.

"We need to be careful," Morgana hissed to Arto. "Any remaining Riders will be on their way back to their tunnels."

Her brother nodded his understanding, and his pace remained steady. Staying quiet, Morgana ignored the tug of the mud in her shoes and mentally cursed their luck of being called to the area during the rainy season. It was no trouble to follow the deep tracks up the valley, but Morgana and Arto paused as they found more tracks leading away from the Riders they had already destroyed.

"Hard to say how many more there are," Arto said.

Nodding in agreement, Morgana started moving forward again, her eyes tracing the sides of the valley for either the entrance of the Sídhe or a place to hide until dawn. Then her light illuminated the space behind three large trees and a boulder, revealing a tall opening in the side of the hill. Morgana took a sharp breath and swallowed painfully at the sight of the smooth round opening. She was unable to contain the shiver that rushed through her body at the sight of the gaping hole in the hillside.

Even at her current distance, she could see the smooth edges of the round opening with dark stone lining the tunnel that she knew stretched deep underground. Through the tunnel, the Riders could escape back to their realm or travel to a distant corner of the Isles. Memories of her childhood in the clutches of the Sídhe washed over Morgana, making her stomach turn painfully. She'd only been saved by virtue of being a mage and Queen Scáthbás' eagerness to turn her into a weapon against her homeland.

"Morgana," Arto called gently, reaching towards her cautiously. "We've found it, time to find some cover and wait for dawn."

"I know... it's just-"

Her words were cut off by the neigh of a horse behind them and the frantic beating of hoofs against the ground. There was the slide of metal as Cathanáil was pulled out of its sheath by Arto. The sight of the tunnel made Morgana slow, her distraction leaving her fumbling for her dagger. Behind her, there was a crash and a shout of anger from Arto.

A scream of fear that turned into a sob made Morgana spin around in horror. Running towards the tunnel entrance was the Rider, now without his horse, but dragging a small child behind him who was bound with a golden rope. Eyes widening in alarm, Morgana gathered magic in her hand as she measured the rate of the Sídhe Riders' paces and the distance to the tunnel entrance. She exhaled softly before shoving her magic forward, but the orb vanished and instead stretched out into a long rope of light. It snapped through the chilly night air, illuminating the space around it before colliding with the back of the Rider.

Crying out in pain, the Rider fell forward, dropping the golden cord. In the corner of her eye, Morgana saw the young girl squirm away from the Rider and stumble down the hill. Snapping her hand, Morgana brought the shimmering river of magic down against the Rider again with a crack. Magic sparked against the Rider's armor, and his body began to dissolve before Morgana's eyes. Weakly the Rider pulled himself forward towards the tunnel entrance, but his body faded into mist long before he reached it.

Fingers clenched in a fist; Morgana couldn't stop her hands from shaking in rage. Behind her, she heard Arto trying to calm down the small child that they'd just rescued. Morgana turned to look towards Arto who was holding the small girl against him in a protective one-armed hug. Raising his eyes towards Morgana, he gave her a forced smile as the last traces of silver blood vanished from the long blade. He inspected Cathanáil for a moment before sheathing the Sword.

"That wasn't so bad now was it," Arto told her, his grin widening. "Now aren't you glad that we came now and didn't wait for day."

"I suppose so." Morgana's eyes dropped to the little shivering girl before going back to Arto. "But you should have hidden, this was a bad position to be battling the Sídhe in, and you are too important," Morgana added angrily, ignoring her inability to keep her body from shaking in rage.

For a moment the young man looked ready to snap in return, but he took a slow breath after closing his eyes. When he opened them again, he met his sister's gaze calmly. His grin was gone with a serious expression replacing it.

"I know that I'm important, Morgana," Arto replied in an even voice. "But I will not have everyone else rush into danger in my place. I have an obligation to fight as well. I may be more than a mage, but I am still a mage."

Without another word, Arto marched towards the tunnel entrance and glared at it. He raised his hands slowly and breathed deeply. Stepping back, Morgana glanced over at the little girl who was shivering and clearly resisting the urge to run to Arto. Morgana sighed softly and walked over to the little girl. She felt the small child grab at the fabric of her dress as she crossed her arms over her chest and waited. Arto's hands moved apart slowly, white lightning sparking between them dangerously. Strange shadows danced through the dark valley as the light crackled and sparked in his hands.

Morgana straightened up as the grip on her dress tightened and lowered her hand to place it on the small girl's head. "It's alright," Morgana promised tensely. "This is good magic."

The lightning in her brother's grip was beginning to spin out of his hands erratically as he slowly turned his palms towards the entrance. Magical lightning burst forth, striking the ground around the entrance with sharp cracks and booms. Rumbling filled the valley as the ground began to twist around the entrance, warping the round dark hole out of its smooth shape. Arto groaned as the tunnel's edges began to glow gold, growing brighter and brighter. The white lightning cracked as it collided with the golden glow, sparks of magic flying violently away from the entrance. Then the golden glow slowly faded, flickering out suddenly as another bolt of white magic hit the dark stone. The rumbling grew louder, and suddenly a section of stone fell away inside the tunnel, followed by another and another. The small girl cried with alarm, tucking herself behind Morgana as the tunnel collapsed and the earth surrounding it began to cover the rumble.

Watching patiently, Morgana chuckled as the grass rolled over the debris and a small flower poked out of the ground. "Well done," she complimented as the little girl stepped away from her and Arto lowered his hands.

Her brother leaned forward, supporting himself against his knees as he struggled to catch his breath. Rushing out from behind Morgana, the little girl ran up to Arto and leaned over to peer at him. Arto chuckled softly when the girl asked him something in too quiet a voice for Morgana to hear. Arto picked up the little girl and started to walk back the way they had come out of the valley, not looking at Morgana as he passed her. Sighing, Morgana's shoulders slumped, and she glanced back towards the remains of the tunnel. She could remember the Sídhean Realm so clearly and the face of her former mistress, Queen Scáthbás, pushed itself to the forefront of her mind. Shaking her head, Morgana turned and started after Arto, her body aching too much for speed.

The weight of the little girl meant that Morgana caught up with her brother as the sun finally rose above the horizon, sending warm rays of light over the dales and casting long shadows into the valleys.

"Sorry," Morgana muttered softly, glancing at the little girl who had fallen into an exhausted sleep in her brother's arms.

"You hate being near the tunnels; I know that," her brother assured Morgana. "I don't take what you say personally when you're near them."

Giving him a weak smile, Morgana nodded to express her gratitude and released a soft sigh of relief. In the distance, she could see the small village that had called for their help a month ago and where they'd arrived less than a week ago after traveling from the southern end of the island. Already there were signs of movement in the village as people began to go about their days, running the life stock out of their evening pens and carrying their tools out towards the surrounding fields. Gently, Arto shook the small girl in his arms awake.

"Ceana," Arto called with a smile. "We're safe now."

The little girl blinked her large brown eyes at Arto and turned to look over her shoulder and into the village. Ahead of them, an older brown-haired woman in a blue dress ran towards them along with several other people.

"Did you kill any Riders?" one man demanded.

"Yes," Morgana answered shortly, looking around for Merlin. "Where is Merlin?"

"We rescued this girl from a Rider," Arto interjected, ignoring questions being asked of him. "Can someone please look after her and find her family?"

One of the women stepped forward and collected Ceana from Arto's arms. The little girl struggled against the strange grip, reaching for Arto, but quickly relaxed. Reaching over, Morgana gripped her brother's shoulder and steered them out of the crowd. When another man kept trying to ask her questions, Morgana fixed her angry and tired green eyes on him. A smile tugged at her lips as he scampered away and her brother laughed. They reached the roundhouse that the village had offered them for the duration of their visit. One of the villagers was inside starting up a fire with a basket of food waiting beside the hearth.

"Thank you," Arto told her gratefully with a wide smile.

"You did us a great service." The woman gave them both a small bow. "Merlin destroyed two Riders who tried to enter the village in the night and if you killed more than perhaps…"

"You will be safe for a few months," Arto promised gently. "The Sídhe's tunnel has been destroyed. If they wish to return to this area, they will have to rebuild it."

The woman's brown eyes lit up, and she bowed once again, stumbling over herself as she insisted that they eat and rest. Sighing, Morgana sank onto the stool by the fire and picked up the waterskin that the woman had left them. After gulping down several mouthfuls, she handed it to Arto and began to sort through the basket. The animal skin that served as the cover of the entrance was shoved back with a flap as Merlin entered the roundhouse. From his seat by the fire, Arto looked up at the older mage with a warm smile as they both checked the other over for signs of injury.

"We found the tunnel," Arto announced with a grin.

"You severed the connection between the Iron Realm and the Sídhean Realm?" Merlin asked calmly, glancing between the siblings.

"Yes, Merlin," Arto replied with a tired smile. "We were able to track the Riders back to the entrance, and we even saved one of the children that they managed to grab tonight."

"I heard that already," Merlin told them with a smile. "The little girl is resting right now. She's not from this village, but a messenger has already been sent to tell her family that she is safe."

"Good," Arto sighed, rolling his shoulders. "And with the entrance closed they should be safe, at least for a little while.

"Indeed." Merlin sat down with them at the side of the roaring hearth, leaning forward on his staff as he fixed his eyes on Arto. "We received a request from the Northlands: they are facing almost nightly raids by the Sídhe in large numbers."

Arto's cheerful expression vanished in a moment, melting into a stern look of anger and determination that Morgana still found startling on her younger brother's face. "We all need rest, so we'll leave first thing tomorrow morning," Arto announced, not waiting for any agreements from Merlin or Morgana, but judging from Merlin's smile and Morgana's sign of acceptance he needn't have been concerned.

"The Northlands..." Morgana said thoughtfully. "I've never been that far north; how will we get there?"

"I've sent a messenger ahead to request a boat for us," Merlin assured Morgana. "It will take a few days to follow the shore, but it will get us there faster than over land."

Morgana nodded her acceptance of the plan and looked back over at Arto who still looked angry, but was beginning to calm. "You've been to the Northlands before?" Morgana asked, hoping to distract her brother.

"Years ago," Arto said with a nod, turning to look over at her. His anger faded a little more, and he managed a small smile. "We went to the furthest northern islands; the wind is so terrible there that everything is built out of stone."

Nodding, Morgana allowed her brother to tell her about his other memories of the northlands even though she had heard his stories before. The tension finally drained out of his shoulders and Morgana could see the exhaustion from their battles finally taking hold. Yawning, Morgana stretched and rolled her shoulders to loosen them up. In the corner of her eye, she saw a yawn escape Arto and caught a pleased smile from Merlin.

"We should all get to bed," Merlin proposed gently. "It will be important that we leave first thing. I'm afraid that our days will be spent in the boat from dawn to dusk and we won't have the luxury of a roundhouse each night."

Morgana flinched at the notion of sleeping under the night sky again after several days of proper accommodation. They'd done it plenty before, but it was always one of the rare times where she truly missed the Sídhean Realm and the comfortable beds she'd grown up with. It was the only thing she missed about being raised by the creatures now threatening her world, but a rock in the back would do that to anyone. Rising from her spot near Arto, Morgana moved over to one side of the room and curled up on the bed their host had provided. She didn't close her eyes and instead waited until Arto was settled on a bed, with Cathanáil in reach of his hand. Merlin gave a nod of approval and walked to the doorway.

Raising her head slightly, Morgana watched Merlin draw a few symbols in the trodden dirt floor right in front of the door with the end of his staff. The older mage waved his hand, and a soft blue light covered the doorway. Knowing they were safe, Morgana exhaled slowly and set her head down, closing her eyes. The fire dimmed, and she heard Merlin move to his bed. A few moments later the roundhouse was silent, and Morgana fell asleep listening to the deep breathing of her younger brother and Merlin.

7

Sídhe Hill

— ☙ —

Breathing in the fresh air, Alex did her best to ignore the slight chill hanging in the air as she followed the line of mages up the game trail. She was still tired from the past week, but that hadn't stopped Morgana from insisting that they hike up to the tunnel early Saturday morning. She needed a lot more sleep to recover from dodging Jenny and Lance while acting like nothing was wrong than a lousy six hours. Her stomach turned sharply at the direction of her thoughts, and Alex focused on a nearby bare tree where a robin was perched to distract herself.

"I'm not much of a hiker," Nicki protested. She was in front of Alex and grumbling. "Did the Riders seriously use this trail?"

"The Sídhe have limited control over where their tunnels appear," Merlin explained from the back of the line. "They make do with what they get, and I suspect that the animal trails throughout the forest made it easier than you think to navigate."

Alex heard the slow thump of Bran's cane behind her, teamed with the taller walking stick that Merlin had given him when they started. So far, he was keeping pace with them, but Alex slowed down a little as they began to climb over a rockier section. Above their heads, the rising sun was shining down through the tops of the evergreens, casting shadows around them. While the trail they were on was mostly clear of snow, the shadowed slopes of the hill were still covered in a layer of snow streaked with dirt and showing small animal tracks.

Mid-February wasn't the right time to go on a hike in Alex's mind and judging from how the others had reacted to the news, they didn't think much of the idea either. Still, Alex had to admit that it was a nice day. She didn't feel cold at all because of the hiking and birds were chirping around them. Small sounds from the underbrush every so often assured her that they weren't alone in the woods.

"Hey," Aiden called from up ahead. "You can see over the trees from up here."

Aiden was standing on a small rocky twist in the trail up ahead and pointing south towards the lake and town. After a moment he kept following Morgana up the hill, letting Nicki take his place while Alex waited behind her. Pulling out her phone, Nicki snapped a quick picture and grinned at Alex before moving on. Alex climbed up the slope of the trail to take Nicki's place and turned to look towards town.

They were above the lake on the first hill that led up into the Middle Santiam Wilderness. From the outcropping of rock, Alex could see across the shimmering surface of the lake. A few houses followed the curve of the lake nearby, but on the far side she could make out several familiar buildings. Hatfield Hall was just visible above the bare trees of the arboretum on the western side of the lake with the buildings of the city proper dominating most of the shore until they faded into a few scattered houses here and there on the eastern shore.

"It's a nice view," Alex agreed with a small smile before she turned to follow Nicki. She glanced over her shoulder to see Bran and Merlin pause to take in the view.

Focusing on the trail, Alex tried to relax and enjoy the fresh air away from the university. There wasn't much talking from the group as Morgana led them up an old game trail, probably made by deer towards the site of the tunnel entrance.

"How are things with Jenny?" Nicki asked ahead of her in a gentle voice. "Any better?"

"Well, I haven't thrown up again from being around them." Alex nearly tripped on a rock. "It's still weird, and I'm just not sure of the state of things."

"Do you think the affair has started?" Bran asked from behind her.

"I don't know," Alex admitted with a shrug. "I thought that maybe it had, but I've been watching all week with no new reasons to worry."

"You know it's possible that they had a one-time thing after drinking too much," Aiden offered from ahead of them. "If they decided to put it behind them then maybe they've figured out how to act normal."

"Maybe..." Alex said slowly.

"If it was a one-time thing then that would be a change," Merlin informed them, finally speaking up. "Something you need to understand about Jenny and Lance's previous lives is that they are always drawn to each other. I like to think that they truly love each other, but are always meeting in the wrong circumstances."

"Can we not talk about them today," Alex interrupted without turning to look at Merlin. "I've finally got a day where I'm not watching my friends like a hawk for signs of betrayal." The words came out more bitter than she intended and the others fell silent. Sighing, Alex looked down at the ground and kicked at a rock.

"Remind me to give you the spare key to my dorm room," Nicki said gently from in front of Alex. "In case you need someplace else to crash sometimes. I'll get some blankets and another pillow."

Alex relaxed slightly at the words, nodding despite Nicki not being able to see her. "Thanks."

"Course," Nicki replied, sounding a little more cheerful. "It'll be fun to have even a temporary roommate. Singles are nice, but they get a bit boring."

"Nothing about you is boring," Aiden interjected from ahead of them.

"It's true," Nicki answered with a laugh. "I had the strangest dream last night." Nicki stepped around a root growing over the game trail they were following.

"Oh, strange by your standards?" Aiden asked from ahead of Nicki. "This should be interesting."

"Earth had been attacked by aliens," Nicki continued, ignoring Aiden's remark. "Then another race of aliens came. They looked like flamingos, and the pink ones were ninjas."

Alex blinked at Nicki's back and heard Bran and Merlin chuckle behind her while Aiden started laughing.

"Were the purple flamingos pirates?" Bran asked with a chuckle as he navigated around the large tree root.

"No, there weren't any pirate flamingos," Nicki told him, glancing over her shoulder with a cheerful smile. "At least I don't remember them."

"That's almost as good as your space ship dream where you bluffed the aliens into leaving despite having no working engines," Aiden observed with another laugh.

"The ship wasn't finished yet," Nicki protested, tossing her long red braid over her shoulder. "We had to think of something."

"Do you keep a dream journal?" Alex asked, looking through the trees towards the lake.

"No, the interesting ones I usually remember without too much trouble. Most I forget as soon as I climb out of bed."

"We're here," Morgana announced as they moved over the small crest of the slope.

They stepped onto a small level area free of trees with a drop to the east that seemed artificially flat and empty. Where the ground sloped up with the hill was a strange pile of rocks that made Alex come to a fast stop. She stared, unmoving, at the pile of rocks and shaped stones that spilled out of the side of the hill. Anyone else may have suspected a mine, but Alex knew better, remembering the feel of those stones as she struggled to leave the tunnel. She'd been exhausted, drained from using magic and weapons soaked in her own blood against the Sídhe guards and Riders. A shiver raced through her body that she couldn't contain as the memories rushed back and the urge to flee rose up in her chest.

Bran stepped up next to Alex, placing a hand on her shoulder even as she heard him struggling to catch his breath. Merlin patted Alex's other shoulder as he stepped around her to join Morgana. Everyone had fallen silent, and Alex found herself searching for the spot she'd first stepped out and seen the sunrise. Taking a few steps forward, Alex moved past Nicki and Aiden towards the pile of collapsed stone. She stopped near the rocks and turned towards the east, looking over the trees below the sudden drop. In the distance was the horizon where she'd glimpsed the first rays of daylight before dropping unconscious to the ground.

Swallowing, Alex struggled to calm down. The injury she'd taken to her head while fighting a Síd guard meant that much of her battle out of the tunnels was a blur, but there were brief moments that she remembered vividly. As she'd stepped out of the tunnel with the children she'd rescued from a future of slavery under the Sídhe, she'd seen the rising sun and heard Morgana's voice.

"It's alright, Alex." Morgana stepped up next to her, placing a hand on Alex's shoulder.

"How did you get me out from here?" Alex asked Morgana when she found her voice.

"Magic," Morgana answered simply, looking out towards the horizon beside her. "We put the children to sleep and floated all of you down the hill to avoid injuries after we destroyed the tunnel."

"That must have been exhausting," Alex replied after swallowing. "I don't remember if I even thanked you for coming when you did. Thank you," Alex added softly.

"You're welcome," Morgana answered, squeezing Alex's shoulder gently before turning back to the others. She pointed to the rocks that spilled out of the hillside in a rough sloping pile. "This is the remains of the original entrance to Ravenslake."

"As you can see, the area is rather bare." Merlin gestured around at the flat patch they were standing on. "This can vary: sometimes the Sídhe are able to blend their tunnels into the surroundings, but if they are rushing to create a tunnel then their magic often alters the terrain around it. Trees often wither and dissolve." Merlin paused and held a hand up to his ear. "If you listen you won't hear birds or animals nearby. They sense that something is not quite right about this place."

"Are we safe here?" Bran asked, looking at the remains of the tunnel carefully even as he lowered himself to the ground.

"We are, none of their magic is coming out at present," Merlin promised. "The magical link between the Sídhean Realm and our world has been cut for now. I have no doubt they are working to repair it, but I doubt they will do us the courtesy of reopening the tunnel in the same spot."

The others sat down to rest, setting down blankets on the rough ground and pulling out water bottles. Nicki tossed Alex a granola bar which she nibbled at without really tasting it. Merlin laid his staff across his lap and smiled at each of them gently.

"Well," Merlin said slowly with a widening grin. "Morgana and I brought you up here to show you where the Sídhe were coming through and the remains of the opening. This opening was very artificial in appearance with smooth stones showing on the outside, but if the Sídhe do take their failure to heart, it is likely that the next attempt they make will be done much more cautiously. They may make sure that the entrance looks like a natural opening and prevent their magic from killing the plants around it to add to the illusion. Additionally, it is likely that they may add security closer to the tunnel's entrance and only pull back during the day."

"There were guards in the tunnel," Alex reminded Merlin, feeling her body throb at the reminder of the pain they'd inflicted on her.

"You were lucky," Morgana told Alex firmly, meeting Alex's gray eyes sternly with her green ones. "The Sídhe will learn from this event and reinforce their security. It may not be as extreme as it used to be, but you can be sure that they will not have only roving guards."

"As it used to be?" Alex asked, feeling faint at the idea of the tunnels being worse.

"The original tunnels throughout the British Isles had multiple sections. The outer tunnels had some roving guards, but where the stone began to turn white was a large heavily guarded door which kept prisoners away from the travel tunnels. There were guards every few rooms and a massive door protected the Sídhean Realm from intruders through the tunnels. Everything was very precise, and guards were always in pairs."

Swallowing, Alex nodded her understanding even as she glanced towards the small pile of rubble. She never wanted to go back to those dark, alien tunnels; much less if it would be even harder to fight her way out.

"If we're captured, what do we do?" Nicki asked softly, her freckles standing out against her very pale skin.

"You fight if you can," Morgana answered, her expression fierce. "But know that you fight alone. Once someone is taken into the tunnels, we do not go after them."

"Never?" Aiden pressed, horrified. "But what about Alex-"

"We would not have gone in after her," Merlin answered, his shoulders slumped and his expression sorrowful. "The tunnels are too dangerous. As terrible as it sounds, it is better to lose one mage than two or three. Our primary duty is to protect the Iron Realm, not each other."

"Hopefully it will never be a point of concern," Morgana said, raising her chin. "I suspect they only took Alex because they didn't know she was a mage. It is not the Sídhe habit to take their enemies underground. If they see you use magic or sense it in you, they won't seek to capture you; they will seek to kill you."

"That's so much better," Bran muttered only to receive a piercing look from Morgana.

"It is." Morgana turned her eyes on each of them. "The Sídhe are not known for hospitality or mercy and what would await a captured mage would be years of torture and experimentation. Do not let them take you: die fighting if you must, but never allow yourself to be taken into the tunnels."

"You cannot fathom the relief we felt when we arrived to find Alex climbing out of the tunnel with those children," Merlin added much more gently with a soft smile in Alex's direction. "There are few moments, even in my long life, that compare to the relief, pride, and renewed hope of that moment."

Aiden reached over, catching Alex's hand and gave it a quick squeeze. Blushing, Alex looked down at her boots and drew nervously in the dirt as she felt the eyes of the others on her. "I just... I didn't want to leave the children," Alex said uncomfortably. "I'd been dreaming about the tunnels for months and heard them crying in my dreams. I couldn't leave them down there."

"And that is why you found your magic and your connection to the Iron Realm," Merlin told her proudly. "Choices are the most important part of who we are, Alex, and in making that choice, you found yourself. The Sídhe will not forget what you managed any time soon."

"Does that put Alex in extra danger?" Aiden asked with a hint of alarm.

"Not really," Morgana answered with a slight huff. "The Sídhe want all mages dead: they may care about killing Alex a bit more than the three of you, but if given a choice they will still come after Merlin and I. Our half Sídhe 'abomination' status is an insult in their eyes."

"But the Sídhe made you that way," Nicki pointed out carefully, glancing between Alex and Morgana.

"Indeed," Morgana agreed with a nod, looking at Alex. "They took me as a baby and years later fused me with the Changeling they left in my place. But I don't think they were prepared for what that would mean. After all, they just wanted me to have the memories of my human life so I could blend in and take the Changelings place."

"Plus, the Sídhe never admit to mistakes," Merlin added. He looked over at Nicki. "So, Nicole, do you have any other questions?"

"Uh..." Nicki paused at the direct approach to her frequent questions but recovered quickly. "The Connection that we had to each other as magic users, those visions about each other's pasts, does that happen with the Sídhe?

"No," Alex said quickly. "Thankfully there wasn't anything like that."

"Thankfully, no indeed," Morgana answered with a shake of her head. "That would be extremely dangerous for us if we were caught in a vision each time we encountered one. Their tendency to travel in pairs would be the end of us."

"Why is that?" Nicki asked, raising her hand before quickly lowering it.

"Remember when I said that similar magic triggers Connections? That is the reason at its simplest form, but those who have loyalty to the Iron Realm can also trigger Connections. It is the loyalty, the tie to the Iron Realm that causes Connections to form as the magic reaches out to link us together. Cyrridven, the Lady of the Lake, for example, is not originally of our world, but has been in our realm so long and is truly loyal to it that when I first met her, she and I had a Connection. I saw the moment of her exile to the Iron Realm."

"Where is the Lady of the Lake?" Nicki asked, leaning forward eagerly. "Is she in the lake here?"

"No, she is not," Merlin answered with a shake of his head. "I have not seen Cyrridven for some time, nearly four hundred years. She slumbers deep in the waters of the world to keep herself untainted."

"Untainted?" Alex repeated with a frown.

"Yes, untainted," Merlin told them seriously. "You must remember that the beings that enter our world sometimes come from places in other dimensions: they come from worlds with very different physical laws and properties. The transition to our world can cause transformations to them. Cyrridven comes from the world of Avalyen, the homeworld of many of the Old Ones. Many of her people were exiled here for a variety of crimes, but our world has a strange effect on them. Many gain great power and in ancient times were mistaken for gods, and some go mad from the effects our world has on them. Cyrridven along with others discovered that staying in water had a purifying effect on them and allowed them to keep their minds intact."

"Many Old Ones spend centuries at a time sleeping deep underwater," Morgana explained. "It is one of the reasons water features as a purifying element in so many religious traditions."

"So, these Old Ones are the ancient gods?" Bran asked with wide eyes.

"Some of them," Merlin confirmed. "Not all mythology is based on them. However, the majority of stories are just that; stories thought up by humans, but in some cases, an Old One was worshiped by humans or something from another world impacted ours."

"The Realm of Avalyen is very unstable politically," Morgana told them. "They tend to banish anyone who doesn't fit into their view of things to Earth. Despite the conflict, there is a strong taboo against killing, so the common punishment is exile even though Avalyen is largely an energy world and coming through badly damages them." Morgana shook her head and sighed in displeasure.

"Lovecraft was right," Aiden muttered darkly earning a snort from Nicki.

"I don't want to fight Cthulhu," Nicki whispered back getting them a look from Merlin.

"Or they send any travelers who enter their world here," Merlin added with a sigh. "They are one of the reasons Earth has such... colorful mythology."

The students stared at them, Alex resisting the urge to fall back in frustrated, worried laughter. Aiden caught her eye and shook his head, revealing his disbelief at the conversation. Nicki suddenly moved, reaching for her day pack and pulling out a small notebook. She flipped it open to a scribbled list that Alex couldn't quite make out and raised her hand.

"Ah, I see Nicole found her list of questions," Merlin chuckled, glancing at Morgana. "Keep in mind, Nicole, that we brought snacks, not lunch. Go ahead and ask your questions."

8

Study Night

Nicki's car came to a sharp stop, bumping against the curb of the street as Alex jolted forward. In the driver's seat, Nicki laughed and gave Alex a sheepish shrug before unbuckling her seat belt. Alex turned to look out the window at the crème-colored two-story house they had parked in front of. It was normal looking with small stairs and a ramp leading up to the covered porch. Two cars were parked in the driveway, and she noted Aiden's truck a little further down the street.

"So, this is Aiden's house," Alex muttered as she climbed out of the car.

"Yep." Nicki walked around her car and joined Alex on the sidewalk. "He's lived here his whole life."

It was remarkably normal at first glance, but as she followed Nicki up onto the porch, she noticed the green man wood carving hanging to the right of the front door, and the horseshoe hung above it. There were several small stone gargoyles placed on the windowsills as if guarding the doorway. Nicki didn't bother knocking, pulling out the screen door and pushing open the front door.

"Nicki is here!" she shouted as they moved into the entryway. "Hello to all Boscos!"

A long bench with shoes piled underneath it and a long row of coat pegs filled with jackets dominated the small entry. Humming, Nicki kicked off her sneakers and set her bag down so she could pull off her coat. Alex followed her example but placed her shoes together next to the door so she could find them again.

"Hello, Nicki," a warm female voice called.

A woman in her late fifties came around the corner with a wide smile on her face. When Alex had first met Shannon Bosco in the bookstore that she owned, Alex hadn't known that she was Aiden's mother. Her light brown hair had hints of gray showing in the light of the ceiling lamp.

"And you're Alex," Shannon Bosco greeted with a wide smile as she turned her eyes towards Alex. Her eyes dropped down to Alex's stocking feet, and she chuckled. "Welcome, please make yourself as at home as Nicki does."

"Then trouble is here," the familiar voice of Professor Bosco laughed from around the corner. A moment later the tall chemistry professor and fencing club advisor with dark brown hair appeared with a wide smile. His laugh lines were very pronounced in the light as he stepped up next to his wife.

"Sorry to make you kids relocate the study session here," Professor Bosco apologized.

"It's fine," Nicki rushed to assure him. "I'm just sorry about your friend. Hopefully, the funeral will go smoothly."

"Thank you." Shannon looked over at the clock hanging on the wall opposite the coat pegs. "Speaking of which, John, we need to get on the road."

"Of course," Professor Bosco agreed with a nod. "I'll grab the bags and meet you at the car." Professor Bosco vanished up the stairs a few feet away, and Alex shifted a bit uncomfortably as Aiden's mom asked Nicki about her grandmother.

"Hey, Alex," Aiden said nearby causing Alex to jump. "Hi, Nicki."

"Hi, Aiden," Alex replied as she looked over to see Aiden standing behind his mom. "Come on this way; we've got snacks." Aiden gestured for her to follow.

"Is Bran here already?" Alex asked with a hint of confusion.

"Yeah, he arrived a bit before you. Come on." Aiden nodded his head for them to follow as his mother headed for the stairs.

They followed him out of the entry into the living room where Bran was already sitting in an armchair with his cane propped up beside him and a book in his lap. Looking up as they entered, Bran nodded in greeting to the two girls.

"Hi, Alex, hi Nicki," Bran said, leaning back in the armchair. "Did you bring your stuff?"

"Course." Nicki rolled her eyes as she held up her bag. "Don't worry so much, Bran. We'll nail this project."

Alex sat with Nicki on the sofa and set her bag down on the large coffee table where Bran could reach it. She unpacked her tablet and pulled out the book she'd checked out from the library.

"At least for once I'm not lying when I say we're working on a project," Alex said as she flicked through the book on Celtic mythology with a bored expression.

The others gave her sympathetic looks but didn't try to say anything on the topic of Alex being the mage unlucky enough to be stuck watching over Jenny and Lance, waiting for their betrayal of Arthur.

"At least I managed to get us signed up as a group for Celtic mythology," Nicki announced with a pleased smile. "We could have gotten stuck with something else."

"Well, I'm sure that most people wanted Greek or Roman mythology," Bran observed dryly.

"Yeah, but imagine being assigned Japanese and trying to sort through the various Shinto kami and different spirits," Nicki countered with a shake of her head. "That would have been tough, interesting, but tough."

"An ingenious pantheon could have been fun too," Aiden offered with a smile as he pulled the other armchair in the room over to the coffee table so he could join them. "I bet writing and presenting about Coyote could be fun."

"We have Celtic mythology," Alex reminded the others. She tapped on the book with a chuckle. "Something we wanted for our own purposes," she added in a softer voice before looking over at Nicki. "So, Miss 'I'm actually an anthropology student,' where do we start?"

"I'd say start with a list of the principal deities and heroes, but also note reoccurring themes in the stories as we go through them," Nicki answered, completely ignoring the teasing tone that had been in Alex's voice. With a dramatic motion, Nicki handed Alex one of the books.

"Aiden!" Shannon Bosco called from the entryway. "We're heading out. The money is by the fridge. Make sure your sister isn't up too late."

"Yeah, Mom," Aiden called back without leaving the living room. "Hope things go well."

"Bye, Shannon!" Nicki added, waving over the back of the couch as she picked up her tablet with her free hand. "Wi-Fi password still the same?" she asked Aiden.

"Yeah, we haven't changed it in forever," Aiden replied with a shrug. "Probably should."

"The biggest issue I see with this topic is the massive range of stories," Bran said, looking up from his book. "I mean there are all these different cycles and parts of Celtic mythology even suggest that some heroes were descended from the Sídhe."

"Which we know isn't true." Alex scanned the table of contents of the book in her hand. "Not to mention the fact that the records of their mythology come from Christian accounts during the period the Celts were being converted with no earlier chronicles since the Romans restricted the use of their written language," Bran continued with a frown. "Can't we just ask Merlin and Morgana?"

"They predate the Celts remember," Aiden said. "Celts are Iron Age; they're Bronze Age. There are centuries of cultural evolution between them and the recorded version of these myths."

Nicki huffed slightly at them, looking up from her tablet. "Look, guys, its mythology. Of course, it isn't perfect — mythology changes from generation to generation, especially when recorded by outsiders. I'm not suggesting that mythology is totally accurate for us to study, but it couldn't hurt. After all, we've already been researching some of the creatures. How bad could the rest of the mythology be?"

Bran shifted in the armchair and glanced towards Nicki before adding, "And if King Arthur is based on an ancient Bronze Age hero, then maybe one of these stories has roots with another incarnation of the Iron Soul."

Aiden made a considering face as he pondered the statement and sighed, "That would serve me right for ignoring most of Grandfather's stories from 'the old country.' Aisling always paid more attention to them than me."

"Is your grandfather dead?" Bran asked, looking over at Aiden.

"No," Aiden answered quickly with a shake of his head. "He lives at Lakeside, it's an independent living center. We visit a couple of times each month."

"Maybe part of our project should be talking with him about growing up with these stories," Bran suggested with a growing smile. "That would be distinct."

"Oh!" Nicki squealed, sitting up straighter on the sofa and nearly sending her tablet crashing to the floor. "That's a great idea! Oral histories are a really important part of understanding the tradition of stories. We could record an interview with him!"

"I'll talk to him," Aiden promised before Nicki could get too excited. "Just calm down before you hurt yourself."

A crash from upstairs followed up a masculine muffled shout made Aiden look up and sigh while Nicki chuckled. The noise continued for a few more moments until Professor Bosco came down the stairs and into view in the entryway. Aiden started to rise from his chair, but his father headed for the door with the two small suitcases.

"Bye, kids!" Professor Bosco shouted. "Aiden, don't let Aisling drink a whole bottle of pop again!"

"Yes, Dad," Aiden called back, sinking back into the armchair. "See you on Thursday!"

The door closed a moment later with a thunk and Aiden shook his head, turning his attention back to his book. Alex tried to hide a smile as she looked down at her book, flipped it open to the Ulster Cycle and glanced over the long list of names. It was all she could do not to sigh as she adjusted her tablet on her lap so that she could start typing a few notes.

A rush of footsteps on the stairs made Alex look up quickly just in time to see a preteen girl come skipping into the room. She had dark brown hair tied in a pair of pigtails and a wide smile that resembled Professor Bosco's. Alex had never met Aiden's younger sister but had heard a bit about the girl from Aiden. Yet it had been from Morgana that Alex had learned that Aisling Bosco had battled and beaten cancer when she was younger. As she watched the preteen rush over to hug Nicki, glance at the books laying open on the table and quickly take in Bran and herself, she wouldn't have guessed that the girl had ever had cancer.

"Hi, I'm Aisling," she greeted Alex and Bran with a smile. "You're Alex and Bran, right?"

"That's right," Bran replied with a nod and a small smile of his own. "It's nice to meet you, Aisling."

The girl looked at Bran, her eyes dropping to the cane and the metal leg braces that he wore. For a moment the girl's eyes darkened, and her smile faltered before she turned back to her brother. "Mom and Dad just left," she informed him with a grin.

"I know, I heard them," Aiden replied calmly. "And that means I'm in charge and no I won't be agreeing to any crazy requests."

Aisling rolled her eyes dramatically at her brother and picked up one of Nicki's books. "Celtic mythology, huh? What class is this for?"

"We have to do a presentation on Celtic mythology for our world mythology class," Nicki explained patiently. "We're just getting started with an outline of some of the core elements."

"Make sure you talk about the Otherworlds," Aisling told Nicki. "Grandpa likes to talk about some of those stories, and I don't think there's anything like it in other mythologies. The Greeks were big on sex, not alternate realities and parallel dimensions."

"Aisling!" Aiden snapped with a horrified look on his face only to receive another eye roll.

"Bro, I'm twelve, not five despite what you and Dad think. It's stupid that Mom and Dad even made you be here tonight."

"They don't want you alone overnight," Aiden countered seriously. "That's just not safe, Aisling."

"Then you could have come over later," Aisling told him, crossing her arms over her chest and glowering at her brother. "You didn't need to bring your study group over."

"This is more comfortable than the library," Nicki interrupted with a grin as she slumped back dramatically on the sofa.

"Nice try," Aisling muttered, glancing at Nicki before looking back at her brother.

"Look," Aiden said slowly after taking a deep breath. "Mom and Dad... Aisling, they worry about you being alone. It's not that we don't trust you, we worry. We're always going to."

Something in her brother's tone made Aisling's shoulders drop, and she sighed loudly. Aisling tilted her head to look at the screen of Nicki's tablet, still slumped over the back of the sofa. "The Irish fairies huh." Aisling leaned on her elbow with a bored expression. "Grandpa told me about them. The Túatha Dé Dannan were the original gods of Ireland according to myth. They came to the island in dark clouds. When the new Celtic people defeated them, they were forced to live underground after the victors claimed the surface." Alex looked up at Aisling, twisting her body so that she could see the girl's face. Aisling seemed pleased with the attention and continued with a smirk, "Of course the stories changed after the Christians came. Then the fairies were believed to be fallen angels who either sided with the devil or wouldn't take a side. That's why some are truly evil and torment humanity while others are more neutral and occasionally kind."

Aiden looked over at his sister with a small smile. "I'll be sure to tell Grandpa that you remembered his stories."

"Some kids get fairy tales, and others get the really really old kind of fairy tales," Aisling replied. Then Aisling looked over at Bran with a thoughtful expression. She nodded towards his leg. "How'd that happen?"

Alex flinched at the blunt question, but Bran didn't seem bothered by it. Instead, he calmly answered, "Car crash." Bran paused and studied Aisling for a moment. "My mom still feels guilty about it since she was driving. She worries a lot."

Aisling nodded in understanding, her eyes darting to her brother before returning to Bran. "That's rough," Aisling told him. "I had bone cancer so I couldn't walk right for a long time. First the wheelchair and then the braces." The preteen fixed her eyes on Bran and leaned forward. "I'm sure you'll walk without that brace someday."

Silence hung in the air of the living room as Alex held her breath and slowly looked towards Bran. He was peering at Aisling with a stunned expression that grew serious after a moment. Nodding to Aisling, Bran smiled slightly, and Aisling nodded in return. Then with a sudden mood change, Aisling swung around to her brother.

"Mom left money for ordering pizza; I'll go do that!" Aisling scrambled around the coffee table and headed back towards the entry hall.

"She's optimistic," Bran observed slowly, still looking a bit stunned.

"She beat cancer," Aiden replied with a smile. "She's allowed to be."

"Well, it made for a nice change someone not beating around the bush," Bran said before dropping his eyes back down to his book.

"Grandpa says that coming so close to death left Aisling with insight into the world," Aiden explained softly as he studied Bran's reaction. "That she sees things more clearly. He calls it being touched."

"Maybe," Bran replied thoughtfully, "We know of stranger things." Bran adjusted himself in the chair. In the stillness of the room, the sound of the metal brace moving seemed to echo.

Looking down, Alex tried not to blush as she remembered her reaction to seeing Bran for the first time. She'd tried not to stare, but his leg brace and cane had been one of the first things she'd noticed about him. Before their eyes had met and she'd had a vision of dried flowers, jazz music, and the smell of baking. Alex paused; she didn't know much about Bran. She knew he'd been injured in a car crash; one he'd survived only due to a magical vision that had compelled him to grab the wheel from his mother. Of her new friends, he was the only one whose family she'd never met, and he'd never mentioned his father.

They all read through their books and internet articles in silence, occasional snorts and laughs interrupting the stillness. Nicki huffed and shifted on the sofa next to Alex, bringing her feet up onto the cushions. In the kitchen, there was some sound of movement and Alex heard Aisling's muffled voice across the house. An outline of the various stories that made up the Ulster Cycles swirled in front of Alex's eyes.

"Pizza's ordered," Aisling announced as she wandered back into the doorway of the living room. She was looking down at her cell phone and waved from the doorway. "Let me know when pizza gets here," Aisling told Aiden before heading for the stairs.

Her footfalls hit the stairs with loud rhythmic thumps, making it sound more like she was jumping up the stairs. Aiden grimaced at the noise, looking towards the stairs while Alex tried not to laugh at the expression on his face.

"Younger siblings," Alex observed with a chuckle and a small smile.

"You can say that again," Aiden muttered. "How much younger is yours?"

"Ed is four years younger than me," Alex answered. "And to be fair, I'm three years younger than Matt."

The sounds of Aisling faded slightly after a door closed above their heads. Aiden glanced up towards the ceiling and then back at the book in his hands. Shaking his head, he wrote something down in the notebook on his lap.

"So have Morgana and Merlin told you anything about plans?" Aiden asked suddenly, looking back at Alex.

"What?" Alex asked, blinking in confusion at Aiden and frowning as Nicki and Bran turned their attention to her as well. "Why would they?"

Nicki chuckled softly and shook her head at Alex. "You're Morgana's favorite," she answered with a soft smile.

"I am not," Alex protested, surprised by the idea. While the Professor had certainly warmed up to her and no longer intimidated Alex as she had the first day of history class, Alex certainly didn't consider them close.

"You are," Bran told her with a nod, meeting her eyes and revealing the seriousness of his statement.

"Yeah," Aiden chimed in. "She watches you most closely during magic lessons and always smiles when you manage something new. With us, she's a bit more... distant."

"I don't think so," Alex replied with a shake of her head and a slight blush. "But anyway, to answer your question, no they haven't told me about any new plans. Why, do you think something is changing?" she asked after a moment of consideration.

"They don't pay as much attention in magic class," Bran answered calmly. "And we've pretty much got control over our current magical manifestations. I'm pretty good at moving objects, Nicki's got water control and freezing it down, and Aiden can juggle his fireballs."

Aiden and Nicki both smiled at the descriptions of their powers. "And you've got control over forming your energy balls. I figure they'll have you trying to take over our powers soon."

"I hope not," Alex exclaimed with a shiver of nervousness. "I don't want to risk hurting you guys. In the tunnels when I took over the Sídhe's magic and turned it against them... I didn't have much control. I barely remember it, but it was explosive. Honestly, I think I'm lucky I didn't hurt any of the kids I was trying to save."

"Yeah, but you'll need to learn how to control it at some point," Nicki reminded Alex in a gentler tone. "And it won't be in battle, I'm sure, they'll just have you start with a few experiments."

"And that might not be what the professors are planning," Aiden added quickly with a wide grin. "No sense worrying about it right now. We were just curious if you knew any other mage news."

"No," Alex snapped, feeling a familiar icy knot settle in her stomach that had become more and more frequent around Jenny. She hated the thought that it would become normal around her fellow mages now. "I don't have any other news."

"Okay then," Nicki said with forced cheerfulness. "Then let's get started on this project. I don't know about you guys, but I don't want anything less than an A in my chosen field of study."

"And now you're about to see Nicki's dark side," Aiden joked, giving Alex and Bran a mock serious expression before looking towards Nicki fearfully.

"I have so much blackmail material, Bosco, don't make me call your lovely girlfriend," Nicki retorted without looking at Aiden, keeping her eyes fixed on her tablet screen.

"When you call my girlfriend it's to flirt with her," Aiden countered with a laugh, but he raised his book once again with a smile.

When Nicki glanced back at Alex, she gave her friend a small smile to ease whatever worries the redhead may have had. Looking back at her book, Alex took a slow breath to calm down and tried to focus on reading more about Celtic mythology. Suddenly above her head, loud pop music began to play. They all looked up, and as Aiden groaned, slumping back on the couch. Alex giggled in response.

9

The Test

8 09 B.C.E. Shores of Loch Torridon

Arto's eyes traced the rocky shore as the boat moved smoothly along the coast. Mountains loomed just past the edges of the water, sloping up towards the sky with snow covered peaks. Despite the summer sunshine, there was a chill in the wind that Arto wasn't able to shrug off. No matter how many times he came to the north, he was always surprised by how cold the summers could be. Above them, the fast winds pushed clouds beyond them allowing the sun to shine down again. Turning his face up towards the sun, Arto barely contained a bored sigh. When they'd left their camp this morning, their escorts had been certain that they would reach their destination today and Arto desperately hoped that they were right.

At first, taking one of the big trading boats north along the west coast had been a treat and much more relaxing than the usual walking they did. He'd gotten a rare chance to spend several days with the same people and hear about their daily lives rather than just hearing about the Sídhe. In total, the crew had fourteen strong men who were happy to tell him about their families, but at the moment they were all focusing on the strong tidal currents rocking the boat. Glancing upward, Arto tried to amuse himself by finding shapes in the clouds, but he'd grown tired of that activity after the third day at sea. He huffed slightly and looked back at the shore, but even the scenery was becoming dull.

Normally they walked which while exhausting meant that he could always talk to Morgana or Merlin. His mentor had a tendency to test his knowledge of magic or make up puzzles for Arto to solve, but usually, it was Morgana that solved them. He'd been more than a little surprised when news had reached them that a trading ship was waiting to take them north due to the urgency of the situation. It may be boring, but Arto had to admit it was a big improvement on his usual trips. The boat was nearly six feet wide and almost forty feet long made of elegantly fitted pieces of wood. Despite knowing little about wood crafting, Arto had been able to appreciate the workmanship. Covering the hull were stretched animal hides, adding another layer of protection from the water. Down both sides of the boat were fourteen men all paddling while Arto watched. He'd tried rowing a few days ago but had tired rather quickly, not used to the motions.

Behind him Arto could hear Merlin and Morgana speaking, their voices carrying softly on the wind. They were debating the merits of something new that Merlin wanted to try with Morgana pointing out every little thing that could go wrong. A smile tugged at the corner of Arto's mouth as he caught fragments of the conversation. Listening to or watching his mentor and his sister was almost always amusing. They were very different with Merlin's greater age and status often irritating his sister who insisted that she had greater knowledge of the Sídhe. Merlin liked action and often encouraged him to test himself, while Morgana was cautious and preferred for Arto to stay away from danger. As his sister's voice grew angrier, Arto shook his head and quietly wondered if they would ever get along. Absentmindedly, his fingers traced over the leather sheath of Cathanáil resting on his lap before moving up to the hilt. Arto glanced down at his Sword and studied it for a moment, taking in the way the gold glinted in the sunlight before sighing once again.

One of the rowers suddenly leaned over towards Arto and called over the wind, "We're nearly there, the shore where we're taking you is just around this mountain!"

"Thank you, Manias." Arto gave the man a grateful smile.

He glanced over his shoulder in time to see his sister and Merlin stop speaking and begin to gather up their things. Merlin nodded to him and adjusted his staff across his lap as Morgana tightened her cloak around her shoulders and put her bag back on. Nodding to them, Arto slung Cathanáil over his back and slipped his bag back over his shoulder. He tugged carefully on his Sword to confirm that Cathanáil was secure. Satisfied, Arto turned towards the front of the boat again and watched the cliff side with more interest as they paddled around it.

The men rowed harder than before, forcing the boat to turn towards the shore and push them out of the movements of the sea. A sudden jolt made him laugh with excitement, but he heard Morgana gasp behind him. Glancing over his shoulder, he saw his sister uncomfortably clenching and unclenching her hands while Merlin watched with a fond look of exasperation.

"Calm down, Morgana," Merlin told her. "These large ships are capable of crossing to the west island and the mainland to the south. They can handle the shore waves."

She didn't reply to Merlin's remark which did not surprise Arto at all. Instead, Morgana reached into her side bag and pulled out a small root that she chewed on nervously. Merlin stretched his back and rolled his shoulders. The boat jolted again, less this time and Arto smiled when Morgana didn't react, catching his eye with a gleam of stubbornness in her own. The waves eased as they turned further into the inlet and followed the shore away from the sea. Long rocky beaches lined the loch with hills sloping up towards the mountains. On the northern shore, he could make out a small building and a thin stream of smoke rising into the sky. Manias shouted to his men, and they increased the speed of their rowing, pushing the boat towards the north.

Arto kept his eyes fixed on the shore as they approached, leaning forward slightly with eagerness. He could just see a pair of people. One of them started running up the steep hill behind the beach and vanished from Arto's sight as the other one came closer to the water. Rocks scratched the underside of the boat as they entered the shallows. Manias and three others leapt out into the water and pulled the boat onto the beach. They came to a sudden halt, and Arto jumped out of the boat, using the side to leverage himself out with one graceful movement. His body swayed, and he spread his stance to combat the sense of motion that his body seemed determined to keep.

"Welcome," the man who had remained on the beach greeted. His eyes were dark brown and exhausted, so Arto merely nodded in greeting and allowed Merlin to take over.

"Thank you," Merlin said, stepping closer to the man.

Morgana moved over and checked him over quickly. "Do you have everything?" his sister asked in a low voice.

"Yes," Arto answered quickly, resisting the urge to say something he shouldn't.

"I am, Merlin," his mentor stated to the man who had welcomed them. "These are my companions Morgana and Arto."

"Cailean, our priest is coming," the man replied quickly. "He'll be here soon."

"Excellent," Merlin answered with a gentle smile before turning back to Manias. "I thank you for your assistance, Manias. Our arrival would have been greatly delayed if not for yourself and your crew."

"You are most welcome, Merlin." Manias nodded and smiled. "My lads and I were glad to be of service." Manias looked up towards the sun. "But if you're safely delivered then we will be on our way. A shipment of tin is waiting for us."

"Of course," Merlin replied with a nod of understanding.

"Thanks," Arto told them with a nod towards the crew, allowing his eyes to settle on one of the back row men. "I hope your wife's delivery goes well, Beagan."

"Thank you, Manias," Morgana repeated before nodding to the other rowers. "Safe travels."

"And to the three of you," Manias told them before the rest of the crew wished them well.

The waiting villager shifted nervously as the crew pushed the boat back into the loch and began rowing towards the sea. Arto's eyes lingered on the boat for a moment as he wondered if he'd see any of them again before he turned his gaze to the waiting man. The villager was shifting in place, his hands in fists and seemed to be barely containing himself. Sighing when his sister stepped closer to him, Arto stayed silent and studied the man's face. He found only a familiar look of fear that often plagued the places they traveled and barely contained grief.

"You've lost someone," Morgana suddenly observed next to him, having noticed the same thing, her voice nearly vanishing on the wind. "My condolences."

Eyes widening, the man looked at her before giving a shaky nod. "Yes," he answered in an unsteady voice. "My wife was killed trying to save our young son, and the Sídhe took our boy."

Merlin stepped forward just enough to place his hand on the man's shoulder. "I am sorry for the pain suffered by your village. We will do everything we can to stop this."

"Cailean says there is no hope of getting the children back... is that true?" the man asked Merlin, looking at him with a spark of hope.

"I am sorry," Merlin repeated. "Your priest speaks the truth. Once someone enters the realm of the Sídhe, they are beyond our power to reach."

Dropping his eyes, the man nodded as the wind howled past them. Merlin stepped back to give the man some space and looked past him towards the hill where several more figures were moving into view. Arto's sister pushed him forward gently and took a small step back. Silence descended on the beach with only distant sounds of approaching people offering any escape.

Arto averted his eyes from the man who had greeted them, focusing instead on the group of three men who were approaching them quickly. One of the villagers was dressed a bit more finely than the others with a golden pin holding his cloak and walking straighter with a sense of urgency in his strides. He had graying brown hair and sharp brown eyes that glanced over the three of them before settling on Merlin.

"Thank you for coming so far," the first man told Merlin gratefully, his shoulders relaxing slightly and a look of relief overtaking his face. "My name is Cailean, and I'm the priest here. I'm afraid that the Sídhe have opened a tunnel somewhere near our village. Our neighbors in the next valley and we have suffered several raids."

"Have you lost children?" Merlin asked calmly with concern.

Cailean swallowed and nodded. "Yes, I'm afraid we've had limited success in repelling the Riders; so far, they've taken two infants and three smaller children. Three nights ago, they came again, but burned down several houses when they discovered that the village is nearly empty of small children."

"I'm very sorry," Merlin told Cailean, lowering his eyes and shaking his head. "There is no way to retrieve the children. That is beyond our power."

"But you can kill the Sídhe?" Cailean asked desperately. "You can keep them from coming back?"

Morgana nodded to him and stepped forward to stand next to Merlin. "We can, but we need any information you have on the location of the Sídhe tunnel. Have you noticed a direction that they ride from or found any trails?"

Cailean nodded quickly even as a sickened look crossed over his face. "Recently they tried to take my daughter," he explained in a shaky voice. "But it was nearly dawn, so they released her in order to get the youngest captives underground."

Arto felt a swell of relief that at least someone had been spared, but Cailean's words only reminded him that others had been taken. He wondered just how young they had been and how many, but couldn't bring himself to ask.

"That's rare," Morgana observed with a raised eyebrow and a slight frown.

"She is very fortunate," Merlin added quickly to cut off anything else that Morgana might say. "Did she see the tunnel?"

"I'm not sure..." Cailean admitted slowly. "When she returned... well, we performed some of the ritual tests on her to be certain that she was truly safe and they hadn't tricked us with a Changeling."

Arto saw his sister tilt her head in consideration. "So, no one has spoken with her about what she saw?" she questioned him with a deepening frown.

"She was very distressed upon her return." Cailean straightened up and regained some force in his voice. "We didn't want to make things worse once we were certain she wasn't a Changeling. Besides..." Cailean swallowed, "What could we have done about it?"

"We will speak with her," Merlin informed Cailean respectfully. "I have experience in such discussions, and I give you my word that I will do my best not to upset the girl further."

"Thank you," Cailean sighed with a nod before glancing towards Arto. His eyes lingered on the visible hilt of Cathanáil.

"We have much to do," Morgana added with a raised eyebrow as she studied the priest.

Cailean jumped and nodded sharply at her words, flushing as he turned away from them. "This way," he called over his shoulder as he began walking.

Merlin gave Morgana a displeased look, but she merely smiled and pressed a hand to Arto's shoulder to steer him forward. Sighing softly, Arto adjusted Cathanáil to be more comfortable for hiking and began to follow Cailean and the other villagers up the slope of the nearby hill and into the mountains.

It was a short hike up the hillside that surrounded the loch, and the terrain evened out slightly. In the distance, Arto could see walls and buildings and the smells of a village were carried on the wind towards them. The heavy scent of livestock nearly made him gag after so much time on the sea. Cailean looked over his shoulder at them many times as they came closer and closer to the village. Uneasiness settled over them all as the villagers accompanying them tensed up.

Arto wasn't sure if he liked northern villages better than the ones in the south. He personally thought that the stone roundhouses were a bit more impressive than the wooden woven walls in the south. Merlin had explained it to him when he was young as being due to the relative shortages of forests in the north compared to the south. Roundhouses filled the area of the fort, but their bases were made of stone with timber and grasses making up their sloped roofs. He'd never asked about how they were constructed, and despite his interest, he decided against it given the circumstances.

Arto shifted a bit uncomfortably as they moved through the village. Men and women were working outside their houses to take advantage of the sun, leaning over small tables with their tools or sitting on the ground working on various crafts. The sound of animals could be heard, but otherwise, the village was very quiet. People looked up at them as they passed and Arto swallowed as he noted the sadness lingering in the faces of many. A quick examination revealed that there were almost no children in the village. People were working on their chores, but almost no one was speaking. A glance towards Merlin and Morgana told Arto that they had noticed as well.

"Gwenyvar!" Cailean called towards a group of girls and women who were at work at a large loom set up in the yard.

All work suddenly stopped, and all of the women looked towards them. One of the girls rose from a kneeling position and quickly brushed off her dark dress before moving towards them. Arto studied her with interest for a moment: she was about his age with long brown hair in braids. He was rarely around people his own age, but the mixture of nervousness and eagerness in her face dampened his excitement. One thing he noted was that a dagger hung on her belt, something which surprised him. The girl stopped in front of them next to Cailean, folding her hands hesitantly in front of herself.

"This is my daughter Gwenyvar," Cailean told them with a stern expression as he introduced them to the young woman.

"You're the one who saw the Sídhe last?" Merlin asked, leaning on his staff and smiling gently at the girl.

Gwenyvar nodded slowly, her eyes shifting between Morgana and Merlin uncertainly. For a moment her eyes stopped on Arto, and she relaxed slightly as he gave her what he hoped was a comforting smile. It was nice to have her look at him too; usually, people glanced over him in favor of his mentor and sister.

"Yes," she finally managed to say. "I was. I guess they ran out of darkness or thought I wasn't worth it since I was struggling so much. They dropped me off the horse, and I started to run. Once dawn came, I was able to find my way home."

"How many Riders were there?" Merlin asked, his eyes staying on Gwenyvar.

"Three of them were on the horses," Gwenyvar answered. "But there were also two Sídhe not on horses nearby."

"You must have been very close to the entrance," Merlin observed thoughtfully. "The guards rarely go far from the tunnel. You are very lucky."

"I suppose," Gwenyvar replied, dropping her eyes. "But the little ones..."

"I know," Merlin agreed, placing a hand gently on her shoulder. "I know, but there was nothing you could do."

The young woman nodded uncertainly, glancing towards her father who merely nodded for her to continue. "If I show you where they took me can you stop them?" Gwenyvar asked Merlin, glancing between the three of them.

"We can prevent them from returning to this area," Merlin told her. "It may not hold forever, but it can give you some peace."

Gwenyvar opened her mouth to reply, her body relaxing slightly until loud shouts from the other side of the village made them all turn sharply. Cailean moved towards the shouts which were indistinct, but Arto was able to catch the name Sadb. There was a sudden rush of people moving that had Arto reaching instinctively for Cathanáil. Gwenyvar's eyes widened at the name, but she drew back as the villagers pushed past them. Reaching out, Arto touched the girl's arm and stepped closer to her. Merlin and Morgana were looking towards the source of the noise along with Cailean who shouted at the villagers to make way. As the people parted, Arto gave Gwenyvar a gentle push in front of him as they followed her father, Merlin, and Morgana.

Up ahead of them, the roundhouses spread out, forming an open area in the center of the village where everyone was gathering. After a moment of searching the area, Arto's eyes settled on the small little girl clutched in the arms of a crying woman who was beaming with joy. Her dark hair was tangled in knots, and dirt covered her face, but the child was smiling and toying with the necklace around the woman's neck. Around them, villagers were staring, some of them smiling, others looking worried and others looking around hopefully. Cailean strode forward and studied the woman and child with a darkening expression.

"Prepare the Changeling test," he announced to the crowd. "Quickly."

Several men quickly moved away from the woman and child, vanishing past a roundhouse in a rush of activity. The woman turned towards Cailean with wide eyes and clutched the child closer, shaking her head. Cailean looked out over the assembled villagers, raising his chin.

"She was taken by the Sídhe," Cailean declared sternly to the crowd. "We must test every child that returns or else the Sídhe may seek to trick us with a Changeling."

There were mumbles of agreement around them, and Arto noticed several men nodding even as the women began to draw back. The few remaining children in the village were being pulled away from the area. Moving forward, Cailean stopped in front of the woman who was still clutching the child.

"Roshen," he said in a quieter tone. "I understand your fear. I tested my daughter when she returned after being taken. This is something that must be done for the safety of everyone. We cannot wonder and worry."

Her grip on the toddler loosened and Cailean scooped the child from her arms. Moving away from Roshen, she joined one of the men who had taken off running in the center of the village. The man set down a large earthen basin with a huff and stepped back. Arto's eyes widened slightly as a calf was led forward towards Cailean. One of the two men leading it carried a long dagger that made Arto swallow at the sight of it. He heard Morgana inhale sharply, but didn't turn to look at her.

The men pulled the calf forward to the basin and in one smooth motion, sliced a long cut in the calf's neck. A weak bellow echoed through the village, but the three men were able to hold the calf in place. Blood gushed out of the long wound and spilled into the large earthen basin below. A few of the villagers watching flinched and Roshen glanced with worry between the small child and the filling basin. Looking towards the child, Arto frowned at the lack of worry being exhibited by the child. She was squirming in the hands of the man holding her and reaching towards her mother.

"That's enough." Cailean's eyes shifted towards Gwenyvar for a moment as she stepped back and nearly collided with Arto.

Placing a hand on Gwenyvar's arm to steady her, Arto glanced towards his sister and frowned as he noted the anxiousness in her eyes. He looked back towards the basin, a feeling of dread rising in his stomach as Gwenyvar began to shiver. The thud of the calf collapsing dead on the ground resonated through the now quiet village.

"Sadb!" Roshen yelled, lunging towards her daughter only to be caught around the waist by one of the villagers.

They said something to her that Arto couldn't make out as he turned his eyes back to Sadb who was being carried towards the basin. The small girl eyed the blood-filled basin with a frown and kept looking towards her mother; confusion and fear clear on her face. Roshen took a pained deep breath and forced a smile.

"Just do what Cailean says," Roshen managed, tears still shining in her eyes. "It will be alright, sweetheart."

Setting the girl down in front of the basin, Cailean nodded to the men who pulled the carcass away. Arto turned slightly to look at Merlin and Morgana who were both standing perfectly still with their eyes locked on the basin. Swallowing, Arto looked back towards the basin just as Cailean pushed the young girl's arm down into the blood. There was a moment of silence other than the sniffing of the little girl and Arto began to relax.

"Hurts," Sadb suddenly shouted, trying to pull her arm away from Cailean and the blood. "Hurts!" the girl screamed. Tears poured out of Sadb's eyes as hissing sounds filled the air only to be drowned out by pained screams and a horrified wail.

"This is a Changeling!" Cailean shouted, his voice carrying over the noise. "The Sídhe have tried to trick us!"

Shouting erupted around them as the villagers all began yelling different things. A hand reached out and gripped Arto's shoulder, pulling him back sharply. Stumbling back, he looked over his shoulder to see Merlin trying to guide him away. His mentor was also gripping Morgana's arm and trying to move her. Arto's eyes widened, and he frowned at the look of horror and shock on his sister's face. A sob from Gwenyvar made Arto twist against Merlin's grip to look back towards the basin.

Roshen had collapsed on the ground sobbing and ignoring Sadb or rather the Changeling as the child reached for her. Before Cailean a crowd was clearing the way, exposing an outdoor fire pit in a nearby yard. Several men rushed forward, piling on more wood as another used the bellows to fan the flames. Arto was suddenly grabbed by Morgana and forcibly turned along with Gwenyvar. Screams erupted behind them followed by the smell of burning fabric and hair.

"This way," Morgana ordered, tugging him and Gwenyvar.

Despite his sister's efforts, Arto turned his head and caught a glimpse of flames rising to surround a small body in the fire. Men with long sticks held the form down in the flames and prevented escape. He couldn't move, his eyes locked on the twisting form as it screamed and coughed in the thick blackening smoke.

Gwenyvar choked back a sob, turning quickly away from the flames and into Arto. Pulled out of his shock by the sudden jarring, Arto looked down at the top of Gwenyvar's head and brought his arms up around her. He swallowed and closed his eyes, trying to banish the image of the rising flames from his mind, but the sounds of screaming and the smell were not easy to dismiss. A yank on his arm forced him to follow awkwardly with Gwenyvar still clinging to him. Merlin had a tight grip on his upper arm and turned them, so they were moving down the path towards the village gate.

No one spoke, Gwenyvar shaking against Arto with her face still pressed into his shoulder even as she walked along beside him. Arto's pace was quick, eager to move away from the horrible event, but shaky from shock. Next to him, Morgana and Merlin were walking just as fast with Merlin's eyes moving between him and Morgana, checking them both over. They didn't stop their rapid pace until they were standing beyond the gates of the village. Morgana stopped first and took in a slow breath, closing her eyes and tilting her face up towards the sun.

"Arto," Merlin called gently, reaching towards him.

"I'm alright," Arto answered quickly, finally loosening his grip on Gwenyvar. "It's okay," he told the girl softly. "It's over."

"That was horrible," Gwenyvar whispered, her voice muffled against Arto's shoulder. "They had a fire ready when they tested me."

His stomach turned, and Arto feared that he'd be physically ill. While Morgana and Merlin wouldn't judge him, he didn't want to upset Gwenyvar further. He closed his eyes, raising his face towards the sun like Morgana had and breathed deeply. After taking several slow breaths, Arto felt in control enough to look towards his sister.

"Was that the test they used on you?" Arto asked softly without releasing Gwenyvar or looking at Morgana.

"It was," Morgana confirmed in a tight voice. "Mother preferred you not see it. Besides, children aren't supposed to be around for the test."

"I remember hearing that there had been a test, but..." Arto paused and turned to look at his sister. "You never told me about that."

"You didn't need to know. The priest came, he tested me and left satisfied," Morgana answered shortly, but she didn't hide the slight shiver that went through her body.

"Enough of this talk," Merlin ordered from ahead of them with a deep sigh. "It serves no purpose and will bring only sorrow." He paused and looked back at Gwenyvar, leaning on his staff and looking very tired. "Gwenyvar, are you well enough to lead us to where you escaped?"

Gwenyvar who had finally stopped shivering, tensed at the question and inhaled sharply. She released Arto, stepping away from him and looked back towards her village. In the distance, the sobbing of Roshen could still be heard. Swallowing, Gwenyvar nodded quickly and gestured towards a distant hill even as she stepped close to Arto once again.

"That way, if we leave now, we can reach it before nightfall."

10

Instructing Magic

Chewing nervously on the black plastic cap of his pen, Bran couldn't look away from the display of magic taking place in the classroom before him. Professor Yates and Professor Cornwall had pushed all the desks, even the professor's desk, back against the walls in order to create a large open space. The only remaining desk was the one he was sitting in. Nicki stood shifting nervously on her feet next to him. He shared in her nervousness and didn't notice as a spurt of black ink spilled onto his hand.

Alex stood in the center of the room; her gray eyes focused on the fireball that Aiden was casually tossing between his hands. Bran studied both their faces with worry, biting down harder on the pen cap. Alex's fingers were twitching, probably resisting her habit of talking with her hands and her feet were moving softly against the carpet as she shifted her stance uncertainly. Aiden was doing his best to seem relaxed, but a small crease between his eyes betrayed his worry. Bran couldn't blame him, even with Merlin and Morgana watching and knowing that it was necessary for Alex to learn to control her powers, he wouldn't feel right about throwing a fireball at an ally and friend.

"I'm ready." Alex raised her chin slightly and tried to look confident, but her voice wavered. Not much, but just enough that Bran could detect it.

Next to him, Nicki was biting at her left thumbnail while her right hand was poised at her side where a bucket of water waited in case of trouble. "This is a bad idea," Nicki muttered softly around her thumb. "Very bad."

"It'll be alright," Bran promised gently. He pulled the pen away from his mouth and set it aside before he choked on it. Bran was torn between giving her a reassuring look and keeping his eyes on Aiden and Alex.

The fireball flared in Aiden's hand as he shifted it anxiously, eyeing Alex cautiously. Tiny flames escaped from the orb like small solar flares, casting a bright orange glow around Aiden. Neither Aiden or Alex moved or spoke; there was only the soft sound of the fireball churning and crackling.

Morgana lost her patience from her vantage point on the other side of the room. Her voice echoed through the space. "Honestly, just give it a try," she scolded them.

Bran saw Aiden bite his lip before he launched the fireball towards Alex. Sudden heat filled the room as the fire left Aiden's careful control and raced towards Alex. Throwing her hands up, Alex leaned back as if fighting an instinct to run. The mere second of movement slowed down and Bran's breath caught painfully in his throat.

The fireball stopped inches from Alex, and the smell of singed hair wafted in the room. With trembling hands, Alex reached towards the still fireball and exhaled a shaky breath. The fireball sputtered in the air, still trying to finish the movement, but Alex's magic kept it in place. A small shower of metallic gray sparks burst from her hand and swirled around the fireball. Leaning forward, Bran finally let himself exhale and unclenched his hands.

Magic began to enclose the fireball, the tiny sparks meeting the small flares in flashes of light. Alex's hands were shaking, and Bran's eyes flew to her face. Blood was trickling from her lip where she was biting it. A sheen of sweat glistened on her forehead, and her body was shaking. A gray color began to take over the side of the fireball closest to Alex, canceling out the fierce orange and red coloration of the flames. Alex's hands were shaking worse now even as the gray sparks of magic began to seep further over the fireball, calming the flames and turning them a metallic color. Then the fireball began to vibrate wildly, flares of fire lashing out in the remaining red and orange half of the orb. In the corner of his eye, Bran saw Aiden take a few quick steps forward and reach towards the fireball.

"Careful," Merlin shouted, breaking the silence in the room.

Gasping, Alex moved her hands as the red half of the fireball flared, and another wave of heat surged through the room. Aiden moved his hand sharply, and the fireball spun wildly away from them both as they lost control. Bran shoved his desk back with a grunt, his legs protesting. The fireball hit the floor just in front of him and Nicki, flashing brightly and sending fiery sparks scattering over the floor. Bran inhaled the scent of singeing fabric and smoke, pushing the desk further back with his legs and cane.

"Oh god!" Nicki shouted nearby quickly followed by a loud splash of water and a sharp hiss.

It took a moment for the dark smoke to clear enough for Bran to see without his eyes burning. He coughed twice to clear the smoke and shifted to ease the pressure on his legs. His eyes dropped to the patch of floor that the fireball had hit. There was a small indent in the hard concrete with black burn marks spread around it like a star.

"Ah..." Alex trailed off and twisted her hands together.

Aiden didn't look much better, gritting his teeth together and eyeing the burn spot with worry. Bran's nose curled up against the scent of the scorched fabric. Nicki made a small sound of displeasure next to him while Alex looked over at the burned area of carpet with a guilty expression. Turning back to Morgana and Merlin, Alex stepped forward.

"I'm sorry about that." Alex's eyes darted between the two older mages nervously. "I tried to stop the fireball, but I just couldn't-"

"It's alright," Merlin assured Alex. Smiling, he placed a hand on her shoulder. "We wouldn't have done this inside if we couldn't deal with the potential consequences."

Bran tilted his head in consideration of the statement as Merlin stepped away from Alex and moved over towards the smoldering patch of floor. Morgana joined Alex and gave her a surprisingly soft smile and nodded to her. Tension melted out of Alex's shoulders, and she turned to watch what Merlin was doing with a relieved smile on her face. Bran heard Nicki sigh in relief.

"You sure you're okay?" Aiden asked softly, but his voice carried through the room as he stepped over by Alex.

"I'm fine," Alex promised him with a warm smile.

"It was pretty crazy to see you taking over my fireball," Aiden offered with a growing grin. "I knew that was the goal, but actually seeing it-"

"Shush," Morgana cut in, looking at the two of them in the corner of her eye with a small smile. "You'll want to see this."

At her words, Bran quickly looked back to Merlin, leaning forward. The older mage was looking down at the burn spot with an amused expression. He glanced around and chuckled as he noticed the attention that was fixed on him.

"I think that you will all enjoy seeing this," he announced before holding his right hand in front of him.

Sparks of green magic danced around Merlin's hand and shifted into flowing streams of green light. He smiled as he pointed his finger at the burn spot, completely ignoring the lingering bad smell, and the sparks jumped from his hand to the floor. Bran leaned as far forward as he could in the desk and bumped Nicki softly with his cane when she nearly stepped in front of him. The sparks settled into the ruined carpet and vanished from their sight, their glow fading away. Blinking, Bran was about to look back at Merlin when the carpet suddenly began to shift. Fibers stretched out from the burned remains and knitted around each other over the concrete which was suddenly clean. Carpet pad rolled out from under the frayed carpet edges, filling the space over the concrete just before the carpet finished knitting back together.

"It's a bit too clean." Merlin tapped the now repaired spot with his foot. "Maybe we should spill something on it, lest the janitor wonder."

"It will be fine," Morgana told him with a small smile as she surveyed their expressions.

Alex spoke up first, turning to Morgana and asking, "Can we do that?"

"Not quite yet," Morgana said. "But very soon."

"All of you are still learning to control your current manifestation of magic," Merlin explained as he moved away from the bright blue patch of carpet.

Merlin beckoned the main desk that had been pushed towards the wall, and it slid out over the carpet in one smooth movement that Bran couldn't help but admire. Merlin sat down on the edge of the desk so he could face all of them and beamed. "The form your magic takes is what is easiest for you at this stage; you can visualize how it works and understand it." He glanced towards Alex and added, "At least to an extent."

"What Merlin just demonstrated is using magic to enforce your will on reality," Morgana explained patiently. "Changing things beyond just the manipulation of a form of energy." She waved her hands, and the stacked desks began to float through the air around them to return to their previous positions throughout the classroom. "This is something that all mages can do once they have control of their internal flow of magic. Using too much magic for a task causes things to go wrong while not using enough can leave magic only half done and cause damage to the thing you tried to affect."

Nicki stepped forward, nearly blocking Bran's view once again, but he decided against tapping her with his cane. "So, are these like spells?" Nicki asked with excitement creeping into her voice.

"No." Morgana looked disgusted. "We don't need spells, Nicole. We are mages. We instruct magic in what we want done, and it is done."

"Spells are used by those tapping into the ebb and flow of magic," Merlin added more gently. "Throughout history, there have been some humans who have learned through focus and practice to access magic, but as they are not mages. They need rituals to command the magic."

"Wait!" Bran called out, now reaching out his cane to gently push Nicki to the side. "I thought mages were the only magic users on Earth."

Merlin chuckled and opened his mouth, but Morgana spoke first. "We are the natural magic users," she told them, glancing over all four of them. "The others are... plugging into magic in a sense. For them it is not natural, they are not chosen or born to be a mage."

"Wizards in lore are an example," Merlin explained. "There have been very few real ones, but on occasion, they do appear. Different mystic traditions have had different levels of success, but they do not have the same access to magic as us."

"Nor do they carry the responsibilities that come with our connection to the Earth's magic," Morgana added seriously.

"Indeed," Merlin agreed with a nod. "If you encounter someone claiming such a thing, be cautious, there have been cases of a human bargaining with invaders for access to their world's magic, and it has never ended well."

Bran wasn't sure if he wanted to hear that story, Merlin's eyes were dark, and Morgana's lips were twisted in a harsh frown. Out of the corner of his eye, he saw Alex and Aiden exchange a quick look and Nicki shifted her feet uncomfortably.

"Enough of this gloom," Merlin said a moment later, clapping his hands together. "Morgana and I have decided that all of you are making excellent progress. We're going to move onto the next step of your magical education," Merlin announced with a glowing smile as he shifted his eyes over each of them one at a time.

"The Sídhe will be returning soon, and you are going to help us prepare to seal this area against them," Morgana continued with a small smile of her own. "The best day to seal the tunnel once we locate it will be on the summer solstice, June 21st, but there is a great deal of preparation that is needed."

"That is where you will come in," Merlin added, picking up the conversation smoothly. "Starting this Saturday, I'll be teaching you to work iron."

"And I'll be working with each of you in refining your abilities to visualize your magic so you can start using your magic for a wider range of things beyond your current abilities." Morgana turned her eyes towards Alex and added, "And hopefully it will help you learn more control when taking over the magic of another."

Alex blushed brightly, folding her arms over her chest and nodding awkwardly. When her eyes found the spot on the carpet her blush deepened, and Bran gave her what he hoped was an encouraging smile when she looked at him.

"Awesome." Aiden glanced towards Nicki. "It would be nice not to have to worry about setting things on fire." He set his hand on Alex's shoulder for a moment and added, "It was cool for the first week, but then it got a bit irritating."

"Yeah," Nicki agreed weakly, managing a small smile. "I still think that Bran has the best power."

Smiling, Bran gestured to his bag and concentrated on a mental picture of his container of trail mix rising from the front pouch. It took a moment, but he felt the soft tug in his gut that he'd come to associate with his magic working and the messenger bag shifted slightly. The most difficult part was envisioning the small plastic bag floating through the air. He'd tried just picturing it appearing in his hand, but that had just caused the bag to tear and drop to the floor. It was getting easier, and the bag moved faster than it had when he first started, floating into his open hand. With a smile, he propped the bag open and reached in to grab a piece of chocolate, tossing it into the air and catching it in his mouth.

"Most useful in everyday life at least," Bran agreed with a widening grin. "But you're better at fighting the Sídhe."

"You each have your own strengths," Morgana announced in a voice that left no room for argument. "Now, it is getting late. We will send you details of when and where to meet. Dress comfortably, but nothing too loose."

The dismissal was clear, and Bran nodded, hoisting himself up from his seat as the others moved to finish straightening out the desks. He paused and adjusted his posture to make sure that his brace was secure and his footing was stable before scooping up his coat and bag. Stepping back, Bran pulled his desk sideways to fit it properly into the row and adjusted the two around it without a word to the others. Merlin and Morgana were speaking to each other in the unfamiliar language that they used on occasion, but neither looked upset, so Bran joined the others. Alex pulled on her coat and swung her bag on as they stepped out into the hallway and headed for the stairs.

"You okay, Alex?" Nicki asked softly, her voice echoing in the tiled corridor.

"I'm fine," Alex assured them all with a rather forced smile. "Just a bit tired and feeling... I don't know. I'm just disappointed that I couldn't get it. I managed it in the tunnels."

"Not as much adrenaline," Aiden suggested, leading the way up the stairs. "You knew that the Sídhe would hurt you." He glanced over his shoulder at her. "I hope you know that I wouldn't hurt you."

"And you were worried about it hurting us too." Nicki put her arm around Alex's shoulders. "You'll get it, don't worry about it so much."

Bran nodded in agreement, taking a deep breath of fresh air as they stepped outside. "Then you'll have the best magical ability," he added with a smile. "Turning the Sídhe's magic back on them."

"Well...." Alex trailed off and then smiled slightly. "That would be pretty cool."

"Then don't worry about it so much," Aiden insisted. "We never thought we'd manage magic in the first place and now we're moving onto something new and more powerful. We're awesome."

Shaking his head at the comment, Bran couldn't help but smile. By silent agreement they all stayed together and near the street lamps as they headed back towards the dorms, turning their conversations to classes and homework instead of magic and invading Sídhe.

11

Seen and Heard

As the elevator doors opened, Alex hummed softly to herself and twirled her small key ring on her index finger. The keys clinked together as Alex waved at one of their neighbors. It was odd, she decided with a soft hum, to suddenly have a free Thursday night. She'd grabbed dinner with her fellow mages in Michaels Dining Hall at six o'clock as usual, but instead of heading to Kittell Hall they'd split up to return to their dorms. Since the start of magic lessons after Halloween, she'd become used to the schedule of practice and lectures, excepting only Thanksgiving and Christmas breaks. To take advantage of the extra free night, Alex was already mentally listing the upcoming deadlines that she had for papers and the reading she still needed to finish.

Stopping in front of the door with the number 321, Alex spun her keys and fit the correct one into the lock. Inside she could hear muffled sounds, presumably a movie or Jenny humming. With a smooth motion, Alex turned the key, unlocking the door and eased it open. The main light was off, and the curtains were drawn with only Jenny's desk lamp illuminating the space. The sounds were no longer muffled, and Alex blushed bright red as her eyes were drawn to the figures in Jenny's bed. Limbs were tangled around sheets, and a dark, muscular back blocked her view of Jenny. A loud moan echoed through the small space and snapped Alex out of her shock. Slamming her eyes closed, Alex stepped back and eased the door closed. As the lock clicked back into place, Alex opened her eyes and darted back to the elevator. An embarrassed giggle escaped Alex, making her blush even redder and she shook her head.

"Sock on the doorknob, Jenny," she muttered as she opened her bag and looked inside of it. "I mean seriously if you and Arthur-"

Alex froze in place, her stomach twisting and a cold feeling rushing up her spine. She didn't even notice when the elevator doors opened and a pair of girls stepped inside. The skin of the person in bed with Jenny had been dark.... Arthur was white. Every worry about Jenny cheating with Lance on Arthur crashed through her, making her knees buckle. Reaching out, Alex caught herself on the wall and fought to keep the sick feeling surging through her in check.

"Hey?" a female voice cut in. "You okay?"

Alex's eyes snapped to a short brunette girl who was giving her a worried look and awkwardly shifting in place next to her friend.

"Yeah," the other girl said with a shake of her head and a shrugging motion. "You don't look so good."

"Feeling a bit sick," Alex replied weakly. "Just need to go to bed."

When the elevator opened again, Alex jumped out without even looking to see which floor she was on. There were sounds behind her as someone called after her and people moved to the elevator, but Alex didn't stop. She rushed into the stairwell, shivering at the cold air in the cement space and leaned against the wall, the icy feel of the cement through her shirt distracting her as she struggled to focus.

"Dammit," she hissed, clenching her hands into fists and slamming them back against the wall. "Dammit, Jenny!" Letting her head fall back against the wall, Alex took several deep breaths in an attempt to calm down, but her mind was racing. She couldn't remember a calming thought; couldn't remember the tricks she'd used to meditate while trying to learn to control her magic. There was only a sense of betrayal and a feeling of worry.

Biting back the urge to swear or scream into the stairwell, Alex pushed herself off the wall and glanced at the floor number before heading down the stairs. She kept moving when she reached the first floor and stepped outside. Indecision made Alex pause as she looked towards the other dorms and started to reach for her phone. Telling the others would be a good first step, but Alex wanted to speak with Morgana. Maybe she'd have some ideas of what to do now. Watching and being Jenny and Arthur's friend hadn't achieved anything. Closing her eyes, Alex took in another slow breath in hopes of calming down.

Another burst of bile surged up her throat as the image of Jenny tangled up with Lance sprung unbidden to her mind. Shaking her head, Alex opened her eyes and started heading for the Hamilton Building. Questions were echoing through her mind: how long had this been going on? Did Arthur suspect? Was this the first time? Did this happen every time she was at magic classes? What would they do now? How could they protect Arthur from the fallout of finding out the girl he'd been dating since he was sixteen was cheating on him with his best friend? How much choice did Jenny and Lance have in this? Had it always been inevitable?

Without meaning to, Alex thought back to Halloween. Despite being chased by Sídhe Hounds and finding out from Professor Cornwall and Professor Yates that magic was real, she'd made it home before Jenny. Lance had taken Jenny home... he'd promised to pick her up too but never returned. She hadn't thought much about it, but suddenly Alex couldn't help but pour over every detail of Jenny coming home that night. At the time she'd been too overwhelmed by the revelation of magic and fear that the Hounds might have hurt her roommate to think about it, but now everything took on a much worse possibility.

"Alex!" a male voice shouted behind her, "Wait up."

She recognized the voice and swallowed painfully. Sucking in a sharp breath, Alex turned slowly and looked over to see Arthur Pendred walking up the sidewalk towards her. His backpack was tossed over one shoulder, and his letterman jacket was hanging open to reveal a Ravenslake University t-shirt. Alex barely kept herself from running away as he jogged toward her, his blond hair shining in the light of the setting sun.

"Arthur." Alex's entire body tensed up as her smiling friend reached her.

"What's up?" he asked.

"Not much," Alex forced out. She resisted the urge to drop her eyes. Her fingers twitched awkwardly, and Alex folded her hands in front of her to keep them from moving.

"Alex?" Arthur called, his smile falling away. "What's wrong? Are you okay?"

He started to reach for her, his blue eyes darkening with concern. Instinctively, Alex stepped back and did her best to ignore the hurt that flashed in Arthur's eyes. Instead, she gestured over her shoulder and forced a sad smile.

"I got a really poor grade on a test," she lied quickly. "I was going to see if I could catch my professor before she leaves for the day."

His shoulders relaxed slowly and Arthur retracted his hand, letting it fall to his side. Alex was sure that he didn't believe her, but he seemed ready to let it go for the time being. Once again, the image of Jenny and Lance together and the sounds flashed to the front of her mind. Her stomach turned, and the need to tell him surged through Alex. Biting her lip, Alex shoved her hands in the pockets of her coat to hide how badly they were shaking.

"Okay," Arthur said slowly. "Good luck with your professor." Alex lowered her eyes only to feel one of Arthur's large hands settle on her shoulder. He squeezed it gently, sending a spark of warmth through her arm and upper chest. "If there is anything I can do, just let me know."

"Thanks," Alex whispered, barely managing the word. "You're a good friend," she added, keeping her eyes down as moisture began to gather in her eyes. "I've got to get moving."

Pulling away from him, Alex turned and started walking quickly down the sidewalk, her eyes locked on Hamilton Hall in the distance. She managed a quick wave over her shoulder and shouted for him to have a good night. When Alex reached the doors of Hamilton Hall, her hands were shaking badly, and it was becoming harder to breathe. A professor coming out of the building held the door open for Alex and called to her after catching sight of her expression, but Alex waved him off quickly and headed for the staircase.

Turning sharply to the right at the top of the stairs, Alex locked her gaze on a door down the corridor. There was no light on, but the main door of the history department was still propped open. She forced herself to slow down as she stepped inside and glanced over the department administrator's desk, but everything was packed up for the night. The only light was coming from a small crack in a doorway at the end of a small hallway leading off the main office space. A sigh of relief escaped Alex as she heard the voice of Professor Cornwall coming from her office, muffled slightly, but distinctly hers.

When she reached the door, Alex raised a shaking hand to knock on the doorframe, but then she heard her name. "I'm not sure about having Alex stay with Jennifer," the voice of Professor Yates said. "She's been losing weight since she found out."

"That could be any number of things, Ambrose," Morgana countered. "Besides, it is the middle of the semester. Alex would have to give a good reason to change roommates at this point and risk alienating herself from Jennifer. Neither of us has classes with the girl, Lance, or Arthur. We need Alex to be our eyes."

Pausing, Alex swallowed and lowered her hand to her side. She knew she should knock or maybe go back to the main door and call for Professor Cornwall, something to announce herself. Still, she didn't move from her spot by the door.

"There are other options," Merlin insisted, and Alex could hear the frustration growing in his voice.

"This is the twenty-first century. We can't just take an interest in random young people without suspicions coming forth. None of them have majors in our department," Morgana scoffed. "The world makes the Iron Soul easy to find, but this era makes him hard to reach."

"We may be worrying too much." Merlin's voice took on a gentler note. "Let's stay to the original plan, train up the mages first so they can help protect the Iron Soul and protect themselves, and then we worry about the Iron Soul. Even we can't manage five novice students at once."

"I don't think that Jennifer Sanchez and Lance Taylor can be trusted." The volume of the conversation was becoming louder. "Their public behavior may be normal, but they will follow the same path as before and the consequences-"

"Morgana, I understand your concern, but we cannot take justice into our own hands," Merlin said. "We don't know if the betrayal has taken place yet; it may not take place for many years."

Alex's hands shook as she reached for the doorknob of the office, but she didn't touch it. A sense of illness overtook her once again, stronger than before. Alex kept her eyes glued to the doorknob rather than close them and risk seeing Jenny and Lance once again.

"Ambrose," Morgana sighed, her volume dropping as a weary note entered her voice. "I recognize that it is not their fault, but the Sídhe are invading again. We cannot risk facing them without the Iron Soul. I –we can't manage without his powers." The professor's voice became soft and thin making Alex step closer to the door. "When they find us... I can't.... if Arthur isn't able to stop them."

"I'm sure that-"

"No, Merlin," Morgana hissed. "Nothing is certain. We can be sure of nothing, but our responsibility to protect and teach the Iron Soul. The other mages are almost ready to help protect him and aid him in this fight, you and I both know that we will have to reach out to Arthur Pendred soon."

"I am aware that time grows short."

"If they are approaching the moment of betrayal then we must prevent it," Morgana said. "Even through extreme measures. Otherwise, the consequences will be far worse than the actions we take." There was silence for a long moment, and Alex couldn't breathe. "I know that forcing the Iron Soul to reincarnate could be an option... one I even suggested, but things are moving so quickly. The political turmoil amongst the Sídhe makes things too unstable."

"I know," Merlin answered quietly. "The only thing more dangerous than a Sídhe is an unpredictable Sídhe."

"Arthur's rebirth isn't an option," Morgana said firmly, but with a hint of sadness. "And we cannot allow him to be broken by their betrayal." Morgana paused, and her sigh was audible even through the door. "It wouldn't be the worst thing that we've done."

"No," Merlin agreed after a moment. "It wouldn't be." There was the sound of a chair moving, and on instinct, Alex drew back slowly from the door. "Yet I mourn for Gwenyvar and Luegáed almost as much as I mourn for Arto. He would not have wanted it this way."

"No," Morgana replied, her voice tight and pained. "I'll not debate you on that, Ambrose, but what else can we do?"

"Killing them will still cause Arthur great pain," Merlin reminded Morgana. "It will not be their betrayal, but ours. It would have been kinder to kill him and force his reincarnation as you suggested."

"There is no time for him to be reborn and grow up once more," Morgana insisted, anger creeping into her voice.

"I know, three thousand years old and yet time is still our enemy. Please, Morgana," Merlin implored. "You promised me a year before you exercise your pragmatism."

"I did," Morgana agreed, her voice stronger, but resigned. "You said that you wouldn't agree to that."

"And you said that you didn't require my agreement."

Alex was back near the main reception desk, but the words seemed to be ringing down the hallway to her. Only her beating heart and struggle to breathe interfered with her ability to hear their conversation. But she doubted that anything could have prevented her from hearing Merlin's final words on the subject.

"You also said that you knew that I wouldn't stop you," Merlin said, his voice sad and defeated. "You are right, Morgana, I won't stop you."

Sucking in a sharp breath, Alex stumbled back and hit her hip on the edge of the desk. The shock of pain spurred her into action, and she dashed for the doorway. Racing out into the hallway, Alex was grateful that the building was closing down for the night. She barely it made it down the stairs without tripping and staggered out into the setting sun.

She couldn't go home, Jenny wouldn't be expecting her for at least another hour, and the idea of seeing her roommate with Lance again made her knees shake. Licking her lips, Alex swallowed and tried to moisten her mouth. A groan of pain escaped Alex as she walked towards the library. Her body ached as if she was truly carrying a heavy weight on her shoulders. Normally she would have paused to admire the shimmer of the red and orange of the setting sun off of the elegant sloping glass of the library's front and the way it made the old red bricks gleam, but tonight Alex kept her head down and went inside quickly.

Finding a table hidden back in the corner of the literature section, Alex laid her hands on her arms and took slow deep breaths. Tears prickled at her eyes, but Alex closed her eyes tightly, refusing to let them fall. Still, the tears slipped out of the corners of her eyes and traced the contours of her face.

"Dammit, Jenny," Alex whispered. "Dammit, Lance." A thick lump in her throat made her cough and Alex had to fight to breathe. "And damn you both, Merlin and Morgana!"

12

Battle in the Gorge

809 B.C.E. Near the shores of Loch Torridon

Arto was careful to keep his eyes roaming the landscape but found himself glancing back to Gwenyvar with every few steps. Her shoulders were squared with determination, and her mouth was set in a stern expression. Turning his gaze, Arto focused on a rocky outcropping ahead of them. Mountains covered in lush grass and accented by long ridges of stone surrounded them.

Merlin's voice from behind them cut through the heavy silence, "How much further?"

"Not much further," Gwenyvar promised, raising a hand to shelter her eyes from the low sun as she looked around. Arto saw fear flash over her face, but it was quickly gone. "But it will be dark soon. There will be Riders," Gwenyvar cautioned them in a neutral voice that hid her worry rather well.

"I'm certain of that," Merlin remarked calmly.

Arto knew without looking that the older mage was leaning on his staff and surveying the mountains and hills around them with a small smile. It was likely that Merlin's fingers were drumming a tune on his staff in time with the wind and the soft clinking of the many amulets around his neck. He'd be watching for unexpected movement, but showing no concern at the danger, they were walking into. In the many years he'd lived and traveled with Merlin, Arto could only remember a handful of times that he'd ever seen his mentor openly worried.

A change in the lighting made Arto turn back towards Merlin just in time to see his mentor's green magic swirling together and brightening to form a small orb of light. Ignoring a gasp from Gwenyvar, Merlin hummed softly and placed the orb at the top of his staff. Small vines of green magic snaked out of the orb to secure the light source firmly at the top of the staff. Arto struggled not to smile as he caught the look of surprise and wonder that washed over Gwenyvar's face. Morgana nodded in agreement, drawing Arto's eyes to his sister. Morgana opened her palm, and her silvery magic spun together to form a glowing silver cord that twined itself around her hand, wrist, and fingers.

"We'll be fine," Arto promised Gwenyvar. He was trying to sound confident for her sake and pulled himself up to his full height. "We won't let you be harmed," he added more gently.

It was a foolish promise to make her, things went wrong all the time, and a large enough force of Riders and Hounds could easily distract them to the point that Gwenyvar would be an easy target. Still knowing that and knowing the fate that awaited Gwenyvar if she was captured made Arto only want to protect her more. After all, she hadn't been forced to show them the way; she'd chosen to. Otherwise, it might have been days of tracking and risking more attacks on the village. But the heat in his chest and cheeks reminded Arto that he wasn't just expressing gratitude or doing his duty as a mage.

Gwenyvar smiled at him, her facial features finally relaxing, making her even prettier in the setting sun. She nodded to him; her eyes lighter than before like she truly believed that they could keep her safe. The thought both pleased and worried him. As she started walking forward again, Arto glanced back to find Merlin watching him with an amused expression and barely suppressing a chuckle. His sister was looking at Gwenyvar with a small thoughtful frown. Blushing, Arto turned around quickly and followed Gwenyvar. He nearly stumbled on a rock, just catching himself as Merlin stepped forward and caught his shoulder.

"We aren't staying, Arto," Merlin cautioned him gently in a low voice.

Arto swallowed and gave Merlin a sharp nod. Moving quickly, he rejoined Gwenyvar and scanned the hillside. His fingers twitched, and Arto thought about drawing Cathanáil, but Merlin had lectured him many times over the years about moving in unfamiliar terrain with the drawn weapon. There was an itch at the back of his neck that he couldn't quite shake off.

"What will you do at the tunnel entrance?" Gwenyvar asked him, her brown eyes glancing between him and the landscape.

"Break the connection between their world and ours," Arto answered, slipping back into more familiar territory.

Looking forward, he sighed softly and recited the speech he'd given many times before to explain how the Sídhe tunnels functioned and limitations on the tunnels. Gwenyvar listened attentively, her gaze jumping to Cathanáil strapped to his back. Arto figured that even with the two-foot blade hidden and protected in the leather sheath, the golden hilt still made for an impressive sight.

"But they can rebuild the tunnel?" Gwenyvar frowned at the sudden thought and bit softly at her lip.

"It takes time and if a region doesn't have much more that they want than they may not rebuild at all," Arto told her, gesturing vaguely around them. "I'm sorry to say it, but there aren't many more young people in your village right now. The Sídhe Queen may target another area."

"But-" Gwenyvar bit harder at her lip, clearly torn about his remark. "Can't you... can't you stop them? Do more than kill the Riders and break the tunnels?" She asked in a rush, her voice almost hysterical. "Otherwise, they'll just come after us again or go after another village."

Shifting uncomfortably, Arto resisted the urge to duck his head and look away from her. Instead, he swallowed quickly and said, "There isn't anything else we can do yet." He paused and licked his lips before adding, "We're working on it."

"I'm sorry," Gwenyvar replied with reddening cheeks. "I didn't mean... I didn't mean to sound ungrateful. What you're doing now... I couldn't do it."

"It's okay," Arto assured her quickly.

He didn't like the idea that his response had upset her and didn't like the hurt that he was feeling at her words. Of course, he wanted to do more than stop a few Riders, he wanted to save those that had been taken like his sister and after the test he'd just seen, he even wanted to find a way to help the Changelings. Swallowing, Arto forced down the bile that was threatening to make him physically ill as the memory of the screams echoed in his ears.

"That was the first time I ever saw the test," he admitted, forcing himself to keep walking. "It was terrible, and I do want to be able to do more against the Sídhe."

He saw her nod in the corner of his eye and the tension in his shoulders eased slightly. Breathing deeply, Arto frowned as his fingers began to tingle and the itch at the back of his neck worsened. He reached back and scratched the spot quickly as they began to descend into a small narrow gorge. Long shadows stretched out around them, and Arto put a hand on Gwenyvar's arm to stop her from walking into the shadows.

"Merlin." Arto studied the darkness around the rocky outcropping and the shade cast off the hillside in the setting sun.

He didn't turn his attention away from the gorge, fearing that Hounds might already be coming out, but he heard Merlin's footfalls as he came towards them. A few moments of silence passed, and then Merlin calmly stepped around them to take the lead. The orb of light at the top of his staff brightened, illuminating the immediate area of the gorge. It was deeper than Arto had assumed, dropping down sharply with large rocks limiting his view. The steep slopes of the gorge were a mixture of sharp rocks that were falling apart and pale green vegetation. There was no sound of movement from down the ravine, no birds or small creatures. Carefully, Arto unsheathed Cathanáil and waited for a signal from Merlin.

Finally, Merlin slipped forward, taking careful steps on the slope as he led them in. Arto stayed beside Gwenyvar but was mindful of giving Merlin plenty of space. Behind him, he heard his sister following them to bring up the rear. He exhaled and forced his muscles to relax, gently rolling his shoulders. The familiarity of the situation was soothing, this he understood. He knew what to expect. Cathanáil's hilt fit perfectly in his hand, and the weight was comforting. As Merlin led the way forward, Arto pushed his magic into Cathanáil. His skin tingled as the magic he'd pounded into the iron when the Sword was forged awoke and Arto closed his eyes. The metal turned warm as white sparks of magic gathered across his skin and seeped into the hilt. With a mental nudge, Arto visualized the magic flowing from the hilt down the blade of the Sword.

Opening his eyes, Arto smiled as his magic pulsed down the long blade like cascading light, illuminating the area around him and Gwenyvar. He allowed his eyes to linger on the Sword for only a moment, drawing pride and strength from its very existence. The Sídhe were dangerous, they were an illness to his realm, and they had used and badly hurt his sister. This part of his life was simple, and he enjoyed the moment of clarity.

"Stay close to me," Arto ordered Gwenyvar in a low voice.

They moved forward slowly, taking care to illuminate the shadows behind the large rocks while another guarded. The sun continued to sink in the sky and was gone from their sight as they carefully moved further into the gorge. Small sharp rocks rattled under Arto's boots and clinked softly with each step despite his best efforts.

A howl echoed through the gorge, high-pitched and menacing. Growls and snarls joined the howl, creating a terrible din that rang against the rocks. Gwenyvar stepped closer to him, placing herself just behind his left shoulder. He could hear her breathing become harsh as she fought the urge to run. Sounds of movement echoed towards them, hooves against stones and the snarling of hounds. Reaching out, Arto gripped Gwenyvar's shoulder and pushed her towards a large boulder jutting out the side of the gorge.

"Hide," he growled, raising Cathanáil in front of him.

The blast of a horn echoed down the gorge and into the night air drowning out the Hounds and the hoof beats. He stepped towards the right to give Merlin more space just as a Rider on a tall shimmering steed charged into the light of Merlin's staff. His mentor moved quickly, whirling the staff back and thrusting his right hand forward. The ground rumbled, and green sparks glistened across Merlin's skin. Underneath the Rider's steed, the rocks heaved up and struck the beast in the belly. The steed stumbled, its Rider gripping the saddle with both hands to stay on the beast.

Morgana stepped up next to Arto in a graceful leap and unfurled the glowing cord in her hand. It lashed out through the air past Merlin and struck the horse in its chest. The Rider was thrown to the ground as the steed dissolved in a shower of golden dust that was carried away by the wind. Jumping forward, Arto gave the Rider no time to recover and raised Cathanáil over his head. The Rider twisted, trying to stand, but his movement exposed the back of his neck to Arto. Cathanáil crashed down on the Rider, and the Síd vanished in a flash of magic.

In the corner of his eye, Morgana's magic flared once again and flashed through the air to strike down a Hound that was leaping through the air towards him. Two more Riders were charging alongside three more Hounds. One of the Riders, dressed in the most elaborate golden armor Arto had yet seen, gestured towards Merlin and unleashed a pulsing orb of energy. Merlin's green magic swirled before him as the Síd's attack collided with the magic. Sparks showered down around them, flashing brightly and blinding everyone for a split second.

Unable to see, Arto swung Cathanáil when he heard the snarl of a Hound. He stumbled when Cathanáil collided with something but threw his weight against the blade. An animalistic cry reverberated around him as his vision began to clear. A Hound vanished with a small flash of light and Arto fell forward, his knees scraping against the rocks.

"Arto!" Gwenyvar shouted as he shook his head.

The pain cleared his mind and eyes, and once again his gaze swept the area. One Rider was rearing up in front of Merlin with no sign of the other, and two Hounds were snarling at his sister. Taking one hand off of Cathanáil, Arto breathed and willed his magic into his palm. A tingling sensation swept up his arm as white sparks gathered in his right palm. Turning his hand, he shoved the magic towards the Hounds. A bolt of magic burst from his hand, twisting through the air with a crack and striking both Hounds. There were twin cries before the animals fell to the ground.

Morgana glanced at him and nodded quickly before rushing to join Merlin. Moving quickly, Arto swung Cathanáil down on the first injured Hound before it could stand and watched it vanish. The second Hound managed a weak snap of its teeth at him, but Cathanáil's blade pierced its side, and it was gone. Looking back toward Merlin, Arto tensed as he saw two more Riders rush into view along with a strangely dressed Síd. The new Síd wasn't dressed in the familiar golden armor of the Riders. Instead, the newcomer wore a long blue robe with an intricate embroidery design that glistened in the magical light. Violet eyes met his gaze before swinging away towards his sister. Even from his position down the gorge, Arto heard a sharp intake of breath from Morgana.

"The Traitor," the strange Síd hissed towards Morgana.

His sister moved quickly: a silver blast of magic rushed from her hand towards the newcomer. The Síd gestured, and a golden wall appeared before him, catching Morgana's magic. A swirl of gold and silver mixed in the air, making the hairs on Arto's arms stand up and everyone took a careful step back. A growl of anger escaped Morgana, who ran around the small magic storm and unleashed another blast of magic. The newcomer leapt off his steep, crashing to the ground as the animal reared and dissolved. Hounds jumped over the ridge and into view, snapping at Morgana who drew back in surprise. Merlin waved towards Morgana, and a wall of rock rose up between her and the Hounds, allowing a breath of relief to escape Arto.

Two Riders and three Hounds were blocking access to the newcomer, placing themselves between him and the mages. Morgana screamed something that Arto didn't understand, and her silver magic swirled around the wall that Merlin had made, sending it crashing down on the Hounds trying to attack her. Their whimpers were barely heard over the huffs of the horses and the snarl of the Hound which hadn't been caught in the rockslide.

Arto ran towards the fight, his eyes focusing on Morgana long enough to see his sister release two small magic orbs that dissolved the Hounds. A Rider swung his sword toward Merlin who gestured quickly. The Rider was thrown off his steed and against the rocky side of the gorge. Morgana's magic lashed out once more to strike the horse which dissolved with a sharp cut off cry. Fighting to stand, the Rider gathered a ball of magic which dissipated into the night air when Merlin's blast hit its chest.

Arto's eyes locked with those of the remaining Rider who spurred his horse forward. Merlin jumped out of the way of the Rider and grunted in pain as he hit the rocky ground. There was a shout from Morgana, but Arto didn't properly hear it. Cathanáil glowed in front of him, and he glared at the coming Síd. Arto saw Morgana start to run towards him only to be attacked by the strange robed Síd with a shower of golden strings that formed a net around her. The sight distracted him: the Rider released a burst of magic that sent him falling to the ground.

His back ached as the sharp rocks dug into him through his clothing. Cathanáil clanged against the ground as it fell from his hand. There was a mixture of shouts from Merlin, Morgana, and Gwenyvar and the sound of hoofs against rock. His skin tingled, and he felt the pull of Cathanáil as his magic sparked between his hand and the Sword. Opening his eyes, he felt more than saw the Rider bearing down on him. Rolling abruptly to the side, Arto narrowly avoided the sharp hoofs of the Sídhe steed. He opened his hand and tugged on his magic, pulling it to him like a fishing net. Cathanáil flew into his hand and Arto fell to the side, swinging Cathanáil down on the leg of the Rider's steed.

He stumbled to his feet, leveraging himself up awkwardly against a small boulder and looked around. Merlin was running towards him while the strange Síd in blue was still throwing spells towards the distracted Morgana. Suddenly Merlin stopped and swung back, throwing a blast of green magic against the mysterious Síd, forcing it back. The last Hound lunged toward Merlin's right side. On instinct, Arto raised his hand and pictured the Hound being struck by a bolt of white magic. A shock traveled through his fingers and a small, bright spark of magic escaped his grasp. The magic intercepted the Hound, knocking it away from Merlin.

"Arto!" Gwenyvar shouted behind him. "The Rider!"

Spinning, Arto brought up Cathanáil as he saw a flash of gold. His knees buckled as the Síd's sword collided with his. His right foot moved back, giving him more leverage against the strength of the Rider. The blades hissed against each other as the metals scraped together: enchanted iron versus Sídhe gold. Arto looked at the Rider, meeting its violet eyes once again. The Rider's face looked strange in the glow of Cathanáil, every sharp angle of its otherworldly face standing out more than usual and its skin and hair shining almost translucently.

Behind him, there was more shouting. Arto stepped back quickly, hoping to throw the Rider off balance. His foot collided with the boulder he'd used to stand. Sliding his foot up the boulder, Arto huffed in pain as his arms protested holding back the Rider any longer. Pushing himself off the boulder with a scream, Arto knocked the Sid back and pulled Cathanáil away.

Swinging Cathanáil, Arto aimed for the Rider's head. The golden sword blocked the attack, but they both kept moving. Arto shifted his weight and removed a hand from Cathanáil, planning to use more magic, but the Rider lunged at him forcing him to turn his body to avoid the blow. Bringing Cathanáil up, Arto lashed out towards the Rider. His Sword shuddered as it struck the Rider's golden armor which pulsed with magic.

The Rider retreated as his armor began to dissolve and glanced down at itself. They were left only in a shimmering white undershirt. Sucking in a quick breath, Arto gripped Cathanáil with his right hand and summoned forth magic in his left hand. With a sudden cry, the Rider swung and leapt towards him. The golden sword cut into Arto's left arm, leaving a long bleeding slice up his forearm. Gritting his teeth, Arto brought up Cathanáil to block another attack even as his magic dissipated.

Gwenyvar shouted, there was a soft thud, and the Rider suddenly stopped, violet eyes wide with shock. Past the Rider's shoulder, Arto caught a glimpse of Gwenyvar throwing another rock. It hit the Rider in the back with a soft thump, surprising both Arto and the Rider. He recovered first and swung Cathanáil just as the Rider started to move back. The Sword sliced down the Rider's front, cutting into the Rider's flesh. Arto only saw the pale blood for a split second before the Rider vanished in a flash of magic. His sister was at his side in a moment, gripping his injured arm and studying it carefully. Merlin stepped up behind her. Arto closed his eyes, took a deep breath and then reopened his eyes to look at Merlin.

"The other Rider and Hound?" Arto asked.

"Dealt with," Merlin assured him, studying Arto with some concern. "One fled back into the tunnel. If we move quickly, we should be able to collapse the tunnel before anymore try to come through."

"I doubt they will even try." Morgana released his arm to pull out some long strips of fabric from her belt pouch. "They know that this tunnel is lost, for the time being at least."

"Gwenyvar threw rocks at the Rider," Arto told them, a laugh escaping him as he said the words.

Merlin's eyebrows went up as a look of genuine surprise took over the older mage's face. "Good for her," Merlin said with a soft chuckle, turning to look at her. "I will make sure she is alright. Arto, allow your sister to bandage you and then we will finish the task at hand."

As Merlin stepped away, Arto examined the gorge. There were scorch marks on many of the rocks, and he found himself wishing he'd had the time to observe the robed Síd's powers properly.

"Which one escaped?" he asked despite being confident of the answer. "The robed Síd?"

"Yes," Morgana muttered. "The last Rider and Hound protected him, and he ran back into the tunnel on foot. Coward," she hissed as she tightened the bandage around his arm with a sharp tug. "At least this was only a scratch: you must practice with Cathanáil more, Arto."

"Who was he?" Arto asked, watching his sister's face.

Her expression was angry, embarrassed, and ashamed all at once as her green eyes darkened with heavy thoughts. He regretted the question and the desire to reach out and comfort her rose up sharply in Arto. It was only the sharp look that said she wanted no pity that she gave him that stilled Arto's hand. Morgana said nothing and Arto shifted awkwardly, preparing to step away now that the bleeding in his arm had been stopped.

"He's a servant of Queen Scáthbás; his name is Murden." Morgana sighed in resignation. "He was the Sídhe mage who fused me and my Changeling counterpart." Morgana's frown deepened, and she looked around. "I wonder why he was here. Riders are simple Síd with low-level magic, Murden is a highly trained Sídhe mage. Scáthbás wouldn't send him lightly." Lines appeared between her eyes as Morgana considered the problem.

Remembering what Murden had called his sister, Arto touched her shoulder gently. "You're not a traitor; I'm sorry he called you that."

Morgana laughed bitterly, her voice rough and sad. "Oh, I've been a traitor to both the Iron Realm and the Sídhe," Morgana replied shrugging off his hand. "It hardly matters why Murden was here I suppose." Morgana glanced down the gorge. "Still, something to keep our eyes open for."

Nodding in agreement, Arto managed a small smile for his sister and looked over to where Merlin and Gwenyvar were waiting, neither of them looking at him nor his sister. "Shall we?" Arto asked with a forced smile, nodding his head down the gorge.

Merlin smiled gently and moved forward, quickly taking the lead once again. Arto waited for a moment to allow Gwenyvar to walk next to him. She gently reached out and touched his arm, studying the bandages with a frown before dropping her hand and looking up at him. Smiling gently, Arto let his hanging hand brush against hers. A moment later, Gwenyvar smiled and took his hand, twining their fingers together.

13

Merlin's Smithy

Bran took in the surprisingly small one-story light green house with white trim on the large lot, half hidden by a massive oak tree as Aiden brought his car to a stop. Despite being one of only three houses on a long road leading out of town, there was a neat white picket fence that marked a large front yard with an iron wrought bench curved around the trunk of the oak tree. A pair of winged stone gargoyles stood amongst some shrubs on either side of the short set of stairs that led up onto the narrow porch of the house. On both sides of the property, thick tall bushes formed a hedge that blocked the view of the backyard.

"This is it?" Nicki asked incredulously from the back seat of Aiden's car. She leaned forward to peer up at the house from between them.

"It's nice," Alex insisted with a slight chuckle. "What were you expecting? A large warning sign saying: Home of Merlin or a castle?"

"Well maybe a mini-Stonehenge or a more impressive house," Nicki answered, sounding a little embarrassed. "Morgana at least has that big classic Victorian," she finished with a huff making Bran and Aiden chuckle.

"I like the gargoyles." Aiden unbuckled his seat belt and studied the house. "It's a nice touch, but otherwise Merlin does have to blend in as Professor Ambrose Yates."

"Yeah, Ambrose is such a common name," Nicki muttered. Bran could almost hear her rolling her eyes. "It means 'immortal' and is a name often linked to Merlin. And I looked up the name meaning of Yates; it means Gate! As in the gates that hold back the Sídhe. Seriously the man is not blending in at all."

"He's an English professor," Alex said. "I'm sure he enjoys a little symbolism and hidden meaning in his name. A lot of character names are significant after all. It's not uncommon in fiction for an author to choose a meaningful name." Alex paused for a moment before adding, "Or for readers to link a name to an aspect of the character's personality or actions."

Her statement made Aiden laugh out loud, his laughter filling the car as his head fell back against the back of his seat. Bran stared at him as Aiden struggled to get his breathing under control. The full laugh lessened into chuckling until Aiden finally sucked in a deep breath and relaxed.

"Sorry," Aiden told them as he recovered. "It's just that my name means fire."

"You're kidding right?" Bran raised a doubtful eyebrow at the statement, but he could see no teasing in his friend's face.

"No, I'm not," Aiden promised him with a wide smile.

"That's why your mom always blamed your temper on your name when you were a kid," Nicki suddenly added before giggling. "I'd forgotten that."

"You have a fiery temper?" Alex asked doubtfully from the back seat. "Seriously, mister take everything in stride with a calm smile?"

"When I was younger, I was a bit difficult to handle," Aiden explained with a shrug. "That was before Aisling got sick."

Aiden didn't offer any further explanation, but he didn't have to. Everyone, except Alex, had personal experience in how much change a family tragedy could bring. Bran shoved away the memory of how everything had changed in his family when his father was killed in action and then after the car crash that injured him. Even his success in physical therapy and getting out of the wheelchair hadn't allowed things to go back to the way they used to be.

"Anyway." Aiden turned to look over his shoulder at Nicki. "I think you're the one who wants a mini-Stonehenge in her yard."

Twisting, Bran looked back at Nicki who grinned and shrugged. "It's true," she replied, catching his gaze and winking at him. "But then doesn't everyone want a hedge labyrinth or small Stonehenge in their yard. That can't just be me."

With the tension broken and their friendly equilibrium mostly restored, everyone gathered their things. Bran noted the others moved slowly, stretching as they climbed out of the car despite Merlin's home only being a couple of miles from campus, across the river and up into the hills near the lake. It was a subtle ploy that he was familiar with, but appreciated, to make sure they didn't rush him leveraging himself out of the car with his cane. In the past he'd been around polite coughing, tapping feet or people who kept trying to be helpful and just made it more frustrating, so he found his friends' method an improvement. Bran slung his bag over his shoulder and returned his gaze to the house, already examining the stairs which were wide and solid looking.

"Who else is nervous?" Nicki's eyes swept over the red sports car that belonged to Professor Cornwall.

"I am a little," Aiden admitted as they started heading for the house. "But a new level of magic, learning to do more with it, that's exciting and good, right?"

Bran made a small sound of agreement with Aiden's statement. Nicki was nearly skipping up the walk, but her fingers were drumming on the strap of her messenger bag nervously. Alex was quiet as she walked along beside him: she kept glancing up towards the house with a slightly ill expression. Even only looking at her in the corner of his eye, Bran could see that she was nervous. Her fingers were twitching like she didn't know what to do with herself until they finally wrapped tightly around the strap of her bag, nearly turning white with the force of her grip. Alex stopped walking when Aiden climbed up the set of steps onto the porch and rang the doorbell.

"You alright?" Bran asked softly, turning to look at Alex.

She looked tired: Bran could see traces of dark shadows under her eyes despite the makeup she had on, including a touch of golden eye shadow to brighten up the dark patches. When they'd had dinner together last on Thursday night, she'd seemed normal and excited for Saturday's lesson. He frowned; Alex had been quiet during World Mythology on Friday and had said that she hadn't slept well. Now he wondered if she'd slept at all last night. Something was bothering her, but she didn't look ready to share.

"I'm just tired," Alex replied after a moment of silence, her reaction to his words slow. "I was too excited last night."

That was a lie, but Bran gave her a small nod and looked back towards the door. He was considering how to challenge the lie or inform the others just in case it was something important but was distracted by a call from the right.

"This way!" Professor Yates shouted.

Turning, Bran caught sight of the professor leaning through a gap in the tall hedge around his house, waving his arm towards them with a beaming grin. Next to him, Alex tensed but took a stumbling step forward. Professor Yates gestured them towards him, waving them faster as they stepped off the gravel drive and headed across the lawn. When they reached Professor Yates, Bran took in the wrought iron gate that filled the space between the tall hedges that still managed to form an archway above the gate and mostly hide the iron supports of the gateway. He studied the hedge, unsure of exactly what they were.

"Lilacs," Merlin said, catching his curious look and patting a nearby small branch fondly. "Marvelous when they are in bloom, but nice now that they are budding." Merlin opened the gate with a small squeak and gestured them inside. "And they still do a reasonable job of sheltering the back in the winter."

A small stone path wound from the gateway through the lilac bushes, that were more than two feet thick, and into the backyard which sloped down the hill. To the left, behind the house, was a patio made of smooth fitted stones with a large fire pit surrounded by heavy wicker patio furniture. The back side of the house was similar to the front with white trim surrounding each of the prairie style windows, but large iron designs were fixed on the house. There were seven in total, each of them a little different than the previous one, but all of them formed spirals with small variations that almost looked like lettering of some kind.

"This way," Merlin called, distracting Bran from his study of the symbols.

He looked to see their professor now ahead of him, walking towards a large metal shop just down the sloping yard. It was about the same height as the house but seemed much longer with one carport entrance on the side and one doorway. Several windows were scattered over the wall, but Bran couldn't see anything inside yet.

Then the door of the shop opened, and Professor Cornwall stepped out. Bran was taken back for a moment at seeing the normally elegant, almost formal, professor dressed in blue jeans with a simple blue t-shirt that was too faded to make out what it may have been before. She was wearing leather gloves, and her hair was twisted up in a tight braid bun on the top of her head.

"Ambrose," she called impatiently. "Where is my small hammer?"

"I reorganized a bit for the students to have room to move," Merlin called back with a thoughtful expression. "Check the table by your workbench." Morgana nodded, her eyes moving over the students before she vanished back into the shop. "Morgana and I share the shop," Merlin informed them, answering the unspoken question. "She finally learned some iron working in the 3rd century."

"But you're three thousand years old," Aiden protested next to Merlin as they headed for the shop.

"Yes, but well.... Male and female division of labor has been around a long time. Morgana was personally happy to have me do the forging." Merlin smiled wistfully. "After all, as a young man, I was trained in bronze metalwork. Had things not turned out the way they did I probably would have spent my life in my village casting bronze axe heads and the occasional sword."

Bran managed to catch a glimpse of his professor's face. Despite his physical age, Merlin's face always seemed bright and energized. Today not only was his voice wistful, but there was a faraway look in his brown eyes that dulled them. Small wrinkles were visible between his eyebrows, and his shoulders were tense.

"Still," Merlin added in a lighter voice. "I wouldn't have been able to see all the wonderful things I have. Did you know that Morgana and I rode the first train for passengers? At the time there had been insistence that traveling so fast would damage a person's body." He opened the door and gestured them into the shop. "Not to mention some of the less entertaining events I've been witness to."

Stepping into the large shop was like walking into a wall of heat despite the ventilation system that could be heard humming loudly. The carport door was open allowing a slight breeze into the shop, but the temperature was still higher than Bran had braced himself for. Long tables near the windows were stacked with iron bars of various sizes, boxes of unknown items, and finished projects including several fire pokers, a weathervane in the shape of a western style dragon and on one table there was even a chandelier like the one in Book Nook, the bookstore owned by Aiden's family. On the far wall were small racks attached to the wall, three levels of them, with hammers, tongs, and other tools of widely varying sizes.

In the center of the shop, several feet apart were large metal and brick furnaces with arched openings. Anvils were set up in front of each of them. Strange square tables with small racks hanging off the sides of them were placed near each of the anvils with a variety of hammers hanging from the racks. They were mostly organized by size, but from his place near the door, Bran could see several out of order on the nearest table. A large vise was set into each of the tables, open and waiting for something to be placed inside. There was a heavy smell of charcoal and metal in the air, so strong that Bran thought it must have seeped into every item in the place. Merlin hummed softly and reached over to a hook by the doorway and pulled a leather apron off it. He said nothing as he pulled it on over his head and tied it behind his back.

"Iron was a critical turning point in the war against the Sídhe." Merlin moved further inside and allowed all of them to stare and take in the large workshop. The professor stopped to examine the chandelier waiting on one of the work tables and sighed. "I've been neglecting my craft," he muttered. "I suppose with the Sídhe returning and training you four that was to be expected."

He reached out and selected an iron sword that was leaning in a rack partially hidden from view by one of the tables. Raising it with both hands, Merlin showed them the long blade. It was different than the ones Bran usually saw in films or even museums with a simple metal hilt with a triskele on the guard and an unmarked blade. Despite having less decoration, it was beautiful in the light of the hanging fluorescent lamps, gleaming smoothly and showing off the sharp edge.

"Ironworking existed other places on Earth when the Sídhe were spreading across the British Isles, but when I was young bronze still dominated Europe. In fact, at the time bronze was a measure of wealth and the British Isles had both copper and tin mines making us critical to the production of that wealth." Merlin sighed softly and gently placed the sword back onto the rack. "Cyrridven, however, was a master at traveling across the Iron Realm through water and observed iron working. She brought the knowledge of it to Britain and with that knowledge the first Iron Soul incarnation forged the first iron sword in northern Europe. However, as strong as iron is against the Sídhe there are limits which is why the Sword, Cathanáil, which you know as Excalibur was forged with magic. Today we are going to start teaching you not only how to work with iron, but how to infuse it with your magic."

Merlin rubbed his hands together and moved over to the first forge, watching as Morgana shifted around the edge of the room to observe them for a moment. Without a word, Merlin loaded charcoal into the furnace and started a small fire inside. He watched the flames begin flickering over the charcoal and nodded in satisfaction.

"Adding magic to iron makes it resistant to Sídhe magic," Morgana explained as she finished circling the room and came up next to them.

"It makes the metal stronger beyond its natural limits, able to survive thousands of years unrusted."

"There is some magic in all of your daggers." Merlin pointed to the dagger that Nicki had pulled from her bag to inspect. "A spark of my magic."

"But this has its limits," Morgana said to recapture their attention. "Magic can be directed through objects to help channel visualization or a way to control larger uses of magic. A familiar example of this would be a staff or a wand, but magical iron can amplify your magic if infused by you, making it the most powerful kind of focus object."

Nicki raised her hand earning a small chuckle from Merlin who pointed to her. "Can you channel your magic through someone else's iron object?" Nicki asked as she held up the dagger Merlin had forged for her. "Could I use magic with this?"

"You can use magic with it," Morgana told her. "But you won't have the amplification effect as the iron was not made with your magic. The magic in the blade will simply protect it from natural breakdown and damage from other magic."

"The Sword Cathanáil, for instance, was so important and powerful because it was an iron blade that carried the magic of the Iron Soul," Merlin added. "Every time Arto used that Sword with magic it grew a little stronger."

"The magic level of Cathanáil is so strong, in fact, that only the Iron Soul can use it," Morgana told them with a slightly proud note to her voice.

"In theory," Merlin added, earning him a stern look that he shrugged off. "Three thousand years ago only Arto could use the Sword's power successfully."

"Hasn't it been used since?" Bran heard himself ask before he thought about the question.

"Cathanáil was the key in the construction of the Iron Gates to hold back the Sídhe, and its magic was invested in keeping those gates standing," Merlin began to explain.

"We eventually entrusted the Sword to the Lady of the Lake after Arto's death," Morgana cut in. "She has the power to travel all over the world and could, in theory, deliver the Sword when we could not. However, the Iron Gates stood for three thousand years, and Cathanáil remained hidden away from any who might try to misuse it after its legend began to spread." Morgana paused and then added, "If they could use it."

The sentence hung in the air for a moment, and Merlin chuckled before stepping over to a nearby work table and picking up a thin piece of metal. He held it up to show them with a widening smile.

"Let's start with the basics, shall we? Iron one of the most common elements on Earth. It's in the blood of humanity and all vertebrates. It is even important to the life of plants. Hence why our world is known as the Iron Realm. And as you all know, the Sídhe are weak against it making it also our greatest defense."

Merlin turned sharply and tugged on a bellow on the side of his furnace several times. The opening of the furnace flared with light, becoming a bright orange as the black and gray of the fuel all but faded. "We'll start simple today," Merlin continued. "Since you don't need to worry about smelting iron, thank you, modern technology, I'll be demonstrating how to work it." Brown eyes met Bran's suddenly before sweeping away from him and to each of his fellow mages for a moment. His chest felt tight, and he struggled to breathe even once the eyes were off of him. "It is in that, the working of metal, the shaping of metal... the creation of something from it that magic is done."

Then Merlin began to move: his actions were graceful and practiced with no hesitation and almost a sense of delight. Bran blinked and tried to collect his scattered thoughts as the small piece of metal, no wider than an inch and only a foot long was thrust into the inferno of the furnace by a pair of tongs. Turning away from the fire with one hand still holding the tongs, Merlin's fingers danced over the selection of hammers before settling on one of the smaller ones which he pulled out with eager fingers.

Merlin began to hum a soft tune as green sparks jumped over his hand. There were only a few at first, glistening in the air and orbiting his hand as if they were planets and it was the sun. More green sparks jumped from his hand, swirling together until Merlin's hand and the hammer clutched within it were glowing brightly. The sparks seeped into the metal, dimming the glow, but the metal shimmered in the light. Not like Bran would have expected it to, but instead with a distinct green tint. Merlin didn't even look down at his hammer or the soft glow that had settled on his hand.

Merlin turned and smoothly pulled out the small piece of metal. Now a few inches of it were glowing bright orange and even from his place a few feet away, Bran could feel the heat. He'd seen this before in movies, but the almost pulsing heat and the fiery color seemed too sharp to be real. It was too intense to be anything natural, and yet it was. Next to him, Alex gasped softly, and Aiden shifted, almost moving closer. Gripping the metal band with the tongs, Merlin placed it on the narrow, rounded part of the anvil that jutted forward.

"This is called the horn," Merlin explained without looking up at them.

Then Merlin lifted the hammer, and the green glow intensified with a flash of magic before the hammer smashed down with a resounding ring. Flinching back, Bran felt the air being forced from his lungs as Merlin's magic jolted from the hammer to the metal. Merlin lifted the hammer away from the iron, giving Bran a glimpse of the impacted metal, now with a small curve. With another ring of metal to metal, Merlin's magic rushed into the small piece of iron. After each blow, Merlin adjusted the metal with the tongs, allowing each strike to force the metal into shape around the arc of the horn, slowly curving the piece evenly.

The metal was cooling quickly, the glow fading with each blow of the hammer. Without a word or any indication of concern, Merlin turned once again to return the iron to the furnace. Gray coals framed the inferno, and the near absence of the flame created a false sense of safety. It was only the heat rolling forward and hitting him straight in the chest that reminded Bran how dangerous the furnace was. Flashes of blue rolled over the coals like waves of water before being swallowed up once more by the glowing orange. Then the iron was withdrawn again and returned to the anvil.

Metal crashed against metal with loud, sharp ringing sounds. Merlin brought the iron back the anvil again and again. Time slipped away as Bran watched the mage work the metal before suddenly setting it aside and picking up a shorter piece of iron. He fit it into the tongs securely without a word of explanation and Bran could not find his voice to speak. Magic pulsed around Merlin, swirling strongest around the hand holding his hammer, but also orbiting him like a gentle breeze. The question if nonmages could see magic in this raw form was on the tip of Bran's tongue, but he couldn't manage the words. The air was thick and hot from the furnace, but also alive with the beating pulse of energy that he was coming to recognize as raw magic, raw energy of Earth being released to aid the mages.

There were no shadows in the coals as the new piece of metal was thrust back into the furnace. There was a sharp hiss and a rush of heat. Deep in the fiery furnace, the red and orange changed to brilliant gold, lining the edges of the charcoal. Merlin did not have to wait long before withdrawing the small piece of metal. He repeated the earlier process, carefully curving the iron around the horn of the anvil. Then he reclaimed the first piece he had shaped and gently placed it in a second set of tongs that he drew from his workstation. Both sets of tongs, both pieces of metal were then thrust back into the fire of the forge, and Bran held his breath.

When Merlin pulled the two pieces out, he quickly set them both on the anvil and using a much smaller and more delicate tool that resembled the tongs, curved the end of the shorter piece so that it was overlapping the center. Eyes widening, Bran took in the now three-armed shape and its gentle curves. Green magic flashed as Merlin picked his hammer back up, this one a smaller and narrower tool that shimmered with magic in an instant. Tearing his eyes away, Bran looked at Morgana who was watching the display with a small smile. She sensed his gaze and turned just enough to catch his eye with a widening grin.

It was the crash of metal to metal that made Bran look back as the red-hot pieces of iron were crashed together. With a quick movement, Merlin used the tongs to flip the piece over and struck the backside of the metal as well, flattening the center slightly. The metal was cooling as Merlin returned it to the fire, now as a single piece. When he withdrew it, the hammering continued, carefully joining the two pieces together. Where they joined now had a triangular shape which Merlin worked on with a small chisel to smooth out the shape. Then after one last reheating,

Merlin leaned over the iron piece one last time and dragged the tip of his chisel over the glowing orange metal.

With a smile, he blew on the iron gently, releasing a wave of green sparks that swirled around the iron before falling upon it like rain and being soaked up like the ground would rain on a hot, dry day. Merlin grasped the piece in the tongs and lowered it into the waiting barrel of liquid. A hissing filled the room, and a moment later, Merlin withdrew the tongs and dropped the iron piece into his hand. Stepping around the anvil, Merlin held out his hand to reveal a small, but beautiful triskele. All three branches spiraled in even, gentle curves. In the center, where the two pieces of metal had been joined, was engraved a perfect circle with another triskele within it.

"That, my students," Merlin said breaking the silence. "Is a demonstration of what it means for a mage to create with iron." Grinning Merlin looked at Morgana and down at his watch. "We still have a little time. Alex and Bran, you're with me, Nicole and Aiden, you're with Morgana. We'll explain to you the different parts of the furnace, and then you can go home. We'll start teaching you the practical skills next weekend."

All Bran could do was nod, his eyes moving between the iron triskele, the furnace, and the selection of tools. Excitement churned in his belly and the childish urge to jump around to demonstrate his eagerness was held in check only by his leg. Glancing to the side, he was relieved to see an awed expression on Alex's face, and her eyes were sparkling with interest. It was better than the sadness and exhaustion that had hung over her earlier. Bran grinned, turning his attention back to Merlin as their professor moved to the cooling forge and began the lecture.

14

Broken Circle

The woman wasn't dressed like a nurse or anything that Alex was expecting for the blood donation drive at the school. Instead, she was dressed in slacks with a blouse and a white lab coat. As Alex glanced around nervously, the woman simply smiled at her before turning her gaze to the much calmer Arthur standing beside her. Alex resisted the urge to scratch her finger where a bandage covered the small prick in her finger from when they tested the hemoglobin in her blood, whatever that was.

"First time giving blood?" Alex glanced down at the forms they had handed her.

"It is for Alex," Arthur replied, nodding towards her. His calm smile was a little irritating at the moment. "I used to give blood in California."

"Well, you've already finished the registration and what we call the mini-medical," the woman said looking back to Alex. "That's the longest part of this." She gestured towards the waiting chairs.

The donation chairs looked odd in the lounge area of the commons, their clearly medical purpose a stark contrast to the broken-in-sofa that had been pushed to the side to make room. The metal frame looked uncomfortable, and the fabric stretched between the parts of the frame didn't look that strong, but while answering all the questions about her medical history, Alex had seen plenty of other students sit in them.

Behind them, Alex could hear more students talking with the people at the registration desk.

"You can change your mind," the woman told her. "But please keep in mind the importance of giving blood."

"I'm fine," Alex assured her in a rush. "I just don't like needles much."

"It only pinches for a moment." The woman pointed towards the chairs again. "Go ahead and take a seat."

Alex obeyed and sat down, leaning her head back and placing her hands on the arms of the chair. It was more comfortable than she'd thought it would be and didn't smell as strange as the chairs in places like the dentist's office. She nearly jumped when a wet piece of light cloth was moved over her arm and looked down to see the woman tossing it away. Her eyes widened as she looked at the needle in the woman's hand and the tube that connected it to a bag.

"We'll be taking roughly a pint of blood," the woman reminded Alex. "This won't take long. Just try to relax. Closing your eyes usually helps at this point."

Alex nodded and closed her eyes, exhaling slowly and turning her face away from the needle. Deciding to make sure she didn't jump or do anything to disrupt the woman, she forced herself into the breathing pattern she'd learned for magical meditation. It helped and the sudden pinch she felt in her arm barely registered. Her head fell back against the back of the chair, and she exhaled again, trying to decide if she was brave enough to look down. The needle was fixed to her arm by a piece of tape that felt a bit itchy, but Alex forced herself to ignore it.

"See, Alex," Arthur called from beside her. "Not so bad."

Nodding, Alex leaned back against the chair once again and exhaled slowly. It wasn't so bad really, and Alex could hear the voices of other students milling around and the other donors talking. Arthur seemed to recognize that she preferred listening to everyone else over talking and started talking with someone else.

"That's it," the woman suddenly said to her, causing Alex to snap her eyes open. She looked down only to quickly turn her head away as the needle was removed and the bag filled with her blood was sealed. "Thank you for your donation," the woman told her cheerfully before offering a hand to help her out of the chair. She then gestured to a table with cookies and juice boxes. "Be sure to get something. You'll want to hold off on driving for a bit and make sure that you drink plenty of fluids."

"Thanks," Alex replied with a quick nod.

Alex wanted to wait for Arthur, but another donor was already coming over. Arthur turned his head and grinned at her while giving her a quick nod. Smiling in return, Alex nodded and headed for the table. She selected a chocolate chip cookie and an apple juice box before leaning against the wall. Arthur was slipping something into his messenger bag as he walked over to join her. Behind him, the woman shook her head awkwardly before smiling at the latest students to step up.

"Thanks for coming." Arthur had a beaming smile when he joined her. He grabbed a juice and took a slurp before adding, "Too bad that Jenny and Lance couldn't join us."

"Yeah," Alex muttered with a swallow. "They've got chemistry now, right?"

"I think so," Arthur replied with a shrug. "That sounds about right." He pulled out his phone, and his eyes widened slightly. "Oh man, not much time before class, but I think we've got time to grab one of the readymade sandwiches."

"Sounds like a good idea."

Arthur grabbed her hand and guided her out of the lounge and towards the food court. Fighting down a blush, Alex forced herself to breathe and focused on her mission. It was her job to protect Arthur, not let her silly crush get worse. The little voice in her head nagged at her that she wasn't doing a good job at either. Jenny and Lance were having an affair, maybe even using their shared chemistry class to plan their encounters while she was keeping everyone in the dark.

Her thoughts were interrupted when Arthur opened the door that separated the lounge from the food court. It was like slamming into a wall of noise with too many voices to make sense of any one of them. People moved in front of them, trying to find tables while others were throwing things into the trash and recycle bins on their way out. Arthur didn't let go of her hand, keeping her close to him as he maneuvered through the throng of people and crowded tables to the large display of ready to go sub sandwiches and bottled drinks. Arthur finally released her hand as he snatched up a roast beef sandwich and a bottle of pop. Shoving the rest of her cookie in her mouth, Alex grabbed a turkey sandwich and considered her juice before deciding to grab a bottle of water too.

As they were moving through the checkout line Arthur asked, "What have you got next?"

"World Mythology in fifteen minutes," Alex answered as she glanced down at her phone. "I can just make it."

"Me too, only Persuasive Writing. I'm sorry, I forgot how long the medical questions can take."

"It was worth it," Alex assured him quickly as she handed her student card over, grateful once again for the easy campus money system. "I think I could have been forgiven; besides I've got three friends in class. Surely one of them would have given me notes."

Arthur grinned again and started making a path for her towards the main door. As people began to swarm out to head for classes, Alex made sure to stay close behind the tall football player who easily cleared the way. Just outside the door, they split up with Arthur heading towards the Carlson building and Alex moving up the sidewalk leading to the Kittell Building.

Arthur gave her one more wave and smile before Alex had to turn and pay attention to where she was walking. She ripped open the plastic of the sandwich and managed three large bites, barely maneuvering her juice box enough to take a few slurps.

World Mythology was held in one of the two large lecture halls in the Kittell Building, with long rows of fixed chairs with the small fold-out desk that only tablets fit on. Professor Weaver was already up on the dais making notes on the whiteboards while her teaching assistant was handing out their last quizzes as the students filed inside slowly. Alex accepted her quiz at the door and glanced around to find her friends. A fast-waving hand in the air helped her spot Nicki sitting in the fourth row from the front with Bran and Aiden. Smiling, Alex adjusted her bag and moved down the aisle to join them. Alex sat down and handed Nicki her sandwich so she could pull the desk up and get out her tablet.

"Miss lunch?" Nicki asked.

"I gave blood and didn't have much time," Alex explained as she reclaimed her sandwich.

"I doubt Weaver will care," Bran added, glancing forward at the Professor.

Nodding in agreement, Alex set up her tablet, balanced her juice on the edge, held her sandwich with her other hand and finally looked at her quiz. Gritting her teeth, Alex glanced over the three questions she got wrong and sighed. Next to her Nicki made a small sound of surprise.

"Bad test day?" Nicki ventured carefully.

"Yeah." Alex remembered how ugly Friday had been after staying at the library in shock after hearing the Professors potentially plotting to kill her roommate and friend. "Wasn't a good day. I really do know that Athena was the Greek goddess of wisdom."

"It was just one quiz." Nicki reached over and touched her arm gently. "Don't worry too much. We're going to blow the grade curve!"

Alex wanted to smile at Nicki's enthusiasm, but just thinking about last Thursday night had killed all positive emotions that she did have. Avoiding Jenny all weekend hadn't helped her think up a solution, but at least hiding in the library all day Sunday to avoid her fellow mages and the professors had allowed her to finish all her remaining mid-term papers. With luck, she could turn in the papers and wrap up her tests early in the week and get the hell out of Ravenslake. She could at least catch her breath; maybe she'd even figure out a solution. Something other than murdering Jenny and Lance just because they were stupid reincarnations who couldn't help themselves and-

"Alex?" Nicki interrupted softly leaning closer and ignoring Professor Weaver as she called the class to order. "You okay?"

"Spring fever," Alex told her with a forced smile. "Just need to get out of here for a bit I guess."

Nicki probably didn't believe her, but she nodded and turned her attention forward. Alex took another bite of her sandwich, but now it tasted rotten and gritty. Forcing herself to swallow the bite in her mouth, Alex quickly washed it down with a gulp of apple juice that tasted sour before shoving the sandwich into her bag. She exhaled slowly, trying to balance herself like Morgana had taught her and did her best to focus on the teacher.

After World Mythology came the most awkward class that Alex now found herself suffering through Elementary Spanish with Arthur and Lance. It wasn't the Spanish that bothered her; she'd taken a year of Spanish her final year in high school after she and French officially parted ways. But last Friday, sitting with Lance and Arthur with Arthur in the middle and knowing what was going on behind his back was physically painful. Alex looked up at the Meier Building from behind a tree as Arthur clapped Lance on the back and they headed in together. The temptation to skip class was extreme, but knowing Arthur's tendency to worry and even Lance's usual gentleman manners, they'd probably come to check on her. Jenny had class so she wouldn't be home until almost 4:30, but she wasn't sure how she'd react to having Lance in the same room as her. As far as she knew, the last time he'd been in the room he'd been in bed with her roommate.

Students gradually moved inside, but Alex stayed put until the last second. She tossed her sandwich into a nearby trashcan and ran towards the classroom. Professor Diaz had just started talking and fixed her with an irritated look as she smiled sheepishly. Sitting down in the seat closest to the door, Alex gave a small wave to Arthur as he twisted to look back at her. When he turned to focus on the teacher, Alex left out a sigh of relief and slumped back in her chair, urging time to move faster and wondering if any mage was powerful enough to affect that. Finally, Professor Diaz was finished and turned off the projection system as the light came back on. Alex quickly packed up and slipped out of the room.

"Alex!" Lance's deep voice shouted behind her. "Wait up."

Caught in the act of running out, Alex sighed softly and stepped to the side as the other students moved past her. A few moments later Lance was followed by Arthur out the door. Lance grinned broadly at her, but Arthur looked at her with consideration.

"Alex?" he asked, "Are you alright?"

"Yeah," Alex assured him with a nod and giving him a sheepish smile. "Sorry, my brain just keeps jumping around to all the stuff I have to do."

"It's only midterms," Lance reminded her with a warm chuckle. "You'll do fine, and if you don't, then there is lots of time to talk to your professors and ace finals."

"Besides, it's still only freshman year," Arthur reminded her. "No one is at their best just yet."

"I hear that doesn't come until junior year," Lance added. "When you finally get out of the general education classes and get to study what you want."

"I just... I want to do well," Alex told them with a small shrug. "My parents are paying for most of it, so I don't want to be a brat."

"I get that," Lance agreed with a softening smile. "But don't let yourself get sick."

"Maybe giving blood wasn't a good idea if you're so stressed." Arthur frowned as he studied Alex's face. "You're a bit pale."

"I didn't eat much of my sandwich," Alex confessed awkwardly. "And I've been rushing between classes since. But I'm fine."

Arthur exchanged a look with Lance who merely smiled and nodded. Turning back to Alex, Arthur smiled and told her, "Well we were thinking of hitting the weight room for a bit, but why don't we go to Michaels and get a sandwich."

"It's only 3:30," Alex protested even as Arthur reached over to grab her hand.

"They're open all day," Arthur countered. "They don't have anything fresh or hot right now, but there's sandwich makings and fruit. I'm a bit hungry myself so we'll join you, head off to the weight room and then meet you and Jenny for dinner later."

"He's not going to concede on this," Lance warned her as he calmly walked towards the door ahead of them.

Recognizing that Lance was right, Alex relaxed and allowed Arthur to tug her out of the building and towards the dormitories. She did her best to prepare herself for acting calmly and most importantly normally around her broken little circle of friends. It was only early March and avoiding her friends wouldn't work and would only draw attention to issues in the group. Forcing a smile, Alex resigned herself to her now much more difficult fate as a mage, wishing that she could go back to when not be able to access magic was her biggest problem.

15

Broken Symbol

8 09 B.C.E. Near the shores of Loch Torridon

Arto's senses were sharper than they had ever been, despite the low light and the long shadows of the gorge, he could make out the sharp ridges of the rocks and the softer lines of the plants scattered around them. His heart was pounding in his chest, and the air smelled sweeter than before as Gwenyvar squeezed his hand. Turning, he helped her step down the slope covered in small chunks of broken up rocks. Ahead of them, Morgana came to a stop, her back straight and her shoulders tense. Arto released Gwenyvar's hand and gestured for her to stay back, relaxing with relief when she nodded in understanding. He tightened his fingers around Cathanáil's hilt and stepped forward to stand next to his sister.

The tunnel entrance was one of the largest that Arto had ever seen, dominating the end of the gorge with a smooth archway of stone. Raising Cathanáil in front of him, Arto sent another burst of his magic into the Sword to illuminate the passage. Small symbols were carved into the stones that made up the archway, and he could just see glowing orbs of light down the tunnel. Some symbols curved elegantly in places while others were made up of sharp straight lines, but Arto didn't understand the meaning of any of them.

"Wait," Merlin commanded Arto in a sharp voice as he stepped past him and Morgana.

Reacting based on years of obedience to Merlin, Arto stepped back by Morgana and lowered Cathanáil slightly. His mentor approached the archway carefully and after a moment of examination reached out with his hand to brush over the symbols. They flared gold under Merlin's touch, and the older mage pulled his hand back quickly. Shifting his staff in front of him, Merlin was still as the symbols glowed.

"Merlin," Morgana called with concern.

Morgana placed herself in front of Arto before he could protest. He twisted to see around his sister; his chest tightened with worry as he looked at Merlin's back. Then the glow coming from the symbols faded slightly, and Merlin took a few steps away from the entrance.

"I'm uninjured," Merlin reassured them without turning around. "But I dare say this is why the Sídhe mage was here. These symbols are charged with their magic, perhaps to keep us from severing the connection."

Arto jumped as his sister made a strange angry and horrified sound before she marched forward towards the tunnel entrance. As she moved, Morgana summoned her magic in the form of an orb of silver sparks. He glanced over his shoulder toward Gwenyvar who was watching them with a frown. She forced a little smile for him that calmed him.

"I think you're right," Morgana agreed as she looked at the symbols. "I haven't seen marks like this before, but this one looks similar to the sign for eternity. And this one looks like the mark for passage."

"There isn't much magic in these marks," Merlin observed, turning to study Morgana.

Arto couldn't see his sister's face but could imagine her expression from the angry tone of her voice. "It doesn't matter, Merlin, how much magic is in this entrance," Morgana snapped. "If the Sídhe find a way to make their gate eternal then-"

Gwenyvar made a small frightened squeak behind them that Merlin and Morgana ignored, but Arto spun back to her. Her brown eyes were wide and glistening in the light of Cathanáil. Arto took a few steps towards her, Gwenyvar lunged forward to grab his free hand. She said nothing as they both turned their attention back to Morgana and Merlin.

Arto watched the other mages speak in front of the entrance for a few moments. Morgana summoned her magic in a swirling silver cloud that floated across the entrance, creating a shimmering magical field over all the stones. Light filled the gorge and the air crackled with energy, smelling like a thunderstorm. The light was gone in a moment, and Morgana shouted words that Arto had never heard her use before.

"Morgana," Merlin snapped. "Calm down! We'll find a way to deal with this."

"We can't allow this!" Morgana spun to face Merlin as she gestured towards the arch. "Nothing! It did nothing, worse I think the symbols absorbed some of the magic!"

Arto's stomach churned, and he swallowed thickly, unused to hearing his sister sound so distressed. There were only a few times since she'd joined him and Merlin that he'd seen her as anything other than calm. Even in his childhood memories, the foggy recollections that he had of his birth village and parents, Morgana was always calm and rational. Merlin gripped Morgana's arm and said something to her far too quietly for Arto to hear.

Then Merlin turned towards the entrance and raised his staff. Green sparks of magic quickly gathered around Merlin's hand and flowed into the wood. Arto waited, unable to breathe as Merlin gathered more and more of his magic until the staff was completely bright leaf green and shimmering with power. With a sharp movement, Merlin smashed the staff against the side of the gorge next to the stone archway, channeling his power into the steep slope of rocks. The ground rumbled, but the symbols on the stones flashed brightly. Merlin grunted as he was shoved back by an unseen force and his magic suddenly dissipated in the air. Morgana lunged forward to stabilize the older mage as Arto stared in horrified awe.

"What is going to happen to my village?" Gwenyvar asked him in a soft voice full of defeat and sorrow. "If the Sídhe's tunnels can't be destroyed..." Her grip on his arm tightened painfully.

"No," Arto replied with a shake of his head. "If something can be made then it can be destroyed," he argued as he narrowed his eyes at the archway.

In his hand, Cathanáil's glow intensified, and Arto dropped his eyes to look at his Sword. His magic was pulsing, charged by the strange mixture of emotions flowing through him. At the back of his mind, there was a sense of something that he couldn't pin down. If they couldn't destroy the Sídhe tunnels, then mages wouldn't be able to do much against the Sídhe. Right now, when they destroyed a tunnel, they moved on to the next one and then the next one. There were always more than they could deal with at once, but this would change everything. Exhaling slowly, Arto forced down the worries and turned his eyes back to the archway of stones.

"Stay here," Arto told Gwenyvar firmly, tugging his arm away from her.

Arto stepped forward slowly, his eyes darting down every so often to check his footing as he approached Merlin, Morgana, and the tunnel entrance. Cathanáil somehow felt lighter in his hand as he lifted his arm to raise the Sword. He was just to the right of Morgana, studying a nearby symbol when his sister turned towards him.

"Arto, you should stay back from this," Morgana insisted, reaching towards him.

Shaking his head, Arto moved away from his sister and stepped closer to the entrance. "I think..." Arto paused and considered his own words for a moment. "I want to try using Cathanáil on the entrance," he told Merlin and Morgana. "Maybe the Sword can severe the magic and the connection."

"Arto-" Morgana began to argue, but Merlin reached out and put a hand on her shoulder.

"Morgana, let the boy try," Merlin told her seriously. "The Iron Soul was created by this world to protect it; he is connected to the magic of this realm in ways you and I cannot understand."

A glance at his sister revealed that she was watching him with a careful expression, looking like she had swallowed something distasteful, but she said nothing. Trying to keep his hand from shaking, Arto reached towards the stones. They began to glow as soon as he brushed his fingers over them earning a hiss of alarm from Morgana. Merlin must have held her back because she did not try to pull him away. Raising Cathanáil, Arto gripped the hilt with both of his hands and studied the archway carefully.

"Arto," Merlin called uncertainly, "That may not be the best approach. We have time to test a few options-"

Arto ignored Merlin and swung Cathanáil as hard as he could against the stones. Halfway through the movement, a rush of panic went through him, and the urge to stop the swing took over him. But it was too late, the sharp edge of Cathanáil collided with one of the stones, striking one of the symbols with a sharp ringing sound. The strange clang of metal on rock echoed through the gorge as Cathanáil sank into the stone, slicing into the symbol. Everything went still in the gorge, Arto, Gwenyvar, and the older mages holding their breaths.

"Hope I wasn't wrong," Arto whispered just before Cathanáil began to shudder in his grasp.

Gripping the Sword with both hands, Arto began to tug on it, trying to dislodge Cathanáil from the stone. The symbol glowed around Cathanáil, magic seeping out of it in tiny sparks that illuminated the other stones. Around him, the other symbols began to flash, slowly at first and quickly speeding up as they glowed brighter and brighter. The air thrummed, and Arto could taste a raw charge on the air, it wasn't of his world. It tasted too sweet, and a strange scent swirled around him.

"Arto! Let go of the Sword!" Morgana shouted behind him, but Arto didn't release the sword.

He grit his teeth, grinding his back molars together and used the discomfort to ground himself as the smell and taste of the air tried to pull him away from his senses. Forcing the stale air from his lungs, Arto glared at the symbol. He pictured it burning, smoking from his magic and crumbling into ash as he pushed magic into Cathanáil. The Sword shook, causing Arto's teeth to chatter as he locked his body into position, no longer trying to remove Cathanáil, but now imagining it rammed into the heart of the Sídhe's magic.

Magical lightning crackled out from the symbols, linking them together. A wall of magic hit Arto in the chest, trying to force him and his magic back. The power of the broken symbol exploded in a shower of golden sparks that illuminated the darkness before burning out like dying embers around Arto's feet. Smoke spilled out from the broken symbol, and magical lightning flashed between the remaining symbols. His grip on the hilt of Cathanáil was so tight that his fingers were white and ached from the pressure, but Arto tightened his grip further, feeling his own pulse in the blade. His white magic shimmered down the blade, flowing into the dead symbol like a river. A bolt of Sídhe magic struck his arm, but he made no sound.

In his mind, he saw his magic spreading, using the broken symbol as an anchor in the Sídhe's magic. It was spreading like his blood had over the tor near his sister's village covering the Sídhe's magic with his own. He would smother it like earth did a fire. Arto chuckled at his thought and looked up as the next symbol began to flash and smoke before it exploded in a flash of magic that threatened to blind him. Another symbol exploded, sending a sharp ripple of magic into Cathanáil.

Forcing himself to inhale, Arto pushed Cathanáil deeper into the stone, and then he screamed. He saw the little Changeling girl being tested, he saw the faces of those who knew the fate of the ones they lost, he saw Gwenyvar's fear for her family and friends, and he saw his sister collapsed in front of him as the blood spell attacked the Sídhe taint in her. The scream echoed in the gorge, and Cathanáil turned a brilliant white. Slamming his eyes closed, Arto forced it all into the stones and watched in his mind as their magic was snuffed out, covered in his power, the power of iron and the power of Earth. There was the sound of a dozen explosions suddenly ringing in his ears, his eyelids went white, and he felt drained as a moment later everything was still and silent.

Exhaling was one of the most difficult things he had ever done; he was fearful of disturbing the calm that had settled around him, and his body protested the muscle movement. Yet a soft sigh escaped him, and he gulped in air before the action even occurred to him. His knees were locked, and Arto was certain that if he tried to move them that he would fall over onto his face. Cathanáil felt far too heavy and threatened to fall from his grasp. To the right, he could hear the others moving over the rocks, but he didn't open his eyes.

A warm hand touched his shoulder gingerly as another hand gently wrapped around the hilt guard of Cathanáil. Releasing another pained breath, Arto loosened his grip and allowed the hand to take the weight of Cathanáil, but did not relinquish the Sword.

"Are you injured?" Morgana asked, her voice soft and comforting.

"No," he gasped before swallowing to soothe his dry throat. "No," he repeated, stronger this time.

Morgana tried to pull Cathanáil from his hand, but Arto tightened his grip and shook his head. Opening his eyes slowly, he had to blink away the stars that lingered in his vision from the magic. He turned and forced a small smile for his sister's sake.

"Arto?" Gwenyvar called gently, pulling his attention to where she stood at Merlin's side with a frightened and worried expression.

"I am fine," Arto announced, rolling his shoulders to loosen the stiff muscles.

He carefully bent his knees and widened his stance, motioning for Morgana to step back and give him space. His sister did so slowly, her hand lingering on his shoulder longer than necessary. Turning his head, Arto let his eyes trace the archway of blackened stones as smoke slowly rose off of them. The symbols were cracked beyond recognition, and already small pieces of the stones were falling away to land at his feet.

"The magic is gone," Morgana assured him as she backed up a few more steps. "It worked." Morgana paused, and Arto turned to see a slight frown on her face. "I can't even feel any traces of the Sídhe's magic. It's like it has all been burned away."

"Remarkable," Merlin breathed as Gwenyvar made a happy sound followed by a sob of relief, but Arto didn't look in their direction.

"It was the Sword," Arto told them, his eyes examining Cathanáil with a new understanding of what he was holding. "This iron.... it is more than just their physical weakness. It has power over them." He reached out and carefully brushed his finger down the blade, noting that the collision with the stone had left no marks, something that stunned him. Beneath his fingers, he could feel the magic that he'd forged into the blade jumping to meet his skin.

"What are you thinking?" Merlin asked in a careful voice that Arto recognized as Merlin's mentor and guiding voice.

His teacher thought or maybe simply felt that he was close to an idea. Indeed, Arto could feel an idea forming, the memory of the magic failing before the magically infused metal of Cathanáil's blade pushing tiny strands of thoughts together until they finally coalesced.

"They want to build arches to grant themselves eternal access to this realm, to our people and our lands. Their Queen won't settle for slaves for much longer," Arto said lowly, almost growling. "I won't let her," Arto added fiercely, looking up at his sister. "No more of this! They can build their arches and Cathanáil will tear them down, and we will build gates to keep them out."

"Gates?" Merlin repeated as Arto turned to look at him, seeing slight confusion on the man's face.

"Iron gates forged with magic," Arto announced, straightening his back and tightening his grip on Cathanáil. "We block the path and allow the magically charged iron to disrupt their magic. The blood spells keep them from returning to an area, but that is tied to the surface. If we go underground and block their pathways, then they won't be able to rebuild."

Merlin and Morgana exchanged a look, a glint of hope and excitement in his sister's eyes while Merlin turned back to him with a cautious expression.

"It might not work, Arto," Merlin told him gently. "You'll have to pull a great amount of iron out of rocks, or we'll need the smelters that they use in the east to make enough iron, and even then, the magic and power of the iron may not be able to spread far enough to block off the Iron Realm."

"It may not work," Arto agreed, the words pouring from his mouth smoothly and easily without any effort on his part. "But we know the pattern of defense that we've been using isn't going to be enough soon. It is time to try something new, time for us to not just fight the Sídhe, but drive them back."

A slow smile appeared on his sister's face, and she raised her chin slightly as she regarded him. There was pride in her eyes that made his spine straighten further. She nodded and looked over at Merlin to say, "He's right, and it's time that the islands banded together to protect themselves."

"Perhaps," Merlin agreed with a small nod to her before looking over at Arto. "But they will need a leader," he told Arto seriously before adding in a voice so soft that Arto barely heard it, "They will need a king."

16

Confrontation

Sighing softly, Alex turned the page of her well-worn copy of *Pride and Prejudice* as she stretched out on her bed. It was the first time she'd allowed herself to get distracted from the multitude of problems that had taken over her life as of late. Yesterday she'd attended black-smithing class and had her first go with the hammer, actually doing much better than she'd expected. Her homework was done, and for what felt like the first time in forever she knew where Jenny was and what she was doing. Her eyes moved over the page, more remembering the scene and dialogue than actually reading it.

Suddenly, the dorm door flew open, and a humming Jenny skipped into the room, dressed in tight exercise clothes with an overly large letterman jacket that Alex recognized to be Arthur's from high school. Her roommate's face was flushed with a wide smile lighting up her features.

"The tryouts were amazing!" Jenny announced before Alex could even ask. As she shrugged off the jacket and tossed it on her bed, Jenny added, "I was the best of the potentials." She sat down on the edge of her bed and toed off her shoes. "You should have seen me!"

"That's great," Alex replied, giving Jenny a wide smile. "I know you've been practicing really hard and looking forward to this." Her roommate was practically glowing, showing no worry or guilt and Alex felt a touch of anger seeping through her.

"I've missed it," Jenny confessed with a giggle. "Sort of a silly thing to miss, but I did miss spirit squad this fall. Next football season will be so much better." Jenny paused and gave Alex a more sheepish smile. "Course the boys, and I will be practically abandoning you."

"I'll be fine." Alex closed the book she'd been reading and set it on the desk by her phone, doing her best to act normal and ignore the anger that was slowly rising. "Besides you won't be traveling with them. And I've got other friends too."

"And maybe next year you'll have a boyfriend." Jenny reached up to pull out her hair tie and let her long dark hair fall around her shoulders. "That would be nice."

"Maybe," Alex replied with a shrug. "I suppose I could always date Lance and make our little foursome a pair of pairs," Alex added, trying to tease Jenny, but unable to put enough humor in her voice.

Instead, she watched her roommate's reaction, waiting for signs of guilt or anything other than the happiness that Jenny was presenting all the time. There was a slight flinch in Jenny's shoulder, and her mouth twitched into a short-lived frown. It was a brief display of something; Alex didn't know if it was jealousy, irritation, distaste at bad humor, but there had certainly been a reaction. She felt triumphant, promptly followed by a heavy feeling of guilt that Alex did her best to ignore.

"Oh, I don't know," Jenny answered with a forced smile so wide that her eyes squinted. "I'm not sure you two would make a good couple. Maybe you should ask Aiden out. He's pretty cute or that other guy, uh, Bran wasn't it. He's a good-looking guy too as long as you don't mind..." Jenny trailed off and blushed.

"That he needs a cane," Alex finished. She raised her eyebrow and felt a bit vindicated when Jenny's blush deepened.

"Yeah... sorry, that wasn't me trying to be nasty," Jenny apologized.

"It's fine." Alex set her feet on the tile floor and reached down to retrieve her slippers. "I was like that at first; I guess it's normal that it takes some getting used to. Honestly, I think we're more hyper-aware and embarrassed by it than he is."

"Maybe," Jenny answered hesitantly before shaking off her embarrassment. "Well do you ever think about dating Bran?"

"No, actually it hasn't occurred to me," Alex told Jenny as she put on her slippers.

"Don't you miss having a boyfriend?" Jenny put her hands on her hips, a dubious look on her face.

Blinking at the question, Alex paused and considered it for a moment before she shook her head. "No, I haven't actually," she answered with a small chuckle. "Things have been changing so fast that I've barely had time to think about it." She could suddenly feel the strain that the last few weeks had put on her as she shrugged, her shoulders ached along with a constant headache right between her eyes. "Which is kind of funny since I know that Tom has a new girlfriend already." Alex forced herself to smile, feeling angry and exhausted all at once.

"But you must like someone," Jenny pressed with renewed curiosity in her voice even as she tried to look nonchalant grabbing her towel.

Staring at Jenny's back as her roommate grabbed the last of her things and put on her sandals, Alex wondered if Jenny was trying to be cruel. The mere thought brought the anger to the surface that she'd been shoving down for days. Alex's fingers clutched at her comforter as she forced herself to speak.

"Yeah, but he's taken." She inhaled, nibbling at her lip for a moment before adding. "You already know I like Arthur so what's with the question?"

"I know you like Arthur," Jenny replied softly without turning around. "I guess I was hoping that you'd found someone else." Then in a more cheerful voice, as she spun around to face her again, Jenny added, "You'll find someone wonderful soon."

"Cause you'd never cheat on him," Alex blurted out before the words processed in her mind. Whether she was lashing out at Jenny for mocking her feelings or for hurting Arthur, Alex wasn't sure which. "Or be honest and break up with him when you're sleeping with his best friend and teammate."

There she'd said it; she'd admitted at least to Jenny that she knew what was going on. Alex had expected that she'd feel better once someone knew, but as she saw guilt, shame, and resignation flash across Jenny's face, she just felt sick as her fiery anger vanished in a crashing wave of guilt. Questions about how much real say Jenny had in the events of her life raged through Alex's mind. Neither of them spoke as they stared at each other until Jenny lowered her eyes, but not quickly enough to keep Alex from seeing a few tears.

"I haven't told Arthur." Alex lowered her eyes and looked at her slippers. The soft blue material didn't feel so comfortable now. "But, Jenny, you need to sort this out."

"I know," Jenny replied in a voice so low that Alex could barely hear her. "On Halloween... I don't know what started it. We said it wouldn't happen again, but-" A dry sob escaped Jenny, sounding raw and painful. "I don't want to be this girl, Alex!"

"Then don't be that girl." Standing up, Alex took a cautious step towards her roommate. "Just tell Arthur you need some time and space, when he's adjusted you can come clean and apologize. It isn't perfect, but it's better than this."

"I keep telling myself to do that." Jenny shook her head and raised a hand to wipe away her tears. She released a shuddering breath and looked up at Alex. "I don't want to be this kind of girl!" Alex managed a soft smile and started to reach toward Jenny to comfort her, but Jenny jumped back like a stray animal about to be kicked. Her roommate shook her head, pointed at her and snapped, "Stop lecturing me, Alex! You just want to steal Arthur!"

In a rapid movement, Jenny grabbed her shower tote and keys and rushed out the door. The door didn't close all the way, falling open as Jenny headed down the hall. Sighing, Alex reached over and shut the door, leaning her forehead against it. She took in slow deep breaths, trying to calm her thoughts and make sense of the conversation. All of Jenny's behavior since Halloween made more sense: her arrival home after Alex after the dawn of November first, her bouts of near depression and her deciding against moving in with Arthur.

Her fist hit the wood of the door, crunching her fingers and sending a jolt of pain up Alex's arm before she even knew what was happening. Despite the pain, she had a strong urge to strike the heavy wooden door again. She took a deep breath and held it, fighting to keep her shaking hands still. Slowly Alex exhaled and tried to calm down, but she could barely focus on anything other than the churning blend of anger, pity, guilt, and what she recognized as jealousy in her stomach. Her chest ached, and breathing was becoming more and more difficult as tears pricked at her eyes. Pushing herself away from the door, Alex spun and threw herself onto her bed. She grabbed the pillow and allowed herself a weak scream into the soft fabric. Her fingers reached out and gripped her plush dog Galahad, drawing her favorite stuffed animal to her chest.

Alex lay there, fighting back tears in a losing battle and struggling to breathe as she refused to pull her face out of her pillow. Jenny had not returned by the time that Alex had cried herself out. Giving one last weak scream into the pillow, Alex slowly pushed herself up and sat on her bed. Everything was blurry, and she blinked rapidly as she tried to think. Jenny could only stretch a shower out so long and would be back soon. Alex's stomach turned, she couldn't face Jenny, not now and maybe not ever again.

Jumping up from her bed, Alex grabbed a duffle bag from the back of her closet and began stuffing some clothes into it. She forced herself to slow down a little and packed some of her toiletries and makeup along with some hair supplies. Turning to her desk, Alex picked a few of the school books she might need and stashed them in her messenger bag with her tablet. With more care, she placed Galahad in the top of the duffle bag and zipped it up. Kicking off her slippers, Alex stepped into her sneakers and collected her wallet, phone, and keys. Before she could change her mind or Jenny could return, Alex headed out the door with the bags.

No one paid her much mind as she headed out of Hatfield Hall and across the lawn to Michaels Hall. There were a few people out playing volleyball and sunbathing despite the chill in the air. Others were milling around the cafeteria, heading for an early dinner as Alex waited for someone to come out of the locked side corridor. She slipped past them as the door opened and headed towards the dorm rooms that made up the side wing and upper floors of the building. It took Alex a moment to get her bearings, the other times she'd been up to Nicki's room they'd gone in through one of the side doors, but she found the elevator after looking down a few hallways.

Nicki's room was in the middle of the main hall of the fourth floor, just to the right of the elevator. The original paper name tag that the RAs had placed on the door at the start of the school year was still there, proclaiming Nicki's name in a mixture of red and orange construction paper. It only occurred to Alex as she knocked on the door that she probably should have called first, but then the door opened revealing Nicki beaming at her with a smile.

The smile fell away in a split second as Nicki's sharp blue eyes took her in. A moment later, the door was pushed open all the way, and Nicki gestured her inside the small dorm room. Giving Nicki a grateful smile, Alex stepped into the room and glanced around. Unlike at Halloween, Nicki had accepted that she wasn't getting a roommate and had spread out. The second desk had her microwave, a pile of dishes on the top and her mini-fridge shoved under it. The second bed had been set up like a sofa with sheets covering the mattress and a blanket adding color with piles of small pillows creating a nest-like structure. With a sigh of relief, Alex set her bags down and turned to face Nicki as she shut her door.

"Sleepover huh?" Nicki asked with a soft smile. "It's been a while, but I think I've got enough junk food stashed around here to make it work; I warn you that I don't do romantic comedies. We're watching action flicks."

"Thanks," Alex replied, "That sounds good."

"Take a seat," Nicki told her, nodding to the second bed. "I've got another blanket stashed in the closet that you can have if you're too cold."

Nodding, Alex turned and unpacked Galahad, setting him on the bed and stroking his fur gently. She could feel Nicki watching and waiting for her to talk. After a moment, Nicki returned to her desk and pulled out something. The smell of nail polish quickly filled the small room, and Alex sat down on the bed with a sigh, sinking into the pillows.

"Ready to talk?" Nicki calmly asked from across the room.

Swallowing, Alex didn't look at Nicki, reaching over and petting Galahad as she tried to sort through the mix of emotions that were still thrumming through her. Alex's fingers tapped nervously at a soft blue pillow under her hand, and without thinking, Alex raised her other hand and bit at her fingernail. When she caught herself, Alex pulled her legs up to her chest and wrapped her arms around them, resting her chin on her knees.

"Do you ever think it's okay to kill someone?" Alex asked in a low voice.

If Nicki was surprised by the question, she didn't show it and instead quickly answered. "Yeah, I do." Alex looked over at her friend only to find Nicki calmly painting her toenail a bright shade of blue. She didn't know how to respond to Nicki's answer, having expected a more cheerful answer. "That surprises you," Nicki said without looking up at her. "But come on, Alex, we've killed Sídhe and haven't cried any tears over them. They may not be humans, but they are living and sentient beings so on some level you already know it is okay to kill someone."

"Well not like that then," Alex countered, "Not in combat. What about if they are defenseless and you're safe, what if they haven't actually tried to hurt you?"

"I'm still fine with it," Nicki replied calmly as she switched her feet and started painting her other toenails. "If this... person or being is someone who has hurt others willingly and will do so again then I think it is worse to risk it. When you kill them, you are saving their next victims."

"But don't people deserve a second chance?' Alex asked.

"Nope," Nicki told her, shaking her head slightly. "People can earn a second chance. Take my parents for example. They brought me to Gran and ran off, letting me believe that they were coming to get me after their trip was over. They show up again once I'm in college and want me to forgive them. I'm trying to forgive them, not because they've done anything to deserve it, but more that I'm just tired of being angry with them. But I'm not giving them a second chance. They've done nothing to earn it. They've done nothing to demonstrate any intention to really change. They haven't earned a second chance."

"I think this conversation has gone the wrong way," Alex groaned. She turned to look straight ahead at one of the photos on Nicki's wall of her and Aiden as young teenagers. "Say you know that someone is going to do something that has terrible consequences, but they don't know that the consequences will be so bad. Would killing them be justified?"

There was silence at the other side of the room for a long moment before Alex heard the glass bottle of nail polish being set on the desk. The smell of the acetone hung in the air as she heard Nicki stand up and pad across the room. Nicki sat on the bed next to her, causing the mattress to sink a little more.

"Jenny is cheating on Arthur, isn't she?" Nicki asked, a note of worry and sadness in her voice. Her hand came up and gripped Alex's shoulder gently. "You okay?"

"How did you know?" Alex asked, still not looking at Nicki.

Her friend laughed, weakly and sadly, but she laughed. "Oh, sweetie, you've been avoiding Jenny and Lance, and now you've shown up to stay with me despite me being a known lesbian while you're straight even with the potential gossip that could cause. Something pretty significant must have happened with Jenny, and that's the only thing that would get you this sad."

"Nailed it," Alex grumbled, lowering her head again.

"Alex, it's not your fault," Nicki assured her, moving her hand from her shoulder around her back, tugging Alex to lean against her. "But judging from your questions, you're worried about something pretty serious. You're not thinking about-"

"No," Alex said quickly, lifting her head and shaking it fiercely. "But I overheard Merlin and Morgana; they were talking about killing Jenny and Lance to protect Arthur."

"I see," Nicki replied thoughtfully. "I suppose they believe that the emotional pain of losing his friend and lover would still be better than the pain of discovering they were betraying him. Hard to imagine that the betrayal could be that bad, but I suppose they've seen it before."

Alex flinched at the observation, wondering exactly what sort of consequences had arisen in their past lives. Had Gwenyvar and Llewelyn really done something so terrible that they were doomed to repeat it over and over? The distress on Jenny's face flashed in her mind's eye; maybe they had no control over what was happening at all.

"And Merlin is okay with this plan?" Nicki asked, breaking into Alex's thoughts. "Morgana I can believe, but Merlin is usually so optimistic. He strikes me as the more idealistic of that pair."

"He doesn't like it. But he also said that he wouldn't stop her."

Nicki rubbed her back gently, but Alex was barely aware of it. Maybe just maybe Jenny would think about their conversation and stop her affair or at least break it off with Arthur until she could sort out her feelings. That wasn't ideal, but this problem had no ideal solution. Maybe Arthur would have time to get over her before finding out that she'd been cheating and it wouldn't hurt so badly. She could be his friend and support him dating someone new, and maybe he'd even consider dating her. Alex shook her head and banished the stray thought. Grand scheme of things it was a foolish thing to be worried about, but then again grand scheme of things maybe Morgana had a point.

"Nicki, it's our responsibility to protect this realm and the Iron Soul so he can stop the Sídhe," Alex sighed in defeat. "So, what if keeping it a secret means that Arthur gets hurt or killed? Is Morgana right to think killing Jenny and Lance is the best option?"

"Okay, one I know that finding out your girlfriend is cheating on you with your best friend is terrible, but it isn't the end of the world," Nicki said sternly. She held up a finger in front of Alex's face. "Arthur doesn't seem so overly emotional that he'd kill himself over it so what is the danger?"

"Maybe not kill him, but the original betrayal didn't kill him like that in the stories," Alex reminded her. "It left him heartbroken, it lowered morale at a critical moment and left him open to Mordred's backstabbing."

"We don't know if that story is true: Merlin and Morgana don't talk about it and evade all my questions," Nicki countered with a dismissive wave of her hand. "And two Arthur has you. When he finds out, you'll be there as the friend who didn't betray him and be able to help him cope."

"But aren't I betraying him by not telling him the truth?" Alex huffed, sinking into the pillows of the bed. "Omission of the truth is another form of a lie; I'm trying to protect him, protect all three of them, but maybe that just isn't possible."

Nicki paused, her mouth twisting into a grimace before she shrugged. "I think Arthur may already suspect it. I get the sense that he knows more than he says."

Alex's eyes widened at Nicki's statement as fear and guilt flooded through her again. Nicki grabbed her face with both hands and forced Alex to meet her eyes. "But I could be wrong," Nicki rushed to assure her. "And the professors won't find out from me. I'll keep it a secret if that's what you decide," Nicki told her gently, releasing her face and giving her a soft smile. "So don't worry about that. Bran might guess, but Aiden isn't the most observant person when it comes to relationships. Why Sarah puts up with him, I'll never know."

"Oh, I don't know," Alex mumbled as she leaned her head back against the pillows. "He has his moments." Inhaling slowly, Alex closed her eyes. "I don't know what to do, Nicki," she admitted. "They haven't committed a crime worth the punishment, even if it is to prevent a greater tragedy. Jenny, when I told her, was so... she looked so torn and heartbroken. I think she hates cheating on him, and I think she's miserable. I don't, God, I don't know what to do."

"I believe in trusting your instincts. Your instinct was to protect Jenny and Lance too by not telling Morgana and Merlin. I know that your feelings for Arthur... well, now's not the time, but you care about all three of them. That's okay, sweetie, that's human."

"Yeah." Alex stared up at the ceiling. "I'll remind myself of that when I come to regret this."

17

Archetype

She was dreaming again: Alex knew it as she walked slowly down the long dark tunnel, but the knowledge wasn't enough to wake her up or give her control over the dream. Dark stone surrounded her, creating smooth walls around her and an almost slippery floor beneath her feet. The small orb of light that Alex held in her left hand illuminated the long gradual curve of the tunnel. She could feel her magic sparking over her skin and in the corner of her eye saw the small dark silver sparks shimmering around the orb. In her right hand, Alex clutched a long golden dagger coated in her red blood that glistened dangerously in the light of the orb.

"Just a dream," Alex whispered to herself, but her voice echoed down the tunnel.

In the distance, she could barely hear the voices of the Sídhe. Their soft and musical voices floated up the tunnel to her, but she couldn't understand what they were saying. Then came the sound of armored footfalls in the tunnel. Alex looked around for someplace to hide, but her feet were suddenly stuck to the floor of the tunnel. Struggling to move and to wake up, Alex pulled desperately at her feet, but she could not move them. The heavy footfalls were getting closer and closer, approaching Alex in the darkness. She raised her light orb to illuminate the passage better.

A Síd stepped into view, golden armor glinting in the light and a long golden sword raised in front of it. Cold violet eyes studied Alex and their thin, pale lips twisted into a smirk. Long twisting horns rose from the Síd's forehead, decorated with golden ornaments with long translucent hair coiled around them. Alex couldn't breathe; her limbs felt heavy as she stared at the creature. A soft laugh from the Síd as it stepped closer to her shocked and terrified Alex. Swinging her dagger forward, Alex lunged as far as she could with her feet still stuck to the ground. Metal hissed as it struck metal, but Alex didn't relent and shifted the dagger up. The tip caught on the edge of the Síd's armor for a split second before snapping up and slicing into the Síd's neck. Silver blood poured out of the wound and turned to dust as it mixed with the red blood on the dagger.

Then the silver blood turned red, spilling out over Alex's hand and flowing down her arm. Gasping, Alex's eyes flew to the face of the Síd. Instead of violet eyes, she was staring into Jenny's brown eyes. Her roommate's face stared at her in shock, betrayal, and sorrow, her lips wide in alarm. Suddenly Alex's feet were free, and she stumbled forward just as Jenny collapsed to the ground. The golden armor clattered as the body hit the tunnel and Alex cried out, reaching for Jenny.

Alex's eyes opened, and she sucked in a desperate breath as the sense of falling woke her up. She didn't move, glancing around her dorm room carefully. A hint of sunlight was shining through their thin curtains, offering low illumination to Alex. From her spot on her bed, Alex looked over to Jenny's bed where she could just see a hint of her roommate's dark hair spilling out over the pillow. Alex's mouth went dry, and her stomach heaved violently, forcing Alex to pull up her legs against her chest. Wrapping her arms around her legs, Alex tried to stop shaking even as she kept her eyes on Jenny.

She didn't know how long she lay there before the fear and horror of the dream finally faded enough for Alex to move. Reaching up to the desk, Alex retrieved her phone and quickly checked the time before turning off her alarm. Alex moved slowly and as quietly as she could, swinging back her comforter and stepping into her slippers. Exhaling slowly, Alex stood up and closed her eyes trying to banish the nightmare from her mind. She rubbed her arms, fighting off the chill of the tunnels that somehow seemed to have followed her back into reality. When that didn't work, Alex walked across the room and grabbed her robe and shower supplies. Making sure she had her keys in her pocket, Alex glanced at Jenny one more time and slipped out of the room, locking the door behind her.

Alex lingered in the heat of the shower, enjoying the benefits of waking up and showering before the others on her floor. There was plenty of hot water and high pressure, but it wasn't enough to completely banish the strange nightmare from Alex's mind. She couldn't help but remember that her dreams mere months ago where she was trapped in the tunnels had been a warning of things to come. Surely this couldn't be a warning dream. Alex knew it was far more likely that it was combining the lingering fear of the Sídhe and their tunnels with her guilt and confusion over Jenny, Lance, and Arthur. But knowing that didn't make it any easier to return to her dorm room to get dressed.

Alex tiptoed through her room, careful not to wake Jenny who was still asleep as she pulled on a pair of jeans and selected a t-shirt for the day. Picking up her messenger bag, Alex gently placed her cell phone in one of the pockets and slipped her keys inside as quietly as she could. She toed out of her slippers and shoved her feet into her still tied sneakers, shifting her foot until the shoe was on and then repeating the process. There was a soft snore from Jenny that made Alex turn sharply towards the bed, but her roommate only shifted slightly before becoming still once more.

Exhaling softly, Alex began to slowly move across her room towards the doorway, her eyes darting between her slumbering roommate and the door. It felt stupid, sneaking out like this, but Alex wasn't sure that she'd get away otherwise. At the party that had lasted until early this morning, Jenny had stuck by her side, laughing and acting like everything was fine. Hopefully, none of her things being absent would prevent Jenny from overreacting.

There was a sudden soft cry from the bed that made Alex stop in her tracks and turn towards the bed slowly. Part of her just wanted to jump for the door and run for it, but she stepped closer to Jenny when the soft crying sound came again. Alex leaned over her roommate's comforter wrapped form carefully to see Jenny clutching her plush teddy bear Zoe tightly to her chest. Small shimmering tear tracks were visible down her face, and Jenny was sniffing quietly in her sleep between soft sobs.

"I'm sorry," Alex whispered as she studied Jenny's profile. Her roommate looked so miserable, vulnerable, and small. The questions over how much control Jenny even had over her actions returned to Alex. "This whole situation sucks but for you most of all."

"Arto," Jenny breathed softly, Alex barely hearing the name. Startled, Alex leaned closer and strained her ears. "Arto, I'm sorry." More tears slipped from Jenny's eyes.

Stumbling backward, Alex moved quickly to the doorway and didn't let herself think about the name Jenny had called until she was in the stairwell. There was a sense of panic churning in her stomach as she rushed down the three flights of stairs. She couldn't help but wonder if Jenny remembered her previous life, but that just seemed crazy. Maybe she'd misheard her, and she was calling to Arthur. Maybe it was a nickname that she didn't know about. But as she stepped outside into the bright sunlight, Alex sighed, and her shoulders slumped, defeated by the certainty that she was grasping at straws. She didn't know what it meant, but in her sleep at least Jenny seemed to be remembering.

Alex's feet scuffed the ground as she headed for Michael's Cafeteria, trying not to think too hard about what this new development could mean. Her stomach gurgled, a mix of her tension and hunger. The cafeteria was nearly empty with only the basic breakfast bar set up and two staff people, one swiping cards at the door and the other tidying up tables. Alex handed over her card and said the obligatory hello before heading to the breakfast bar.

Nothing appealed to Alex despite her hunger, but she finally picked a bowl of oatmeal with blueberries. She sat down alone at a small table and began to pick at her food. After forcing down a few bites, Alex began moving her spoon through the oatmeal, making random shapes in it. Suddenly another tray was set down across from her, loaded up with toast, cereal, juice, fruit and two cinnamon rolls. Alex looked up sharply to see Nicki watching her with a pensive expression. Forcing herself to smile, Alex straightened up and greeted Nicki. Her red-haired friend raised an eyebrow at her, looked pointedly at the flower drawn in the oatmeal and then sat down while shaking her head. Sighing in return, Alex slumped back in her chair and toyed with the spoon of her oatmeal.

"Don't judge me," she grumbled, not looking up at Nicki.

"So..." Nicki said slowly, "I'm guessing that the return to your dorm room hasn't been pleasant."

"Oh, it's been fine," Alex replied before shaking her head and setting down the spoon. "On the surface at least. Jenny and I have been eating every meal with the boys; that's why I haven't seen you guys since fencing club."

"Wow." Nicki took one of the glasses of orange juice and set it in front of Alex. "Any chance it's because she missed you?"

"I don't think so." Alex sighed, slumping down further. "She's worried I'll crack and tell Arthur." Pausing, Alex looked at the glass of orange juice. "Plus side, I've at least known where she is, and today she's got spirit squad practice while we're at magic lessons."

"I don't understand why they call it spirit squad and not cheerleading," Nicki said, changing the subject. She moved one of the cinnamon rolls over to Alex's tray. "Just seems a bit silly to me."

"According to my darling roommate it is because they do more than just cheer at games, they are ambassadors to the community and help with school events." Alex poked at the cinnamon roll.

"Ah so, in theory, they build school spirit," Nicki confirmed with a nod. "Well, that's nice I suppose."

"I guess. I was happy for her, I really was. She had something to get involved in that didn't require her spending time with Arthur or Lance and finally seemed to be acting more normal. Then I go and lose my cool and blow everything." Alex muttered with a shrug, leaning forward to rest her elbows on the table.

"Okay, Alex honey, sit up and eat something or I will tie you down and shove food down your throat," Nicki told her in a sweet voice that had a hard edge to it.

Alex looked over at Nicki only to be met with a very stern expression and firm blue eyes. She straightened up in her chair and ripped a piece off the cinnamon roll, looking away from the satisfied smile. They were silent as Alex forced herself to eat half of the cinnamon roll and drained the glass of orange juice.

"So do you think Morgana and Merlin noticed me staying with you?" Alex finally asked as Nicki pushed a piece of toast onto the small plate with what remained of the cinnamon roll. "It was for three days."

"Probably," Nicki said. Shrugging, she spread grape jelly generously over a piece of toast. "But I told the boys that we were working on our papers for the Epic and you just needed a break from Jenny watching."

"Well, part of that was true." Alex sighed before looking back at Nicki. "Thanks for covering, I don't like lying to the boys-"

"I get it," Nicki interrupted gently. "Now do you want to say what is bothering you?"

"You know what is bothering me." Alex looked away from Nicki towards the main doors where a few more people were trickling in.

"Alex, honey, I am very capable of recognizing when you go from constant depression to having some new hellish thing dumped on you," Nicki replied, watching her with a soft smile. "Something else happened, didn't it?"

"Promise you won't tell?" Alex asked softly, still not looking over at Nicki.

"I promise," Nicki told her solemnly. "But bottling this shit up isn't healthy. None of it's healthy, but I don't want you having a heart attack or an aneurysm."

"Well..." Alex faltered, wondering not for the first time if she was putting too much of her current crisis on Nicki. It was her job to watch over Arthur, Jenny, and Lance as their friend and as a mage, but the ache in her chest practically demanded that she answer the question.

"Jenny was talking in her sleep this morning," Alex slowly answered, tapping her fingers nervously on the armrest. "She said Arto and apologized to him."

"Arto," Nicki repeated thoughtfully. "Wasn't that the name-"

"Of the first Iron Soul?" Alex sighed and nodded, "Yes it was." Nibbling at her lip, Alex shook her hands nervously in front of her, twisting her fingers together. "What if she remembers, Nicki?"

"Calm down," Nicki ordered, setting down her glass and holding up her hand. "Dreams are subconscious, and most people can't even remember them. There is a big difference between that and remembering. It may just be some part of her that feels guilty connecting to the ancient part of her that felt guilty."

"You're just making this up as you go along aren't you." Alex sank back into the seat and ran a hand through her hair. "Course I am too. Damn it, why does this have to be so messy?"

"It's the price we pay for being able to use magic," Nicki answered with a slight shrug. "Anything else?" Alex thought about the nightmare but shook her head no. "Alright then," Nicki sighed, giving Alex a small nod. "On a more cheerful note, so that you aren't upset when we get to Merlin's, I moved a peanut last night," Nicki announced with a widening smile.

"You did?" Alex asked, looking at her with wide eyes. "With magic? How far?"

"Yes, with magic," Nicki assured her with a little laugh. "Don't tell the boys. I want to show them when I can manage more than just pushing it two inches across my desk."

"Good for you," Alex told her softly, a small smile on her face. She paused and hesitated, pushing a strand of loose hair back behind her ear. "Look, Nicki, thank you for helping me through this. I know I'm kind of... up and down a lot lately."

"Alex, you're facing a terrible situation. You don't have to thank me for trying to be a good friend during that." Nicki shrugged and grimaced.

"In my worst moments, I'm grateful that I'm not the one dealing with it."

A snort escaped Alex's throat, and she shook her head. "No offense taken," Alex replied as she pushed her tray away, happy that Nicki didn't push it back. "I'm not thrilled with the role I was cast as in this retelling of the Arthurian myth."

"Hey, Alex! Nicki," a voice called across the room, making them both turn to see Aiden standing near the breakfast bar with Bran. Both boys waved to them, Aiden with more energy than the still sleepy looking Bran.

Raising her hand, Alex gave them a little wave while Nicki chuckled and gulped down the last of her juice. When Alex turned her attention back to Nicki, the redhead smiled. "So which archetype are you in this particular story?"

"Regular person probably," Alex replied with a soft laugh. "Driven to connect with others and help the hero of the story."

"And which one am I?" Nicki asked as she settled back in her chair.

"You'd probably be either the caregiver if this morning is anything to go by," Alex said gesturing to the tray that Nicki had been stacking food on for her. "But I suppose that you could also be the creator depending on which archetype list you're going off of, artistic and driven to make a vision a reality."

"Really?" Nicki asked with a widening smile. "I think I like the sound of that one. Can a person be multiple archetypes?"

"Sometimes," Alex replied with a thoughtful nod. "Archetypes are more... trends and traditions that are seen in literature, there aren't really rules about it."

A new tray was set down next to Alex on the right followed by one on the left. As Aiden dropped into his seat, he glanced between the two of them with a warm smile. "Morning, girls, what are we talking about?"

"Our roles in the strange story we live in," Nicki said. She turned to Bran as he sat down, giving him a welcoming smile.

"Our roles?" Aiden repeated. "Do you mean like stock characters?"

"Exactly." Alex leaned forward on her hand as she looked at him. "For instance, Bran is the seer."

"Obviously," Bran answered even as he kept his eyes focused on his breakfast and worked on his cup of coffee.

"Merlin is well…. Merlin the wise old man or sage," Alex continued with a chuckle. "Morgana could fit that archetype as well, but I'd be inclined to put her down as the explorer or maybe the ruler."

Aiden huffed and looked across the table at Bran. "This mean anything to you?"

"Nope." Bran shrugged before taking another bite of his toast.

"Hurry up, boys." Nicki pulled out her phone and checked the time. "Merlin and Morgana wanted us there early, remember?"

"So, what about me?" Aiden asked, ignoring Nicki's comment to look at Alex. "Which one would I be?"

Alex paused and considered him for a moment before smiling. "I'm torn; you'd either be the hero." Aiden grinned. "Or the fool."

Nicki laughed and knocked on the table to get everyone's attention. "And on that note, come on everyone it's time to go."

"But I'm not done eating," Aiden protested with a huff.

"Too bad, time to go," Nicki told him as she stood up. Alex paused and waited for Bran to stand, helping him collect the trays to take to the front with them. Nicki rolled her eyes at Aiden as she slung her bag over her shoulders and grabbed her tray. "Aiden, get your butt moving."

"Bossy," Aiden grumbled as he grabbed his last piece of toast and dumped strawberry jelly on it before jumping up and heading after them.

The Return

808 B.C.E. Northern Cornwall

Breathing in the salty air that carried the scent of the sea, Arto licked his lips and looked towards the village of his birth from his vantage point on a nearby hill. Smoke curled up from the village's roundhouses, and the soft sounds of animals could be heard. Arto listened to the dogs barking, and it made him wonder not for the first time what had become of his childhood pet. A vague memory of the animal disliking Morgana sprang to mind and Arto barely held back a sigh at his naivety. Even now the idea that his sister had been watching him for the wicked Queen of the Sídhe still felt foolish. He turned back and glanced at the sloping hill beyond him and wondered if this was where that Sídhe attack which had led Merlin to conclude he had to be taken away from his home had occurred.

"Arto," his mentor's voice called gently just before a hand was placed on his shoulder. "Are you alright?"

"I just..." Arto struggled for a moment, taking in a deep breath. "I am conflicted about being back here," he admitted in a softer voice, looking at the ground.

"I understand," Merlin told him in a soothing voice, his hand just brushing the hair at the back of Arto's neck. "I do wish that removing you from your parents had not been necessary-"

"I know," Arto interrupted, uncomfortable with hearing Merlin's explanation again. "Once the Sídhe knew where this new 'weapon' was they would never have left the village in peace. Constantly moving protected me." He swallowed thickly as he watched people move into the village through the gate in the distance. "I'm not angry at you, or Morgana," he added quickly.

"But the questions linger," Merlin said. "What might your life have been like? That is natural. In quiet moments I ask the same thing about my mother's death and my time serving as your guardian. Just be mindful that questions about what the past might have been, do not ruin your ability to shape your future." The hand on his shoulder tightened as Merlin fell silent and for a moment Arto was content to know that the old mage was standing with him.

The wind swirled around them, and Arto inhaled the scents of spring, grateful that the winter had finally receded and made travel easier once more. The sinking sun was reminding him that he really should be making his way towards the village, but Arto did not move. He glanced at Merlin when the sounds of metal shifting told him that the man was moving, but his mentor was simply adjusting the long sack slung over his shoulder. From his position next to Merlin, Arto could just see the hilts of the swords carried within.

"Do you remember your mother and father?" Merlin asked in a calm, conversational tone, breaking the silence around them.

"Not really," Arto confessed softly. He looked down at his feet and studied how his leather shoes crushed the wild grasses. "Just some impressions, little feelings. There are a few images that I'm not sure if they are memories or just dreams."

"You were only seven," Merlin comforted him. "I hope that you'll be able to make some memories now."

"Except I'm here as the Iron Soul and wielder of Cathanáil now," Arto reminded Merlin, straightening up and raising his chin. "It has taken a year to organize this meeting, to have so many leaders and powerful traders in one place. I have to be the Iron Soul."

"Before the assembled men yes," Merlin agreed with a nod. "But please, Arto, be willing to take at least a few moments to be the son of Uthyrn and Eigyr. For their sake and Morgana's."

Arto flinched at the reminder of the role his sister had played in his removal from their parents. Eigyr had been unaware that the Sídhe had stolen the infant Morgana and left a Changeling in her place. Years later the Queen of the Sídhe fused her servant Morgana and the Changeling to serve as her spy. Arto rarely saw his sister show any signs of guilt, but he knew her well enough to know that guilt shimmered beneath the calm she showed the world.

"I will," Arto promised quickly, licking his lips nervously.

"We've given Morgana long enough to speak with your parents, don't you think," Merlin suggested calmly a few moments later as he gestured towards the village.

Arto's voice deserted him, his mouth suddenly dry and he only managed a quick nod of agreement. Merlin seemed to understand and carefully pushed him forward to get him moving. The grass and plants seemed thicker than usual as Arto nearly tripped twice as they followed the worn trail to the gate of the village.

An older man with gray in his beard straightened up as they approached, his eyes locking onto Cathanáil's hilt. The instinct to shrink away from the stare rose quickly in him, but Arto shoved it down forcefully. Doing his best to look confident, he strode towards the gate and nodded to the guard who jumped to attention. As they passed through the gate, Arto heard Merlin chuckle behind him. Looking over his shoulder, Arto raised an eyebrow at his guardian who shrugged slightly.

Looking around, Arto waited for something to trigger a memory, but the village looked like all the others he'd ever been in. Roundhouses were scattered about with worn paths leading to a central dirt road and there were small fenced areas where animals were kept. People looked over at them with curiosity and wonder but soon returned to their tasks. As they began to walk forward, Arto could see a group of weavers and a bronze caster working nearby in small yards by different roundhouses. Others were carrying baskets and earthen jars through the village.

The path cleared in front of them as they walked further into the village, everyone moving smoothly out of their way. Merlin's staff thumped on the ground with each step and Arto tried to relax as he listened to the familiar rhythm. He caught sight of several older men that he vaguely recognized from his travels who were talking together. Arto just hoped that they were feeling positive about the talks that would begin tonight.

They followed the bend of the path around the hill and Arto nearly stopped when he caught sight of Morgana up on the hill by a roundhouse. A sudden strange feeling gripped him as he saw the curve of the path up to the door and the large rock that was in the fenced yard. Morgana was standing there alone, but the pelt that covered the door was moving as someone inside the house lingered and peeked out.

Taking a deep breath, Arto climbed the hill. It was familiar, slowly coming out of a thick haze. His height made it seem strange even as it felt familiar, his legs were too long, and he was seeing the house at a new angle. He looked back at his sister, aware that he was moving far more slowly than usual, but Morgana was waiting calmly with her hands folded in front of her. Lowering his eyes from her knowing gaze, Arto forced himself to take the last few steps to join her without further delay.

"I know," Morgana whispered, wrapping an arm around his back as she turned to face the roundhouse. "I haven't seen them in years either."

"But you at least grew up here," Arto hissed as he stumbled towards the door. Morgana sucked in a sharp breath, and Arto flinched as he realized his words. "Morgana, sister, I didn't mean-"

"It's alright," Morgana said quickly. "Just go inside. Uthyrn was insistent that he and mother not embarrass you in front of the visitors."

Nodding mutely, Arto reached for the animal pelt that covered the door slowly. Morgana reached forward and pulled it back, clearing the way for him, and Merlin gave him a sudden push, forcing him into the roundhouse. It was greatly changed from the foggy memories he had and seemed far barer. A large set of shelves stood directly opposite of him, holding elegant bottles, jet necklaces, golden rings, and bronze axe heads. There was only a small fire in the hearth, giving Arto enough light to see a figure rise from a short seat at the right side of the roundhouse. Turning his head, Arto saw that it was an older woman who was staring at him with wide, teary eyes.

Tensing up, Arto swallowed thickly as his mother approached him. There were small wrinkles around her warm brown eyes, and they were shining with unshed tears. Eigyr's long dark brown hair had strands of gray running through the braid that hung over her shoulder. Her hands shook gently as she tentatively reached for him.

"Arto," she breathed in a soft broken voice. "Oh, my baby."

Eigyr's arms were suddenly around him, clasping him tightly against her. A warm hand was stroking his hair and tears fell onto his shoulder. Arto could barely breathe, his chest felt tight, and his arms were hanging limply at his sides, too heavy to move.

"Mother," he choked out, stumbling over the word.

The arms around him suddenly loosened and Eigyr stepped back. Her eyes were still teary, but she straightened up and lifted her chin with a forced smile. "Welcome... back, Arto," she greeted, stumbling for a moment herself. "I understand that this must be overwhelming for you."

He didn't want to feel guilty, but Arto couldn't help it as he saw the sadness and hope blended together in his mother's eyes. Giving her a small smile, he managed a simple nod. He licked his lips, desperately searching for something to say. Eigyr watched his face for a moment, her shoulders sinking before she turned to Merlin. She didn't smile at him, giving him a cold look with barely concealed anger.

"And you return to our little village after all these years, Merlin," Eigyr said as her eyes took him in with a sharp glance. "It has been too long."

"Indeed," Merlin agreed, giving Eigyr a small bow and showing no reaction to her cold reception. "Sadly, the Sídhe have kept us very busy over the last few years and before that simply keeping those creatures away from Arto made all things in life much more complicated."

Arto watched his mother fight internally, her eyes flashing with anger and sadness before they settled to a dull shade of brown. A resigned sigh escaped her, and she looked back at him.

"I'm glad to see you," Eigyr whispered, carefully reaching out a hand and straightening the metal clasp of his cloak. "I've often wondered what you would look like."

There was movement at the side of the roundhouse and the sounds of a large person moving. Looking away from Eigyr, Arto saw a tall broad-shouldered man with light brown hair which was streaked with gray. Brown eyes were nearly hidden under thick eyebrows. A jet necklace that seemed familiar hung around his neck, and small golden decorations were woven into his braided hair. Swallowing again, Arto was left realizing that he didn't look as much like his father as Morgana tended to say.

"Father," Arto greeted, his voice higher and more nervous than he wanted. He cleared his throat and repeated the greeting in a more normal voice, barely resisting the urge to deepen it.

"Welcome, son," Uthyrn replied moving closer slowly. The older man limped slightly but walked with a straight back. A hazy memory of being carried by his father returned making Arto's throat tighten.

"Thank you, Father," Arto said with a nod before looking over at Eigyr. "I am happy to see you both. I wish it was under better circumstances." Arto shifted uncomfortably, wishing he could turn to Merlin or Morgana for guidance in the situation.

Then Uthyrn stepped forward and clasped his shoulder with a small smile. Uthyrn looked over at Morgana and nodded to her, getting a small nod of acknowledgment in return. "Come, son," Uthyrn said, the word hesitant. Arto barely held back a flinch at the reminder of what Merlin taking him had cost his parents. "There is someone you need to meet."

"As you wish, Father." Arto allowed his father to turn him towards the doorway.

Morgana and Merlin stepped out of the way, clearing his path. Glancing over his shoulder, he saw his mother be wrapped in a hug by Morgana and cling to her daughter. His stomach churned, and his mouth went painfully dry, but his Father led him out of the roundhouse without another word. Uthyrn kept a firm grip on his shoulder as he steered him gently through the village. All around them, people stopped and looked at them, some even coming out of their roundhouses to catch a glimpse of the pair. Arto wondered how his parents had reacted to some of the tales about him, Merlin, and Morgana that had spread across the land over the last few years. It was strange to think that this village was where he had been born and that had things gone differently, he might have spent his entire youth here.

They suddenly stopped at a roundhouse near his parents' and Uthyrn pushed him towards the doorway, finally releasing his shoulder. Nothing about the roundhouse stood out, it was of good construction, and it looked like the roof had been redone within the last summer or two. A thick hide served as a doorway but was pushed open to let air flow into the house. Glancing back at his father, Arto saw Uthyrn nod to him and walked up to the house. Behind him, he heard his father follow and wondered just who it was that he was going to be meeting. The discussions about the Sídhe wouldn't begin until near sundown.

Arto hesitated for a moment at the doorway but stepped into the roundhouse after taking a quick breath. In front of him was a shelf with several small bottles and a gleaming bronze sword on display along with two bronze axe heads. There was only one bed at the side of the roundhouse, and the fire in the central pit had gone out. Movement on the left side made Arto turn his head and look over to see a young man about his age standing up from a small seat.

The young man had long dark hair pulled away from his face with small golden ornaments. Like Arto, he didn't have much facial hair and was dressed in a simple tunic and pants. As the man stepped closer, Arto nearly frowned as he recognized a strong resemblance between the young man in front of him and Uthyrn. Dark eyes took him in quickly, and a nervous smile appeared on his face as the young man stepped closer to him.

"Arto," Uthyrn spoke up from behind them, stepping up next to him and placing a hand on his shoulder. "This is your cousin Medraut, the son of my brother Adair."

"It's a pleasure to meet you, at last, cousin." Medraut stepped forward and gripped Arto's forearm with a smile. Arto returned the gesture and nodded to his cousin with a relieved smile. His father's tone had made him worry.

"Arto, Medraut lives here because he is my heir," Uthyrn informed him gruffly. "I'm sorry, son, but when it became clear that you were never going to return here to live, I needed to determine the succession. We have valuable trading connections that must be protected."

"Oh," Arto breathed, blinking in surprise. He'd never really thought about the political situation that his father oversaw in the region with the bronze trade to the southern lands. Arto felt a bit silly for a moment, remembering that Morgana's marriage had been in part a political arrangement once Morgana agreed to accept Airril. "I see, Father," he forced himself to say and gave Medraut a more welcoming smile. "I am relieved that my gift and responsibilities haven't caused any lasting harm to the family."

His response seemed to put Uthyrn at ease, and his father clapped him on the back. "A fine answer, son. You would have been a fine leader, but it seems that you may become one anyway."

"I am of course at your service, cousin," Medraut assured Arto with a widening smile, standing a bit taller with a spark in his brown eyes.

Uthyrn made a small sound of relief behind Arto and squeezed his shoulder before excusing himself from the roundhouse. Trying not to appear nervous, Arto smiled warmly at Medraut and studied the young man quickly. Medraut greatly resembled his father's side of the family with a strong jaw and broad shoulders, making Arto suddenly feel small in comparison, but he forced such thoughts aside.

"How long have you lived here?" Arto settled on for his first question.

"Four years," Medraut answered with a small shrug as he gestured to the doorway. "My father died, and Uthyrn invited my mother and me here. She passed last year."

Arto allowed Medraut to lead him out of the roundhouse and the two stood in silence as they watched villagers rush around preparing for the gathering. His father was mingling with the men he'd noticed earlier in the largest open area of the village where a large circle of stools had been placed. More men were joining the group with each passing moment causing Arto's stomach to turn.

"Quite a sight," Medraut murmured next to Arto before chuckling. "I don't think anyone other than the traders and the priests usually come so far." He glanced over at Arto and added, "And mages of course."

"This is important." Arto's eyes found Morgana and Merlin speaking nearby. Both of them were ignoring the people staring at them. "It's rare that something affects everyone."

"Some leaders from the western island are even coming," Medraut said. "The rumor is that you have a plan to stop the Sídhe for good."

Arto didn't even have to look at his cousin to know that his eyes were on Cathanáil. People seemed to know more about the Sword than him.

"Arto!" a female voice called to their right.

Turning, Arto's eyes widened in surprise as Gwenyvar came running up to him, her long brown hair flowing loose behind her with only a few small braids holding it back from her face. Arms were suddenly around him, and a cheek was pressed against his bare neck. Next to him, he heard Medraut chuckle as he slowly brought his arms up around Gwenyvar.

"Excuse me, cousin," Medraut said, giving Arto a quick nod and turning to walk towards Uthyrn.

"Hello, Gwenyvar." Arto glanced around to make sure that Morgana and Merlin weren't watching.

She released him and stepped back, blushing slightly, but smiling widely. "It's very nice to see you, Arto."

"It's nice to see you as well," Arto replied uncertainly. "Are you here with your father?"

"Yes," she told him seriously. "He wanted me to come since I have some personal experience with the Sídhe and saw you destroy that tunnel." Gwenyvar glanced down at the ground, her hands trembling the tiniest bit as she clutched the fabric of her dress. "I want to be sure that everyone understands what you can do."

His mouth went dry again even as his palms suddenly felt sweaty. Gwenyvar raised her eyes to meet his and gave him a small smile. His heart jumped, Arto nearly flinched at the strange feeling but returned the smile.

"I'm really not-"

"You were very brave that night," Gwenyvar insisted with a stern expression, giving him no room for argument. "You refused to back down and were able to destroy that wretched tunnel." Gwenyvar's expression softened. "Arto, you're the best chance we have. Well, you and your sword," she added quickly with a nervous giggle.

"I- thank you, Gwenyvar."

Arto barely caught sight of Morgana in time to jump back from Gwenyvar as his sister walked towards them. She raised an eyebrow and looked over at Gwenyvar, her lips forming a thin line. Morgana nodded to Gwenyvar but turned her attention to Arto without a single word of greeting.

"Arto, its time, the last priest from the east just arrived."

"Alright." Arto took in a deep breath to try and calm himself as his stomach felt like it flipped and his throat tightened.

"We'll talk later," Gwenyvar assured him, giving a deep nod to Morgana before she turned and rushed down the hill. Arto watched her long enough to see her reach her father and take a spot standing behind him.

"Shouldn't Merlin-" Arto began to ask.

"No," Morgana answered quickly, cutting him off. "You are the Iron Soul. You are the one who created this plan." His sister stepped closer to him, placing a hand on each shoulder. "I know that this is frightening, but we wouldn't have you address them if we didn't think you could do it."

"It's the Sword that everyone cares about," Arto told her, hating the whine in his voice.

"The Sword is easier to understand than the one who wields it. You created Cathanáil, Arto: it may be iron, but unlike those lesser iron blades that Merlin brought here, it carries magic. In your hands, it is capable of things that no other blade can do."

Arto nodded, not completely swayed by his sister's words, but knowing that he could not argue. Her faith in him and the knowledge of Merlin's faith in him made him feel stronger physically, but worries of disappointing them now joined the brew of fear and nervousness churning in his gut. Morgana walked ahead of him down the hill, leading him to where Merlin was seated and waiting for them. Morgana sat down gracefully on an empty stool, leaving one between herself and Merlin. Swallowing, Arto turned and lowered himself onto the wooden seat, trying to appear every bit the hero that his sister and mentor thought he could be.

Merlin raised his staff and brought it down on the packed earth with a flash of his brilliant green magic. All the voices stilled and almost as one, the sea of heads all turned towards them. Before him sat dozens of men, some large and young and some older and more frail, but all were watching him. Arto found the familiar face of his brother-in-law Airril amongst them and for a moment focused on him, trying to gather his strength and courage.

The desire to shrink back behind Merlin nearly overwhelmed him despite knowing that he'd lose whatever respect he did have from them. Morgana discreetly placed her hand against his back, silently telling him that she was there.

"Welcome," Arto greeted as loudly and clearly as he could manage. "I thank you all for coming; I know that it has been a very long journey for many of you." Cold sweat was trickling down his back, and he wasn't sure what to do with his hands, settling for folding them in front of him. "We are gathered together to-" Screams erupted from the gate cutting Arto off, and everyone turned to look behind them.

"Riders!" a man shouted in the distance. "Dozens of them!"

Without thinking, Arto reached back and pulled Cathanáil from its sheath in one smooth action. Merlin grabbed the bag of swords and held it out in front of him.

"Quickly," the elder mage shouted. "Arm yourselves! It seems we will have a demonstration of the power of iron tonight!"

19

In the Furnace

Heat from the furnace hit her back, but Alex forced herself to focus on the metal strip gently placed over the horn of the anvil. She could hear the sounds of hammering nearby and voices mingling with metallic scrapes. There was a small grunt to her right followed by the scratch of a wooden cane against the concrete floor that confirmed Bran's presence. Exhaling slowly, Alex forced herself to keep her eyes open even as she visualized her dark silver magic gathering in her right hand and traveling into the hammer she was clutching.

Her skin tingled with warmth as the magic flowed just over the surface of her hand. It became easier to breathe, and the heat of the furnaces no longer seemed so heavy on her body. Tiny sparks zinged over her palm, making the wood of the hammer's handle pulse in her grasp. She brought the hammer down sharply on the metal, hearing the ring of the impact. The iron band bent to the curved shape of the horn, twisting slightly to start the shape of a circle. Alex exhaled as she brought the hammer down once again. Dark silver magic flowed into the metal, causing a soft glow to cover the iron. Sparks flew off the hammer, jumping over the surface of the iron and into the anvil which began to glow. The magic darkened the steel of the anvil, branching out slowly like veins.

Pulling the hammer back, Alex struggled to contain her magic which was sparking wildly around her hand and flowing into the medium-sized hammer with barely any instruction. The dark silvery sparks were visible in the corner of her eye as she adjusted the thin piece of iron using the tong around the horn of the anvil. Gritting her teeth, she considered the cooling piece of metal.

"Careful, Alex," Bran cautioned her from his vantage point a few feet away.

The desire to snap at him rose through her, but Alex shoved it down and brought the hammer down on the metal. She almost missed the strip of iron and was left with concerns about her hand and eye coordination. As the hammer struck the metal and a loud, dull ring echoed around her, Alex's dark silver magic flowed from the hammer and into the metal. The iron shimmered, magic running not just through it, but over the surface as well. Lifting the hammer again, she tried to keep her magic from surging into the tool too quickly, but it was proving to be difficult.

The hammer was glowing so brightly in her right hand that it was difficult to have it in her peripheral vision. Sparks of magic began to spring out of the metal of the tool, making her panic. She swung the hammer down and pushed the magic into the piece of iron desperately, picturing a wave of magic hitting the metal band like a tsunami. The iron piece curved around the horn sharply and the magical glow was constant now, glittering brightly with dark silver sparks that were falling to the ground. Behind her, Alex heard Morgana and Merlin suddenly stop talking about modern blacksmithing methods.

"Alex, you're putting too much magic into the metal too quickly," Merlin shouted, worry apparent in his voice.

Someone grasped the hammer around her hand, and another smaller hand took the tongs from her. Moving smoothly, Merlin pulled the hammer from her grip and gently pushed her away from the furnace. Morgana shifted the metal with the tongs as Merlin selected another hammer from the rack quickly and switched the one still glowing with magic to his left hand. With several quick strikes with the uncharged hammer, Merlin forced the metal into a smoother curved shape and then motioned for Morgana to put it back into the fire. Once the iron was back in the furnace, both professors turned to face her.

"I'm sorry," Alex told them quickly. "I couldn't get the magic to slow down."

"Slow down?" Merlin repeated with a quizzical expression, raising an eyebrow. "I've never heard that before. Most of us have a hard time channeling magic in that fashion."

"Well, she has the ability to control magical energy at an unusual level," Morgana chimed in, giving Alex a small smile. "No harm done, but you don't want the magic building up to that level. In theory, it could activate and explode or cause some other nasty event."

Nodding in understanding, Alex carefully accepted back the hammer which was still shimmering with her magic. Morgana and Merlin stepped aside to give her access to the furnace and anvil once again. Fighting down a blush, Alex pulled out the iron and carefully struck it with the hammer again, doing her best to keep her magic from flowing so quickly. It was harder, like forcing up a wall in a channel that she'd been digging for hours. It felt unnatural, but Alex inhaled slowly and swung the hammer, exhaling as it struck the iron once again. Both the hammer and the iron shimmered with magic as her magical flow slowed to a gentle trickle.

"Better," Merlin said. Alex relaxed, hearing the smile in his voice. "That's it. You don't want to let the iron take in too much magic too fast. It should always be dimmer with magic than your hammer."

"What about at the end," Aiden asked from the other side of the shop where he was working with Nicki on a piece of metal.

"As the magic settles into the iron it rapidly dims in brightness. At the end, you push the last of the magic out of the hammer and into it. But you can underestimate how quickly iron absorbs magic."

Nodding slowly, Alex carefully picked up the iron piece with the tongs and studied it. She'd already managed to make all the necessary spiraled pieces for the triskele.

"You're almost done," Bran observed with a smile as he reached over and grabbed the first piece. "Just have to finish that spiral, and then Merlin said he'd weld them together." He gave her an encouraging look. "Weird that we're allowed to work with furnaces, but not a blow torch."

Alex managed a weak laugh before a sigh escaped her. Glancing over her shoulder, she saw Morgana and Merlin talking with Aiden. Apparently, he was having the opposite problem of not putting enough magic in.

"Can't blame him for that," Bran remarked, leaning back against one of the work tables. "When your primary form of using magic is fire, I can see not wanting to use much of it."

"I wonder how long it will take for us to be good at this." Alex looked back at the furnace, watching the flicker of blue flames deep in the nest of red-hot coals. "We've been at it for weeks now."

"This is a pretty different skill set than we're used to," Bran pointed out with a shrug. "Come on. You're almost done with your first iron piece. That's great. I haven't made nearly as much progress."

"You know that if I finish today, you'll probably have to work all next Saturday." Alex pushed the iron band back into the furnace.

"I doubt that," Bran replied. "Morgana and Merlin worry about making me stand without my cane for too long. I've told them I can lock my brace to keep the leg straight, but they won't have it."

"I don't blame them," Alex admitted. "They don't want us getting hurt in lessons. Ironworking is important, but Morgana said that she didn't do it for years, so it isn't vital."

"Yeah, but I hate people thinking I can't do something." Bran crossed his arms and glared at the furnace.

Nodding, Alex wondered what she could say, but couldn't think of anything. She pulled out the iron band, now glowing a soft orange and brought it over to the anvil. The curve was so small now that she had to slide it carefully down the horn to the proper narrowness. Alex picked up one of the smallest hammers and pictured a slight glow, just a flicker of magic in the hammer. Her skin hummed, and then there was a tug in her gut that stole her breath for a moment. Her magic flowed through her limbs, but more gently this time. It felt like a small trickle of water under the skin instead of a full water burst. The hammer began to glow softly in her hand, and she sighed in relief.

"Well done," Merlin complimented from behind her. "Oh my, you're nearly done."

Alex brought the hammer down on the band of iron and watched as it curved tightly. She had to pull with the tongs to shift its position and pulled the iron band further down the horn, making the curve even tighter. Keeping a tight grip on the flow of the magic, picturing it as a special nozzle on a hose, Alex reheated and hammered the metal twice more. Then after the final heating, four more hammer strikes sent magic flowing into the metal and finished the tiny curve of the spiral.

Bran clapped from his vantage point, still leaning against the work table with his cane propped up next to him. More applause joined his a moment later, and Alex blushed as she turned to see a grinning Nicki and Aiden. She set down the metal spiral and put the tongs and hammer aside.

"What is all this?" Morgana asked as she came through the doorway, startling Alex who hadn't noticed her leave. She caught sight of the curved piece of metal and glanced at Merlin who was grinning. "I see. Congratulations, Alex," Morgana said in a warmer tone. "You've completed the hardest part."

"I'll help you weld the pieces together and put a metal ring around the triskele after lunch," Merlin added before gesturing to the door. "Speaking of which, Morgana, I assume you found the sandwiches?"

"I did, and it looks like Aiden and Nicki have already stopped for the morning," Morgana replied with a glance towards the two young mages. Aiden shrugged and grinned while Nicki gave Morgana a sheepish smile. "Lunch is on the patio, come along."

Alex let the others head out first, waiting with Merlin as he closed the furnace covers and tidied up the tools. She picked up the two pieces of iron that she'd spent days hammering into the gentle curves and brushed her fingers over them, studying them carefully. It was still rather rough, she could see hammer marks all over the metal, unlike the more refined pieces made by Merlin and Morgana that filled the worktables, but she was still pleased.

"An excellent first effort," Merlin said gently at her right as he placed a hand on her shoulder. "But come along, time to eat. You're probably not feeling it yet, but the amount of magic you were trying to use earlier will have made you ravenous." He took the metal pieces from Alex and set them down on the tool bench. "We'll take care of the rest after lunch. You're the first of your class with a finished item."

Smiling at the praise, Alex headed outside to the patio. Six wrought iron chairs with bright red cushions were set up around the oval wrought iron table, probably made by Merlin. A large tray of sandwiches was set out along with a bowl of Caesar salad and a setting for everyone.

The sight of the food made Alex's stomach rumble. Merlin chuckled next to her as she sat down before taking his seat. Already the others were talking with Morgana, Nicki had probably asked some historical question judging from the snippets that Alex caught of the conversation.

"Yes, we've made some good investments over the years," Morgana said.

Morgana picked up the tray of sandwiches and held it out for Alex. With a grateful smile, Alex grabbed one of the thick turkey and Swiss sandwiches and took a large bite out of it. Nicki passed her the salad a moment later, and she focused on the ongoing conversation.

"One of my fondest memories is the steam engine," Merlin said with a chuckle as he selected a roast beef sandwich from the platter. "At the time many people were afraid that going at such a high speed would destroy internal organs and kill passengers."

"On a train?" Aiden asked doubtfully.

"It was the first time something like that had been seen," Morgana told him as a smile tugged at her lips. "Merlin and I bought tickets for it." She looked over at Merlin and chuckled, "Of course, he wasn't so confident about flying when commercial airplanes were built. I bought a ticket and flew more than a decade before he was willing to give it a try."

"It was still a relatively new science," Merlin protested, sulking slightly as he gave Morgana a look. "Trains stayed on the ground and followed a set path. Planes were an entirely different thing." Merlin straightened up and pointed at Morgana, shaking his finger. "And I'll remind you that I used an automobile before you did."

"Smelly and slow," Morgana huffed dismissively. "It wasn't until the 1930s that they finally got some style. I do miss some of the elegance that cars had back then, but I can't argue about modern gas mileage improvements." Morgana shrugged and glanced around at the students who were staring at them. "We've lived through a lot of changes," she reminded them before delicately taking a sip of her iced tea.

"I'll say," Nicki said with a smile before her expression turned quizzical. "Has anything ever frightened you in history? I mean wars and natural disasters?"

"Wars are never pleasant," Morgana agreed with a sigh and a shake of her head. "We've been around for at least part of several, the worst one I spent any real time in the midst of was the Thirty Years War. For the population at the time, it was devastating." Morgana shivered and shook her head.

"We were a little involved in World War II," Merlin admitted carefully. "An incarnation of the Iron Soul was active, but I'm afraid that we couldn't get into contact with him and he died very soon after. Thankfully magic was very low during that period, so we didn't have to worry about the Sídhe or other invaders on top of the destruction of that war." There was an odd note to Merlin's voice that was distressing.

"So, you two don't get involved most of the time?" Aiden asked. He leaned back in his chair. "But doesn't it bother you, all the fighting, death and destruction?"

"You forget how old we are," Morgana told Aiden gently. "We've seen civilizations rise and fall, wars seemingly destroy beyond any point of repair, governments overthrown, tsunamis, volcanic eruptions, hurricanes, earthquakes, warming periods, cooling periods, and fiction become reality." Morgana shook her head. "At a certain point, you recognize that all of this is just humanity trying to move forward and the natural cycle of nature. After a while you realize that destroyed civilizations survive with small reminders carried by the people and the land, you realize that nothing is ever beyond restoration if people have a mind to do it and you realize that a three-thousand-year-old person shouldn't have a say in the government of those who have but one lifespan to live." Morgana took a sip of tea and chuckled, "And as a mage, you realize that the Earth is far stronger than you or any humans will ever be and you just need to adapt to what she throws your way."

"But surely you've been concerned at some point," Aiden pressed. "Just once at least?"

Merlin chuckled and set down his drink with a nod. "Indeed, I'll admit that during the Cold War Morgana, and I tried to make plans to ensure that Mutually Assured Destruction failed and at least some of the planet wasn't left completely wiped out."

"Were you successful?" Alex asked, speaking up for the first time.

"We have plans to prevent a total loss of life on Earth," Morgana informed them as she glanced Alex over and smiled. "In fact, once you have full control of your powers you may be helpful in that." Morgana sipped her tea and said nothing more on the subject despite the look of confusion and curiosity on Alex's face that made Merlin chuckle.

"To change the subject," Bran said after swallowing a bite of his sandwich. "There's some things that I've wanted to ask you about the Tree of Reality."

Merlin set down his iced tea and looked over at Bran, nodding to him encouragingly. "Go ahead," Merlin told him. "We'll answer what we can."

"Okay." Bran paused to gather his thoughts. "You said that the tree connects different worlds, even ones with different physical laws which means that they are actually in different universes."

"Yes, I believe that to be the case," Merlin agreed. "It's only recently that science has advanced to the point of giving us the concept of other universes instead of just different worlds."

"But you have no idea about why they are connected?" Bran asked with a frown. "Even though according to the theory of the multiverse the different universes are moving further away from each other."

"We do not," Morgana told him, setting down her plate. "The fact is that we know what the Tree of Reality is, but we don't know anything about why it exists."

"We don't know if the thirty-nine worlds of the Tree of Reality are the only inhabited worlds with sentient life in the whole multiverse or if there are others," Merlin continued with a shrug and a smile.

"How do you know there are thirty-nine?" Alex asked, leaning forward with a hint of curiosity herself. "Have you two been to the other worlds?"

"Morgana has been to Sídhean, but I have never left the Iron Realm," Merlin informed her calmly. "We know the shape of the Tree of Reality because of magical connections that can be traced. On certain days of the year, the alignment and seasonal change days, it is possible to reach out into the Tree of Reality. Dangerous, but possible. I believe it likely that each world has some point when they can perceive the Tree of Reality."

"The issue is, do they understand what they are seeing," Morgana chimed in.

"So how do you know that all the worlds have life on them?" Aiden asked causing Morgana to look over at him.

"In truth we don't," Morgana informed him calmly. "But over the years we have had contact with beings that have had more direct contact with the other points on the tree and their reports all include life." Morgana paused and made a small nod as she considered something. "However, I suppose that it is possible that some of the worlds may have died. Just like a branch of a tree can die."

"Do you think it's possible that new branches could grow in the future?" Bran asked. "I mean if it might be possible for a branch to die then could the tree connect to a new world."

"I don't know," Morgana answered, shaking her head. "As I said Merlin and I know only some of the secrets of the tree. You're asking questions that I have no answer to."

"Perhaps you will find some of the answers," Merlin said with a smile to all of them. "After all, Morgana and I have great experience, but we are a bit stuck in our ways of thinking. Bran, you are a student of physics, perhaps in time you will unravel some more of the mysteries."

Bran smiled at the idea and exchanged a look with Aiden who grinned in return. Nicki giggled softly and set her empty plate down.

"Well, if everyone is finished with lunch then it is time to return to work. Switch off who is working in the forge," Morgana instructed.

Alex nodded and caught Bran's sigh of relief out of the corner of her eye. Nicki stood first and started helping Morgana and Merlin gather up the plates and glasses. Jumping to her feet, Alex grabbed the plate of sandwiches just before Aiden snatched the last turkey sandwich. She followed Morgana and Merlin inside with Nicki trailing after her.

Merlin's kitchen was large with natural wood cabinets that shined brightly in the sunlight streaming through the two picture windows. There was a kitchen island separating the main kitchen from a cozy looking living room. Alex glanced around with interest to distract herself as Merlin set the dishes on the counter.

"Just leave them here," Merlin told them with a smile and gesture to the counter. "I'll take care of it once we're done for the day."

Nicki gently set down the pitcher of iced tea and the two glasses she'd managed to carry carefully. Alex followed the action and put down the plate on the kitchen island only for Merlin to pick it back up. He opened the refrigerator and placed the sandwiches on an empty shelf leaving Alex shifting on her feet wondering if she could help with something else. Aiden followed them inside with the last of the dishes and nodded to Alex before heading for the door. Alex smiled at Aiden and glanced at Merlin to make sure that he didn't need any more help.

"Alex," Morgana called, reaching out and catching her arm gently as she turned towards the doorway. "I need a word."

"Yes, Morgana?" Alex asked, trying to keep her voice even.

Behind them Alex caught sight of Merlin leading Nicki out of the house and her friend glancing back nervously. Alex looked at Morgana as calmly as she could and waited for whatever terrible questions she was about to be asked.

"Have there been any new developments between Jennifer and Lance?" Morgana asked bluntly, glancing towards the door.

"No," Alex forced out, unsure if she should smile or look distressed. She hesitated and carefully met Morgana's eyes. "Does it have to happen?"

Morgana's features softened, and her green eyes darkened sadly. Moving her hand, she brushed a strand of long blonde hair that had escaped Alex's ponytail behind her ear. "I'm afraid so," Morgana answered as she drew her hand back. "I wish it was not so."

"Maybe you're wrong, and it isn't Arthur," Alex offered weakly lowering her eyes. "I mean none of the others have even had a Connection with him, so maybe he isn't the Iron Soul."

"Alex," Morgana said gently, reaching out and gripping her arm carefully. "His magic just isn't flowing correctly... but he matches every sign of the Iron Soul. Merlin and I recognize him."

"They're not bad people," Alex insisted with a small sigh of defeat, reaching up and pulling her hair back into her ponytail. "They're just... stuck."

"I know that." Morgana sighed and turned away from Alex. "I know."

Morgana turned on the sink faucet and began running water into the sink. Morgana grabbed a small bottle of soap and squirted it into the water without a word. As she placed the dishes into the water, Alex took a step back and moved slowly to the back door. When Morgana said nothing else, Alex stepped outside and with a sigh of relief headed back to the blacksmith shop. Merlin was waiting for her with his leather apron and goggles already on, the welding torch in his hand.

"Alright then, Alex, I'll show you how to work with this, and then we'll finish up your triskele."

"Great," Alex agreed weakly.

She accepted a pair of leather gloves and goggles from Merlin. He waited until she put them both on and then fired up the torch. Alex did her best to focus on Merlin's words and the way that he slowly used a small piece of iron to fuse the two curving pieces together in the shape of the triskele, but her stomach kept flipping over with worry about what would happen when Morgana discovered the truth.

20

In Passing

T he words blurred in front of Alex. She'd been staring at the same sheet of notes for the last half an hour. The Spanish accent marks were the only way that she even remembered what she was looking at. She'd tucked herself away in a quiet study room in the library to think, but her mind kept going in circles without offering any solutions. Not that she'd honestly expected to have a sudden epiphany that would solve the issue of the dangerous love triangle between Arthur, Jenny, and Lance.

Groaning, Alex pushed the book away and rested her elbows on the table, dropping her head into her hands. The days had turned into weeks and then dragged into more than a month with no progress. Once Jenny had become convinced that Alex hadn't told Arthur the truth, she'd finally eased off watching her, but the recent string of late nights made Alex wonder if she wasn't back to her bad habits with Lance. Her phone chirped with an incoming call, providing a distraction that Alex jumped on. With a quick tap, she answered Nicki's call and brought the phone to her ear, glancing towards the door to make sure no one was around.

"Hey," Nicki greeted warmly. "What you up to?"

"I'm at the library," Alex replied. "Reviewing my Spanish notes to be exact."

"Sounds like a fun way to spend a Friday night."

"Not what I imagined doing with my Friday nights in college," Alex agreed with a sigh. "But then I wasn't expecting what I spend my Saturdays doing."

"True, I remember when I was worried about being pressured about drugs, date rape drugs, and having a slob for a roommate."

"Well two out of the three wouldn't be so bad," Alex conceded. "I almost wish that I trusted my magic enough to go and get drunk at a party."

"But then you think about blasting the jerk who won't back off through a wall," Nicki chimed in. "Right there with you, sweetie. Only I worry about turning them into a popsicle or causing rain indoors."

"You can't cause rain," Alex reminded Nicki, leaning back in her chair as a small smile tugged at her lips.

"Hey rain is water, someday I'll pull it off," Nicki countered, sounding like she was pouting.

"I'm not as sciency as the guys, but even I know that there is more to weather than just water."

"Yeah, but Morgana and Merlin say that we'll be able to use our powers beyond our current limitations. My goal is to make it rain."

"Morgana and Merlin don't do anything that flashy," Alex pointed out, glancing towards the door again. "Probably for a reason."

"There's a reason, it's called they're old with no imagination and ambition. I'm sure that once a time they pushed themselves and had fun with their magic. You know back when they wouldn't be dragged in for study."

"Fun with magic," Alex repeated, her lips twisting doubtfully. "Nope, can't imagine that."

"Give it time, I mean once we can move objects like Bran, then we'll have some fun. I'm looking forward to painting without having to touch a brush. I'm thinking little floating balls of paint splatting against the canvas."

"Sounds like painting with a paintball gun, nothing revolutionary there."

"Don't tell me that you lack imagination too," Nicki demanded. "Come on there must be something that you want to do with your magic."

Alex paused at the comment and blinked as she turned the words over in her head. "Not really," she answered slowly. "I haven't really been in the frame of mind since I got control to think about such things."

There was a moment of silence on the other end of the call before Nicki sighed softly and said, "Okay I get that. So, stop thinking about Spanish for a moment and think: if you could do one thing with magic, anything at all without having to worry about consequences or magical drain, what would you do?"

"Heal Bran's leg," Alex replied before she even thought about it. When she heard her own words, a soft laugh escaped her. "Yeah, final answer. That's what I'd do."

Nicki chuckled on the other end, and then a softer voice added, "And you say you're not the Hero of the story."

"Oh, shut up," Alex grumbled into the phone, glad that Nicki couldn't see her blushing.

"Alright I'll leave that alone," Nicki sighed loudly over the phone. "On a serious note, then, are you going to be okay watching them on Beltane?"

Alex swallowed at the question, leaning back in her chair, and licking her lips. "I'll manage," she finally said. "I assume the plan is still that you guys will be trying to keep the Sídhe at bay."

"Morgana and Merlin say it's the best plan. Someone needs to be near the Iron Soul, and you're the only one of us friendly with him."

"Yeah," Alex sighed. "But I hate the idea of you guys being out there without me."

"Hey you faced down the Sídhe already and did the conquering hero thing, it's our turn."

"I collapsed as soon I reached the surface, hardly conquering hero."

"You got those kids out," Nicki reminded her seriously. "You were a hero to them and their families, even if they don't remember you." In a more cheerful voice, Nicki added, "We can handle it, we may be greenhorns, but we'll have Morgana and Merlin with us. And we know the area of the tunnel so we can just cut them off before they even reach town. Think of it as our rite of passage for becoming mages. We'll look after each other."

"I know but-"

"Don't worry so much, it's still a week away, and you've got to figure out a way to keep Arthur close." Nicki chuckled and then added in a teasing tone, "Just don't forget when it starts this time."

"I'm never going to live Imbolc down, am I?" Alex groaned.

"Nope, sorry, sweetie, but definitely not."

"Alex?" A voice called from the doorway, making Alex turn to look over with wide eyes.

Arthur was standing in the doorway, smiling softly at her, and holding onto a backpack with one hand. He was in his usual university t-shirt, making Alex wonder just how many he had and if the school provided them.

"Oh sorry," he said quickly seeing the phone. "I didn't mean to interrupt."

"No problem, Arthur," Alex said quickly as he began to turn and leave. "It's not important."

"Arthur's there?" Nicki asked through the phone. "Is Jenny?"

"No," Alex answered quickly before forcing a smile for Arthur and greeting him. "Arthur, how's it going?"

"Fine," Arthur told her, glancing back at her phone. "Uh, if this is a bad time-"

"I'll talk to you later, Nicki," Alex said into the phone. "Meet you for breakfast." Before Nicki could answer her, Alex ended the call and put the phone to the side.

"Sorry," Arthur apologized, running a hand through his hair. "I didn't mean-"

"It's fine," Alex interrupted. "I really do need to spend some time going over my Spanish notes."

"You too? I brought mine as well. I only got a C on the last test. Finals are coming up in less than a month." He shook his head and added, "Hard to believe that the year is almost over. May's the last month of the semester. We won't be freshman for much longer."

"Yeah," Alex agreed as her stomach flipped uncomfortably.

As the first of May approached, it was getting harder and harder to focus on school work. Beltane was the next seasonal shift when the natural defenses of Earth were at their weakest: the Sídhe would certainly be invading with force and this time they'd surely be more careful. Alex doubted that their security would make escape possible for anyone they captured.

"So... uh can I join you?" Arthur asked, breaking into her worrying thoughts. He gestured to the chair across from her and shifted awkwardly on his feet.

"Oh, yes of course." Alex blinked at him in surprise and embarrassment.

She gestured quickly at the empty chair only to blush, realizing she was repeating his gesture. As Arthur moved towards the chair, Alex quickly tried to neaten up her side of the table, putting her notes back into a stack and pulling the bottle of water and contraband in the library chips closer to herself. Arthur didn't say anything as he sat down and put his backpack on the table next to him. Alex glanced up to see him pull out his Spanish book along with a statistics book, a spiral notebook, and several sheets of problems from his backpack. He settled quickly, bringing out his bottle of water and a small bag of trail mix.

As she watched Arthur, it suddenly hit Alex that this was the first time they'd been alone since she'd told Jenny that she knew about her cheating with Lance. This was the event that Jenny had been so worried about. Her mouth was suddenly dry, and Alex quickly grabbed her water and took a long sip. Smiling at him, Alex tried to think of something else to say before lowering her eyes to her notes, not trusting herself to keep the secret.

The small room was silent with only the occasional sounds of turning pages, the beeps of their tablets, and the sounds of them consuming their snacks. In the distance, Alex could hear other people in the library, but no one came by their little study room. Glancing up, Alex studied Arthur for a moment. He seemed normal, but his jaw was unusually tight, and his shoulders were tense. Suddenly Arthur looked up from his book and met Alex's eyes. His blue eyes weren't as bright as they usually were and after a short staring contest, Arthur sighed, closed his eyes, and placed his book back on the table.

"Did I... did I do something to upset you, Alex?" Arthur asked her as he opened his eyes, shifting uncomfortably in his seat. "Did Jenny or Lance? Or me? You've just been…" Arthur shook his head and took a breath. "I feel like I've barely seen you and when I do, you're just so quiet." He was looking at her earnestly now, his right hand coming up and running quickly through his hair.

"No, you haven't, Arthur," Alex rushed to assure him, nearly tripping over the words. "I've just been busy and distracted. My other friends… well one of them Nicki has been going through a family issue, and I've been trying to be there for her."

There was a stab of guilt for using Nicki as an excuse, but it was the first thing to come to mind and not completely untrue. After all her parents had returned earlier in the year after being absent for years and Alex had done her best to be there for her in the aftermath.

Arthur's shoulders visibly relaxed, and he swallowed thickly, taking a shaky breath. "Wow… uh, I misread the situation. I'm relieved," he said before his eyes widened. "I don't mean about your friend having problems, that's horrible, and I'm glad that you're there for her. I just mean," Arthur paused again and seemed to struggle with his thoughts. "I'm grateful to have you as a friend, Alex, and I don't want to lose that. It's just seemed like I only see you at meals."

"And when you drag me to blood donations," Alex added, reaching up to rub her arm dramatically. "How many has it been, two in the last month?"

"Something like that," Arthur agreed with a widening smile. "So, everything is okay? Really okay?"

"Yes," Alex lied with a smile. "Nothing too insane, just college and life stuff."

"Yeah, I get that. Funny isn't it how nothing in high school actually prepares you for college."

"I remember everyone saying how hard college is, so far the classes are pretty easy," Alex observed, leaning on her hand. "But it's the social interactions that are the strangest. High school at least had structure, here's there just throngs of people and too many stereotypes about college to ever sort anything out."

"Expectations versus reality, I think it's supposed to trip us up from the moment we leave high school until we're in our sixties."

"I hope to figure it out before then," Alex groaned, looking back at her book. "I just want to finish the semester with decent grades right now."

"Then we'd both better study." Arthur reached over the table and pushed her Spanish book closer to her.

Sighing dramatically, Alex made a show of picking up the book and starting to read it. Arthur chuckled at her and picked up his book. He glanced towards the door before swinging his feet up onto the table. When Alex looked up, he held a finger up to his lips making her smile. She reviewed all the Spanish vocabulary, mouthing each word slowly and trying to remember the different tenses for the verbs. Her professor had gone over what would be on the final but hadn't gone into much detail about the format. Alex was hoping that she didn't have to remember the spelling or else she was in trouble. When she was tired of Spanish, Alex pulled out the latest reading assignment for her epic class, knowing that Professor Yates was sure to call on her and Nicki.

"Excuse me," a voice called from the doorway, pushing it open. "We're closing."

Arthur dropped his feet down from the table and smiled at the girl, but she was already walking away.

"It's already midnight," Alex groaned, picking up her phone. "Man, I feel like I got nothing done."

"That's not true," Arthur said as he began to pack up his things. "You're a lot further in that book than you were earlier."

"But I only understood some of it," Alex complained, shoving the Tale of Gilgamesh back into her bag. "Maybe Nicki understood it," she added hopefully.

"Come on," Arthur said, gesturing to the door. "I'll walk you home."

There were only a few students in the library, and everyone was quiet as they headed towards the entrance. The student workers were leaning over the checkout counter watching them leave one by one. Alex shivered as they stepped outside into the chilly wind. Above her head, a few stars were shining through the light of the library and street lamps.

"Cold?" Arthur asked, adjusting his bag. "Hold on a second."

A moment later he produced a large sweatshirt with the school logo on the front and handed it to her. Arthur accepted her backpack and waited patiently as Alex pulled the sweatshirt on. It hung past her hands, but the smell of Arthur's aftershave and shampoo reached her nose and warmed her instantly.

"Thanks," Alex whispered as she took back her bag. "I should have brought something."

"It's cool," Arthur assured her.

He led the way down the main walk of campus, their path illuminated by street lamps. Exhaling slowly, Alex forced herself to stop thinking about Arthur and reached into her bag to grasp the hilt of her dagger. The night was still and quiet, and Arthur didn't seem to be in a talkative mood, which suited Alex just fine. She was waiting for the howl of a Hound or any other sign of the Sídhe, but there was only the occasional noise of other students. A few cars were still on the roads, and Alex could hear laughter from a parking lot in the distance.

Hatfield Hall slowly came into view, dotted with illuminated windows. A group of students was camped out on the front steps smoking and laughing. Alex turned and smiled at Arthur. "Just a second and I'll give this back to you."

"Don't worry about it," Arthur told her warmly, shaking his head. "I've got several when I picked this school; Mom ordered a ton of stuff. Just give it back to me later."

"If you're sure," Alex replied slowly only to get a wide smile. "I'll see you later then, maybe breakfast on Sunday?"

"Sounds good," Arthur agreed with a nod. "Enjoy your Saturday." He turned and started heading down the sidewalk that led to Michaels.

"Arthur, wait," Alex called impulsively, a small half-formed thought pushing to the front of her mind.

He stopped and turned around to look at her, standing directly under the street light. Swallowing, Alex hurried up to him as her hand dove into her bag, searching for the iron triskele. Her fingers brushed over the leather of the dagger sheath, making her shiver slightly. Finally, she felt the bumpy curve of the iron sign at the bottom of her bag and tugged it out.

"Here," Alex said awkwardly as she held it out to him. "Uh, Nicki and I have been doing blacksmithing on the weekends with Bran and Aiden. Just a friendly activity to keep her occupied." She was rambling, but couldn't seem to stop herself. "Anyway, I finished this one a couple of weeks ago, it's not perfect: the one I'm working on now is a lot better, but I'd..." Her face felt hot now, and she was grateful for the low light, maybe just maybe it would help hide it. "Here, I'd like you to have it. I know I've been kind of flaky lately and I'm sorry for that. I'm still your friend." Her mouth went dry at the words as a fresh wave of guilt crashed over her.

Arthur's eyes widened before dropping down to look at the iron piece. It was rough certainly, hammer marks showing all over the spirals, but the shape of the triskele was clear. Merlin's welding was the best part of it and the band circling the triskele to give it more stability was smooth due to Merlin heating the metal and twisting it into shape. It hadn't even needed much hammering.

"Alex, you must have worked really hard on this with Nicki. Don't you want to keep it?"

"I'm making another," Alex told him, shrugging nervously. "Besides I don't want to end up like Professor Yates with a whole workshop full of these piled up." Arthur chuckled lightly at her remark, helping Alex relax enough to wet her lips.

"Thanks," Arthur told her, reaching out to take it from her. "That's a pretty cool thing to be learning, Alex."

His fingers brushed Alex's as he gripped the outer ring of the iron sign. It felt warm, and Alex risked a glance down to see the metal shimmering, sparks of magic swirling just over the surface. Alex released the metal as if burned and opened her mouth, desperate for an explanation. Arthur laughed and suddenly shifted the metal in the light of the lamp, but it was gone.

"Weird," he muttered as he looked up at the street light. "It doesn't look that polished."

"Yeah," Alex managed. "Anyway, have a good night, Arthur." She gestured to Hatfield Hall behind her. "I should be getting inside."

"Oh right. Sleep well, Alex, I'll see you at breakfast, right?"

"Yeah, Jenny and I will be there," Alex promised, climbing up the stairs at an angle so she could keep watching Arthur. "Goodnight," she forced out as she swiped her card.

Arthur nodded and adjusted his backpack so it hung off only one shoulder, dropping the iron triskele into a side pocket. He raised his hand and gave her a wave before turning and heading down the sidewalk towards his dorm. Breathing out, Alex pushed open the door and stepped inside Hatfield Hall, her hands shaking.

21

Blood Spilt

8 08 B.C.E. Northern Cornwall

He could hear drumming as the warriors rushed forward to snatch up the iron swords from Merlin. It took Arto a moment to realize that it was the pounding of his own heart echoing in his ears as adrenaline pumped through him. Warriors pulled out their weapons, some with swords, but most with bronze axes. The priests and traders fell back and moved to the walls ready to provide what help they could. His feet were moving of their own accord towards the gate of the village, maneuvering him around the fleeing women and children. Behind him, Arto thought he heard Morgana shout for him to wait, but the sound of the screams of fear and the crying of young children teamed with his heartbeat was drowning out everything.

Then he heard a long howl that echoed across the sea of grass and through the village. A fearful silence fell over the village, followed a moment later by the hiss of swords being drawn. A heavy hand came down on his shoulder, and Arto turned to see his father gazing out the gate.

"Should we meet them beyond the gate or wait until they break through?" Uthyrn asked, the question hanging in the air like an icy breath.

"They usually have the Hounds attack first to distract the warriors," Arto heard himself say. "We don't want to give the Riders time to line up and attack as one."

"Agreed," Merlin said. He strode over to join him and Uthyrn. "Beyond the gates, we can spread out and thus force the Sídhe out of their attack pattern."

"You heard them," Uthyrn boomed, raising his sword, and motioning to the gate. "We came here to strike back against the Sídhe. Let's start now."

He became lost in a crowd of men rushing out the gate and beyond the wooden walls. The slope of the hill would offer them some protection Arto realized as he came to a stop and looked around. Against the mounted Riders, it would give them a chance, especially with the iron swords. Tightening his grip on Cathanáil, Arto exhaled slowly and scanned the horizon. Another howl ripped across the land and Arto heard sharp intakes of breath.

"Arto," he heard Morgana call and felt her move to his side. "We're here."

He exhaled, and things snapped back into focus. There were twenty-two of them including himself, Morgana, and Merlin spread across the hillside in a rough formation, guarding the gates. Only seven of them, including his father, were holding iron blades while the others were armed with bronze swords and axes. Near his father, he saw Medraut shifting between his feet, in nervousness, fear, or excitement he did not know. As the thundering sound of the Riders came closer, Arto could see those armed with bronze swords and axes examining their weapons nervously.

"Cut your arms," Arto commanded as he eyed the bronze weapons. "Those of you without iron blades do your best to coat the blade in fresh blood. The Sídhe are weak to human blood!"

Some of them reacted with surprise at the notion, but several nodded in understanding. One man, tall with a thick beard sliced deep and coated his sword with a laugh before offering his bleeding limb to another.

"Maybe I can use the spell," Arto said in a low voice, knowing that Morgana would hear him.

"The blood spell is dangerous," Morgana cautioned him. "If you make a single mistake-" Then another Sídhe horn blew across the hills, and thirteen Riders charged into view, a hound running alongside each of them. Morgana sucked in a pained breath. "But perhaps that would be best." Her hand reached out and squeezed his shoulder, comforting them both. "Just please be careful, little brother. I-we can't lose you."

Swallowing, Arto nodded in response, not trusting himself to speak. He raised Cathanáil and glared at the Riders as they approached. The Hounds rushed out in front, snarling, and leaping at the nearest warriors. In a flash of movement, Arto saw two men go down as Hounds attacked them only for the Hounds to be struck by the blood coated blades of two more men. A Síd Rider held out its hand and formed a golden orb of magic.

Morgana jumped past him, swinging out her hand as silver magic spun around her. In a split second, magic swirled together in her hand. She moved gracefully, throwing the magic out in front of her, striking the Rider in the chest. He fell from the horse which reared in alarm as a warrior charged at its Rider. Swords flashed, one covered in blood and the other iron, both striking at the Síd's unguarded neck.

The ground shuddered beneath his feet, nearly in time with the dying screams of men to his far left as five of the Riders charged through the line. Merlin's voice thundered above the din before a crack and lurch of the earth sent Arto stumbling. Turning quickly, he saw the ground rise in front of three Sídhe Riders. It blasted forth like a great wave of water upon a shore, throwing the Riders from their horses before swallowing them and their steeds.

There was a roar from the humans led by his father, Uthyrn raised the iron sword which glinted in the low light of dusk. Two Hounds lunged towards his father, Uthyrn swung the sword downwards catching one of the Hounds in the head and knocking it into the second. With a sharp tug, Uthyrn ripped the blade from the skull of the disintegrating Hound just in time to slice into the chest of the surviving Hound as it leapt at him.

Screams erupted from the left and Arto spun, barely avoiding a snarling Hound. Swinging Cathanáil, Arto spared only a small glance at the Hound to confirm that it vanished in a flash of magic as the blade of his Sword sliced into the flesh. He turned to look where shouts and screams were coming from loudest. A Síd dressed in long robes rather than armor was rearing up on his steed, a scepter gleaming in his hand. Fire lashed out around him, sending the human warriors scattering. One brave man sliced at the steed with his blade before a blast of fire hit him. Arto tried to ignore the agonized scream and focused on watching the horse shimmer and begin to vanish. The Síd leapt off the horse and landed on the ground, sending a wave of magic out and throwing back the warriors. As the man on fire fell to the ground, the light of the flames illuminated the face of the Síd.

He recognized the Síd; it was the mage Murden who had been at the tunnel. Judging from the way that the Síd's eyes widened, Murden recognized him as well. Arto glared at the Síd mage who curled his lips in a snarl. Pulling sharply at his magic, Arto commanded it to gather in his hand. The telltale tingles up his arm and the warmth spreading from his chest assured him it was working even as he refused to move his gaze away from Murden.

A cry to look out came from his sister just in time, and a snarl reached Arto's ears. Spinning to the right, he brought up his hand and released the magic, letting it burst forth without clear instructions. For a moment he was blinded by the white sparks that zinged all around him, but the Hound was jumping back and yelping in pain as the magic rushed over its body like lightning.

Arto hissed as he flexed the fingers of his left hand. The skin felt tight and hot as if burned by the uncontrolled burst of magic. Murden was observing him, his violet eyes darting away only to check the battlefield and Arto shifted into a defensive stance, waiting. Shouts and battle cries could be heard around them, coming from both sides. Arto jumped back as a Sídhe horse ran by without its Rider, rearing and neighing in fear. In the corner of his eye, as the steed passed, Arto saw his father Uthyrn dash forward and swing his iron sword at the beast's neck. Another Hound rushed him, forcing Arto to spin away from Murden and bring the blade crashing down on the head of the creature. He averted his eyes from the flash of light as Cathanáil's magic vaporized the beast.

"The Weapon, the Traitor, and the Abomination," Murden suddenly shouted. Looking back at him, Arto found Murden calmly watching him and risked a glance towards his sister who was throwing balls of silvery magic rapidly at advancing Sídhe rushing towards her on foot. "In the name of Queen Scáthbás, destroy them!" Murden called to the Riders. "Kill the Weapon!"

"Arto!" Morgana shouted as the Riders turned their attention towards him.

His hand ached, but his magic flowed freely. Picturing a bolt of light-ning flashing through the sky, Arto pulled sharply on his magic, raising his hand, and focusing on exactly what he wanted to happen. There was no raw explosion of magic this time. Instead, the white magic flashed off his fingertips through the air, cracking sharply and making the hairs on his arm stand on end. The bolt split, striking the first two Riders in the chest. Their mouths opened in silent screams, magic jolting over their bodies. Then they both began to shimmer and disintegrate.

An animalistic snarl made Arto spin, and he brought Cathanáil up to guard himself. The blade barely caught the bolt of magic that was about to hit his chest. Glowing a violent orange, Cathanáil shook in Arto's hand, fighting off the effect of the enemy magic. Arto grit his teeth, clutching tightly to Cathanáil with his right hand. Magic crackled over the fingertips of his left hand, eyes widening as Murden charged another attack. Arto brought his hand up, releasing a burst of magic. Murden dodged smoothly, his robe flaring around him. Pushing out more magic, Arto risked a moment to gather an orb of magic and threw it right at Murden's chest. The Sídhe mage crossed his arms in front of him, releasing his golden magic into a swirling mist. Arto's orb crashed into the mist, exploding, and knocking Murden back a few steps, but not touching him.

Biting back a growl, Arto flexed his fingers on Cathanáil, still feeling the foreign magic lingering on the blade. He turned the Sword quickly, pointing the blade towards the ground. Before he could second-guess himself, Arto thrust the Sword into the soft soil to his right. There was only a moment of resistance before the blade slid several inches into the earth.

Another Hound rushed him as Murden began to gather his mag-ic. Cathanáil shuddered in Arto's hand, pulsing with magic. Risking a glance down at his Sword, Arto gasped as Cathanáil's soft glow intensified, burning off the taint of Sídhe magic. Murden stopped moving, an orb of magic resting in his palm as he eyed the Sword. Arto used the moment of hesitation to lash out with a blast of magic, pulling on it quickly. His stomach flipped, and there was a moment of vertigo, but the sparks rushed out of his hand and struck the oncoming Hound. Silver magic lashed out to his right, forming a whip in the air that collided with the shimmering fur of the Hound. A terrible cry of agony escaped the creature's mouth as it began to fade away.

Murden moved first, turning his attention from Arto towards Morgana as an orb of her silver magic sailed towards him. Arto was still as the strange mist appeared once more and protected Murden before a wave of magic blew towards his sister. Moving her hand quickly, Morgana summoned a breeze, dispersing the glittering smoke up above the heads.

"Arto!" Morgana snapped without looking over at him. "Hurry!"

Nodding, Arto tugged Cathanáil from the ground, feeling the remnants of the connection to the Iron Realm thrumming in the Sword. He promised himself that they'd explore the potential of this more in the future as he brought Cathanáil up. The blade slid over his palm, slicing open the skin and sending both a sharp pain and a rush of warmth through his hand. Arto bit back a hiss as the pain spread and settled around the wound, but forced himself to focus on the blood gathering in the valley of his palm. His eyes closed and he exhaled slowly, focusing on the beat of his heart. Around him, the sounds of the clanging swords and snarls faded. Even with his eyes closed he was aware of Morgana nearby and saw a flash of silver on his eyelids as she lashed out with her magic. Another inhale and exhale.

He reached for his magic, imagining the flow of energy that tied him to the very ground beneath his feet and following it down into the soil.

There was a pulse; he could feel the world moving and smell the sharp scent of the iron in his blood. Grinding his teeth together, Arto pulled on the swirling magic that he could feel gathering in his gut. His flesh began tingling, and small bolts of heat blasted over his skin randomly. White sparks of magic sprang from his fingertips and swirled around his hand before sinking into the pool of red blood. The liquid shimmered white and began to glow as more magic flowed into it.

Holding out his hand, Arto breathed slowly and ignored the sounds of battle. He heard Merlin shout something, but the words were lost to him as the wind began to swirl around them. There was the whimper of a Hound followed by a cry of death and the frightened neigh of the Rider's steed behind him, but he did not move. His arm was shaking and burning as the rush of magic became painful. Gasping for air, Arto opened his eyes and tilted his hand. Blood rolled out of his palm in large shimmering droplets. The first drop fell towards the ground shimmering both red and white. It hit the soil, and for a split second, everything went still. The next drop hit and then the next. On the ground, the blood began to glow bright red and crackle with magic.

A roar filled Arto's ears drowning out everything around him. The world slowed down and his vision blurred, colors blending together like rain on the horizon. Murden was on his knees, mouth open in a scream Arto could not hear. Morgana was smiling, drawing the iron dagger they'd forged only three weeks ago. In slow motion, Arto saw the dagger driven into Murden's neck. Everything shifted around him. People were glowing red in his vision as the rest of the world darkened, like hot coals against dark ash in a low fire. Sídhe were on their knees, a pale unnatural green that began to vanish like smoke in the wind.

His heartbeat was increasing, a rhythm of drums through his body and Cathanáil. Magic was flowing out of him leaving Arto grasping at it, but it was like trying to stop a river with his hands. The roar was too loud to think; he needed to do something, but nothing would come into focus. In his eyes he saw two red figures moving towards him, their movements slow and sluggish to him. Cathanáil felt too heavy as his magic drained out of him, illuminating everything around him in a fiery red glow as his blood trickled over the landscape. The heartbeat drumming in his ears began to slow, and the roar lessened to a throbbing pain. Unseen to Arto, everyone was drawing back save Morgana and Merlin. The hilt began to slip from his fingers, but instinct made him tighten his weak grip. The tip of the blade touched the soil.

Warmth rose through the blade sharply, returning heat to his body. He inhaled, and the world began to come into focus. Grinding his teeth together, Arto closed his eyes and shoved a wall in front of his magic, cutting off the flow out of his body. He swayed on his feet at the sudden stop but kept the visual firm at the front of his mind. A pair of hands caught him and pushed Cathanáil deeper into the ground. Arto slowly opened his eyes and relaxed the tight hold on his magic. The river calmed into a lake, ready and waiting, but contained for now.

"That was harder than I remember," Arto groaned. His body dehydrated and heavy.

"You put more magic into the spell this time," Merlin explained gently. The older mage was standing so close behind Arto that his breath drifted over his cheek. "I suspect the number of Riders triggered a fear response."

Arto snorted at the words earning a soft chuckle from Merlin. A softer hand gripped his bare forearm, gently massaging the tight muscles that were gripping Cathanáil. "Thank you, Morgana," Arto whispered as his eyes opened and drifted to where he had last seen Murden. "The Sídhe mage?"

"Dead before your spell could kill him," Morgana informed him, satisfaction ringing in her voice. "But thank you, it certainly simplified killing him when he could no longer move or use magic."

"It didn't harm you?" Arto asked softly, not wishing for anyone to overhear him.

"I am the Iron Realm's," his sister replied simply. He smiled at the remark and breathed a little easier.

"Arto!" A familiar voice called. "Please! Over here!" Arto recognized it as Medraut and turned sharply towards it.

Men were gathered around them, many injured with bloody wounds visible and more bodies were scattered about. Many of them in multiple pieces thanks to the Hounds. It was difficult to survey the battlefield, but Arto forced himself and was grateful when the onlookers shifted to grant him a clear view to Medraut. His cousin was on his knees, his bronze sword still smeared with red blood and a man collapsed on the ground next to him.

"Uthyrn," Morgana called out in alarm. She tugged on his arm, causing Arto to stumble forward, but she paid no notice.

It wasn't until they were right by Medraut and Uthyrn that Arto realized what he was seeing. His father was on his back with a bleeding wound through his stomach and blood already soaking the ground beneath him. Morgana dropped to her knees and tenderly adjusted her step-father's head to rest it in her lap.

"Father," Arto called, moving closer to the man. He started to reach for Uthyrn's hand before pulling his hand back and letting it drop to his side. "Merlin?"

"The wound is grave," Merlin answered carefully, shaking his head. "I am sorry."

"Got me in the back," Uthyrn mumbled, blood seeping out of his mouth. Moving slowly, Uthyrn shifted his face towards Arto, his father's dimming brown eyes meeting his own wide ones. "It's alright, son."

Unable to watch his father's face, Arto looked up at his sister. Morgana's green eyes were bright with unshed tears, and she gently cleared a loose strand of gray hair from Uthyrn's face. From the crowd of warriors, Airril stepped out and knelt next to Morgana. His brother-in-law wrapped one arm around his sister who leaned into him, but neither said anything.

Swallowing, Arto struggled to breathe. His throat closed, and tears burned his eyes. He didn't know what to say or what not to say. This was important; he wouldn't get this moment back and yet no words would form. All he wanted to do was pull away, pretend it wasn't happening. His father, the father he'd only just gotten home to, couldn't possibly be dying. If he didn't watch then maybe-

"Uncle!" Medraut called as he shifted closer to Arto and Uthyrn. "Uncle," he called again, but the man didn't look away from Arto.

"Arto," Merlin urged him, his voice both soft and commanding at the same time.

Sniffing, Arto felt a tear slip out of the corner of his eye and roll down his cheek. He reached forward and moved his father's hand onto his chest, resting his hand over it. "I'll stop them," Arto promised in a low voice, struggling to form the words. "The land will be free of them." Uthyrn's lips moved weakly, trying to form words, but his breathing was slowing down. Blood seeped over Arto's palm. A sob escaped him as his father's face blurred behind tears. "Father," he gasped barely managing the word. "I'm sorry!"

"Arto," Morgana whispered, "He's gone."

Her hand moved over his back awkwardly, nearly embracing him, but she did not. Swallowing thickly, Arto tried to control the tears rolling down his cheeks. He heard the others moving nearby and realized that while Morgana wished to embrace him, and offer him comfort, she could not without the others seeing his need for it.

"He's with the ancestors now," a strong male voice that Arto was not familiar with said behind him. There was a pause of hesitation before the voice continued, "The swords did well; never before have I seen Riders fall. And your magic... they were powerless."

"Arto," Morgana's voice urged softly, her breath tickling his cheek.

He began to move, began to stand, but Medraut jumped to his feet and took a deep breath.

"Uthyrn is dead," Medraut announced, turning to face the crowd. "He died protecting those he led. When Midwinter arrives, we will honor him at the Great Circle."

There were sounds of agreement and Arto forced himself to stand, grateful when Morgana rose with him. It was painful to turn away from his father's body to face the crowd. Several bodies were lying amongst them, all with someone kneeling beside them. Swords were gripped in the hands of everyone still living, even if a few of them were swaying dangerously on their feet. He knew that he needed to say something, but his knees were threatening to collapse under him.

"Cousin." Medraut clapped a hand on his shoulder. "Your magic saved the day. I have never seen anything like it."

"The blood and magic mixed with the ground," Arto informed them, finding his voice. "It will protect this area from the Sídhe. They cannot return here."

He flexed his fingers carefully, feeling the skin burn around the cut. He hated the feeling, but at the same time, it grounded him, so he was also grateful for it. Cheers erupted from the warriors and the gates opened behind them. Arto swayed on his feet, Medraut's hand keeping him in place.

"I will accompany you to speak with Eigyr," Medraut assured him in a low voice. "Say what you need to say."

Turning to look at his cousin, Arto took in the strong jaw that was so like his father's and the dark eyes. This boy his age had known his father so much better, had lived here with him for years and yet stayed back while he said goodbye to his father. Arto was torn between gratitude and guilt. Raising his arm, he clasped Medraut's shoulder, accidentally smearing his father's blood on his cousin's shirt and took a breath.

"Gather the fallen," Arto called as his stomach turned over at the thought of seeing his mother with such grave news. "Return to the village. We will rest and resume council at dawn."

There were nods of agreement; some gave him sympathetic looks while others looked at him doubtfully. Merlin cleared his throat loudly, dismissing those who were staring. One of the men stepped forward, stopping right before Arto. In his hands, he held an iron sword which he balanced between his palms.

"This is a good blade," the man informed him. It was the voice of the one who had spoken earlier, Arto realized. "I am Eaban from Inisfail." He gave Arto a small bow. "I came to answer the call, but I did not expect this." Holding the sword out to Arto, he added, "This belongs to you."

"No," Arto countered, shaking his head. "You fought and killed Sídhe with that blade. It is yours now, sir. I have no doubt that it will be needed again."

The man offered him only a slight smile as he nodded solemnly in agreement.

22

Beltane Begins

If Arthur noticed Alex glancing out the window at the setting sun, he said nothing and kept up their shaky Spanish conversation. Alex stumbled over the verb for reading but recovered with a quick correction. She scratched off the clear nail polish on her pointer finger nervously as she read a question out of the open Spanish book. As Arthur answered with slow, but precise words, her eyes moved to the window of the library.

The sun was hanging just above the horizon, slowly vanishing behind the hills to the west of Ravenslake, painting the clouds bright pink and red with shades of violet. On any other night, she might have stopped to enjoy the sunset and a peaceful moment, but Beltane was upon them. She knew her fellow mages would be patrolling the hills of Ravenslake where the defenses of the Iron Realm would be at their weakest due to the tunnel. Alex wasn't sure if she was grateful for the restriction on geography that the defenses of the Iron Realm enforced on the Sídhe or not. On the one hand, it protected the rest of the world from their attacks but guaranteed a strong force would be attacking her friends. And according to Morgana, those defenses were the reason that the Sídhe had been restricted to the British Isles three thousand years ago. They'd been able to expand their influence, but it took time.

Still, a sick feeling churned in Alex's stomach. The desire to grab her phone and text her friends to make sure that they were alright was overwhelming. True they knew the most likely location of the Sídhe gateway, but what if the Sídhe had gathered enough power to create a second one? What if they caught the others from behind? Sure, Merlin and Morgana had survived for three thousand years and the first war against the Sídhe, but they were imperfect. And willing to sacrifice lives to achieve their ends. The sick feeling suddenly became worse, and Alex tried to banish the dark thought that Merlin and Morgana might allow one of her friends to die if it meant stopping a few Riders.

Peeling off more nail polish nervously, Alex turned back to Arthur and asked him to repeat the question that she'd only caught the last part of with a forced smile. She waved her hand absentmindedly as she answered the question, more slowly this time and making sure that she had the right verb and tense. Alex reminded herself that she had to stay focused on Arthur. If the Sídhe did have a second tunnel, no matter how slim the odds of that, then they might get into town around the others and pose a threat. If they discovered Arthur, then they'd kill him for sure, or worse drag him underground and into their realm and try to find a way to make sure that the Iron Soul couldn't be reborn again.

"You're distracted." Arthur closed the Spanish book, snapping Alex back to the present. "Come on," Arthur said, running a hand through his blond hair. "It's Friday night. Just because Jenny is practicing with the squad and Lance is weight lifting doesn't mean that we shouldn't go out and have some fun."

"But finals are coming-"

"We've got a couple of weeks," Arthur said. "And we're not going to improve if we're not focused on it." He pushed out the chair and stood up, rolling his shoulders, and stretching out his arms.

Checking her phone, Alex noted it was only eight o'clock, and there were no messages from her fellow mages. Plenty of time for her and Arthur to find something to do and for her to keep an eye on Arthur. Her instructions had been very clear; the others would monitor the Sídhe, and she was to stay close to Arthur and protect him. The thought almost made her laugh; sure, she was pretty tall for a girl, but Arthur still had several inches and a whole lot of muscle on her.

"So how about a movie?" Arthur suggested.

He pulled out his phone and swung his feet onto the library table. Alex glanced around, grateful that the student worker shelving books nearby didn't seem to notice or care that Arthur had his feet on the furniture.

"Anything good in town?" Alex asked, starting to pack up her things. "I haven't been paying attention."

"Well, there's an action flick playing at Central. It starts in an hour."

"Okay," Alex agreed with a smile. "I could use some car chases and explosions."

"Woman after my own heart," Arthur said, swinging down his feet and grabbing his things. "If only you liked football more."

"I like it when you play," Alex said, feeling her skin beginning to flush. "Watching you and Lance play is a lot better than normal football. I'm not as invested," Alex continued cheerfully, hoping that she hadn't been too obvious.

"I get that," Arthur said with a nod and a smile. "I don't care much for baseball for example, but my best friend in high school, Jason Brown, played on the team, so Jenny and I went to every game. I zoned out a lot when he wasn't on the field or at bat."

"Jenny and baseball..." Alex repeated slowly, trying not to laugh.

"Believe it or not she likes baseball. I think she would have been much happier if I'd kept playing it beyond sophomore year."

"Why didn't you," Alex asked, trying to keep the conversation light as they headed past the library book detectors and out the double glass doors.

"Too busy, by that point I was pretty sure that I was going to get a scholarship for football and I wasn't that good at baseball. I preferred to spend the offseason focusing on school work and weight lifting. Football season was intense, so I enjoyed the quiet and slower pace of spring."

Alex nodded her understanding, and they both fell silent, but it was comfortable this time. She could feel Arthur's presence next to her as they walked up the long sidewalk lined with lights that were glowing brightly in the coming night. Above their heads, Alex could see wisps of clouds shimmering with shades of red and violet. The campus seemed calm or at least as calm as it ever was on a Friday night. Students were lounging out on the lawns in the dying light, and as they approached the dorms, Alex noted a fierce game of volleyball was going on.

"Meet back here in ten," Arthur told her, breaking the silence with a wide smile.

"Yeah," Alex agreed, but he was already jogging off towards Michaels leaving Alex alone in front of Hatfield.

A terrible sense of worry flooded through Alex as she watched him disappear through the main door of Michaels Hall. Finally, she exhaled and shook her head, she was too on edge for this, but then again, she couldn't imagine the others were doing much better in the woods. Alex turned and made her way inside Hatfield Hall and up the stairs to her room. It was dark and silent; a pair of Jenny's shoes nearly tripped her as she stepped inside to toss her book bag on the bed. Alex paused to fish her wallet and dagger out of the messenger bag and tossed them into a smaller shoulder bag, checking that she had her phone and keys. Satisfied,

Alex kicked the shoes back over to Jenny's side and heard them thump into the dresser with a spark of pleasure.

Arthur was waiting for her outside, kicking at the edge of the grass lightly. He grinned as she approached and Alex couldn't help, but smile in return. As they started walking towards the edge of campus, Alex did her best to seem relaxed even as she fingered the phone in her bag. The sun was just above the horizon and would set at any moment. Of course, the hills beyond town were shaded by trees so the invasion may have already started.

"Pretty night," Arthur said as they reached the edge of campus and looked towards downtown Ravenslake.

Central Avenue stretched out in front of them for several blocks with cars parked all along both sides of the road. The street lights were already on and teamed with the neon lights of the town's signage made the street glow. It should have felt safe: well-lit with lots of people walking around, but the sense of dread had settled fully in Alex's stomach. Arthur grabbed her hand and tugged her after him as the traffic paused to let them cross the street. He didn't release it until they were past the crowd of students gathered around the entrance of Bookend Coffee.

It was an odd feeling walking along the streets of Ravenslake with Arthur. They'd walked together plenty of times to class or meals without Lance or Jenny, they were friends after all, but this felt different. Maybe it was the fact that they were suddenly off campus, further away from Lance and Jenny then they'd ever been together before. All around them other students were walking the streets, some slipping in and out of the bars and the shops that were still open. The club on the corner had a line spilling out into the street, and loud dance music poured out from inside.

"Noisy," Arthur observed, filling the silence. "Jenny wishes I was into clubs more."

"We're only eighteen; can you even get in there?" Alex asked, her eyes moving back to the doorway where people were slowly entering.

"They card at the bar so anyone over eighteen can get in," Arthur said. "Jenny and I have gone a few times, I didn't like it, but..."

"Jenny loves to dance," Alex added in a cheerful voice. She was worried by the brooding look beginning to settle on Arthur's face. Thin lines appeared between his eyebrows. "Hey, you okay?" Alex asked softly, reaching over tentatively and touching Arthur's arm.

"Yeah," Arthur replied, slowing his pace slightly.

Looking ahead, Alex could see the glowing neon of the Central Theater sign and a small crowd mingling by the doors. Arthur huffed softly his jaw tightening, a clear sign that he was angry or frustrated.

"Arthur?" Alex called gently. "What's wrong?"

For a moment Alex was certain that he wasn't going to answer her, that they were just going to get in line for tickets and then go in to watch the movie, hopefully, distracted. She exhaled slowly, the question lingering in the air between them. A sigh escaped Arthur, and he moved his shoulder, making Alex think that he was reaching for his wallet. Instead, Arthur gripped her arm and tugged her to the left, onto 3rd street west.

"It's Jenny." Arthur slumped back against the wall into the shadows of a closed shop's doorway. The shadows over his face made his cheekbones stand out while his eyes vanished in the dark. "I'm not sure what we're doing anymore," Arthur admitted in a low voice.

Alex's stomach flipped nervously, and her mouth was dry. There was a tingling in her mouth as words tried to form and escape. Whether to encourage him to work things out with her roommate or break up and date her she didn't know. Her fingers twitched as unease settled over her like an icy mist, clinging to her skin and making Alex want to shiver.

"She's been distant lately," Arthur continued in a rush like he was afraid that she would stop him. "Like she's constantly distracted. Her smiles don't reach her eyes and... I don't know. I guess we're just not happy anymore." Arthur shook his head sadly before leaning it back against the doorframe. "Maybe it's just time to let the relationship go. We're high school sweethearts, for some that works for life, but most of the time it doesn't."

Alex felt herself nod in agreement, but didn't dare speak for fear of what might pop out. She shifted awkwardly and shoved her hands in the pockets of her hoodie, trying to keep a sympathetic smile on her face. In the distance, she thought she heard a howl, but Arthur just sighed and shook his head. He pushed himself off the doorframe and stepped closer to Alex.

"I'm sorry." Arthur's jaw was tightening again, and he swallowed so thickly that Alex could see his Adam's apple moving. "I shouldn't be dumping this on you."

"I'm your friend," Alex whispered with a painful smile. "I care about you."

It should have been a simple sentence, but from the way Arthur's eyes widened, and he stared at her, Alex knew that she hadn't said the words with the necessary distance. Frozen in place, Alex internally debated looking away or holding the sharp look that Arthur was giving her. One would certainly confirm his reading of her words while the other was much more difficult, but gave her a little bit of a chance for dignity. Forcing a smile, Alex tilted her head slightly and did her best to look unconcerned.

"So, movie?" she asked lightly. "Or would you rather find a coffee shop and talk about things?"

"No, movie," Arthur told her, straightening up further and shaking his head. He gave Alex a wide smile and nodded back to the street. "Come on; we don't want to be late."

"Late?" Alex repeated, raising an eyebrow as they walked around the corner and into the bright blue glow of a neon sign. "Do you mean after the previews start late or we actually manage to miss the twenty minutes of ads and previews late?"

"I like previews," Arthur insisted, his shoulders and jaw relaxing as a real chuckle escaped him. "They're fun."

"They give away the best parts of the movie," Alex protested as they reached the short line in front of the small movie theater's double doors.

Two posters hung on either side of the doorway, advertising the four films. The smell of popcorn was wafting out over the street along with the sounds of voices. Alex breathed in the smell and took in the sounds, trying to relax and enjoy having a normal night out. In the distance she again thought she heard a Hound howl and turned around nervously, glancing at the last rays of the sun as they vanished beyond the horizon. As Arthur handed Alex her ticket, only the violet undersides of the clouds provided any hint of the sun, and that would be gone soon enough. Beltane had begun.

23

In the Lights

Night had settled across Ravenslake: it was a starry night though the glow of the neon signs and street lights that illuminated downtown drowned them out. Students and residents were still out in force, stumbling in and out of clubs and bars while others came out of shops that were open late. Alex stepped out into the fresh night air next to Arthur as the movie let out and took a deep breath. She paused to listen, braced for the sounds of any danger, but all she could hear was the normal sounds of a Friday night in a college town.

"Well, that was... entertaining." Arthur stepped up next to her and gestured down the street. "Let's get out of this crowd."

Nodding, Alex followed Arthur down the street towards the university and away from the theater. He was glancing around into store windows, his shoulders more relaxed than she'd seen them all night. A soft sigh of relief escaped Alex, and she told herself to calm down. The movie plus the commercials and ads had been two and a half hours long; surely the Sídhe had made a move and been defeated. Without thinking, she pulled out her phone and checked it, but there were no messages.

"So did you like it?" Arthur asked. He glanced into the window of the Book Nook.

"Huh?" Alex's eyes lingered on the dark store that belonged to Aiden's family as a new wave of worry washed through her.

"The movie," Arthur reminded her, giving Alex a worried look. "I know it wasn't a masterpiece."

"Wasn't a masterpiece," Alex repeated, smiling despite her worry at the very idea of that movie ever being considered good much less a masterpiece. "It was a series of explosions and car chases held together by a barely-there plot and unconvincing actors."

"It wasn't that bad," Arthur protested as they walked towards the dorms. His statement and the slight pout on his face made Alex laugh out loud.

"Come on, Arthur," she argued, shaking her head. "There was a weak main plot that made no sense with plot holes that could swallow a planet, too many subplots, and the movie tried to string everything together with explosions."

"Don't forget about the car chases." Arthur's eyes twinkled in the warm glow of the street lights.

"Yes, fine the car chases were fun, in fact, the movie was pretty fun, but the dialogue was almost painfully cliché."

"Sometimes the point of a movie is just to be fun," Arthur said, smiling triumphantly. "Don't overcomplicate it by demanding anything more, Alex."

"I don't demand great literature or even good characters," Alex huffed, raising her chin and mock glaring at Arthur. "But I do need a decent plot and somewhat decent motivation; otherwise, I don't know who to cheer for."

"That's easy, root against the guys who wear all black or hurt dogs."

"Sometimes the good guys wear black, in fact, they wear black too in almost all action movies-"

"Okay, okay the movie had a messy plot," Arthur cried out, shaking his head. "I concede this argument to the literature major." He shook his head. "But the explosions were still fun."

A small smile tugged at Alex's lips, and she sighed dramatically before conceding. "Yeah, the action wasn't bad." She shrugged and peeked at the smiling Arthur in the corner of her eye. "I guess it was fun and did the job of entertaining me."

"Now you get it." Arthur tossed an arm around Alex's shoulders. It brought them close together, and Alex hoped that the neon lights would disguise her blush. "It's official, Alex, you are now my action movie buddy."

"Action movie buddy," Alex repeated. She glanced up at Arthur with a blend of confusion and nervousness. "That means you're going to drag me to every action flick this theater gets no matter how bad, doesn't it?"

"Not all," Arthur defended with a wide smile and cheerful eyes. "Just the ones that look the most fun. In return, I'll go to all the romantic comedies you want."

"I don't like romantic comedies."

"Oh," Arthur said slowly as if only just realizing that, but with a hint of sarcasm. "That's right you don't do you."

Looking up at him suspiciously, Alex gave him a thoughtful look. "You've got a manipulative and cunning side to you, Arthur. I'll have to remember that."

For a split-second Alex thought she saw a hint of worry in his eyes, but then he tossed her a wide grin and chuckled. Tightening his grip on her shoulder, Arthur caused her to stumble a little as he hugged her closer.

"Yep, I'm an evil genius," he informed her proudly. "I'm just using you."

"Whatever for?" Alex asked, playing along with a smile even though it was a bit hard to walk at the angle she was at.

Arthur realized her trouble and eased his grip at once, releasing her shoulder and swinging his arm down to his side. He bent his arm and offered it to her, allowing Alex to thread their arms and walk normally.

"What are you using me for?" Alex asked, repeating the question.

"Uh..." Arthur paused and chuckled. "Give me a second for a witty reply to that one."

Hatfield loomed overhead, and they stepped into the light of the many lamps placed around the front doors and over the walls. Tightening her grip on Arthur's arm, Alex's mind suddenly jumped back into action, wondering how to keep Arthur nearby until sunrise. Several ideas ran through her mind, mostly focusing on getting him upstairs and knocking him out, but Alex hesitated to use magic on him just in case she did real damage.

"Hey I'll come up with you," Arthur announced, tugging her up the stairs. "Leave a note for Jenny."

"Okay," Alex replied with a small sigh of relief. Maybe she could get them talking and keep him there for the rest of the night. Or maybe he'd fall asleep.

Digging into her pocket, Alex pulled out her card key and opened the doors, smiling when Arthur held it open for her. In the distance, she thought she heard a howl, but Arthur showed no signs of having heard anything out of place. The heavy glass and metal door closed behind them with a thunk, and Alex relaxed a little more.

Pulling out her keys, Alex flicked them around, so she had the right one and slipped it into the lock. She pushed the door open; frowning as she noted the lamp on Jenny's desk was on. The main light was off, but as the door opened fully and light poured in from the hallway, Alex was confronted with the sight of Lance and Jenny kissing and wrapped around each other. She froze in the doorway, barely aware of Arthur taking a step past her, a stunned expression on his face.

Alex couldn't move, couldn't say anything. Her place at the doorway gave her a clear view of Jenny and Lance and Arthur's profile as he gaped at them. The pair in the room hadn't stopped and didn't seem at all aware of them. Hands were moving as Jenny tugged the hem of Lance's t-shirt up and slipped her hands out of view.

"Oh god!" Arthur stumbled back against the doorframe with a soft crash.

Turning to look at him, Alex could barely stand the confused expression of anger, hurt, disbelief, and resignation that washed over his features and warred for dominance.

"Arthur!" Jenny shrieked behind them.

Alex didn't turn around to look at the pair, keeping her eyes focused on Arthur. His face closed, all emotion vanishing as he swallowed and stared at his girlfriend. Alex felt her heart beating painfully fast in her chest and couldn't hear anything over the frantic pumping of blood in her ears. Then without a word Arthur turned on his heel and walked out into the hallway. Alex was frozen in place until she heard the stairwell door slam shut. Lunging forward, she rushed out into the hallway and ran to the stairs. A wave of cold hit her as she entered the concrete structure and looked down. She just caught sight of Arthur and called his name, but he didn't react before he vanished out the first-floor door.

"Damn it!" Alex hissed as she began racing down the stairs.

Horrible thoughts were rushing through her mind: everything she'd ever feared might happen when he found out about Jenny and Lance now mixed with her worries over Beltane. As she pulled open the first-floor door, Alex fumbled with her phone and pressed Nicki's speed dial. There was no answer as Alex ran to the parking lot and caught sight of Arthur climbing into his car. She shouted again, but he didn't turn to look at her.

"Hi this is Nicki, I'm not here right now, so you know what to do," the message played.

Running towards her car, Alex dug out her keys and scraped the side of her car as she tried to unlock the door. "Nicki! Arthur just caught Jenny and Lance. He's taking off! Keep the Sídhe at bay and for god's sake call me!"

"Arthur!" Lance's strong voice shouted behind her, making Alex jump. "God damn it!"

"What idiotic thing is he doing now?" Jenny demanded, her voice both worried and angry.

"You don't get to say that shit!" Alex snapped.

She swung open the door of her car angrily and spun sideways to glare at her roommate and Lance. Jenny ignored her, reaching around Alex to hit the unlock button on the door of her car. The other doors opened with a loud click, and without a word, Jenny pulled open the back door and climbed into the car. Alex was about to argue, but Lance climbed into the passenger side, and Arthur's car sped out of the parking lot. A growl escaped Alex's throat as she dove into the car and fumbled with her keys to get it started. She didn't bother to put on her seatbelt, shifting the car into reverse and swinging her car out. Up ahead she saw the tail lights of Arthur's car and sped after him.

"I'm sorry," Jenny gasped from the back seat. "Oh shit! I never meant-"

"It wasn't like we planned it." Lance looked over at Alex, his face twisted in a grimace. "It just happened."

"I don't care right now," Alex snapped, turning the steering wheel sharply to follow Arthur.

"Alex... maybe you should slow down," Jenny suggested meekly from behind her. "Maybe we should just give him some space and time to cool down."

A howl echoed through the night, high-pitched and long. She could almost see the Hound in her mind's eye, its fur shimmering and its teeth gleaming as it prepared to lunge for her neck. And on Beltane where there were Hounds, there was sure to be Riders. Alex clutched the steering wheel tighter, trying to ignore the churning emotions in her stomach.

"No," she muttered as she kept following Arthur's tail lights. "No, I can't do that."

They crossed the bridge, the river reflecting the street lights on the bank, but up ahead the forest and mountains loomed. Alex briefly considered speeding up enough to slam into Arthur: it might stop him before he got any closer to the Sídhe.

"Alex, I'm sorry," Jenny added from the backseat, her voice quivering.

"Jenny..." Alex's grip tightened even more on the steering wheel, her knuckles creaking painfully at the strain. "I'm not doing this right now. I need to get to Arthur."

"Alex-" Lance started to say, but she glanced at him in warning. He fell silent and swallowed audibly in the tense quiet of the car.

Arthur's speed began to drop as he pulled off the main street and headed up a narrower road that led towards a few outlying houses and the head of several hiking trails. Alex's foot twitched in protest, but she tapped the brakes when the car nearly slid as the pavement changed to gravel. In front of her Arthur's tail lights glowed a bright red and his high beams illuminated the thickening trees on the left side of the road. In the corner of her eye, Alex could see the bright reflection of the nearly full moon shining on the lake. No Sídhe were in sight, yet.

Slowing down, Arthur turned into a small gravel parking lot that linked to the hiking trail. Alex's stomach flipped when she spotted Merlin and Aiden's cars parked. There was no sign of them, but Arthur pulled in next to the cars and without turning off the vehicle climbed out. With shaking hands, Alex pulled a short way into the lot and stopped her car. Her headlights illuminated Arthur who was glaring at the car, scowling with irritation. Jenny jumped out of the back of the car before Alex could stop her and Lance followed a heartbeat later.

"Arthur!" Jenny yelled, rushing past Alex's door. "I'm so sorry! I didn't mean for you to find out that way!"

"Then how was I supposed to find out!" Arthur demanded, turning to his girlfriend. "How long has this been going on?"

Alex inhaled slowly, her fingers aching as she released her death grip on the steering wheel. Exhaling slowly, Alex adjusted her bag to her left side and slipped her left hand in to grip the hilt of her iron dagger. She eased open the door and stepped outside, scanning the trees for any sign of movement. But a soft night breeze was rustling all the leaves, and the moon was casting a silver light that made the forest look like it was moving.

"Arthur," Alex called, interrupting Lance trying to assure Arthur that this hadn't been intentional. "Come on, let's just go.... Jenny and Lance can take my car back, and we can go in yours." There was a pleading note in her voice that Alex didn't like, but ignored as she took a tentative step towards Arthur. "Everyone just needs to calm down, and we shouldn't be out here at night."

She reached out her right hand for his, but Arthur shook his head and stepped back. "I need to think, Alex. I need to calm down." Arthur looked sadly towards Jenny as his shoulders slumped. "I don't want to talk right now, not even with you."

A sudden burst of wind made the trees in the valley sway and groan, their gentle rustling turning into a roar that drowned out Arthur's next word. Tensing up, Alex looked around in alarm. In the light of Arthur's headlights, she could see the branches bending in the strong wind. The crescendo of sound reminded Alex more of waves crashing on a beach than the forest. Then it was gone, and the soft whistling of the trees was back.

"Arthur, please," Alex begged, starting to reach for him again.

"No," Lance protested, straightening up. "Let's get this out now. I'm sorry, man, this wasn't planned, but Jenny and I just-"

"What the hell!" Jenny shouted, jumping back, and pointing towards the trees with wide eyes.

Lunging forward, Alex jumped up next to Arthur as he turned to investigate the trees where Jenny was pointing with a terrified expression. A Síd in heavy golden armor with a drawn sword and a Hound on either side, stepped out into the parking lot, its armor gleaming in the headlights. Violet eyes locked on Arthur and a smile appeared on its face as the pair of Hounds threw back their heads and howled.

24

Tears

808 B.C.E. Northern Cornwall

His mother's soft cries made Arto feel helpless as he lingered by the doorway of the roundhouse. Eigyr had collapsed by her bed, head in her arms smothering her sobs even as her whole body shook in her grief. Arto's eyes were fixed on her and his cousin as Medraut spoke gently to her. Morgana sat on the edge of the bed, gently stroking their mother's hair in silence. The desire to say more, to comfort her rose through Arto, but everything he could think to say just seemed so inadequate.

Yet he lingered and watched the shake of her shoulders as she cried. They brought his father's body in on a stretched piece of hide without a word and gently set it on his bed at the far side of the roundhouse. Despite knowing he shouldn't, Arto looked over at his father's body and froze. Eaban's men had cleaned away the blood as best they could, and a blanket was draped over his chest, hiding the ugly wound that had killed him. Someone had closed his eyes and mouth, forcing his features into a relaxed expression. Arto had heard many times that death could look like sleep, but at the moment he couldn't breathe as he watched his father and waited for some sign of life.

Finally, he inhaled when dark spots began to flicker in his eyes and turned to look back towards his mother. Her fingers were tearing at the fabric spread over her bed as she buried her face in it. There was a hint of panic and unease on his sister's face that worried Arto. As Morgana glanced up at him, Arto's stomach dropped, and his heart skipped a beat. She looked helpless and frightened, two emotions that he'd never associated with his elder sister.

Swallowing thickly, Arto stepped backward, pushing the pelt flap out of his way. The cool night air hit his skin, forcing the air from his lungs. Arto swayed on his feet feeling an unfamiliar sense of weakness. He could feel exhaustion creeping up on him, but there was an angry and nervous energy humming through his skin. Arto turned, and his eyes went to the wall that protected the village, tracing it until he found the gate. Beyond it somewhere was the Sídhe tunnel. He'd certainly killed the one who took his father from his mother and him, but there'd be more. His fingers curled into a fist as the angry energy hummed stronger beneath his skin.

"Arto," a warm deep voice called. He turned his head slightly to catch sight of Eaban making his way up the path towards him. "A moment, lad," the older man requested.

He hadn't paid much mind to Eaban before in the rush of his father's death, but now Arto made a point of committing the man's face to memory as the man moved to join him. It was a strong face much like his father's, with a thick beard with small gold beads. His eyes were honest and a warm brown that communicated his sympathy for Uthyrn's death. Laugh lines surrounded his eyes hinting at his normal nature outside of such events. It was a kind face that belonged to the sort of man that Arto knew he'd be grateful for in the future, but right now his shoulders felt too heavy for gratitude. Eaban smiled gently at him, and Arto felt himself relax slightly at the warm gesture. The older man reached out and placed a hand on his shoulder, squeezing it slightly.

"I am sorry about your father, lad," he told Arto gently. "He would be very proud of you."

"Thank you, sir," Arto forced himself to reply even as his throat tried to close. "And thank you for your support."

"You represent the first chance we've ever had to free our land from the Sídhe. They don't belong here; this is not their world." Eaban shook his head as a dark expression settled on his face. "I must return to Inisfail, but I shall send my eldest son to join you. His name is Luegáed, and he is a fine warrior."

"I look forward to meeting him," Arto replied politely, raising his chin slightly.

Eaban chuckled and removed his hand from Arto's shoulder. "Easy lad, Luegáed is about your age. He'll be a great help in the war I'm sure, but I suspect that you two will become friends." Eaban paused before adding, "I know you'll not want to speak of this now, but I've spoken with Merlin about iron furnaces. If you need anything from us to construct them, simply send out the call."

"Thank you," Arto said again. "Given last night's attack, we'll be starting work on them right away." Arto swallowed and added, "Even with my gifts there is a limit to how much iron I can produce at once."

"Well, you've selected a good location," Eaban reminded him, redirecting the conversation. "My people are miners with limited craftsman, but your father brought copper and tin together here. It may not have the furnaces yet, but there are plenty of metalsmiths here."

Arto nodded in agreement and tried to think of something else to say. Eaban must have understood his sudden silence because the older man squeezed his shoulder once again and bade him a good night. Arto watched the older man walk away silently in the low torchlight, feeling a knot in his stomach ease a bit. Walking down the path, Arto inhaled the night air and tried to think straight.

He wanted to go and deal with the Sídhe tunnel, but at the same time knew that he needed rest to do so. Nibbling at his lip, Arto wondered if he'd be able to track the Sídhe in the morning or if the trail would be cold. It didn't matter he decided: Merlin clearly intended for them to stay here to produce the iron they'd need to arm a force large enough to stand against the Sídhe's magic. There would be time to find the Sídhe tunnel and then.... Arto swallowed and his fingers clenched into a fist.

He wasn't exactly sure what he'd do, but he wanted... he wanted it to be something big, something that would tell the Sídhe just how powerful he was and that he could hurt them. He wanted them hurt, he realized with a start; he wanted them to know that he could destroy them, that he could keep them from ever taking another child. Arto didn't want their Queen Scáthbás to wonder and worry about what he could do; he wanted her to fear what he could and would do to them. Exhaling, Arto raised his chin to look up at the stars and breathed deeply before his anger could get the better of him. His eyes closed and he relaxed his fingers, stretching them out. Silently, he made a promise that the Sídhe's power in the Iron Realm was going to be broken. Broken like a bronze axe returned to the Earth.

"Arto," a soft, warm voice called behind him. He relaxed, recognizing Gwenyvar's voice and turned to see her looking at him with sad brown eyes. "Arto, I'm so sorry about your father," she told him, her voice barely louder than a whisper.

"Thank you," he replied, swallowing thickly. "I'm just... glad I got to see him again before it happened."

Gwenyvar made a tiny nod and stepped closer to him. Her soft hands gripped his own rougher ones, and Arto was horrified by the blush creeping over his cheeks. Gwenyvar leaned forward quickly and kissed his cheek.

"I'm sure that he was grateful to see the man you've become," Gwenyvar assured him, squeezing his hands. She paused and glanced down. "Uh, how is your mother?"

Arto flinched and lowered his eyes. "I'm not sure," he answered. "Morgana is with her. I'm afraid that I didn't know what to say."

He really should have let go of her hands, the thought occurred to Arto, but he didn't ease his grip. Thankfully Gwenyvar didn't either, and they stood there in the low light of the moon and burning torches for several minutes. She said nothing and Arto used the opportunity to collect his thoughts.

"I really should..." he started to say, but he didn't want to go back into his mother's roundhouse.

Medraut was with her, and the sad truth was that his mother knew his cousin far better than she knew him. His stomach twisted and Arto frowned as anger sparked in his gut at both Morgana and Merlin. If his sister hadn't told the Sídhe about him then maybe he wouldn't have missed out on growing up with his parents. It wasn't true of course, a small voice in the back of his head reminded him. Morgana had been fused with a Changeling because the Sídhe knew that he was the Iron Soul, a new kind of weapon against them. His sister's actions had almost nothing to do with how anything had turned out.

"Arto," Gwenyvar called softly. "Don't go too far away," she whispered to him when he raised his eyes to meet hers. "People here want you with us."

Without meaning to Arto smiled, touched by the simple and warm sentiment. "I... thanks," he whispered, highly aware of his cheeks flushing.

"Gwenyvar," an older voice called making both Arto and Gwenyvar turn towards her father who was walking towards them.

Cailean's decorated staff struck the earth with each step as he moved towards them, eyeing them both carefully. He stopped just short of them, his eyes lingering on Gwenyvar who quickly released Arto's hands and stepped back with a soft smile. Meeting Cailean's eyes as they turned to him, Arto was surprised at the twitch of fear he felt. They'd just battled Sídhe, and yet a small part of him wanted to step back from the priest as the man's fingers flexed around the heavy walking stick that he carried. It was straighter than Merlin's and had some symbols on it and a band of gold near the top matching Cailean's more elegant dress style.

"My condolences on the death of Uthyrn," Cailean said. "I didn't know him well, but he was a man of good reputation. I hope that your mother is well."

"My sister Morgana and my cousin Medraut are with her now." Arto once again felt the small twist of worry and guilt in his stomach.

Cailean raised an eyebrow at the statement. "Your cousin," he repeated carefully.

"Uthyrn's nephew," Arto said, tripping over his father's name. "He is my father's heir." Arto was lost when a strange look of concern crossed Cailean's face and then vanished. "He has pledged his support to the cause."

"Yes, I suppose that your responsibilities would... limit your ability to take charge of this area's trade," Cailean observed. "A shame, of course, your father had control over valuable mines and key trading routes with the continent. Your sister's father Kenwyn was an important figure in expanding the bronze production operations here." Cailean glanced towards the Roundhouse. "Your sister's husband is Airril is it not? I understand that his family has control over many copper mines to the north. Has he made no claim as the husband of Kenwyn's daughter?"

"Uh, not that I know of," Arto confessed barely holding back a frown. "But my mother Eigyr, Kenwyn's widow approved of Medraut being trained by my father. He was taken in years ago by them while Morgana and I were fighting the Sídhe. That is our responsibility." Arto was at a loss of what to say about Airril's thoughts on the subject, but Morgana's husband had always struck him as a humble and calm man.

"Indeed," Cailean said with a deep nod and smile. "But I urge you also to consider what you will do with your life once the Sídhe have been turned back. If this plan of yours is successful, then you have the potential to become an important figure in the isles." Cailean looked beyond Arto towards his daughter. "Different than a priest or even a trade leader, something new and important."

"We have to stop the Sídhe first," Arto reminded Cailean. He tried not to shift nervously in front of him. "Can we count on the support of the north?"

Cailean smiled at the question and nodded once again. "Of course, Arto, my people have suffered a great deal and want the end of the Sídhe raids. I recognize how fortunate I am to still have my daughter with me."

"We will stand with you," Gwenyvar assured Arto. Then she brushed his hand with hers as she walked past him to join her father. "But for now, we'll leave you to be with your family. I am certain that your mother would like to see you and your sister would appreciate your support."

Gwenyvar gave him another warm smile, her brown eyes glistening in the moonlight even as she tugged on her father's arm. Nodding in gratitude, Arto was unable to form any words but managed a shaky smile. Cailean watched him for a moment before allowing his daughter to lead him away. Taking a deep breath, Arto looked up at the bright moon and sighed as exhaustion threatened to overtake him. Before he could change his mind, he turned on his heel, strode to the door of the roundhouse and joined his sister inside to offer whatever comfort he could.

Eigyr was asleep now, curled up on her bed, clutching at one of Uthyrn's cloaks. Even from the doorway, Arto could see the tear tracks down her cheeks and the reddish color surrounding her eyes. Morgana looked up at him from a pile of furs by the fire and visibly relaxed in relief.

"Arto," she called in a low soft voice, gesturing him over.

Nodding, Arto moved slowly, his eyes darting between his mother and sister. There was no sign of Medraut, and a cloak had been laid over his father's face. Arto's heart stopped for a moment, and tears prickled at his eyes. He looked away from his father and focused on his sister whose expression softened. Slowly, Arto sank down on the furs next to the fire with her, crossing his legs under him. His fingers brushed the soft hair of the deer hide they were seated on.

"How is she?" Arto asked in a whisper.

"She exhausted herself," Morgana answered, glancing over towards their mother. "I remember... well, she was like this when my father died," Morgana informed him, tripping over the reference to her Changeling memories. "She'll recover, but it will take some time."

"Cailean was surprised to hear that Medraut was the heir," Arto told her, looking over towards his mother as she shifted in her sleep. "He wanted to know if Airril would try to take over as your husband."

Morgana chuckled a sad and resigned sound. "Airril knows that bronze won't matter for much longer," Morgana explained. "I married a loyal and intelligent man. He knows that iron is going to change how everything works."

"It will let us fight the Sídhe," Arto agreed, unable to hide his confusion about her statement.

"Sometimes I forget that you've been all over the isles, but never really lived anywhere," Morgana said sadly, looking at him with watery green eyes. "Most wealth is measured by bronze and gained by trading bronze. That's why the great families have sought to secure control over the regions where tin and copper can be mined. That's why your father ensured that he controlled this region for trading the bronze made here with the south."

"And iron will change that?"

"Tin and copper can only be mined certain places," Morgana reminded him. "Iron on the other hand... it can be smelted, worked, and then reworked. It doesn't have to be recast like bronze. It is stronger and doesn't require the same skill and is found more easily. It is something that the families won't be able to control like they have bronze." Morgana shook her head. "Whatever happens with the Sídhe, win or lose, iron is going to change the land we live in drastically."

"And is that bad?" Arto asked with a frown. "If we beat the Sídhe and keep them out of our world, isn't that good?"

"Yes, it is, little brother," Morgana said warmly. "But it will be a change and change, even good change, is a painful thing."

Frowning at her words, Arto pulled his knees up to his chest and rested his chin on them. He stared into the fire as Morgana brought a hand up to his shoulder. They were silent for some time, the soft crackling of the fire the only sound in the roundhouse. Then Morgana began to tell him about Merlin's plans to build furnaces and begin training the villagers in smelting iron. Arto knew that he should be pleased: it would assure them enough iron to strike back against the Sídhe, ensure that he had the chance to protect his people. But as he watched the outermost orange coals of the fire glow amongst the ashes like tiny dying stars in the night sky, all he could think about was his father's covered and lifeless body only a few feet away.

25

The Defender

Without even thinking, Alex leapt forward to throw herself between her friends and the Síd. The Hounds snarled, their teeth glinting dangerously in the headlights. Behind her, Alex heard Jenny whimper and heard the shuffle of feet on gravel as the others drew back from the sinister looking creatures. In a moment, Alex withdrew her dagger from its sheath and gripped the cool wooden handle tightly, drawing some comfort from its weight. As the Síd stepped forward slowly, its boots grinding down on the gravel, Alex switched her dagger into her left hand and before she could change her mind made a quick shallow cut on her right hand. The Síd paused as the blood gathered in her hand and the two Hounds growled at Alex, their eyes now all on her.

"Alex?" Arthur called.

"Stay back," Alex ordered sharply without looking at them. "Get in the car and go."

Arthur began to protest, but Alex blocked it out as one of the Hounds lunged towards her. Jumping to the side, Alex could feel the brush of the beast's fur against her jeans as it turned to pursue her. She barely stayed on her feet and turned to the side, eyeing the Hound that was thankfully ignoring the others for the time being. Eyes darting over to the Síd who was watching her with calculating eyes and the second snarling hound, Alex sucked in a deep breath and tried to calm down. Opening her right palm, Alex ignored the twinge of pain that shot up her arm as the skin surrounding the cut on her palm pulled and stretched. She could feel blood oozing slowly from the wound, but forced herself to ignore the sensation. Instead, Alex searched for the warm spark in her gut, for her magic.

The Síd raised his golden sword and took a step towards Alex. She watched his eyes move away from her towards the others. Fear clenched at her stomach; did they know about Arthur, could the Síd tell just by looking at him? A spark of dark silver magic shot down Alex's arm, causing her to gasp as the flow of magic opened roughly. Energy surged through Alex, reacting to her adrenaline and urgency. Her fingers felt hot, and her flesh tingled uncomfortably in the moments that it took for the dark silver sparks to gather in her right hand. Resisting the urge to look down at the orb forming between her outstretched fingers, Alex kept her eyes on the Síd.

Snarling reached Alex's ears, and her eyes shifted, catching sight of a Hound lunging towards her. Gasping, Alex stumbled back and pushed her hand out towards the Hound. The magic in her palm shuddered before exploding as a beam towards the Hound, blinding Alex for a moment. Over the hum of her magic in her ears, Alex could barely hear the cry of the Hound. As the light faded, Alex saw the body of the creature vanish in a shimmer of golden sparks.

"Oh my God!" Lance shouted behind her, followed by the sound of shoes scuffing against the ground.

"Get in the car and go!" Alex turned her eyes back to the Síd.

Eyes widening, Alex saw the golden orb of energy only a second before it blasted forth from the Síd's outstretched left hand. A scream behind her, one that Alex realized in fear was Jenny's, distracted her for the critical moment the orb was flying towards her. It collided with her chest, sending sharp jolts of pain through her body. She was falling but in the wrong direction. Her eyes were closed, she couldn't see, and her body was so heavy, how was she even moving?

Her back collided with the hood of her car, stretching too far, and pulling the muscles beyond their limits. Gasping in pain, Alex barely registered the blaring sound of the car alarm. Someone screamed her name, and she shook her head as the world began to clear. Over the sound of the car alarm, Alex heard a terrible howl that made her heart jump in her chest. She needed to move: she was in danger; the others were in danger.

With speed and strength that Alex didn't know she possessed, she scrambled to her knees on the car hood. Blood pounded in her ears, and her breathing was labored as the ache in her back protested every move. In the corner of her eye, she caught sight of another orb forming in the Síd's hand. She exhaled, turning to focus on the glowing orb of magic. Tugging at her magic, Alex pushed the pain in her back and shoulders into the trickle of energy shifting up from her gut to her chest. Her heart beat faster and faster as the sparks of magic coalesced into a shining string of dark silver. With a sharp gasp for air, Alex pulled at the shimmering magic, bringing it outside of herself like drawing a stitch loose from fabric.

The Síd's golden orb flew from his hand, speeding towards Alex. Throwing up a hand, Alex released her magic, wishing for and urging it to stop the attack. The orb slowed, magic sparks flying off it as the energy swirled in a storm of gold and dark silver. Her hand shook, and it was hard to breathe as the energy of the blast brushed against her outstretched hand. Traces of foreign, wrong, and violent magic sparked over her fingers as the orb stopped, pressed tightly against her open palm.

Looking back at the Síd, Alex felt a rush of triumph as it took a step back, his free hand moving towards his horn. The Hound at its side whimpered, lowering its sharp ears. She could feel the foreign magic fading as her magic swept over the last of the Síd's power, consuming and transforming it. Dark silver magic spun around her fingers like the soft caress of water. There was a moment of stillness; even the breeze paused. She pushed, the magic lashed forward, the Síd's eyes widened as he brought up his horn and the Hound snarled.

There was a loud burst of noise on the horn before it was cut off. The magic struck the Síd in his chest, his body froze, his back arched unnaturally and features contoured in pain. It lingered for only a moment before the golden outline fell apart and scattered in the breeze. Panting, Alex smiled and slowly rose from her knees.

"Alex?" The soft thin voice of Jenny called behind her, but Alex did not look back.

Underneath her feet, the thrum of the car's motor seemed in time with her heart. The surviving Hound snarled, eying Alex before throwing its head back. A long howl echoed around them, singing through the trees and down the valley. Alex's right hand, still tingling with magic, came up in front of her. The Hound lunged, jumping towards the car. Alex threw her hand out, sending a wave of her magic at the Hound which rippled through the air and struck it.

The snarls turned to an animalistic cry of alarm as the Hound was sent reeling back into the thick trunk of a tree. The terrible crack made Alex flinch, but the Hound climbed to its feet. Sweeping her hand in front of her, Alex did not take her eyes off the creature. Its fur shimmered in the light, silver much like her magic, Alex realized distantly. Sparks swarmed around her hand, but she did not wait to give them form. An image manifested in her mind: she could see exactly how the magic would act if she released it. Her index and middle finger were pressed together tightly as the energy crackled. Pushing her arm out, Alex pointed the fingers straight at the Hound. Lightning jumped from her fingertips, arcing through the air. The Hound tried to dodge, but its legs couldn't move quickly enough. Energy danced over the shining fur, the scent of burnt hair and flesh teased at the air for only a moment before the Hound vanished in a puff of dust.

Sucking in a quick breath, Alex slid towards the edge of the hood. The slope of the hood worried her as her shaking body fought to stay steady. Arthur rushed forward, coming to the side of the car and staring at her.

"Alex," he gasped. Arthur's mouth moved without any words as he stumbled. "What?"

"I'm okay," Alex assured him, forcing a pitiful little smile.

She began to lower herself down, hoping to slide off the hood of the car, but the muscles in her back protested, tightening painfully. Arthur moved forward quickly, holding out his hands. Blinking in surprise, Alex smiled, and a soft sigh of relief escaped her. Then there was the blare of a horn up the hill in the trees. She heard a horse neigh, though it was quickly drowned out by the sound of crashing trees. Eyes widening, Alex grabbed Arthur's arms and leveraged herself off the hood of the car. She bit back a scream at the pain.

"Arthur, we need to go!" Alex snapped, pulling away from him as Arthur tried to hold onto her waist.

"Alex, what the hell is going on!?" Jenny asked, coming forward with wide eyes, Lance behind her. "Is this some kind of joke? It isn't funny!" Jenny's voice was on the edge of hysteria.

"Lance, Jenny, get in the back seat, don't ask questions," Alex ordered sharply before looking back at Arthur. "Just get in my car, Arthur, we'll come back for yours later."

"Alex? I don't understand," Arthur protested with wide eyes.

The horn blared again making Arthur turn and look towards the woods with a worried, yet quizzical expression. Reaching up, Alex turned Arthur's face back towards her own so he could see how serious she was. "Arthur, get in the car," Alex ordered as calmly as she could.

The sound of cracking branches was getting louder and louder with every moment as something made its way towards them. The wind picked up suddenly, ripping through the valley and making the hills howl as the trees creaked. A scream erupted from up the hill sending ice through Alex's veins. Gasping softly, she turned towards the hill and swallowed down a rush of bile. The scream had been too high for one of the boys, and she had trouble imagining Morgana ever screaming.

"Nicki," she whispered fearfully. Her eyes traced up the tree-covered slope of the hill. Another howl ripped through the night, and Alex sucked in a shaky breath. "Arthur," she said softly. "Get in the car and go. I'll see you in the morning."

"Alex!" Lance snapped coming up next to Arthur. "What is going on? Who or what was that guy?"

"No time!" Alex eyed the tree line. "For the love of God just get in the damn car!"

"Guys we should listen to her," Jenny begged coming up and tugging on Lance's arm. She began to reach for Arthur but pulled her hand away as if burned. "Please come on let's go. This isn't right."

Jenny screamed as the crack of wood came right to the edge of the forest. A tall shining horse bearing its Rider in golden armor burst forth from the trees along the hiking trail, its golden accented saddle and bridle glinting in the headlights.

"Run!" Alex hissed, pulling away from Arthur.

But Arthur reached for her, grabbing her left hand as Alex began to turn towards the Rider. The iron dagger slipped from her grasp, hitting the dirt with a soft thud that was drowned out by the hoofbeats of the horse as it paced anxiously in place and the car alarm still ringing through the night. Gasping, Alex pulled on her arm, feeling her shoulder stretch beyond its limit. Arthur released her, staring in shock at the Rider on his luminescent horse. There was another crash in the woods just before another Rider's horse leapt over a fallen log and crashed into the parking lot.

"Damn it!" Alex shouted, imagining a bolt of magic in her hand. The magic rushed to answer, flowing down her skin like water and collecting in her hand.

The first Rider charged towards them; Alex threw the ball of dark silver magic. It struck not the Síd, but his horse as it reared when its Rider pulled harshly on the reins. Leaping from the back of the dissolving beast, the Síd hit the ground on his knees, but was up in an instant and drew his sword. The Síd yelled to the Rider still on his horse before lunging towards them. Alex dodged the sword, shoving Arthur out of the way. There was the sound of metal scraping against metal to her left. Glancing over, Alex huffed despite the situation when she saw the long ugly scrape in her car's hood.

Golden magic began to gather in the Síd's palm, and Alex reached out her hand toward him. Focusing on the magic, she felt the foreign energies brush against her own unpleasantly, sending a shudder down her back, but she pressed her magic forward. Dark silver swirls appeared in the air, surrounding the Síd's hand while its eyes widened in confusion. As the golden color of the magic faded into dark silver, the magic crackled sending out sparks and tiny bolts of energy like lightning. The Síd tried to throw the orb, but Alex imagined it stuck to his hand and smirked as tiny threads of energy twirled about the Síd's hand. Pushing more magic into the orb, Alex ordered an explosion. She could see the energy blasting outward and vaporizing the Síd. Then it did, but it went further out than Alex expected, blasting the other Rider off his horse which screamed before vanishing in a breeze of golden dust and knocking Alex off of her feet.

Her ears were ringing, and the car alarm going off right behind her echoed in her skull painfully. But a sudden cry to look out from Jenny still managed to reach her. When she heard the shout, Alex had only a moment to look to her left to see a Rider on his steed charging out of the woods. Heavy hoof beats filled her ears as it raced down on her. Without fully thinking, Alex threw up her hands, calling on her magic. She couldn't think straight, couldn't visualize with the pounding in her head. Magic zinged around her wildly, forming a cloud of silver sparks. Rather than charging in, the horse neighed and reared back fearfully.

Grabbing the bumper of her car, Alex leveraged herself up to her knees and climbed to her feet. The swirling magic was tightening around her, reacting to her growing control. Maneuvering his horse back, the Rider watched Alex carefully. The sound of metal sliding against metal filled her ears as the Rider drew his long golden sword. They studied each other for a moment: he had longer horns than the other Riders she'd seen tonight and wore a golden circlet. Still watching Alex, he snapped something that she couldn't make out. It sounded half English, half something else in a jumble that she couldn't understand.

The circlet wearing Rider charged toward her, collecting magic in his free hand. Rushing to the left, Alex felt the horse move past her and heard metal crunch as the horse's hooves hit the hood of her car. The Síd yelled something again, and Alex spun to face him. A bolt of magic struck Alex before she could react. Her muscles tightened as painful jolts shot through her body. She felt the world spin for a frightening moment. Her back hit the dirt, and the air was forced from her lungs. Alex's head knocked against something hard. Her vision cleared enough for her to make out a tree root poking out of the ground.

Forcing her body to turn, Alex looked up to see the Rider coming towards her on his horse. Traces of her dark silvery magic were still swirling around Alex, waiting for a command. She closed her eyes, not trusting them with the pounding in her head. Magic caressed her skin as it flowed down to her palm which she raised in front of her. Under her other hand, she could feel magic seeping into her from the ground, slowly but there, reminding her that she wasn't alone. The thought calmed her, and she smiled even as the horse's slow and deliberate footsteps came closer and closer.

Magic swirled in her hand, spinning like a globe between her curved fingers and palm. Alex opened her eyes to find the Síd's hand glowing. She breathed out and pushed. Magic burst forth as a hundred tiny bolts, but rather than going straight they zipped through the air towards the Rider and his steed in two curves, one on the right and one on the left leaving no place to dodge. The horse reared and tried to back up, but the wave of sparks struck its right side. Moving to jump, the Rider was hit in his back by the left attack. Both figures were frozen for a split second before dissolving. His circlet hit the ground with a soft chink before it too turned to dust.

Pushing herself up with her hands and her feet, Alex felt her back collide with a solid tree trunk and took a deep breath. For a moment she was able to block out the car alarm and breathe. Then grunts to the right made Alex glance over with worry. The Síd she'd rendered without a horse was grappling with Arthur; its sword caught high above their heads as Arthur struggled to hold him in place. Alex began to move, her eyes catching sight of her iron dagger still laying in the dirt. A dark figure rushed up from the shadows, Alex realized it was Lance just before the football player crashed into the Síd, sending them both tumbling to the ground.

Arthur rolled to the side panting but caught sight of the dagger. Before Alex could say anything, he snatched it up. Lance hissed in pain as the Síd he was pinning kneed him in the stomach, but the young man refused to be moved. Arthur crawled back over to them, bringing the dagger into view of the Síd who thrashed out violently.

"Kill it!" Alex shouted as she tried to move, but her knees didn't want to work anymore and her back hurt so badly that light flashed at the edges of her vision. Even from several feet away and in the low light, Alex could see the struggle on Arthur's face. "He'll kill us all!" Alex screamed to him before flinching in pain. Opening her hand, she tried to call on more magic, but the pain was too distracting, overwhelming her ability to focus.

The Síd thrashed again, kneeing Lance once more, lower this time. Lance huffed and fell slightly to the side, catching himself on one hand while still trying to hold the Síd with his left hand. Moving to roll away, the Síd was suddenly trapped under Arthur's knee just before the dagger was brought down into his neck. There was a muted, gargled cry before the Síd began to dissolve into golden dust.

"Alex!" Jenny yelled. Alex turned her head slowly to see her roommate staring at her with wide, terrified eyes. Jenny began walking towards her, ignoring the boys. "Alex!"

"Look out!" Lance shouted, pointing into the woods.

The wind and car alarm nearly kept Alex from hearing the crashing of wood and movement in the trees. A blast of magic knocked a tree over and into the parking lot near Alex. Shrinking back against the tree, Alex grit her teeth and fought back a scream of frustration as three more Síd stepped out into the parking lot, their swords already drawn.

One of them spotted her and pointed to her with his sword. She couldn't breathe, her lungs were weighed down and couldn't operate right even as her heart raced. The car alarm and even the wind in the trees were drowned out by the sound of her blood racing in her ears. Then Arthur was in front of her, his hands shaking even as he ground his feet into the dirt to mark his position.

"Stay back!" Arthur yelled at the Riders, his voice wavering only the tiniest bit as he stared down three armed warriors.

In the corner of her eye, Alex saw her iron dagger glint dangerously in the light of the car's headlights. The first Síd noticed and paused in his movement forward, eyeing the dagger carefully. His sword came up in front of him in his right hand as he gestured to the two approaching Síd behind him. Bile rose in Alex's throat that she could barely force down; her vision was fuzzy, but the sharp violet eyes were horribly clear.

As she watched the front Sid, one of the flanking Riders raised his hand and unleashed a small bolt of magic. A warning cry escaped Jenny far to the right in the shadows and Arthur dropped to one knee to avoid it. Another bolt forced him to roll back out of the way, leaving a small smoking patch of black dust where he'd stood. Now he was so close to her, almost kneeling at her side and leaving the way clear.

Raising her hand, Alex called desperately at her magic. Her connection was weakening, even as she felt the pulse of the earth beneath her body. She was too tired to call, to command and shape the magic. The Sídhe moved closer, satisfaction taking over the face of the closest one as he began to reach for the golden rope coiled on his belt. Tensing up, Alex struggled to breathe remembering the last time she'd seen a Sídhe smile like that. Memories of the tunnels, the crying children, and spreading her blood over a sword sprang forward in her mind. She could feel the chill of the tunnels on her skin and the fear that she'd fought to forget hit her.

Magic surged through her hands, an unstable and sparking mess of dark silver forming. It blasted out of her hand without direction. The Sídhe dodged it easily and smirked at her. Pulling desperately at her magic, feeling like she was clawing to hold onto it, Alex's hand shook so badly she whimpered while trying to keep it steady and focus. Arthur grabbed her hand tightly, his fingers jarring the cut in her palm. Blood smeared on his hand, and Alex hissed in pain, but her eyes didn't leave the Síd marching towards them. Words were lost on her tongue even as Alex tried to yell for Arthur to run. In the distance, she thought that maybe she heard shouting, but between the car alarm and the whimpers escaping her lips, it was impossible to be certain. She tried to move, tried to stand, but nothing seemed to work.

Then there was light around them, swirling like a breeze or a wave over their heads and in front of them. Dark silver streams of sparks were accented with white. Their joined hands were glowing brightly as magic surged out, unchecked and not in Alex's control. The blood in her palm burned against her skin and she could feel more blood flowing out of the cut, feeling like hot lava on her flesh. But she didn't release Arthur's hand, and she didn't move. Perhaps she couldn't move as the field of light and magic suddenly constricted and crashed forward like a tsunami. White and dark silver magic blasted the Sídhe, knocking all three back as their armor and bodies dissolved. Alex gasped, unable to contain her shock as the closest Síd reached towards them, even as silvery bones were exposed in his arm. Then all three were golden dust swirling in the air and being swallowed up by the magical wave as it dissolved and fell apart like a storm of shooting stars.

26

Out of the Woods

Bran's leg was aching as he stumbled forward on the small game trail that wove its way through the woods back to the main hiking trail. Up ahead flashes of magic were visible even over the glow of car headlights. A car alarm was blaring and drawing all the Sídhe and their Hounds towards it. He glanced around, catching sight of Aiden and Morgana a few feet away facing down a Síd that had lost its horse. Merlin was shouting nearby, but Bran wasn't sure where he and Nicki were. Stopping to catch his breath, Bran leaned against a large tree and shifted his leg hoping to adjust his brace which had started to dig into his thigh. He wasn't supposed to be wearing it so long and teamed with the exhaustion he could feel creeping up on him, Bran was amazed that he hadn't fallen flat on his face yet.

A loud snarl jolted Bran from his thoughts. He pressed his back against the rough bark of the tree and scanned the area. A few feet away up the hill, he caught sight of the underbrush moving. Raising his hand, he exhaled slowly and braced himself for the Hound to appear. It didn't disappoint, launching towards him from the underbrush with a growl and bared teeth. Waving his hand forward, Bran pictured the beast flying back against the tree. The Hound's growl turned into a whimper as its trajectory suddenly changed, and it was crashed back against one of the large trees. Branches rattled at the impact, and the Hound was slow to pick itself up.

Pulling out his iron dagger, Bran held the weapon out towards the Hound and sucked in another breath to steady himself. Sparks of bright yellow danced over his hand, surprising Bran with their visible color, but he forced himself to focus on the Hound climbing to its feet. He had to close his eyes as he commanded his magic forward to surround the Hound. Then he focused on his dagger, still not opening his eyes. It was there in his mind, the Hound and his dagger. He was familiar enough with both of them to see clearly. Loosening his grip, Bran felt his magic surround his dagger, like a loose invisible hand. As he opened his eyes slowly, Bran let go of the dagger and watched it fly.

Bran squirmed as the blade sliced into the Hound's neck, spilling silvery blood out over the forest floor. It was difficult to ignore the pained sound that became a gurgle, but thankfully the Hound began to dissolve into golden dust. Holding out his hand, Bran pulled on the yellow magic that was shimmering around the dagger. It was like reeling it back to his hand, keeping careful control of the speed, so he didn't stab himself, but after a moment it floated back into his grip. The hilt was wet from the Hound blood that was already fading away, but Bran tightened his grip around the comfortably carved wooden handle and began to move towards the parking lot once more.

Up ahead he could see Morgana come to a sudden stop at the edge of the parking lot as dark silver and white magic flooded the area. Slamming his eyes shut, Bran pressed his hand against a tree in an attempt to stay still and stable. He felt traces of the magic brush over his skin, but there was no burning or pain. It didn't feel wrong like the Sídhe's did and he relaxed. Opening his eyes, he saw Morgana still standing at the edge of the parking lot and began to move forward.

He stepped to the left to avoid crowding her in the event of another wave of Sídhe. It had seemed like there were hundreds of them, spilling out of the tunnel as soon as the sun began to set. Bran froze at the edge of the woods; Alex was collapsed against a tree at the far side of the parking lot with Arthur kneeling next to her, clutching her hand. Even in the dim light, Bran could see the stain of blood on her skin: both on her hands and her face. Around him, the wind was still whipping through the trees, but the car alarm finally beeped and shut off. Magic sparks were swirling gently around the pair, illuminating their faces as they stared at each other. Slowly the sparks began to fall around them in a shower of light, fading into the darkness of the night. An exhausted and relieved laugh escaped Alex which spurred the others into action.

There was a sharp crack of wood breaking in the forest behind him causing Alex to straighten up and Bran to flinch in sympathy. Nicki rushed past him, their shoulders slamming into each other, but the girl didn't stop. She rushed out into the headlights, her eyes wide and her mouth hanging open as she panted. Bran frowned as he took in her condition, her cargo pants were torn on her left leg with three long scrapes visible, but she was walking. A hand on his shoulder made Bran turn to meet Aiden's bright eyes. Grinning at him, Aiden squeezed his shoulder gently and whispered for Bran to come on before stepping out after Nicki. Aiden was in a similar state as Nicki with his jeans ripped and twigs caught in his dark hair.

"You guys are okay," Alex said. Her voice was exhausted, but her happiness and relief were shining through. Arthur jumped to his feet and stood defensively in front of her with wide, uncertain eyes.

"Most impressive." Morgana stepped out of the trees to his right, closer to Alex and Arthur than he was.

Stepping out himself, Bran noted Jenny and Lance were staring at them with wide eyes and nervous expressions. He could guess what had happened; Alex had taken her assignment of protecting Arthur on Beltane far too seriously to have brought him here herself. Narrowing his eyes at them, Bran noted their clear confusion and discomfort and felt his irritation lessen a little. They hadn't asked for this after all and probably still had no idea of what was happening. He nearly missed Merlin joining Morgana.

"Alex!" Nicki rushed over to Alex and dropped down next to her. "God, sweetie, are you okay?"

"Of course, she isn't," Aiden said. He moved over to join them, glancing at Arthur who was sizing the two of them up. "Look at her."

"Nice, Aiden," Alex sighed, resting her head back against the tree. "Wait, where's Bran?"

"I'm here," Bran called over to her as he forced himself to start walking again. Alex's face fell when she saw how heavily he was relying on his cane, but he forced a small smile for her. He may be in some pain and exhausted, but Alex looked like she'd gone five rounds in a boxing ring; well maybe not that bad. There was slight scorching on her shirt where he suspected an energy blast had hit her at least once.

"Alex?" Arthur's blue eyes darted around at the people who had suddenly arrived. "What is going on?"

Bran saw Alex visibly flinch at the question and felt a great wave of sympathy for Alex being caught in the middle yet again. "Well, you see...." Alex began to say before she swallowed thickly and seemed unable to speak, her lips moving a tiny bit with no sound coming out.

"Alex," Arthur called in a shaky voice. As he moved closer, Bran could see blood smeared over them both and a dark red slice on Alex's right hand.

"I'm sorry," Alex whispered, Bran only just catching the words as he stepped behind Aiden. "I'm so sorry, Arthur."

"Alex, what if there are more of... those things?" Arthur asked her. His eyes jumped back to Alex and then the rest of them for a moment before he turned to look towards the cars.

"I believe that we have cleared the area," Morgana announced, drawing Arthur's attention. She was standing straight with a stern and calm expression on her face. It was no surprise when Arthur mutely nodded. "Now please, everyone, step back, I would like to check Alex's condition."

In front of Bran, Aiden reached out to grip Arthur's shoulder and pulled the football player back. Bran caught sight of fading silver blood sprayed over Arthur's shirt and frowned slightly, wondering if he'd somehow helped in the battle. Turning, he glanced towards the seemingly frozen Jenny and Lance, noting a bit of silver reflecting the light of the car headlights.

Morgana knelt next to Alex with the softest smile that Bran had ever seen on her face and exchanged a curious expression with Aiden and Nicki while Merlin looked on with a smile. "You did very well," Morgana told Alex gently before her eyes dropped to the iron dagger that had fallen into the dirt. Reaching down Morgana picked it up and studied it for a moment. "You know that you don't have to cut your hand to use an iron dagger," Morgana reminded Alex as her eyes went down to her blood smeared hand.

"Yeah, I know," Alex groaned slightly. "Instinct I guess from the tunnels." Bran and the others exchanged another worried look, but then Alex added, "Plus they hesitate more when they see a blade covered in red blood."

A chuckle escaped Bran before he could contain it getting him a stunned look from the still wide-eyed Arthur and a wink from Nicki.

"How are you feeling?" Morgana asked Alex calmly. "How injured are you?"

Bran felt himself tense up as he waited for the answer, certain that everyone else was eager to be reassured.

"I'm not sure," Alex admitted in a low voice, flinching as she moved. "I got thrown around a bit. My back hurts," she whispered earning a nod from Morgana.

"I can take you straight to the hospital or to my home where I'll check you over. I also have some muscle relaxants and pain relievers that I can give you, but your injuries may go beyond bruising."

"Your house," Alex answered quickly. "I don't want to risk scaring my parents just yet."

"Very well," Morgana agreed before she climbed to her feet. "Merlin, I will take Alexandra to my home in your car."

Merlin nodded his understanding, reached into his pocket, and pulled out a small ring of keys which he tossed to Morgana. Aiden moved first, nearly running into Arthur as both of them reached down to help Alex stand up. Bran frowned at the way she was moving and glanced towards Morgana, but the professor was calm and stepped back to allow Arthur to shift over to Alex's other side. Bran moved back to give them room to maneuver Alex to her feet and help her walk over to Professor Yate's blue SUV.

"Wait," Alex called. "The Sídhe tunnel? Is it safe?"

"We damaged it," Morgana assured Alex as she unlocked the passenger side door. "They won't be able to send anything through for a little while." Professor Cornwall glanced back at Merlin, and a significant look passed between them until Merlin nodded, probably promising to call her with the results of whatever happened next.

Bran leaned against the tree and watched in silence as Alex was gently shifted into the SUV and Morgana started it up. Arthur and Aiden moved away to give Professor Cornwall room to pull out, even with Alex and Arthur's cars still in the middle of the parking lot. Headlights filled the area as she pulled back onto the road and drove off. A sigh of relief escaped Bran, and his shoulders relaxed.

"She'll be alright," Merlin said. "Morgana is an excellent doctor and will take Alexandra to the hospital if needed."

"Great," Jenny said, her voice thin and bordering on hysterical. "She's okay, but what the hell is going on?"

Merlin turned to look at Jenny with a sad expression, but he nodded slightly. "Magic, young lady, is real. It is the result of beings from other universes and from other worlds seeking to invade our own. Alexandra Adams along with Nicole, Aiden, and Bran are mages, humans with the ability to use magic for the purpose of stopping these invaders." Merlin gestured towards the woods. "Tonight, we were guarding an entrance that these beings, the Sídhe, made to enter our world, but I'm afraid that our defensive line fell apart and they bypassed us. We were successful in blocking their access for a time, but Alex was required to battle them to protect yourself, Arthur, and Lance."

"Those people... the Sídhe," Arthur said slowly, testing the word carefully. "They're really from another world?"

"Indeed," Merlin said patiently. "Celtic mythology records them and the existence of the Otherworlds, although the records were not created until later accounting for the mistakes in their descriptions and history."

"But they are.... People," Arthur choked out, dropping his gaze to his hands.

Merlin reached out and placed a hand on the young man's shoulder. "They are sentient beings, capable of emotions, forethought, planning, and creativity," Merlin conceded gently before his gaze hardened. "They are also capable of choice, and for more than three thousand years they have chosen to invade and enslave other worlds."

Bran watched Arthur's face carefully, noting the shock, awe, fear, and resignation that flashed over his features. There was an odd glint of excitement and eagerness in his blue eyes that surprised Bran, but he considered that Arthur might be more interested in the idea of magic than Alex had been.

"So how do we fit into this?" Arthur asked, gesturing at himself, Jenny, and Lance. "When I was with Alex, and those Sídhe were attacking us, I felt… I don't know, something passed through me like an energy current. Sort of like a shock, but not painful and slower… maybe."

"Indeed, Arthur, you have magic of your own," Merlin informed him with a widening smile.

"Then why?" Arthur shook his head, trying to formulate a question.

"Why didn't he know?" Lance asked. He shifted nervously and glanced over at Jenny with concern written all over his face.

"In the simplest terms that you'll understand at the moment, you are the reincarnation of the man who inspired the legend of King Arthur," Merlin informed Arthur carefully, watching the young man's eyes widen comically. "And my name was not always Ambrose Yates. To mythology, I am known as Merlin, and the lovely woman who just left with Alexandra is none other than my longtime friend and colleague Morgana le Fey.

Even in the low light and shadows, Bran could see Arthur's Adam's apple move in a thick swallow. He glanced towards Jenny who was hiding in the shadow of a tree with her long hair covering half of her face.

"Jenny is the reincarnation of your former wife Gwenyvar and Lance, better known in the stories as Lancelot, was your friend and her lover," Merlin added, following Arthur's gaze. "I am afraid that the three of you have been caught in a repeating cycle of events in your lives." Merlin gave them a moment before he asked, "May I ask what brought you out here tonight?"

A look of confusion and discomfort came over Arthur's face as he glanced back towards Jenny and then over towards Lance who was lingering near Alex's car. "I was hanging out with Alex, we were studying for Spanish exams, but then we got bored, so we went out to a movie," Arthur explained in a rush. "Just as friends I mean. So, I walked her home thinking I'd leave a note for Jenny since she was out for the evening and I uh... I caught..." Arthur trailed off.

"He found Jenny and me kissing," Lance offered in a low voice, his eyes fixed on a spot on the ground. He kicked at the dirt and pushed his foot down making marks in the soil. "So, he drove out here, and we followed."

"I see," Merlin said slowly. He sighed in relief and slowly smiled. "Then I am pleased to say the betrayal has taken place."

"The betrayal?" Jenny repeated, flinching at the word. "Isn't that a little... harsh."

Merlin looked over at the distraught girl and gave her a small nod. "Perhaps it is a harsh word given that you and Arthur have only been dating as opposed to married, but in the past, the pattern has always been that once Arthur discovers the... cheating between his lover and his friend, it starts a chain reaction that leads to his death." Merlin's eyes went back to Arthur, and his smile widened. "You came out here alone, I suspect to think about what you'd found out, but tonight is the start of Beltane, and the Sídhe were out in force. Had Alex not followed you then they certainly would have killed you."

There was a pained gasp from Jenny before the girl covered her face with her hands and sank into the dirt. Before Bran could say anything, Nicki had quickly walked over to Jenny and knelt next to her, placing a hand on the young woman's shoulder.

"Hey, it's gonna be okay," Nicki said in a low voice that Bran had to strain to hear. Jenny's face was blank, the light from the car making her features shadowed and sharp. Nicki chuckled nervously and tugged Jenny up from the ground gently, wrapping an arm around the other girl's shoulders. "Come on, Jenny, I'll get you home."

"But-"

"We're going to steal Alex's car," Nicki announced as she began to push Jenny towards the vehicle. Nicki glanced towards Bran, her eyes reflecting how nervous she was. He nodded to her, hoping that she understood his promise to catch her up.

"Jenny?" Lance called as he began to move towards her, but Jenny flinched and crowded up against Nicki. She looked like a frightened stray animal to Bran, uncertain if it was going to be kicked or welcomed. Seeing the expression, Lance stopped and stepped back with a dejected look.

"Uh, I'll drive Lance back to the dorms," Aiden said. He awkwardly glanced between Arthur, Lance, and Jenny. Nicki nodded to him as she gently pushed Jenny into Alex's car.

"A fine idea," Merlin said with clear relief. "Right now, Arthur is the priority."

"This wasn't their fault," Arthur muttered, his eyes dropping to the ground.

"No, it wasn't," Merlin agreed with a heavy sigh. "But we must deal with this as best we can."

Arthur nodded but didn't look up as Nicki pulled Alex's car out of the parking lot. Bran sighed as it drove past them and vanished around a turn down the hill. A few moments later Aiden's car pulled out and followed, Lance looking out the window towards Arthur. Bran shook his head; he really did feel sorry for those three, but poor Alex had been stuck in the middle, so he just felt relief that at least this part was over. Nicki had hinted that things were bad, but he'd always had a feeling that it was worse for Alex than she let on.

"What happens now?" Arthur asked, finally looking up and glancing towards him before his eyes settled on Merlin.

"Now, lad, we get you home; you and Bran both need rest. The tunnel will fully collapse within twenty-four hours. Tomorrow we will begin your training in how to use your magic and bring you up to speed on the world you now live in."

Merlin clapped his hand on Arthur's shoulder and began to steer him towards the only remaining vehicle: his own. Bran followed, leaning on his cane, and watching Arthur closely, hoping that this guy, this Iron Soul was worth it. As Arthur climbed in the driver's side, Merlin gestured him towards the passenger seat with a pointed look at his leg before climbing into the back. Bran made his way to the passenger side door and took a breath before he looked back into the woods. As he gripped the handle of the door, Bran suddenly felt faint as a wave of vertigo hit him. His eyes slid shut, his heart began to race, and his legs shook as a haze slid over his mind.

Something was moving in front of him, something large and dark. It moved, and a pair of neon green glowing eyes were suddenly staring at him. Fear gripped Bran; he couldn't move and couldn't breathe. A deep chuckle resonated around him. But there was nothing, just darkness with tiny sparks of light falling around him and dimming. Behind him, Bran heard the scrape of metal as a sword was drawn, and he felt the brush of familiar magic. For a moment relief began to sink through him until abruptly there was a sharp pain in his stomach. It spread up his body, burning and freezing his limbs, heart, and lungs all at the same time.

Dropping his eyes away from the massive dark monster in front of him, Bran looked down. The pointed edge of a long sword was jutted out from his stomach, covered in his red blood. There was a laugh near his ear from someone taller than him, and they exhaled, blowing air across his neck and cheek. A roar escaped the beast in front of him, and the darkness around him shook and shimmered as everything began to fade. Bran sucked in a greedy breath, his legs giving out under him and his hand dropped to his stomach desperate to stop the bleeding.

But there was no sword, no wound, and no blood.

"Bran! Brandon!" Merlin called to him, cutting through the panic and the fog. "It's me, Bran, take a breath and hold it."

He obeyed without thinking it through, sucking in a deep breath and closing his mouth to hold it. There was a hand on his shoulder and another rubbing his back gently. He was on his knees, his brace digging into his leg painfully. Merlin's voice was calm and controlled, allowing Bran to draw strength from it. He slowly released the breath and opened his eyes.

"That's it, Bran." Merlin started pulling him to his feet.

"What happened?" Arthur's voice asked, and Bran became aware of the other student standing nearby, holding his cane out to him.

"Bran is 'gifted' with visions," Merlin explained patiently. "Let's get him in the car, and then he can tell us what he saw."

Bran nodded even as he tried to process how he could describe what he had seen. It wasn't like his tunnel dream or even the vision that had warned him of the car crash that injured him. This was something which he couldn't find meaning in, but he allowed Merlin and Arthur to help him into the passenger seat. He stretched out his leg as far as he could with a grateful sigh and leaned his head back. A few moments later Merlin climbed into the back seat and reached forward to place a warm hand on Bran's shoulder. Arthur climbed into the driver's side and, with a final glance towards Bran, started the car and began driving them back to the University of Ravenslake campus.

27

Changeling Made

8 07 B.C.E. Northern Cornwall

Arto was finally getting used to the metallic smell that hung in the air around his home village now and seeing the trails of smoke curling up into the sky. Furnaces were working much of each day turning the reddish tint in rocks into iron. The clang of hammers was becoming more and more familiar with each passing day as more of the bronze craftsmen accepted the new tools and metal. While the swords and tools they produced were rough and would not stand the test of time like the magic-infused iron of Cathanáil, the ease with which they could be repaired was winning over many. Bronze, when damaged, had to be melted down and recast, but iron had only to be reheated and reshaped. Bent swords could be hammered back into perfect balance in a matter of hours rather than the whole sword being scraped.

Not that everyone was happy with the change; news that bronze was being replaced had caused panic in some corners of the isles. Arto had heard plenty of rumors about artisans and merchants burying caches of bronze axe heads for the day when bronze became valuable again. He wasn't sure if he found this amusing or not, but sometimes guilt crept up on him. His own family had become powerful and wealthy through the bronze trade and was now at the center of the only iron production village in the isles. Introducing iron had changed his homeland, and his people and Arto couldn't decide if it was for the better or the worse.

Rolling his shoulders, Arto sat down on the grassy hill and looked up at the sky. A fast wind was pushing the highest layer of clouds past quickly while the lower ones moved at a more sedate pace. He indulged himself in a few moments of peace and quiet watching the clouds shift and form shapes. Sadly, many of them looked like creatures from the Sídhe realms.

Arto frowned as his thoughts turned back to the war effort. Thus far things were quiet as they focused on creating enough iron to make his dream a reality. Breaking down the tunnels only slowed the Sídhe, but iron seemed to really hurt them. He was going to block the tunnels with iron, keeping them open and allowing the energy of the iron to seep into Sídhean. There was no guarantee that it would have any effect, but as he'd argued; humanity had to try something new if they were going to keep their world.

But change was hard, it was painful, and it was wonderful all at the same time. Falling back on the grass, Arto stretched out his arms and breathed in the smell of fresh air with a hint of metal and smoke. Four months he'd been living in one place, living with his mother, Eigyr. He'd never stayed somewhere so long in his life, well not since he first left the village with Merlin. There were moments when he and Morgana had dinner with their mother that they almost seemed like a real family, a proper family who knew each other well, but then something would come up and remind Eigyr or him that they barely knew each other.

The last four months had been a blur of battles with the Sídhe: he and Morgana would rip down their tunnel only for another to spring up less than two months later which was then destroyed once more. News had come from the isles reporting a drop in the activities of the

Sídhe elsewhere. Almost no children had been taken, and Riders and their Hounds were quickly becoming a rare sight. It made Arto nervous, and he had overheard a whispered conversation between Morgana and Merlin expressing concerns of a traitor. The suggestion was beyond worrying; the idea that when the time came to create the first Iron Gate that their army with iron weapons might not be enough, that the Sídhe might also have new weapons prepared was alarming.

"Deep thoughts?" Gwenyvar asked.

Arto snapped his eyes up, twisting his head enough to see the smiling young woman standing near him. He rolled himself up, so he was sitting on the grass as Gwenyvar lowered herself down next to him.

"A bit," Arto replied.

"How are you?" Gwenyvar asked him gently. She studied his face carefully. Her worry wasn't necessary, but Arto felt warm every time she expressed it.

"I'm alright," he answered serenely, looking back at the clouds. "Just enjoying a moment of calm." He inhaled a deep breath and heard Gwenyvar do the same. "When did you return?"

"Not long ago: I came to find you as soon as we settled in. Father seems glad to be back; he was tense the whole time we were back home. Kept muttering about missing important decisions."

"He doesn't seem to think we can do without him," Arto observed with a laugh before he coughed in embarrassment. "I'm sorry, Gwenyvar, I didn't mean to suggest-"

She just laughed a soft and melodic sound that instantly made him smile. "Oh, I know you don't mean offense," Gwenyvar assured him, tucking a stray strand of brown hair behind her ear and pushing it into her braid. "He is my father; I love and respect him, but you are right. Father doesn't think that most people know what they are doing." She shook her head and leaned back in the grass, spreading her brown hair around her. "He just likes being in control and knowing what is going on."

Arto nodded slowly and laid back in the grass next to her, their hands almost touching. They didn't speak as the soft breeze blew around them. There was the barest hint of a chill to it, reminding Arto that winter was fast approaching. Over the last few weeks, they'd lost several of their ironworkers to the fields to bring in livestock and crops. With so many extra people residing in the village and the frequent visits from the regional leaders and traders, he knew that it would be a busy winter and greater stockpiles of food would be needed.

"Will you be taking your father's ashes to the Procession?" Gwenyvar suddenly asked.

"Of course. Morgana and I will be accompanying Mother." He paused and swallowed, "I think Mother is still sad that we could not wait for his pyre until winter's eve."

"It is a great honor to hold a pyre at the stone circle," Gwenyvar agreed carefully. "But I'm sure he would have understood. The last of the bones can be burned with the great assembly present, and he will be honored at the feast."

Arto nodded but chuckled. "Although young pigs may be in short supply for the winter's eve feast from our region. So many new people living in the village has been a strain."

"I thought the other leaders promised aid?"

"They did; Eaban is having some animals brought over, but it is quite a voyage with livestock on board the ships. Others are starting to send down some animals, no large numbers, but Merlin is certain the village will be fine with all the aid combined."

"Good," Gwenyvar said firmly, and in the corner of his eye, he saw her nod. "They need to demonstrate their support. After all, you're going to save us all from the Sídhe."

"I'm going to try, but it isn't just me. Merlin is the one who learned about iron and the workers are producing the arms that we will need."

"But it will be your magic that brings it all together," Gwenyvar reminded him. "And it was your idea: you are the heart of this effort, Arto."

He swallowed nervously but managed to nod. A moment later, Gwenyvar's warm hand covered his as the soft grass tickled his palm. She said nothing, just gently squeezed and Arto found himself relaxing.

"I'm glad you're back."

"I'm glad to be back," Gwenyvar replied. "I missed you."

Arto turned his head to find Gwenyvar looking at him with a soft smile on her face. Without meaning to his eyes dropped to her lips and he blushed, quickly turning his head away. She laughed softly at his embarrassment and rolled slightly. The next thing Arto knew, Gwenyvar was lying alongside him, their hands still joined, and her head was resting on his shoulder.

"Do you ever think of what comes next?" Gwenyvar asked him in a soft voice, relaxing against him.

"Some," Arto replied, barely keeping his voice even. "Honestly, I'm not sure what my life will be like when the Sídhe are gone. They've been such a central part of my life for as long as I can remember." Arto paused and swallowed again as he tried to gather his thoughts. "It's strange, but in some moments I'm more afraid of what happens after the war than the battles of the war."

Gwenyvar was silent for a moment, considering his words, but then she shifted again and raised herself up on her hands. She was leaning over him and studying his expression with a quizzical look.

"Do you want to live in one place? Have a family?"

"I... I don't know," he admitted. "Airril comes and visits often, Morgana even has her own roundhouse now due to his visits. It seems to make her happy, but I'm not sure it is for me."

"Well maybe when this is all over you can give it a try," Gwenyvar suggested with a growing smile. "It would be a new kind of adventure."

"I'd probably get fat and lazy if I did that."

"No, you wouldn't, you'd be too busy rushing through the village helping anyone who needed you. Helping resolve disputes and traveling to meet with other leaders."

"Medraut is the heir of this region," Arto reminded Gwenyvar gently. "I'm no one's leader."

"Yes, you are," Gwenyvar assured him, lowering herself down and resting her head back on his shoulder. "Just you wait, Arto, when this is all over, you'll be known as a great hero, a great leader and maybe if you're lucky a nice girl will marry you and then you'll be a great father."

A throat was cleared loudly near them, and Gwenyvar sat up with wide eyes. Rolling to the side, Arto relaxed when he saw Morgana standing near them with her hands on her hips and a raised eyebrow. He felt himself blushing as his sister studied him for a moment before her eyes swept over to Gwenyvar.

"I need to speak with my brother."

Gwenyvar jumped to her feet and nodded deeply to Morgana, giving his sister a charming smile that only made her eyebrow arch higher. With a glance toward him and a hasty goodbye, Gwenyvar rushed down the hill and back towards the village.

"Her father suggested a marriage between the two of you," Morgana informed him, her voice giving away none of her feelings on the subject as they both watched Gwenyvar depart. "He had the decency not to raise it with Mother before he left, but now he's making his goal for you to marry Gwenyvar very clear."

Arto was surprised by her statement, but a smile began to tug at his lips without him meaning for it. "Is that such a bad thing?" Arto asked, his heart pumping a little faster at the idea of marrying Gwenyvar.

"You're young, Arto," Morgana chided.

"You were barely older when you married Airril," Arto countered as his sister lowered herself down to the ground and sat next to him.

"When my father Kenwyn died, Mother was lost," Morgana admitted sadly, a bittersweet smile on her face. "Uthyrn wasn't very important then, but he was a natural leader who stepped up and kept things working. It was more than a year before Uthyrn began to pursue mother. I'm not sure if she loved him then, but her position was shaky with her being unable to maintain my father's agreements and ensure the production of bronze. But things changed slowly, and after a while, they were married, it wasn't too much later that you came along in fact. I hesitated at first; I didn't want someone replacing my father, but he made Mother happy. He tried to be a good father and leader while always being respectful of Kenwyn's place as my father." Morgana tilted her head back to look up at the sky. "I was happy during those years."

"You said I," Arto observed quietly. "Not my Changeling."

"True," Morgana agreed with a nod. "I was taken as a baby; the memories of the Changeling are the only memories I have of my father. They are also much better than the alternative memories. They may not truly be mine, but they are good ones and worth holding onto."

"I see," Arto said slowly, wondering where his sister was going with this.

"I wasn't happy when Uthyrn wanted me to marry," Morgana admitted. "He had ideas on who I should marry, selected those who would be suitable since there was no one I was interested in. Out of them, I selected Airril as the best. He was intelligent and gentle, but if I hadn't been pressured to marry, then I doubt I would have."

"But you lo- care about Airril," Arto protested with a sharp look at his sister.

"Yes, I do care about him, but I'm never there." Morgana shook her head. "Airril and I are never going to have children together or raise them. That's not my life; that's not our life."

"But the war will be over soon."

"Perhaps the war will come to an end soon, but you are still the Iron Soul. There may be much more waiting for you when this task is done that Gwenyvar will not fit into." Morgana shivered, tightening her cloak around her as Arto glared at her. "And as for me... it will never be over for me, Arto. I am part Sídhe. I carry as a part of me the remains of that Changeling." She looked down at her hands folded in her lap. "When we were fused together, she was so afraid. I didn't know that they could feel like that. I'm still not sure if she died and I lived, or we both died with something new taking both of our places." She shivered again, making a hissing sound between her teeth.

"What are Changelings?" Arto asked quietly, his irritation draining away at his sister's confession. "They are a kind of Sídhe, but are they born or are they made?"

"They are made."

"How?" Arto pressed, unwilling to back down. "You and Merlin never tell me about these things."

"You've never asked."

He sighed and ran a hand through his messy brown hair. "I know, but I'm older now. I need to understand not just the basics, but the details of what I'm fighting and what I'm fighting for." Arto looked over at Morgana, noting her pressed lips and distant eyes. "Please, I want to understand. I know they took you from your parents, I know that your life was a nightmare, but there is so much that I just don't understand. You're my sister, and I'm not a child anymore."

"No," Morgana replied sadly. "I suppose not." There was a moment of silence; the wind rustling the grass around them. "Changelings are made from the corpses of the humans in Sídhean. By the time a human lives out their life in that Realm, they have been changed by the magic, the very essence of a world that is not their own. Sídhe power lingers in the corpse which is then reshaped using magic into the new shape they need it to carry. Sídhe mages fill it with Sídhe blood and add a spark of magic to animate it. When the Changeling is brought into contact with the person it is replacing, it is capable of taking on the person's appearance and with some extra magic their memories." Morgana paused and swallowed. "The reason Sídhe like taking the young isn't just that they are trainable, but that children are smaller. From the corpse of an adult, they can make two young human Changelings, and less magic is needed to get the memories."

His stomach was turning, but Arto did his best to hide the reaction not wanting to show that maybe he hadn't been ready to hear it. "Why do they even bother with the Changelings?" Arto asked carefully. "Most of the time they just steal children and burn down villages."

"Changelings can be used as spies. Sometimes they don't even know what they are, but with the right spark of magic they can be controlled at a distance and in theory, a Sídhe mage can see through their eyes. If they reach human adulthood, magical abilities sometimes manifest in them making them dangerous weapons. That is rare due to humans discovering the blood test," Morgana informed him sadly. "And sometimes the Sídhe want slaves without announcing that they have a tunnel in the area."

"So how many do you think there are?" He asked before he could change his mind. "Humans in the tunnels and Sídhean."

"I have no idea," Morgana admitted carefully. "Many don't survive long: the Sídhe have rules about not harming humans until they are seven, but... I doubt the Riders always obey. I grew up with a small group, but it was always changing, and I'm honestly not sure if we were the only group. I didn't think about things like that when I lived with them. It was just... the way things were."

"Can't you guess?"

"I don't think we want a number, Arto," Morgana cautioned.

"Morgana."

"I'd say roughly five hundred, including adults and descendants of those taken."

"All those people we won't be able to save," Arto muttered, toying with strands of grass sadly. "Those trapped in Sídhean."

"It won't be forever," Morgana confided. "Humans can last a long time, but not forever. Eventually, the strain of living in another realm kills them."

"But the Sídhe make them... there are breeders," Arto stumbled over the phrase distastefully.

"The Realm itself alters humans in Sídhean, they can have children and their children can have children, but after that... it just doesn't work. The Sídhe must get new... stock all the time to replace the humans who are sterile and deformed by the Realm."

"That's horrible," Arto gasped, his mouth open in shock and disgust. "And we can't help them? Not at all?"

"Arto, few humans ever return: I only returned safely with the aid of a magical potion that strengthened my body, and I believe it helped to reverse some of the changes wrought on me, but I have no idea what was in the potion. For all I know the only reason I am still alive is my Changeling half," she snapped, her anger at the situation showing.

"I'm sorry," Arto whispered, turning his head away from his sister. "I know that you'd help them if you could."

Morgana didn't reply to his apology, but she didn't leave either. They just sat in silence, feeling the wind on their skin, and watching the clouds in the sky. Arto inhaled deeply, in synch with his sister, and smiled when her hand touched his. She said nothing, but her message was clear, and he relaxed, letting himself enjoy the beautiful and calm day.

28

Waking Up at Morgana's Again

Waking up in Morgana's guest room was not going to become a thing, Alex promised herself as she sat up slowly and carefully stretched. The vintage ivory wallpaper in the room was too distinct to mistake. Inhaling deeply, Alex caught the scent of flowers outside the open window and felt a soft breeze tickle her arms as the white curtains floated in the breeze. Alex moved her shoulders carefully, taking stock of how her body reacted. There was some residual soreness that the pain medication would help her take care of, but she vaguely recalled Morgana telling her that the worst of the damage was fixed. Alex frowned as she tried to remember when Morgana had told her that; she certainly felt better, so she didn't think it had been a dream. She'd been in and out of consciousness the last... was it two days or three days now? Alex could remember getting up and eating a couple of times, using the bathroom, and speaking with Morgana, but the details were fuzzy.

Alex frowned at the thought. Beltane had been a Friday, and if she'd been here too long, then she was missing classes right before finals week. Sure, everything was mostly review, and she'd been taking good notes all year, but with the threat of the Sídhe and worrying about Lance and Jenny, her work hadn't been up to her normal standards lately. Pushing back the blankets, Alex carefully swung her legs around and lowered them to the floor. There was a slight twinge in her back, but no sharp pains which calmed her. Standing up, Alex glanced down at the t-shirt and shorts she was wearing; they were her own at least. Alex swallowed, wondering if Nicki had grabbed them when she took Jenny home or if someone else had gone back to get them later. Thoughts of how Jenny and Lance might be coping rushed through her mind and made her feel sick to her stomach.

"Alex?" Morgana's voice called down the hallway. There were footsteps against the polished wood flooring of Morgana's home.

Walking over to the bedroom door, Alex opened it and gave her teacher a reassuring smile. "Hi, Morgana."

Already green eyes were inspecting her carefully. "How are you feeling?"

"Pretty good actually," Alex replied with a widening smile. "I don't feel like I'm going to sleep a whole day again." Alex frowned slightly. "What day is it anyway?"

"It's Sunday." Morgana's lips quirked into a slight smile. "You seem to be doing well enough that you can go back to classes tomorrow."

"Really?" Alex blinked and frowned. "Only Sunday?"

"Your sense of time is off due to the drugs, your exhaustion, and my healing magic," Morgana assured her, holding back a smile. "It's natural, don't worry there is nothing wrong with you."

"That's... that's really good." Alex shivered slightly and quietly admitted, "When I got knocked around like that, I was really worried."

"Don't get me wrong," Morgana cut in as she reached out and placed a warm hand on Alex's shoulder. "There was some bruising to your spine, and you had two hairline fractures. Not to mention a concussion which explains you sleeping so much and your memory. I checked you over this morning while you were sleeping and if you want, I'm comfortable taking you home."

Alex nodded in agreement, but then asked, "If you used magic then why am I still sore?"

"I healed the worst of the internal injuries, but healing magic is very draining, so I couldn't heal everything." Morgana dropped her hand off Alex's shoulder. "I can try to help some of the muscles this afternoon... but I'm afraid I don't have the energy to do much more today."

"Of course, I'm sorry," Alex apologized quickly. "I didn't mean-"

"Don't worry about it, Alex, you and the others are still learning the limits of magic. It is only natural to occasionally over or underestimate what can be done. I often find myself wishing that I could make magic do more and that is after I find myself living for centuries at a time without it at all." Morgana turned and gestured towards the bathroom. "Why don't you take a shower; I have some of your things in there waiting for you. That may help to relax your muscles. After you eat, you can have another pain pill if you need it."

"What about the others?" Alex asked. "Is everyone okay?" She felt guilty for not asking that first thing but was still confident that Morgana would have told her already if someone else had been hurt badly.

Morgana chuckled and nodded. "As I told you yesterday, three times, everyone is fine. Merlin saw Arthur back to his dorm room safely, Bran, Aiden, and Nicki are all safe, and no one suffered serious injuries. A few bites and scrapes, all of which Merlin took care of yesterday. Nicki took care of one of Aiden's injuries for practice. The girl has real potential with healing magic." Morgana gestured towards the bathroom with a knowing smile. "The sooner you clean up and eat something the sooner I can take you back to campus."

Nodding, Alex moved down the hall, pausing at the door to watch Morgana vanish into the kitchen. There wasn't a clock in the bathroom, so Alex was left to wonder the time as she showered and cleaned up, noting the new toothbrush gratefully. A glance out the window told Alex that the sun was roughly overhead so it wasn't too late when she dressed in fresh clothing and went to join Morgana.

The kitchen was a large airy room and the large window looking out into the yard was open, allowing a cool breeze to fill the house. Alex lingered in the doorway, studying the plants that Morgana had hanging from the ceiling and breathing in the scent coming from the forest beyond the house. Another smaller window near the small dining table was open and with a pair of hanging potted plants swaying in the breeze.

"Feeling any better?" Morgana asked as she finished putting something in a cabinet above the sink. Turning toward Alex, she gestured Alex to have a seat at the high island counter that dominated the bright kitchen.

"Much better," Alex replied with a smile which turned into a grin when a pair of grilled cheese sandwiches with pickles was placed in front of her.

Morgana also set a bottle of pills down next to the plate. It was a small white nondescript bottle, and Alex wondered just how Morgana got the pills. Then again, Merlin could apparently alter memories and leave false trails for the police so getting a few pills probably wasn't a challenge.

"Here are some muscle relaxants, but remember not to drive when taking them."

"Will they mess with my school work?" Alex opened the bottle and dropped one of the pills into her hand. "Finals week is almost here, and I haven't had the easiest year."

"They will dull your reaction time, but shouldn't cloud your mind too much," Morgana assured her with a soft smile across the counter. "In fact, you may do better as the edge will be taken off your stress."

Alex wished she had a clever comeback for that remark but settled for taking the pill with a gulp of water and eating her lunch. As she ate Morgana caught her up on the later events of Beltane: Nicki had taken Jenny home while Aiden returned Lance home and thankfully thus far Arthur seemed to have accepted his situation relatively calmly.

"We'll discuss everything in more detail soon," Morgana promised when Alex began to ask about Arthur. "You might be pleased to know that he swung by yesterday. He barely missed Aiden and Nicki. Merlin gave him my address."

"Arthur came here?" Alex asked as casually as she could, but couldn't keep her voice from squeaking.

"He was very worried about you," Morgana said with a small smile. "I didn't let him see you for more than a moment since you were sleeping, but I did assure him that you were going to be fine."

Alex looked down into her glass of water well aware that she was blushing, but also unsure of how to feel about this news. Finally, she took another sip of her water and set it to the side.

"Has anyone heard from Jenny or Lance?"

"Not yet," Morgana replied with a shake of her head. "They were delivered safely back to their dorms."

That wasn't much of an answer, and Alex suddenly found her appetite fading, but after a look from Morgana, she managed to eat the last bites of the sandwich. Her professor seemed to debate with herself in the kitchen as she washed the plate for a few moments before informing Alex that she'd take her back to the school. Returning to the bedroom, Alex gathered up her things and put them in the small bag that Morgana provided her. Picking up her phone, Alex quickly hit the speed dial for Nicki.

"Hey, Alex," her friend's cheerful voice greeted. "How are you feeling?"

"Not too bad; listen Morgana is about to bring me back. Can you meet me and show me where my car is?"

"Not planning an escape attempt, are you? It's nice to hear your voice, but you really should listen to the older, more powerful, trained doctor and all-around scary mage you know."

"Nothing like that," Alex replied, rolling her eyes even as she smiled. "But I would like to know where my car is."

"Sure thing, I'll be outside by Hatfield in say fifteen minutes."

"That should work, thanks."

Alex walked back out to the entry hall to find Morgana calmly speaking on her phone, by the tone and subject she guessed with Merlin. Sitting down on the small bench by the door under the coat hooks, Alex kept her back straight and waited patiently. She caught part of the conversation: they were discussing when to start Arthur's training and something about the summer, but Morgana said only a little on that.

"Alright, I'll be there soon," Morgana promised into the phone. "Sorry about that, Alex," Morgana apologized as she ended the call and slipped her phone into her purse. "I'm sure you're eager to get back to campus." Morgana led her out to her red sports car parked in the drive.

Morgana stayed near Alex as she eased herself into the passenger seat and relaxed against it, finding a good position. "I'll write you a doctor's note," Morgana informed Alex as she climbed into the driver's side of the car. "Just in case."

"Won't they know it's from you?" Alex asked, frowning slightly. "I know you were a doctor until recently, but-"

"They won't know the names of the local doctors," Morgana chuckled. "Besides it is just to explain your pain pills and potentially needing to miss classes, just in case."

Nodding, Alex decided to accept the explanation. It made sense she supposed; after all, she was in college not high school. Teachers here weren't responsible for their students like they were when they were kids. Sighing, Alex closed her eyes and breathed in and out as the vibrations of the car moving irritated her sore muscles. The ride across the river and to campus seemed to take longer than usual, but thankfully they arrived before Alex was whimpering in pain.

They pulled into the largest parking lot for the dorms, and Morgana maneuvered around the cars towards the walkway that led up to Hatfield. Alex smiled when she caught sight of Nicki waiting patiently on the sidewalk. The car stopped, and Nicki jumped forward to open Alex's door.

"The pill will take full effect soon," Morgana promised Alex as she climbed out with Nicki's help. The professor leaned across the car, lowering the passenger side window after Nicki closed the door. "Take another tonight if you need to. If you have any questions, call me, no matter what time it is."

"I will," Alex promised as she straightened her back and sighed in relief as the pain eased slightly. "Thanks again."

"Thank you, Alex," Morgana told her with a softening smile. "You did a wonderful job in keeping him safe."

"Even though he got attacked and ran off?"

"He's still alive," Morgana reminded her. "This is the first time he has survived the chain of events surrounding the betrayal." Morgana chuckled and shook her head. "I hate to say it, but Merlin was right about you, Alex. You did change things. You broke the cycle."

Alex felt heat rising to her cheeks even as a sense of pleasure warmed her chest. Next to her, Nicki grinned and placed a careful hand on her shoulder.

"Nicki," Morgana called drawing the redhead's attention. "I'll leave Alex in your hands."

"Yes, Morgana," Nicki replied with a nod.

Morgana nodded in return, leaned back into the driver's side, and pulled out of the parking lot. Nicki made a small sound of displeasure.

"She took off fast," Nicki huffed with a frown.

"I think she's meeting Merlin and maybe Arthur as well," Alex said to calm her friend. "And she did take care of me. There's just a lot that they need to tell him."

"I suppose," Nicki replied slowly, still clearly displeased. "How are you feeling, sweetie?"

"Sore," Alex admitted. "And my memory is a little fuzzy; Morgana said that I had a concussion, but she healed everything. My muscles are just bruised, but I've got pain pills to help with that." Alex assured Nicki quickly. "I'm going to be fine."

"Man, Alex, it's not fair. The rest of us have never been hurt like that."

"Well maybe that means that I'm not as good a fighter as the rest of you," Alex replied, shrugging only to realize that it was a very bad idea.

"No, it's not that, it's that you keep having to go up against the Sídhe on your own. Speaking of which have you made housing arrangements for next year?"

"Not yet," Alex admitted. "I haven't been sure of what's going on with Jenny..."

"That's fair, anyway listen Gallagher Hall didn't fill up, so they are opening the suite rooms to sophomores for the coming year. We could sign up together. We'd each have our own bedroom, but also share a living room. There are two-person suites left, not perfect, but it would give us young mages a better meeting place.”

“What about the boys?” Alex asked with a smile.

“I’ve told Aiden about the announcement; he’s going to talk to Bran.”

“Well, that sounds like a plan to me,” Alex agreed. “Do you want to take care of that?”

“Sure,” Nicki replied. “I can do that.”

“Good, so where is my car?”

Nicki laughed and gestured for Alex to follow her. They had to go across the parking lot, but up ahead Alex caught sight of her dark blue car with the tolerance bumper sticker in the shade of a tree. Alex braced herself as she walked around the front of her little blue four-door, waiting to see the dents in the hood. Behind her, Alex heard Nicki chuckle and resisted the urge to smack her friend’s head. She was the one who was either going to have to fix it or figure out some kind of explanation for her parents, not to mention the insurance company. But there was nothing; no body sized dent, not even a scratch.

“Seriously?” Alex asked, reaching out and running her hand over the hood, wondering if it just wasn’t visible.

“Merlin fixed your car,” Nicki informed her with a laugh. “Saturday we came to check on you, but you were out cold. He decided to go ahead and fix the dent, and I drove it back to campus for you.”

Alex nodded vaguely as she moved around the car, noting with surprise that some of the small dings and dents that she’d gotten in parking lots over the years were gone as well. Moving to the right side quickly, Alex grinned when she discovered that the small scrape from a mailbox when she’d first been learning to drive was gone as well.

“According to Merlin, restoring an item is pretty easy, so long as it isn’t anything complicated. The body of a car for instance. He checked the engine and said that everything looked fine there which was good 'cause apparently that is a lot more complicated and shouldn't be fixed with magic."

"This is cool!" Alex grinned widely. "Total body job without paying a dime!"

"Yeah, I asked him if I can try on my car." Nicki smiled brightly at her. "He said to wait until summer. And of course, to make sure I'm not in sight of anyone."

Alex patted her car fondly and turned back towards Nicki, catching sight of Hatfield Hall across the parking lot. Nicki must have noticed the smile drop away from her face because her friend turned and looked towards the dormitory and nodded.

"How about you stay with me for the rest of the semester? There's only a couple of weeks left, and I wouldn't mind the company." Nicki reached into her pocket and pulled out a single key. "Here's the spare key they gave me."

Alex looked back at Nicki, feeling churning emotions that she couldn't quite identify. She managed a quick nod and after a moment of fighting to regain control said, "Thank you, I appreciate that."

"It'll be good practice for next year," Nicki said as Alex reached out and took the key. She held out her hand for the small bag Alex was carrying. "Come on."

"I need to get my stuff for classes and some clothes," Alex muttered, turning to look over at Hatfield Hall.

"Do you want me to go?" Nicki asked her gently. "I grabbed your stuff yesterday."

"Did you see Jenny?"

"No, I didn't, I'm guessing she was in the shower. Her robe was missing, but it was yesterday morning and..."

"I'll do it." Alex sighed, handing the small bag she had been carrying to Nicki. "Meet you at your room."

"Are you sure?"

"No, but I can't avoid her forever. We are in some of the same classes after all."

Nicki looked like she wanted to argue and to be honest Alex really wanted to be talked out of this idea, but a moment later Nicki nodded and stepped back. "See you in a few then, but if you're not over at my place in .... an hour, I'm going to call the others and do a mage rescue operation."

A small smile tugged at Alex's lips, and she nodded to Nicki. Taking a deep breath, she turned and walked back to the sidewalk and followed it across the lawn to Hatfield Hall before she could change her mind. Despite the nice weather, Alex felt very cold by the time she entered the building and stepped into the elevator. Breathing in and out slowly, she struggled to stay calm as a hundred different possible reactions from Jenny and potential conversations skittered through her mind. When the elevator door opened on her floor, Alex wasn't very sure about this decision anymore.

29

Conversations

Somehow Alex stepped out of the elevator before the door closed on her and walked down the hall even as her mind helpfully produced a long list of reasons why she shouldn't. Her dorm room door was suddenly terrifying as Alex heard someone moving around inside. She'd been desperately hoping that Jenny would be out, but then the silliness of that thought hit Alex squarely in the chest. Two days ago, the woman had found out that she was the reincarnation of one of the most famous adulteresses in history or mythology and that she'd been reliving the same love triangle over the past school year. Of course, she wouldn't feel like going out. Suddenly having Nicki wait outside didn't seem like such a good idea... after all, she needed to get most of her school things and a few days' worth of clothing.

"Come on, Alex," she muttered. "You can fight the Sídhe; you can face your roommate."

Yet she stood there frozen in fear until one of their neighbors down the hall stepped out while talking on her phone and waved to Alex, giving her an odd look. Forcing a smile, Alex waved back and pulled out her room key. Before she could change her mind, Alex unlocked the door and pushed it open as gently and quietly as she could manage.

There was a lump of blankets and pillows on Jenny's bed. A loud sniff from under it all revealed Jenny's position. Tissues were scattered around on the floor, and the room was dark with the lights off, and the curtains were drawn across the window. Only one small sunbeam managed to penetrate the darkness, illuminating a sliver of the blue rug between the beds. The air was extremely stale, smelling of sweat and heavy with emotion. Some of Jenny's clothing was scattered around her side without any of the usual regard Jenny held for her clothes. The desire to run far away and not face this was back and stronger than ever.

"Uh hi, it's me," Alex announced nervously as she shut the door carefully. "Nicki has offered to let me stay with her, so I'm gonna grab some things." Alex moved away from the door and tried to focus on what she needed to get.

Alex walked past the pile of blankets determinedly and grabbed her messenger bag. She made quick work of disconnecting her laptop and packing it away, stuffing her tablet and a variety of books into the bag until it was full. Placing it on the bed, Alex then dug a backpack out of the top of her closet and packed up the rest of her school books.

"Are you okay?" a weak and exhausted voice asked from under the blankets, breaking the thick silence. The words were followed by a loud, painful sounding sniff.

"Yeah, I'm okay, Morgana took care of my injuries," Alex replied without turning around. She tried to sound friendly and calm. "Good as new."

That was a lie, but the tone of Jenny's voice was more than a little worrying. As much as a part of Alex was still angry at Jenny for cheating on Arthur, she couldn't deny all the times she'd seen Jenny a wreck over it. Sighing softly, Alex shook her head and kept packing, realizing that she didn't have it in her to be angry with Jenny. It was done and over with now, all any of them could do was pick up the pieces. She just didn't know how to start.

"I'm sorry," Jenny whispered, her words barely reaching Alex from under the pile of blankets.

Taking a deep breath, Alex nibbled at her lip for a moment before she dared reply. "This wasn't your fault, Jenny... you couldn't help it, any of it."

"That scares me more."

Alex nodded; she could understand that. Hadn't she and the others wondered plenty of times about how much choice the reincarnations had, how much their emotions were their own and the ramifications about their present lives? Even with all the discussions, they had never found a decent answer, something that made Alex's stomach turn once again.

"But it's past now." Alex forced herself to ignore the sick churning in her stomach. "What was doomed to repeat has and there shouldn't be anything-"

"Did I ever love Arthur?" Jenny asked, her voice on the edge of hysteria. "Or was it just... programmed into me because I was Guinevere? Could I have done anything differently?"

"I... I don't know, Jenny," Alex answered as gently as she could. "I don't know how your feelings worked for Arthur or Lance. That's... it's never been clear to any of us how that worked." Alex shifted uncomfortably as she retrieved a duffel bag from under her bed. "And for what it is worth, I don't blame you for anything."

"Why didn't you tell me?"

"Would you have believed me?" Alex asked, a slightly hysterical laugh escaping her. "Even if I'd shown you magic would you have believed me? Would it have changed anything?" Alex exhaled slowly and shook her head. "I don't blame you if you're angry with me, but please believe me when I say that I was your friend long before I found out about this and it wasn't the reason I spent time with you guys, I honestly like and care about all three of you."

"Nicki said that Professor Yates...."

"Merlin, yeah he's really Merlin," Alex told her. "Crazy, but he's three thousand years old, and the original story took place in the Bronze Age, not the Middle Ages."

"Nicki said that you never told them about Lance and me," Jenny said, her voice clearer.

Turning, Alex caught sight of Jenny peeking out from under the blankets. Her eyes were red, her normal wavy dark hair was limp and greasy, and there was no sign of the usual happy spark or smile. Alex's mind flashed back to the attractive, fashionable, and energetic girl that she'd met on her first day at Ravenslake. Sure, she'd been a bit jealous of her boyfriend and nursed a crush on him, but she'd always liked Jenny. This was... so very wrong.

"No, I didn't tell them," Alex agreed, and for a moment they just looked at each other. Finally, Alex sat on the edge of her bed. Taking a deep breath, Alex tried to find the right words to explain without frightening Jenny, but they wouldn't come. Her roommate was still watching her, so Alex exhaled and said, "I was trying to protect you. Merlin and Morgana.... There isn't much they wouldn't do to protect Arthur."

The flash of panic on Jenny's face told Alex that her roommate understood what she was saying loud and clear. Guilt twisted in Alex's chest again; that wasn't fair, and even though she had kept Jenny alive this was another moment when Alex wished she'd never overheard Merlin and Morgana talking. Jenny swallowed several times and looked down, the blankets shaking around her.

"What happens now?"

"Arthur will be trained now," Alex told her gently. "Merlin and Morgana will teach him to make a new Iron Gate to keep the Sídhe out of our world. Beyond that.... I don't know."

Jenny nodded carefully, clutching her stuffed bear Zoe tightly to her chest. Alex reached over and gently brushed her fingers over her own stuffed dog Galahad's soft plush fur and sighed. She felt exhausted suddenly, not physically, but like all energy had just drained out of her. It was tempting to just lay back on her bed and go to sleep, but then again this wasn't her room anymore.

"What about you?" Alex heard herself ask. "What are you going to do? Are you going to transfer?"

"No," Jenny answered sadly. "I don't have enough credits to transfer, and I don't have a good explanation for my father. I can't exactly tell him that I want to abandon an entire year of school because I'm the reincarnation of Guinevere or Gwenyvar, whatever her name was and just relived the discovery of my love triangle with Lancelot which would have gotten Arthur killed if my mage roommate hadn't stepped in and saved his life."

Alex flinched, feeling another wave of sympathy for Jenny, and nodded carefully. "Yeah, I can see that."

"I'll stay out of your way," Jenny promised softly. "I'm going to finish this year and come back for at least one semester next year, so I can get enough credits to transfer."

"Jenny, no one blames you, I promise. Nicki was the only one I talked to about all this." Jenny flinched under the blankets and retreated into them. "I'm sorry, but I had to talk to someone, it was just too much. But she doesn't blame you; none of us could imagine being in your position."

There was a nod, and the blankets moved, but her roommate curled back into her nest and laid back down. Her normally vibrant and gorgeous roommate looked tiny and vulnerable, and for a moment Alex reconsidered her decision to leave. But the small sniffs from Jenny made up her mind as her roommate tried to keep her from hearing any noises. Jenny needed time to cope as best she could, and she wasn't going to do that with Alex present.

"I'll swing back around over the next week to pack up my stuff."

Alex swung her backpack on which made her flinch and a sharp gasp escaped her. The pain passed after a moment, and Alex could breathe again, making a mental note not to use the backpack for a while. She zipped up the duffel bag and picked it up along with her messenger. She was a bit off balance but had everything she'd need for at least a few days.

"Can you do something for me?" Jenny asked, lifting the blankets just enough that her voice was clear.

"Uh, yes of course," Alex quickly replied as she shifted her position to balance out her burdens.

"Well, that jacket over there..." Jenny poked one hand out from under the blankets, and Alex turned to see a crumbled letterman of red and white on the floor. "It's Lance's."

"Oh," Alex said slowly as she nodded. "You want me to return it?"

"I can't.... please," Jenny cried as she pulled the blankets tighter over her head.

"Yeah, okay. He's in room 221 in Michaels, right?"

"Yes," Jenny's soft voice whispered under the blankets.

"Okay." Alex adjusted her messenger bag enough that she could reach down and grab the jacket. The muscles in her lower back ached but eased when she stood back up. Heading for the door, Alex glanced around to make sure she wasn't forgetting anything urgent and slung the jacket over her shoulder.

"Ah, Jenny…" Alex said as she reached the door. "If you need any-thing…"

"Yeah," Jenny muttered from her bed.

"Okay." Alex opened the door and stepped out into the hall, locking the door behind her with a grateful sigh. "That could have been worse," Alex reminded herself as she headed for the elevator.

Twenty minutes later, after dropping her things off at Nicki's and begging off a recap of her conversation with Jenny, Alex stood in front of room 221 in Michaels Hall and knocked on the door. For a moment there was no sound from inside, and Alex began to hope that she'd be able to come back later. Then there was a small crash from inside the room, and she heard a groan just before the door opened. Alex was hit with the smell of cheap beer, and her eyes began to water, but she looked up to meet the bloodshot brown eyes of Lance. He blinked at her, and his eyes dropped to his jacket. Lance swallowed thickly, and he straightened up, his eyes becoming sharper.

"Alex," he greeted in a gravelly voice before coughing. "How are you?"

"I'm alright," Alex replied with a nod. She glanced past Lance and into the room where she spotted a knocked over trash can and empty beer bottles. "Uh, are you…"

"How is Jenny?" Lance asked, cutting her off.

"She's…." Alex paused, her mouth moving uncertainly. "She's trying to cope."

"Is she leaving?"

"No… not yet, she doesn't have the credits to transfer. Jenny said she'll be returning next year until she can transfer."

"Oh… that's… oh."

"Yeah," Alex muttered before holding out the jacket. "She asked me to get this back to you."

Lance looked down at the jacket for a long moment before he reached out and took it from her. "Thanks."

"You're welcome." Alex swallowed as Lance turned and tossed the jacket on his bed. "Look, Lance, this wasn't your fault."

"Yeah, it is... Jenny and Arthur were happy, and I got in the way of that."

"No, you didn't," Alex protested, shaking her head. "This thing between you and Jenny... well, it's happened before, and you had no control over the fact that you used to be..."

"Freaking Lancelot."

"Well, that wasn't his name... but yeah," Alex flinched at her own words, she wasn't doing this very well. "Look, no one blames the two of you so please don't beat yourself up."

"Jenny won't talk to me." Lance slumped against the doorway. "Kept crying when I tried to see her about not knowing if she had any real feelings for me and won't pick up her phone."

"Just give her time," Alex urged.

"And then what?" Lance demanded, his voice taking on an angry edge. "What happens next in this story?"

"I don't know. Arthur lived this time; that's never happened before." Alex paused and considered her next words carefully. "I think that means that nothing has to happen. What comes next isn't following a script so you and Jenny can do anything. Be together or not, it's up to you."

Lance stared at her, his eyes shining with a hint of clarity as her words cut through the grief and alcohol. He nodded slowly and straightened back up. "Thanks," he said in a clearer voice as he nodded. "I'll try, can't promise anything, but I'll try to... I don't even know what yet, but I'll try."

"Thank you. And give Jenny time, this has always been hard on her even before she knew…" Alex shook her head and trailed off. "Well take care, I'll see you around."

"Alex," Lance called as she began to turn away. He hesitated and rubbed his head nervously. "Please be there for Arthur; this sucks for him too."

"Of course, I'll be there; he's my friend."

Lance laughed a sad and rough sound. "Look, Alex, half the time I was able to justify cheating with Jenny because of you and Arthur, I told myself that in the long term it was probably going to be the two of you together, so Jenny and I didn't matter so much." He shook his head again and stepped fully back into the room. "So, like I said, just… be there for him okay and Jenny if she needs you."

"I promise," Alex managed to say with a firm nod, her stomach fluttering uncomfortably.

The door of room 221 closed a moment later, and Alex was able to breathe again. Turning quickly, she rushed down the corridor to the elevator. She stepped inside the elevator, noting she was alone and hit the button before leaning her head back against the wall. A few moments later the doors dinged and opened for her. Stepping out, Alex pulled out her new key and headed for Nicki's room, wondering if her new roommate would let her ignore everything that was happening around them for a few hours and get some homework done.

30

March of Warriors

8 07 B.C.E. Northern Cornwall

Arto straightened up as Eigyr stepped closer to him, her small hands rising to the clasp of his cloak. He was silent as his mother carefully straightened the pin and tightened the cloth to adjust the fall of the cloak over his shoulders. Swallowing thickly, Arto studied her face carefully. This was one of the first days that she'd woken up without red eyes and he was optimistic that her time of deep grief for Uthyrn was beginning to pass.

"Your father would be so proud of you," she said softly, her voice sad and happy at the same time. "I am so grateful that he was able to see you again." Eigyr stopped fussing with his cloak but left her hands resting on his shoulders as she looked up at her son. "Losing you, even to the protection of Merlin, was one of the most painful things in our lives. He sent messages, of course, assuring us that you were alive and healthy, but it was not the same as raising your child, as holding them." She sighed and shook her head sadly, her hands falling off his shoulders to her sides. "There is a part of me that will never forgive him for that. Yet another part of me has been grateful to Merlin for keeping you safe ever since I caught a glimpse of those horrible creatures that killed your father."

"I miss Father too," Arto offered gently.

Eigyr gave him a watery smile and shook her head. "Oh, my son, you miss the idea of your Father. I fear that you did not have the chance to get to know him."

"Morgana speaks fondly of him," Arto told her quickly. "And the others speak so highly of him."

"Uthyrn made such an effort for your sister," Eigyr agreed with a wistful smile. "She resented him at first, disliked him for trying to take Kenwyn's place." Eigyr brushed a bit of dust that may or may not have been there from Arto's cloak. "And he made sure to give her a choice in her suitors. Of course, he favored Airril, a young man only a little older than her with strong links to copper mining." Eigyr chuckled and added, "But he did make sure that Morgana knew he wouldn't force her. All things considered; he was a good father to the child we still had."

Arto swallowed again, bile threatening to rise in his throat. There was just so much that she didn't know. His sister had long been a Changeling and human fusion, something that had new meaning to him now that Morgana had confessed the nature of the Changelings. Yet her mother suspected nothing, did not realize just how much the Sídhe had taken from her. Had they not.... Arto stopped the train of thought; it would do no good to get so angry. Rage had some power, but it was quick to exhaust. Calm, clarity, and control offered him a better source of power for what he needed to do today.

"I am sorry that things have turned out this way, Mother," Arto whispered to her, leaning forward, and kissing her forehead. "I truly am."

"Such is our story," Eigyr sighed sadly before a smile tugged at the corners of her lips. "But then again, there may be some good news on the horizon."

"Beyond stopping the Sídhe?" Arto asked with a raised eyebrow and doubtful expression.

"You have been seeing a great deal of Gwenyvar, my son," Eigyr teased gently. "Her father makes no secret of his hopes for that friendship."

Arto could feel the blood rush to his cheeks and had a strong strange desire to deny everything and scamper away. A musical laugh escaped his mother, a sound he had never heard from her before, and it rooted him to the spot.

"Oh, Arto." Eigyr laughed with a widening smile. "I like the girl. She is very sweet. I have no objections if when you are a conquering hero, you pursue the girl."

"This war may take some time, Mother," Arto reminded her quickly. "Today... today is the first step. We're testing the Iron Gate today, if it works then, it will give us a clear path, but if it does not..."

"It will work," Eigyr said firmly, reaching down and squeezing her son's hand. "It will and if you wish to distract me from Gwenyvar then I will let the subject drop... for now." Eigyr chuckled warmly. "After all, Morgana and Airril are finally living as husband and wife once again. I may have a grandchild soon."

Arto barely contained a flinch: his instinct was that it could never happen. Morgana's combined nature did not seem designed to grant human life, but he stayed silent. Leaning forward once again he kissed his mother's cheek and gave her a wide smile. His bag and Cathanáil were by the doorway waiting for him. In one smooth movement, he slung the bag over his shoulder and secured Cathanáil on his back.

Stepping outside, Arto glared up at the sky where thick dark clouds churned ominously. There had been some debate over marching to the tunnel with the potential of a storm, but in the end, no one had wanted to wait. Months of work had gone into this, tracking down the tunnel, holding off the Sídhe as they attempted to sabotage the effort to make iron and all the blacksmithing that had gone into arming warriors with iron weapons.

Yet the sky gave Arto pause. He knew that the Sídhe normally only came out at night due to their sensitivity to light, but with the sun buried so deep in clouds it seemed like a day when the Sídhe could easily muster a defense. Arto forced himself to step away from the roundhouse and move down the hill towards the assembled warriors who had volunteered.

Arto stood to the side in the shadow of a roundhouse, watching the others greet each other and talk. His eyes soon found Morgana and Airril standing off to the side, their heads leaning in close to each other and talking in low voices. Airril was holding his sister's hand gently, and a small smile graced his sister's features. Despite the worry and nerves churning inside of him, Arto couldn't help but smile at the sight. A sword was strapped to Airril's back, but he made no move to join the others.

"Good morning, cousin," a calm and cheerful voice greeted him.

Arto turned and forced a smile as Medraut walked up and joined him. "Good morning, Medraut," Arto greeted as calmly as he could manage.

"How are you?" Medraut asked in a lower voice as he studied Arto's face. "Nervous?"

"A bit and I'm worried about the village," Arto admitted. "The weather means that the Sídhe may ride, if we miss them then they could come here..."

"Don't worry," Medraut told him quickly, clapping a hand on his shoulder near Cathanáil. "That was discussed last night; Merlin had the same worry, and Airril agreed to stay here with a few warriors. All armed with iron, of course, they'll keep everyone safe."

"And will you remain?" Arto questioned as he turned to look at Medraut, noting the iron sword strapped to his cousin's back and the dagger fixed to his belt.

"No, while I do have a duty to the village you are my kin. I'll stay near you," Medraut informed him solemnly. "Besides, I'm not the leader of the village yet. With so many coming and going and following you and Merlin's orders, there's not much for me to worry about." Flinching slightly, Arto gave his cousin an apologetic look, but Medraut just laughed. "Oh, don't worry so much, Arto, this will pass in time."

Medraut looked around and grinned, gesturing across the village. Arto followed his cousin's hand and blushed when he spotted Gwenyvar wandering through the crowd, glancing around curiously.

"She's looking for you I'll wager," Medraut said with a grin. "To wish you luck, of course." His cousin leaned closer to him and whispered. "If I was going to be jealous of your life, cousin, it wouldn't be your magic or authority in this damn war."

Arto blushed, and Medraut chuckled loudly, squeezing his shoulder again. Gathering his courage, Arto tried to think of something to say to Gwenyvar, but his mother's gentle teasing and the recent remarks about them throughout the village made him nervous. Then Merlin stepped forward, and Morgana kissed Airril's cheek before moving to join the older man. Arto straightened up and stepped forward, moving out of the shadows and into view. Merlin caught his gaze and gave him a small nod.

"Good morning," Merlin greeted loudly, his voice rolling over the village causing everyone to fall silent. "Today we march to the latest Sídhe tunnel in the hills. This tunnel was cut into our world only days ago, but already the Sídhe have used it to attack nearby villages." There were murmurs of anger throughout the crowd. "As many of you know, we have been smelting and smithing iron to arm the men of our land to ensure that they have a fighting chance against the Sídhe, but this work has had another purpose. Myself, Arto, and Morgana are the mages of our realm, and we have been infusing some of the iron with our magic. We intend to use the power of the realm and the power of iron together against the Sídhe. The warriors who accompany us do so as we do not know what defense the Sídhe may muster."

Merlin gave Arto a significant glance, a silent instruction that he obeyed. Stepping forward, Arto swallowed thickly and tried to look confident. "I thank those who have volunteered to accompany us to the Sídhe tunnel," he announced, surprised at how clear and calm his voice sounded. "I also thank those who will remain to protect the village in light of the weather. As Merlin said, we do not know how the attempt to seal a tunnel rather than destroy it will go. It might be successful; it might fail, but I am grateful for the work and determination that all of you have shown in trying this plan. With the help of the ancestors, may this day be the first day of a new age."

There was a cheer from the crowd that threatened to overwhelm Arto. Iron swords, iron spearheads, and axes with iron heads were lifted into the air as the voices surged into one. Instead of noticing, however, Arto's eyes found Gwenyvar's soft brown ones as the small young woman maneuvered through the crowd.

"Let us depart!" Merlin shouted over the din. He and Morgana circled around the group and side by side began to march towards the gates of the village.

It only took a moment for the first warriors to begin following them, slipping into a two-by-two formation as they followed the well-worn path of the village. A dozen men followed Merlin and Morgana towards the gates, while another ten hung back, moving to stand near Airril as the man watched them go. Gwenyvar slipped out of the crowd and rushed up the hill to Arto. Her eyes moved over to Medraut who coughed lightly and began to move down the hill towards the departing warriors.

"Good luck," Gwenyvar told Arto. "Please try to stay safe."

"I will," Arto promised quickly. "You stay safe too." Arto paused, trying to think of something else to say. "Uh, if you don't need to stay with your father could you please look in on my mother today?" He heard himself ask in a rush, wondering what had possessed him to ask such a thing.

Gwenyvar smiled and nodded quickly. "Of course," she promised eagerly. "With both you and your sister going she must be very worried." Arto flinched guiltily, and Gwenyvar grimaced with an apologetic look. "I'll look after her," Gwenyvar promised. "I won't overwhelm her of course, but I'll make sure that she isn't alone."

"Thank you," Arto told her gratefully.

"Cousin!" Medraut yelled. "Come on; we'll have to run as it is!"

"Coming!" Arto called back, reaching up to adjust his bag.

Already the weight of the iron that he was carrying was becoming an irritation, and he felt a moment of gratitude that Merlin, Morgana, and himself had divided it up between them. He stepped forward, moving past Gwenyvar, but she suddenly leaned forward, gripped his chin, and turned his face towards her. She kissed him on the lips. Softly and it was over in a moment, but Arto stood stunned in front of her. Without meaning to, he grinned at her and Gwenyvar smiled back at him even as a pretty blush appeared on her cheeks. There were soft snickers from the crowd. Then a hand gripped his arm and tugged sharply. Arto nearly stumbled down the hill as Medraut pulled him along behind him.

"Come on then," Medraut huffed, shaking his head. "We have to run now if we want to catch the others. Merlin and Morgana surely thought you were right behind them!"

"I was right behind them," Arto managed to retort, glancing back over his shoulder.

He just caught sight of Gwenyvar waving to him before his view of her was blocked by a roundhouse. Sighing loudly, he shook his head and looked forward. Indeed, the line of warriors was already leaving through the gate. He ignored the smirk on Medraut's face and began to jog, not run with the weight of the iron on his back, but managed a respectable pace. Just beyond the gate, they caught up with the others, falling into step as the new back row and Medraut chuckling next to him.

"Well, cousin, I think we can all agree that you're probably going to marry the girl now," Medraut teased with a widening smile. "But if you please, focus on the Sídhe and not the girl."

Arto wanted to say something witty and clever to Medraut, but he couldn't quite bring himself to be irritated with his cousin. His lips were still curled up in a smile, and his body was tingling pleasantly. He wondered if he should be more surprised by her action, but he wasn't. A roll of thunder overhead made Arto look up and glare at the sky. He was left wondering once again if this was a good idea. Sighing, he returned his attention to the marching warriors and shook his head. Arto breathed slowly, reminding himself to stay calm and focused as the long troop of people moved over the hills. While Gwenyvar's face kept trying to invade his thoughts, Arto managed to keep his eyes scanning the horizon.

His bag clanged at his back, knocking against his hip as he walked. The weight of several iron pieces was both comforting and nerve-racking. He'd been pouring his magic into small bits of iron for weeks to practice and prepare the magic-infused iron needed to make the plan work. But now doubts were seeping in: what if it didn't work, what if all they did was block one tunnel? What if the magic in the iron wasn't enough to protect the area? He knew that they'd made no promises, but if this didn't work then were they doomed to a never-ending war. There seemed to be no end to the Sídhe. Morgana said that they had whole worlds filled with their warriors and slaves. Could they ever truly drive them back? The pleasant tingle in his body from Gwenyvar's kiss was long gone now as nervous and fearful energy began to take its place. His skin itched, and he felt too hot even with the cool breeze and lack of sunlight.

He took another slow breath, focusing on the feel of his lungs expanding and his shoulders relaxing. Around him, energy hissed in the air, and Arto felt it dance across his skin. It was raw power, but he couldn't grab onto it. On such an important day, he wished that he could reach out and grab hold of the lightning, take control of the hum in the air, and use it. Lightning flashed across the sky above them, and the scent of the energy only heightened in the air. But he still couldn't use it.

Shaking his head, Arto forced his thoughts away from magic and glanced over the men who were marching with him. As they turned around the slope of the hill and began to move out their two-by-two formation, Arto caught sight of Merlin and Morgana talking with a rough looking warrior sent by Eaban last week. Arto had yet to see the man fight, but the way he'd swung around his axe when the blacksmith had fixed the new iron axe head to it gave him a healthy respect for the man. Just ahead of him and Medraut were a pair of men from the northland, though different areas and one much taller than the other. They were laughing loudly, their full belly laughs filling the air.

"Nice to see some confidence," Medraut said with a smirk as he nodded towards the pair ahead of them. "Even if their laughing is a bit grating."

"It may help calm the others," Arto offered as he glanced towards his cousin.

"Maybe, but it makes me want to turn around and go back home to be away from the noise."

Shaking his head at his cousin, Arto turned away to hide the slight smile that was growing on his face. The dozen or so people were spreading out more, and more so Arto began to walk a little faster, wanting to be closer to Morgana and Merlin. He was aware of Medraut speeding up and following him up the procession of warriors. As they reached the top of the hill, Arto was a little winded, but much nearer to his sister. The group halted, and Arto moved forward around a large burly man and stopped next to his sister.

Below them was a sloping valley between a few low hills. It wasn't the best terrain, but manageable. But down below on the far side of the valley, Arto could see a dark hole cut into the side of the hill. Glancing towards his sister, Arto blinked in alarm as he noticed her frown.

"Morgana?" he asked carefully.

"There are tracks from horses on the hills," Merlin said calmly. "They may be from before."

"Or the Sídhe may already be out," Morgana replied cautiously, her hand moving down to the iron dagger on her belt. "We must proceed carefully. I doubt that we have the element of surprise."

Nodding his understanding, Arto turned and told the man behind them who had been listening to pass word back.

"Arto stay near us, so you have access to the iron," Merlin ordered quickly. "We can't hesitate."

"Yes sir," Arto answered automatically with a nod.

Carefully they began to descend the hill. Above their heads, the dark clouds rumbled with thunder, and a flash of lightning on the horizon made Arto squirm. A moment later the blare of a Sídhe horn echoed through the small valley making Arto look up at the dark sky.

"Perfect," he groaned as he reached back and drew Cathanáil. "Just perfect."

31

Monday

Sunday night was restless for Alex. The new bed was too soft, the pillows weren't quite right, and she was using spare sheets and blankets. Her thoughts about Jenny, Lance, and Arthur wouldn't leave her alone for more than a few minutes at a time during the day, and once the lights were out, there was no escape. She tossed and turned, occasionally drifting off only to wake up from nightmares of a screaming Jenny, a shouting Lance, and a laughing Arthur. Her skin crawled, and she shivered after each dream, pulling the blankets tighter around her and clutching Galahad closer. Soft snores from the other side of the room indicated that at least Nicki was sleeping and were the only reason she didn't climb out of bed and pace. The dreams didn't last long; sometimes Aiden, Bran, and Nicki were there too and sometimes they weren't. Sometimes Morgana and Merlin were trying to tell her something, but she couldn't hear them.

Now she was dreaming of the Sídhe tunnels, of the perfectly fitted white stones in the deepest area of the tunnels, far outside the safety of the Iron Realm. Musical voices of the Sídhe were talking nearby but soon turned to cackling laughs that filled her with dread. She turned and ran down the tunnels as fast as she could away from the voices. There was crying; it sounded like Jenny and echoed down the tunnels. Then someone was calling her name.

A hand was tapping at her cheek, and the tunnels faded around her. There was a moment of vertigo and Alex couldn't think straight. Her eyes opened only to slam shut as bright light beamed down overhead. After a moment she slowly opened her eyes again.

"Alex," Nicki called softly. "Alex, sweetie, I've got to go to class. The boys are going to meet you for breakfast downstairs at 9:45 and walk you to class."

Opening her eyes, Alex blinked several times before Nicki's face came into focus. Her friend smiled warmly at her.

"Sorry, Alex, but you'll feel better if you get up and aren't rushed."

"Yeah, yeah," Alex groaned as she began to sit up. "I'm up."

Nicki was already dressed for the day in jeans and a simple t-shirt, her red hair in a long neat plait that Alex couldn't imagine how she managed on her own. A travel mug was sitting on the desk, and Nicki's bag was already slung over her shoulder.

"How are you feeling?" Nicki turned and picked up her mug. "Were you at least able to get some sleep?"

"I'm okay." Alex slowly sat up and moved her shoulders carefully. "I... had a lot of nightmares, though."

Nicki turned back to Alex with a thoughtful frown and stepped closer to her. "Do you think they mean something?"

"Yeah, I think they mean I got thrown around by the Sídhe and my relationships are almost all in tatters," Alex grumbled, not looking at Nicki. Instead, she picked up Galahad and stroked the stuffed toy's fur for a moment before setting him on a small pillow. "I'll probably sleep better if I get my bedding and stuff for tonight."

"Okay," Nicki agreed slowly, still frowning. "We'll get it later today then. Slowly move your stuff out. How's that?"

"Sounds like a plan." Alex raised her hand and rubbed her eyes. "So, you said something about breakfast?"

"The boys will meet you downstairs at the main cafeteria doors at 9:45." Nicki raised her mug in a toast to Alex before she turned to the doorway. "Have a good morning, try to eat a decent breakfast, and I'll see you in class."

"Okay," Alex muttered. She lowered her feet down to the plush carpet that Nicki had in the room, curling her toes slightly into the fabric.

"Remember breakfast 9:45 downstairs," Nicki called over her shoulder as she went out the door.

"Yes, Mother."

Alex sighed, but she smiled slightly. At least her friends were trying to look after her and make sure that they all made it through this drama in one piece. Alex sat on the edge of the bed, lost in thought for several minutes before she inhaled deeply and stood up. Her back muscles ached at the movement, but as she stood still and gently rolled her shoulders, there was no horrible burst of pain which Alex took as a good sign. Shaking her head, Alex told herself to get moving, grabbed her robe and headed off to shower. By the time she was done and dressed, Alex had to rush downstairs with damp hair and was still late meeting the boys.

"Morning," a tired-looking Bran greeted from his place leaning against the wall. Aiden stepped forward with a smile and hugged Alex quickly.

"It's great to see you up," Aiden said warmly.

"You had us pretty worried," Bran agreed. "Even with Morgana insisting you'd be alright."

"I was just really tired and sore," Alex assured them. "Still am, but I'll be fine."

"Still, I hope this isn't going to become a habit." Aiden pulled open the main door and held it open as a group of girls came out.

"You know what, I thought the exact same thing yesterday when I woke up at Morgana's," Alex told him with a chuckle as she walked into the cafeteria.

They split up for a few minutes, each collecting their own desired breakfast. Bran preferred oatmeal with berries and a muffin as breakfast while Alex and Aiden tended towards the omelet bar. As they waited for their main course side by side, Aiden thankfully didn't ask Alex any questions and seemed far more relaxed than she was. Breathing slowly, Alex allowed Aiden to take her book bag due to her sore back.

After gathering their respective breakfasts, they found a table in the corner away from any other students. Alex informed them that she'd seen Jenny and Lance both briefly on Sunday and that while neither was doing well, they were both coping in their own ways. Bran gave her a sympathetic look but said nothing else on the subject.

Aiden visibly flinched and shook his head. "Man, I pity those two," he said sadly. "I hope they're able to make peace with it, but how do you approach something like that."

"I don't know," Alex replied weakly, forcing herself to take another bite of her omelet even if it didn't taste nearly as good as it had before.

"They'll just have to find their way," Bran offered with a glance towards Alex. "And I hate to say it but even if they don't then maybe what happened on Friday will mean that they won't reincarnate anymore."

"You think the cycle might be broken?" Aiden asked with a frown, giving Bran an intense look. "Arthur may not have died, but their actions had no impact on that."

"So, you think they'll reincarnate until they change things themselves?"

"Well, no, not exactly anyway," Aiden told him, shaking his head. "But that wouldn't make sense if they always repeat the same action.

People can't learn if they don't remember the lesson. Forcing them to reincarnate like that would be cruel."

"But we don't even know why they reincarnate," Bran said as Alex turned her attention to pouring a glass of milk into her bowl of cereal. "Is it something they accidentally triggered in their grief or guilt, is it something done by the Sídhe or something else, or is the magic of the Iron Realm causing it? The reason it happened in the first place is important to the answer of how to stop the cycle."

"But maybe they can break it this time by admitting their guilt and recognizing the near consequences," Aiden argued in a low voice.

"We lack the data needed to resolve this," Bran said, holding up his hand. "We can debate it, but honestly that is probably in bad taste given what all three of them are going through."

Aiden sighed, slumping back in his chair, but he nodded in agreement. Looking back at Alex while he buttered a piece of toast, he asked, "So did Morgana fill you in on our side of things Friday?"

"No, she didn't," Alex replied as she raised a spoon of cereal to her mouth.

"We tried to set up a perimeter," he explained in a low voice. "We actually held it for a while, blasting the Sídhe as they came out. Morgana and Merlin did most of it of course, but we helped. But then there was this big wave of them, almost all Riders and only a few Hounds. One of them blasted Morgana in the chest; she barely rolled out of the way before the horse crushed her."

"That wasn't long before you got there, we think," Bran clarified. "After that several of them got through, Morgana and Merlin stayed near the tunnel while the rest of us scattered trying to catch them."

"Which is not an easy feat when they are on horses, and you're on foot," Aiden added with a smile, but Alex only shook her head.

"Sorry you had to fight them again," Bran said softly. "We were hoping to let you have an easier night."

"We're all in this together," Alex replied quickly, dropping her eyes. "I'll be okay, and Arthur is alright, things could have gone a lot worse."

She looked up in time to see the boys exchange a meaningful glance and Bran nod quickly. "We're meeting at 4 PM at Merlin's house." Bran watched Alex's face. "Arthur too: he's been told, but now we have to plan for what comes next."

"Four o'clock... yeah okay," Alex agreed with a nod.

"How about we head over together," Aiden offered. "Arthur is going by himself, but the four of us could go together."

"Well, I can't drive safely right now," Alex reminded him, "So that's fine for me."

There was a hint of tension in the air, and Aiden kept glancing at Bran who shook his head which made Aiden sigh. If she'd had more energy, Alex would have asked what was going on, but couldn't bring herself to care at the moment. Instead, they finished breakfast and the boys, despite her protests, escorted Alex to her first class of the day, The Epic, where they found Nicki waiting patiently at the door.

"Did she eat?" Nicki asked Aiden as she accepted Alex's bag from him.

"A bit," Aiden told her with a nod. "We'll see you both later, Alex; take care."

"I'm fine," Alex muttered darkly, but quietly, mindful of the students around them.

"We're your friends." Bran completely ignored her glare. "Indulge us."

Sighing loudly, Alex nodded and lingered by the doorway, waiting for Nicki. Aiden gave her a big smile and nodded. He turned and began to walk back down the hallway, chatting with Bran. Then he waved to Alex over his shoulder. Shaking her head, Alex silently accepted that she was going to have babysitters all day.

"I hate it when he does that," Alex muttered, trying to reach for her bag.

"I got it," Nicki told her firmly. "Now come on, Professor Yates dislikes tardiness."

Deciding not to argue Alex headed into the classroom and took a seat near the door. She flinched slightly at the poorly padded chair and confined space, but managed to settle into a reasonable position. From the front of the room, Merlin looked over at her with a worried expression. Forcing a smile, Alex shook her head a tiny bit to tell him that she was alright. When class started Merlin launched into his lecture, and Alex did her best to pay attention while the professor glanced at her throughout class.

"Don't worry," Nicki whispered. "I'll share my notes."

Nodding, Alex straightened up in the desk chair, forcing herself to exhale. It took some doing, but she was finally able to settle and relax a little. Of course, she barely noticed anything that Professor Yates talked about, but she was there and trying. And for a Monday morning after fighting the Sídhe, Alex figured that was good enough.

But after two classes and lunch, Alex's back couldn't take any more of the uncomfortable plastic and metal backed school chairs or having to sit in an uncomfortable position for nearly an hour. The pain pills, as promised, kept the edge off, and Alex was fine when she was standing and even moving, but she couldn't take another desk. At her insistence lunch was sandwiches from the commons and eaten out under a tree where Alex could stretch out and relax.

Then they'd gone to World Mythologies, and Alex was faced with a lecture style room and desks that were just too small for anything but sitting slumped over notes. Professor Weaver must have had a hard weekend too; today she was yawning and lacked all energy. Alex kept dozing off and waking up when her head began to fall forward. If her back hadn't been sore, she would have leaned forward and at least rested on the tiny half desk that folded up from her chair.

Needless to say, it didn't take much for Nicki to convince Alex to skip her Spanish class in favor of taking a nap before the mage meeting. A tiny part of Alex regretted not going since Arthur might be in class and worry that she was avoiding him, but another part of her was too worried that Lance would be in class. After agreeing with Nicki, Alex was promptly escorted back to the dorm room in Michaels Hall and ordered into bed. Pulling off her shoes, Alex didn't bother to change. Instead, she just emptied her pockets and tossed her bag on the desk before collapsing back on the bed.

"I'm going to steal your keys and go get your bedding," Nicki announced walking past Alex to retrieve her bag.

"Okay," Alex mumbled as she snuggled down into the blankets and wiggled her toes cheerfully. For a bed that hadn't been that comfortable last night, it suddenly felt wonderful.

There was a laugh from the doorway, and then the lights were off leaving Alex in a nice dim room before the door closed. Silently, Alex promised herself that she'd figure out a way to get back at Nicki. Or she'd thank her, one of the two. Sighing deeply, Alex closed her eyes and focused on her breathing. She was asleep by the time Nicki returned with her bedding fifteen minutes later and gently laid her comforter over her. This time there were no dreams.

32

Gathering of Mages

Climbing out of Aiden's truck, Alex gently stretched her back muscles and shoulders as her eyes swept over the house quickly. Everything seemed to be in order, but there was an undercurrent of tension and nervousness in the air between herself and her fellow mages. Standing in the gravel driveway, they glanced at each other. All their eyes expressed the same hesitation, and no one moved. Then a giggle escaped Nicki causing the others to look at her in surprise. Aiden cracked a smile followed by Alex who barely contained a snort at their behavior.

"Ah, right on time!" Merlin's voice called. They all turned quickly to see him coming through the iron gate in the hedge that separated the front yard and driveway from the back. He was beaming at them and said nothing about their delay. Instead, Merlin nodded to all of them, but walked up to Alex. "How are you feeling?"

"Sore and I didn't sleep very well last night," Alex admitted before she forced a smile. "But I'll live."

"Well, that is a relief: we're going to be in the back on the patio. Alex, please go and sit down. If you need any additional pillows or padding just let me know."

Touched by Merlin's concern, Alex gave him a real smile and nodded. He beamed at her in return and gestured them towards the side of the house. Following the others, Alex walked through the waist-high gateway. Paving stones created a small path that led to an elegant patio set of wrought iron furniture. The chairs had back, and seat cushions of a pale sky-blue color and Alex sat down in one of them tenderly, noting with pleasure that it provided good support while also being soft on her back.

Settling back in the chair, Alex relaxed and looked up at the clouds overhead. There was a soft breeze, gently pushing the lower clouds and stretching them into new shapes. Around her, she heard the others puttering and Morgana calling Aiden and Nicki inside to help with refreshments. Bran made a comment about afternoon tea which Merlin laughed at before Morgana informed Bran that she had in fact lived in England when afternoon tea became popular and that the idea of a light late afternoon snack was a completely valid one. Alex chuckled softly at the remark and then focused on the sounds of Nicki and Aiden in the house and Merlin humming to himself as he brought another chair out of the house. For a moment it was easy to forget the insanity of her life and the very strange conversation they were about to have.

"Arthur is late," Morgana said a few moments later. Her words were accompanied by the soft clink of a plate being set on the wrought iron table.

Alex opened her eyes and looked at her professor. "I'm sure it's just a delay in getting out of class. Three thirty and the parking lot gets a bit crazy."

"He's also never been here before," Merlin reminded Morgana with a calm smile as he sat down in his chair.

"We should have picked him up," Morgana muttered, a hint of nervousness in her voice. "Too much could go wrong."

"We cannot keep the boy under lock and key." Merlin poured himself a glass of iced tea and selected a tuna sandwich from the tray. "Need I remind you of how much some of his incarnations have chafed at the very idea."

Morgana stopped, glanced at Merlin, and nodded before she elegantly eased into her chair. "How are you feeling, Alex?" Morgana asked, turning her attention towards Alex.

"A bit sore; I ended up skipping Spanish class," Alex admitted with a grimace. "Couldn't take sitting in a plastic chair another minute."

"Understandable," Merlin assured her. "Iced tea?"

"Please," Alex said. "But I'm afraid I didn't see Arthur yet today... we're in Spanish class together."

Morgana made a small displeased sound but said nothing. Then there was the sound of a car pulling up into the driveway that made everyone straighten up and fall silent. An engine cut off and a few moments later a car door slammed.

"Please excuse me," Merlin said as he rose from his chair gesturing to Morgana.

Alex caught sight of a flash of disappointment in Morgana's eyes, but the woman nodded in agreement and resettled in her chair, raising her tea to her lips and sipping. Bran and Alex exchanged a glance, and he shrugged slightly. It didn't take long for the sound of footfalls and the gate opening to make them all turn. Merlin waved to them as he stepped back into the yard with a pleased smile on his face, humming softly.

Arthur was right behind Merlin, coming through the wrought iron gate a moment later. His blue eyes darted about, glancing at everyone and Alex noticed his hand tighten on the strap of his backpack nervously. Everyone around the table was silent and still as Merlin escorted Arthur over, the only sounds were their footfalls against the paving stones and Merlin humming softly.

"Well now that everyone is here, shall we do more proper introductions," Merlin offered as he returned to his seat. "You know me, Professor Ambrose Yates or Merlin. Obviously please try to call me Professor Yates in public. I am the oldest mage of the Iron Realm, and I raised and trained your first incarnation. Since then, it has been my task to protect the Iron Realm and help the Iron Soul when needed."

"I am Professor Morgana Cornwall," Morgana said calmly, her green eyes uneasy as she looked at Arthur. "Like Merlin, I protect the Iron Realm and aid the Iron Soul. The first incarnation of the Iron Soul, a young warrior leader named Arto, was my half-brother leading to my loyalty to the cause and the Iron Soul."

"Uh... pleased to meet you, Morgana," Arthur replied nervously. "Thank you for taking care of Alex the other night. I'm sorry we didn't have a chance to talk."

Morgana nodded, her shoulders relaxing a tiny bit. Merlin nodded, clearly pleased, and gestured towards Alex.

"Of course, you already know Alex." Merlin paused for a moment. "The other night, Beltane, was one of the nights when the Sídhe are at their strongest in our world and thus why we asked Alex to watch over you. I can assure you that when you two first became friends, she was not aware of your identity."

Arthur looked over at Alex and gave her a small forced smile. "I don't think I thanked you for the other night so thanks."

"You're welcome," Alex managed to say with a forced smile of her own.

"Uh, when I first met Alex... I thought I saw something...."

"Did you?" Merlin asked, sounding very pleased. "What did you see?"

"Lightning: I remember there was lightning."

"Alex had a similar experience when she met you. It is known as a Connection, and it occurs when people with magic meet."

"But..." Arthur frowned and gestured at Merlin and the others. "There wasn't anything like that when we met."

"The magic of the Iron Soul often manifests later and does not always register in the same way," Morgana explained calmly. "We don't know why Alex experienced a Connection with you, but her magic takes a rather distinct and powerful form as energy control. That might have triggered your magic for a moment."

"Or perhaps the two of you just have a more powerful connection," Merlin offered with a grin that made Alex want to kick him. Nicki must have caught the look because she used her position next to Merlin to kick the man's shin lightly making Morgana chuckle.

"In any case, it isn't anything you need to worry about," Morgana informed Arthur with a reassuring smile. "Moving on, I know that you have met through Alex, but the rest of you, please introduce yourselves."

"I'm Nicki Russell, my magic tends to manifest as ice, but I've used healing magic in the past, and I'm starting to experiment with my magic in other ways now," Nicki said in a rush with a big smile. "Just yesterday I was able to remove a spot from my jeans using magic."

"Really?" Merlin asked as a big smile broke out over his face. "Well done, it is always a big step when a mage begins to train their magic to operate in new avenues."

"My name is Aiden Bosco," Aiden greeted with a small wave. "My magic takes the form of fire meaning that I practice with Nicki a lot. I haven't started experimenting, but it sounds like a potential summer project."

"And I'm Brandon Fisher, I go by Bran, and my magic is usually telekinesis, but sometimes I get... well for lack of a better word visions."

"You can see the future?" Arthur asked with a hint of excitement and nervousness in his voice.

"No, not really, not usually anyway." Bran reached up and brushed a stubborn strand of brown hair out of his face. "I have dreams mostly, and they're not clear."

"Speaking of which," Merlin interjected. "I didn't ask the other night due to Arthur's presence, but what did you see."

Alex's eyes widened at the news that Bran had a vision after fighting the Sídhe. He looked exhausted; she noted as she turned to look at him. Alex felt guilty for not noticing it sooner. Bran glanced at her and gave Alex a tiny smile before he turned his attention back to Merlin. It was chilling to hear about his vision: Alex wasn't sure which sounded worse, the great monster in the darkness or someone stabbing him with a sword. In the corner of her eye, she saw Arthur frown deeply at the description of the stabbing.

"Thank you," Merlin said when Bran had finished. "I'm afraid that I am not sure what the stabbing might mean, but I believe that we can shed some light on the dark monster."

"We've told all of you in the past that some beings that enter our world manage to stay and that some of them over time become known as deities in human mythology. We call these the Old Ones," Morgana explained. She paused to take another breath and considered her next words for a moment. "These beings in many cases sleep for hundreds and even thousands of years when magic is not as strong. However, the invasion of the Sídhe has greatly increased the levels of magic in the world and begun waking some of the Old Ones."

"Are they friend or foe?" Aiden asked seriously, a look of intense concentration on his face.

"It varies greatly," Merlin informed him. "Living in our world too long causes many of these beings to go insane and turn very violent. Over the past three thousand years, we have helped fight several such Old Ones. Others like my mentor Cyrridven spend a great deal of time in water to hold off the negative effects of our world."

Aiden and Nicki exchanged a look, both of them fighting back what looked like guilty smiles. Alex figured that they were mentally referencing something, but didn't have the energy for that today.

"Some Old Ones are our allies, but others, as they wake, will travel to Ravenslake to search out the epicenter of magic, usually to consume that power," Morgana added darkly.

Alex's mouth dropped open, and she shuddered, suddenly feeling chilled. Bran reached over and placed a hand on her shoulder from her left and from her right Arthur's hand was suddenly squeezing her hand. Turning her hand slightly, Alex returned the gestured and forced herself to take a deep breath and focus on the conversation.

"Old Ones take time to wake," Morgana was explaining to Nicki. "We probably have a few more months before any will have achieved full consciousness."

"We already knew that many of the Old Ones, both our allies and old enemies, were beginning to wake up," Merlin said sternly, drawing everyone's attention to him. "Bran's vision confirms that we will no doubt be facing them soon, which means that we must address the Sídhe."

"How can we fight both at once?" Arthur asked weakly. "I mean I've seen Alex fight, but I don't know how and those aren't good odds."

"We were hoping that you could make arrangements to remain in Ravenslake over the summer," Morgana admitted to Arthur. "The powers of the Iron Soul while always holding a talent over iron vary greatly, and you will need time to learn."

"Why didn't you just tell me before?" Arthur questioned. "I could have practiced with the others."

"The Sídhe might have found you: we could not protect all of you at once. Better to train the others so they could help to protect you before drawing attention to you," Merlin answered gently.

Arthur bit his lip as his jaw tightened and he raised a hand to mess his blond hair. He was tense and irritated, but a moment later he breathed out and nodded. "Okay," Arthur sighed. "So, the Sídhe are still a danger, I need training, and the Old Ones are coming. What do we do?"

"We need to create a new Iron Gate, sadly we do not have Cathanáil, uh Arthur, you know it as Excalibur," Merlin explained quickly with a reassuring smile for Arthur. "But between all of us and the Iron Soul, we should be able to make things more difficult for the Sídhe."

"Now we don't have much time, the next alignment day when the defense of the Iron Realm and our magic are at the peak is June 21st," Morgana informed them with a nod to Merlin. "We need to gather together with a suitable supply of iron and create a new iron gate."

"June 21st... alignment day," Arthur repeated before he shook his head. "That doesn't leave me much time to learn."

"I am confident that you are up to the task," Merlin replied kindly. "But will you be able to make arrangements to stay at least through the end of June?"

"Yeah, sure I think so," Arthur shrugged. "My mother won't be thrilled, but if I say it's for football, she'll calm down about it. After the 21st I could go home for a bit, right?"

"Of course," Morgana said quickly with a sharp look at Merlin. "We don't mean to keep you from your family, but the iron gates are our best defense, and the first Iron Soul was critical to their creation."

"Indeed, we are at a bit of a loss of how to proceed without your help," Merlin added with a sharp nod. "But don't worry, everyone here will help you, and we will add our magic to yours."

"From that standpoint, we have more magic than we did the first time," Morgana said with a rather forced smile.

"But not Excalibur," Arthur reminded them. "How can we get the Sword? Where is it?"

"Cathanáil was entrusted to Cyrridven, similar to how the legend suggests. She keeps the Sword beyond the hands of the Sídhe and other Old Ones underwater."

"And is she waking up with the other Old Ones?" Arthur's blue eyes glinted with determination and excitement. "Any chance she can get us the Sword?"

"I doubt she will wake completely in time to deliver the Sword before the 21st," Morgana informed Arthur with a hint of regret. "But keep in mind that once she does wake, she will be able to find and come to us quickly. Her greatest ability is water travel; she can move from one body of water to another. If you regain your Sword in the future, then there is nothing that would prevent us from making a new Iron Gate."

"Why is the Sword so important to the Iron Gates?" Alex asked with a frown. "I mean it was made by the Iron Soul, right?"

"Yes: Cathanáil was the creation of the Iron Soul, with some help of course," Merlin said with a grin and a glance towards Morgana who gave him a look. "When Arto made the Iron Gates, he directed his power through the Sword. As a result, we observed a strong connection with Cathanáil and the Iron Gates. It acts as a Key to the Iron Gates if you will; using the sword could potentially open them or lock them. We will be building a gate, but without the key, we lack a way to lock it."

"So, until we get the Sword nothing is permanent," Arthur sighed, messing his hair again and clenching his jaw.

"The gate will be vulnerable to attack," Morgana conceded, "But that doesn't mean that it won't still protect the Iron Realm. It won't last for three thousand years, but it will help."

"Merlin told me a bit about the Iron Gates in the British Isles," Arthur remarked after taking a deep breath. "He said that those are breaking apart; what will happen when those gates fall? How will it impact us?"

"I believe that we need to explain the gates in more detail," Merlin decided, lifting his palm.

Arthur straightened up with wide eyes, and Alex smiled as green sparks twisted around Merlin's hand. Smiling, the old mage opened his palm, and the sparks flew up into the air around them. Next to him, Morgana chuckled softly and waved her hand, sending a swirl of glittering silver magic up into the air. The two colors split with silver sparks forming one glowing sphere above their heads and Merlin's green sparks forming a second.

"Whoa," Arthur whispered, "That's something else."

"They like visuals," Nicki remarked with a grin.

"Imagine these are two worlds, very different from another," Merlin lectured calmly. "In order to travel from one to the other, the beings of a world have to focus their magic on building a bridge or in the case of the Sídhe a tunnel."

Morgana pointed her finger at the silver sphere, and a stream of silver sparks flowed into the air between the two spheres, creating a pathway between them. The magic collided with the green sphere sending off several little sparks.

"And, of course, when the different magic enters our world and brings with it the impressions of that very different world, ours reacts by creating its magic to defend it. Mages act as the Iron Realm's white blood cells and fight back the infection," Merlin told them, and Alex nodded her understanding.

"Now, over time the Sídhe invest more and more energy and power to create additional pathways," Morgana said, releasing more magic from the silver sphere causing several more lines of pale magic to appear and connect the two spheres.

"These multiple tunnels are pushing more and more foreign energy and power into our world," Merlin explained. "In fact, these pathways reinforce each other; they bleed energy into nearby tunnels. The more of them that are stable, than the less power the Sídhe must put into creating a tunnel. It is one of the reasons why in my youth there were tunnels everywhere throughout the British Islands."

"But why the British Islands?" Nicki suddenly asked. "Why didn't they go beyond there?"

"They tried on several occasions," Merlin replied calmly. "But the pathways form at weak points: we don't know why certain places are vulnerable at certain times, but they are. Three thousand years ago the British Isles were vulnerable; the defenses of the Iron Realm faltered, and the Sídhe gained a foothold. Today Oregon seems to be the weak point."

"Due to the power of the tunnels, the Sídhe could have expanded beyond the British Isles given enough time if a way to destroy the tunnels had not been found," Morgana added quickly. "But it takes a great deal of power to create a pathway. Once a pathway has been cut it is far easier to follow it than cut a new one which is why the tunnels keep reappearing for now in the same hillside. Eventually, the Sídhe will stop being lazy about it and will try to create a tunnel further away, but it must still be formed in the vulnerable area."

"So, what do the gates do?" Merlin asked with a wide smile. "Well...." He waved his hand and created a small burst of green magic which formed a line over one of the pathways, blocking the stream of silver magic. "Simply put the Iron Gates when infused with the magic of the Iron Soul block the flow of magic into our world. They are far more than a physical barrier over the tunnel. Over time the magic seeping from them destroys the tunnels and similar to how the tunnels reinforce each other, an Iron Gate reinforces the magical defenses of Earth."

"So, an Iron Gate closes the weakness of Earth's defenses?" Aiden asked with a grin. "How quickly?"

"Well, that is where having multiple gates comes in handy like we did three thousand years ago," Merlin remarked gesturing towards the small green swirl that was holding back one of the silver streams of magic.

Another green swirl appeared over another path, and Alex blinked in surprise as the magical glow from the two swirls began to fade together. Another swirl appeared followed by another, and sure enough, the magical glow surrounding them soon created a small field of green light just beyond the surface of the green sphere and blocking the flow of the silver light.

"That was how we won the war the first time," Morgana said with a smile as she waved her hand and the silver magical sparks dissolved into the air. "Over time by blocking the tunnels with Iron Gates, we gradually shielded the weak point in Earth's magic. That magic spread and created a protective field for the entire Iron Realm. Even when the Sídhe attempted to enter our world at a different point, they paid a heavy price for the attempt."

"At the time we didn't even fully realize that was what we were doing," Merlin chimed in with a laugh. "Most of the Old Ones came through a weak point that existed several thousand years ago. Thankfully the Sídhe hadn't noticed our world yet. These weak points do seem to close up over time as well as open naturally, hence the need for mages. Currently, the shield that was created with the Iron Gates three thousand years ago is fading, but it offers us some protection and is probably what is keeping the Sídhe from expanding all over Oregon."

"So, if we make this Iron Gate that will stop the Sídhe?" Arthur asked carefully. "It sounds like it will need more than one gate."

"Yes, it will," Merlin answered with a large smile. "But if we can get a gate in place, even if created without Cathanáil then our magic will weaken the Sídhe attempts to build stable tunnels and every time they do manage to build one, we can take it over and build a new Iron Gate."

"Make no mistake this is going to take some time," Morgana announced sternly. "Potentially several years, but it is doable with the group of mages that we have now."

Arthur nodded, taking a deep breath, and straightening up in his chair. "Okay, where do we start?"

Merlin grinned almost jumping from his seat. "That's the spirit, Arthur. You're going to be training with Morgana and I. The rest of you," he said turning his attention to them. "We're going to need magically touched iron and a lot of it."

"Great," Aiden sighed dramatically as he stood up from his chair. "Out of the fire and into the forge." He smiled and winked at Merlin before clapping his hands together. "Come on gang; we've got blacksmithing to do."

"You are way too excited about this," Nicki muttered as she stood up.

"We've got a Sídhe invasion to deal with, a magical force field to create, and Old Ones who will be hunting us down soon," Aiden snarked back with a roll of his eyes. "Forgive me if I'd prefer to stay positive."

Alex stood up slowly and heard Arthur chuckle next to her at the conversation between Nicki and Aiden. Turning to look at him, Alex's chest tightened when she met his bright blue eyes.

"Nice people," he said quietly. "I think..." he paused and chuckled again. "I think this is going to work out."

"Yeah?" Alex asked, smiling hopefully.

"Yeah," Arthur said with a nod. "I do."

"Come along, Arthur," Merlin called, eyeing the two of them with a big smile. "Lots to learn and the sooner, the better."

Arthur nodded, giving Alex an apologetic look before he moved across the yard to join Merlin. Alex watched them start talking for a moment, inhaled deeply and then turned towards the workshop. Morgana caught her eye as she moved to join Merlin and Arthur, offering her a soft smile which Alex returned. Maybe things really were going to be okay: sure, as Aiden pointed out they had a long way to go, but maybe things would turn out alright in the end.

33

The First Gate

8 07 B.C.E. Northern Cornwall

There was no hesitation around Arto as the sound of the horn faded. Suddenly swords were drawn, spears were ready, and axes were raised as the assembled warriors began to spread out. Another flash of lightning illuminated the far hill, and golden armor reflected the light. Three Riders stood waiting on the far hill and chuckles from behind Arto told him that the warriors expected no true battle. Then the Rider in the middle raised his hand, and an orb of light appeared. A howl ripped across the landscape followed by the high-pitched sound of a Sídhe horn. More Riders appeared on the crest of the hill. Doing a quick count of the enemies, Arto felt his stomach drop, and his limbs started to shake. Thirteen Riders were watching them, and then the Hounds appeared, one by each Rider. Howls and snarls echoed through the small shallow valley.

"Arto," Morgana breathed. "Stay with us."

Neither side moved, the Sídhe's strange mounts remaining perfectly still with the Hounds panting and snarling at their sides. Cathanáil hissed against its sheath as Arto drew it slowly and pushed a tiny bit of his magic into the blade. Next to him, Arto could see Morgana's silver magic spinning around her hands. Merlin raised his staff, the small carvings on it began to glow the soft green color of Merlin's magic, casting a pale light over Arto, Morgana, and the assembled warriors. Then the Sídhe moved as one, charging forward. Gleaming golden sparks gathered around them as all the Riders called forth their magic and the Hounds rushed ahead of their masters.

"They're giving up the high ground!" Came a shout of surprise behind him.

"Don't forget their magic!" Another voice countered sharply. "Hold your ground and watch them!"

Merlin said nothing through all of this. Arto turned and saw his mentor watching the Sídhe with sharp eyes that were tracing the terrain quickly. Above his head, the soft green glow from his staff was intensifying, and sparks of magic were escaping and swirling around him. Morgana was focused on the Sídhe, her lips moving in silent words that Arto did not recognize. The scent and feel of energy in the air were furthered sharpened by another flash of lightning.

Arto inhaled just before Merlin brought his staff down with a deafening crack. Underneath them, the ground rumbled, and Arto felt a wave of magic roll under his feet. The air was forced from his lungs as Morgana swung her hands forward and released a burst of magic. It crackled in the air but moved like a wave upon the shore spreading out from Morgana across the valley. His heart beat faster, his magic sparking in his gut and up his chest at the feel of magic saturating the air and earth. Cathanáil glowed brightly, turning white in his hands, and thrumming in response to the magic around it.

Rocks jutted out of the ground in the front of Sídhe, sending several horses stumbling. The entire hill shook violently as the eruption of jagged bits of stone spread from the floor of the valley and up both slopes stopping only in front of Merlin's feet. Some of the Riders released their magic in time to blast the rocks close to them while others avoided them.

A cry of pain escaped one of the Riders as his steed fell, crushing him beneath the beast's flank. Yet the rumbling of the earth continued and the rocks released their grip on the side of the hill, beginning to roll down the slope. Those who had stopped their horses or avoided the initial rocks found themselves facing a rock slide.

Blasts of golden magic collided with the stones just before the wave of silver magic reached the Sídhe. Gold and silver twisted in the air, dissolving both opposing magic and leaving rocks rolling down the hill. Cheers erupted from the warriors behind the mages and Arto gasped in amazement. Another flash of silver in the corner of his eye made him turn to see Morgana summoning more magic. A moment later she launched a rapid succession of magical bolts that rained down.

Then the rocks reached the bottom of the hill, and the dust began to settle. For a moment everything was still and silent. Then a snarl cut through the silence, and a Hound raced out of the dust cloud. Arto heard Morgana gasp in alarm, but only a second later a bolt of silver magic struck the Hound in the chest. It growled and lunged, but its body was already beginning to dissolve. Swinging Cathanáil, Arto sliced into what remained of the flesh, and the creature vanished in a flash of white.

"Do you think that's it?" Arto asked softly after a moment. His skin tingled as he stared into the valley trying to see something.

"Perhaps." Merlin leaned heavily on his staff and was breathing hard. "I am reminded why I don't do that very often."

"It did require you to use a great deal of magic," Morgana observed, her eyes darting over to Merlin with a hint of worry. "But it was very impressive."

The dust cloud cleared, revealing nothing of the Riders and the Hounds. Arto caught sight of a glimmer of gold dust in the air and smiled in relief. Behind them, the warriors cheered and shouted in glee, Arto heard stray words including magic, rocks, and mages, but everything was too jumbled to make out.

"Some might have made it into the tunnel," Morgana shouted to the crowd. "We cannot assume the danger is past."

Thankfully the warriors settled before his sister lost her temper. Arto glanced at Morgana only to find her holding an orb of silvery magic and glancing around sharply. Then carefully, Morgana stepped forward and began to move carefully down the slope of the hill. Arto gave her a moment's head start and with a glance towards Merlin began to follow her. He heard Morgana exhale slowly and the magical orb began to float out of her hand, casting light around them. The hillside was a mess with large chunks of the once gentle slope missing and scars from the impact of rocks all over. Stepping into one of the indents, Arto tugged on the magic he could feel around him and shivered as a burst of energy traveled up his body. It wasn't a bad feeling, but it left him lightheaded, and he swayed uneasily for a moment before he could continue forward. Sheathing Cathanáil, he moved down the hill slowly, minding his footing.

They all made it into the bottom of the valley where the rocks Merlin had sent rolling were gathered, many already crumbling from the force of the rockslide. Merlin patted one of the rocks fondly and hummed softly to himself in satisfaction. Morgana shook her head, placing a hand on Arto's shoulder and carefully guiding him towards the tunnel entrance. It was in a more sheltered part of the hill with a small cliff of rocks hanging over it. Arto stared into the darkness of the tunnel and shivered, almost certain that a cold wind was blowing out of it.

Morgana studied the area around the tunnel carefully and then slowly shrugged off the bag of iron she was carrying. It hit the ground with a clattering thump, and she quickly straightened back up with a grateful sigh and rolled her shoulders. A few moments later, Merlin stumbled over still leaning heavily on his staff. With a soft grunt, the eldest mage dropped his bag near Arto's feet.

"You best move quickly," Merlin told him gently, but with a hint of urgency. "I'm not confident that we've seen the last of the Sídhe today."

Nodding, Arto drew Cathanáil forth and breathed in and out slowly, trying to calm down. Underneath his feet, he could feel the soft humming of magic just below the surface of the earth. His gut clenched for a moment before the soft flow of magic began. Another horn blast distracted Arto and made the assembled humans turn quickly to look down the valley. There, just beyond a rocky cliff that cast a shadow over the area was another large group of Riders and Hounds. A curse escaped Morgana who summoned more magic and formed a magical orb in her outstretched hand.

"They knew," Morgana growled in a low voice. "They must have!"

"We don't know that," Merlin replied sharply, stepping away from Arto and towards the Sídhe. "Focus on keeping them back. Arto, focus on the gate!"

Arto closed his eyes and focused on his magic, trying to block out what was happening. He inhaled slowly, focusing his entire consciousness on his Sword, and willing the rest of the world away. Cathanáil thrummed with warmth, the magic sending a soft pulse of energy through the hilt and into Arto's hand. He returned the brush of magic, allowing his magic infused within the blade to connect to the stream of white magic flowing through him. There was a sharp tug in his gut as the Sword pulled almost violently on his magic.

Opening his eyes, Arto kicked open one of the bags to reveal the small iron pieces within. There was no system to their shape: while most were round with the triskelion carved into them, others were simple bars made in the last-minute rush. He could feel a soft brush of magic from them all, his own in some and Morgana's or Merlin's in others.

Behind him he could hear shouting, screaming, cursing, magic striking targets, and the crash of metal against metal. He tried to ignore it, but as the scent of burning hair and flesh reached him it was all Arto could do to keep down a rush of bile. Arto turned his attention back to Cathanáil and pointed his Sword towards the first bag. The Sword's glow sparked, traveling down the blade, and arcing off the tip into the iron pieces. They began to glow, the magic infused in them reacting with his own.

Closing his eyes, Arto reached towards the pieces, pulling the awakened magic towards him. He could feel the metal shudder, and the magic react. In his mind he visualized the metal fusing together, the magic blending and following the movement of his Sword. Arto grit his teeth and opened his eyes: the iron was floating in the air and shaking, magical sparks of silver, white and green jumping between them, but the fusion wasn't working.

Inhaling and exhaling with measured breaths, Arto turned and looked over his shoulder as the sounds of battle came closer and closer. Two warriors tackled and held a Síd in place, twisting its arms amidst its screams and curses. An axe was swung down on the head by a third man, and the body began to turn to golden dust. Arto barely avoided a spear, its point glinting dangerously as it flew past him. A Rider was thrown to the ground but blasted off a wave of magic sending the men flying back. Snarling and growling of Hounds, men, and Sídhe filled the air as both sides abandoned any notion of prisoners.

He turned back to the metal, biting his lip as he tried to pull more magic forth. The iron vibrated and began to glow softly, but it wasn't enough. Moving Cathanáil towards the other bags, Arto repeated his earlier action and pulled harshly on the magic infused into the metal.

Small pieces of iron rushed out of the bag and into the air, joining the first set in a swirling mass of metal shapes. Magic arced between the pieces, different colors sparked and pulsed amongst the iron. A sudden tang of iron hit his tongue shocking Arto out of his concentration. He licked his lip, finding a small wound and blood trickling over his skin.

Blinking, Arto looked back at the pieces of iron and beyond them to the empty darkness of the tunnel. He smiled slightly and slowly lowered himself down to his knees. Beneath him, he could feel magic straining against the surface of the earth. Arto focused on the iron and relaxed his hold on his magic. The pieces floated gently in the air, magic still sparking between them, but Arto slowly relaxed his shoulders and brought Cathanáil up higher. Slicing into his left arm, Arto flinched at the hot pain that spread from the wound and blood began to flow down his arm freely. He quickly raised Cathanáil and twisted his arm as much as he could manage to make the blood drip onto the blade.

Then he pushed the blade forward, into the swirl of magic and iron. His red blood began to glow brightly, the red color startling against the green, white, and silver magic around it. Small drops of blood began to rise off the blade of the Sword, colliding with pieces of iron which flared brilliantly. One by one, drops of blood were pulled from the blade to each of the iron pieces. Slamming his eyes shut against the brilliant glow, Arto gasped for air.

He could still see in his mind the opening in the hill. He could feel the chill from the tunnel on his face and could feel the tingle of the foreign magic on his skin. It was wrong and his stomach twisted at the feeling. His magic thrummed in his veins and danced across his skin as blood slowly flowed out of his wound. Arto pushed more magic through Cathanáil despite his shaking hands. The Sword thrummed and pulsed, so hot in his hands that it was difficult to keep hold of the hilt.

He opened his eyes and gasped softly; the air forced from his lungs in awe. In front of him, the glowing iron pieces began to flow together, the wrought shapes and signs vanishing as the magic turned them red hot. The colors of magic faded away, replaced by a warm red glow that sparkled with hints of his white magic. The metal pieces crashed into each other. The sound of metal striking metal rang through the valley. Sparks of magic flew from each collision as the pieces shimmered and shifted against each other.

Raising Cathanáil, Arto grinned as the iron followed his blade, sparks of magic jolting between the pieces and Cathanáil. Arto turned his eyes towards the tunnel entrance and let his pounding heart drown out the nearby sounds of battle. He studied the tunnel, adjusting the picture he'd been carrying in his mind for months to the size and rounded shape of the entrance. Arto did not blink and did not move his eyes from the tunnel.

A scream behind him made Arto tense, but he dared not look back. He heard his sister's voice shouting something and a pained whimper of a dying Hound, but he did not look back. Cathanáil shook violently, requiring both hands to keep the Sword stable. Magic sparked off the blade like tiny bolts of lightning. Arto gazed at the tunnel one more time before closing his eyes.

He saw a shining gate, iron fused into the very rock around it, reaching into the earth for power and support. Arto visualized the glowing iron flying forward into the darkness and driving itself into the rock. It would form strong bars vertically, twisting around each other. There was the sound of metal striking rock. He felt a blast of magic against his chest, knocking him back a few steps. The iron would create a barrier, locking into the rock of the tunnel, breaking through the Sídhe touched stone and into the earth beyond. There was cracking in front of him, the sound of crumbling stone. The iron would only answer to him, to Cathanáil. It would be unmovable, unbreakable and protect the Iron Realm. A wave of magic hit him in an icy rush as the magical connection to the iron was suddenly cut off with the completion of the gate. Arto fell to his knees in exhaustion.

His lungs burned. He couldn't inhale air quickly enough. Black flickered at the edge of his vision as his limbs turned heavy. Arto groaned between gasps as he forced himself back up onto his knees and tried to regain his composure. Forcing his head up, Arto took another greedy gulp of air. But then he saw into the tunnel and gasped softly in awe and pleasure. There, just beyond the opening in the hillside, stood a glowing gray metal structure. It filled the whole of the opening, the metal twisting into the earth around it and gleaming with magic. Bars of iron crisscrossed, melting seamlessly into one another. The dark stone around the bars was crumbling to dust. No Sídhe would pass this; the iron was infused with magic and solid in its own right. Those bars would bend only for Cathanáil, for him. There would be no opening this gate without his power.

Cathanáil pulsed in his hand even as Arto felt the power he'd called on slipping back into the ground beneath him. He was grateful that he was already on the ground and kneeling. Every muscle ached as if he'd exercised everything all at once for days on end. He forced himself to look around, watching with a grin as the remaining Sídhe warriors stumbled around with dazed expressions at the sudden shift in their magic. His allied warriors seemed surprised, but leapt forward and begun cutting the Sídhe down with roars of glee. Arto looked towards the sky. The dark clouds were still moving over his head, but they somehow seemed lighter. A laugh escaped Arto, and before he knew what was happening, he was laughing hysterically.

Then it began to rain. A fat raindrop hit the side of his nose and rolled down his cheek. Sticking out his tongue, Arto caught the raindrop and sucked it into his mouth eagerly. He could hear voices cheering behind him and laughing as the rain came down. Arto laughed again and felt drops fall straight onto his tongue. Holding his head back, he laughed and welcomed the tingling feeling of the rain hitting the back of his throat. An arm wrapped around him suddenly and he felt a body pressed against his side. Turning his head, Arto relaxed as he took in his sister's long dark and braided hair.

"You did it," Morgana whispered against his neck. "The gate..."

"Can you feel it too?" Arto asked, adjusting his head so he could look back at the gate.

The white glow was fading, but he could still feel the gate itself. Magic was flowing gently from the earth around them into the iron bars. There was a soft hum in the air, warm and soothing. It felt like safety and happiness.

"Yes," Morgana answered. "I can feel it."

"Well done," Merlin said. The older mage sunk to the ground next to them. "I feel very old at the moment." He groaned as he rested his staff on his lap. "Perhaps a few days of rest would be wise before we begin to seek out other tunnels. Once news of this success spreads, we will certainly be in high demand. Not to mention we need to forge more iron and infuse it."

"That will give the Sídhe time to muster their forces," Morgana reminded Merlin, her voice suddenly distant and sad.

"Indeed," Merlin agreed with a sigh. "The Sídhe now know that they have a real fight on their hands." A laugh escaped Merlin, and he sighed happily drawing Morgana and Arto's attention. Merlin's face was relaxed, and the raindrops were washing away the dust clinging to his skin.

"But for the moment," he reached over and put a warm hand on Arto's shoulder. "Well done."

34

Finals Weekend

B ran had to admire the way that Alex smoothly moved around the forge; she was graceful even as she brought down a magic-infused hammer on the bar of iron that she was currently working with. It was rather impressive just how far Alex had come in a matter of months. Originally, she'd been very nervous around the heat and overwhelmed like all of them by the sheer number of hammers and other tools to keep straight. Now she was the most comfortable and precise. Dark silver magic swirled around the hammer just before she brought it crashing down. The thin iron bar shuddered between the hammer and anvil, shimmering with Alex's magic.

He looked over towards the other furnace and anvil where Aiden was hammering a small piece of iron while Nicki stood nearby watching. Bran had the horrible feeling that when they returned to school next autumn that they'd find Merlin had added two more blacksmithing stations to the workshop. The current setup of forging every weekend in preparation for the summer solstice was bad enough. His eyes went over to the nearby table where the collection of flattened iron bars was laid out. They didn't need to do anything fancy like the earlier triskelions right now, just infuse the iron with magic and keep it relatively straight and strong.

Next to the pile of finished bars was a stack of books including Alex's Spanish book and his calculus book. While most of their fellow students were studying and packing so they could leave as soon as they finished their last tests this week, they were spending almost every moment outside of class infusing iron with magic and trying to prepare Arthur for the solstice. Alex placed another iron bar to the side and grabbed a small hand towel from the workbench to clean the sheen of sweat off her face.

"Take a break," Bran urged her. "Go outside and cool off."

"I'm fine," Alex told him with a badly forced smile. Raising an eyebrow, Bran gave her a doubtful look which made her chuckle and shake her head. "I just want to stay busy." Alex touched the hammers hanging on the workbench thoughtfully. "Stopping to think about things hasn't been going very well."

"Things still bad with Jenny?"

"Haven't spoken to her since Sunday after Beltane. She comes to class at the last second so she can sit away from me. When Nicki and I went over to pack up my stuff she left the room and didn't come back while we were there."

"Sorry," Bran offered with a grimace. "She's not really angry at you, Alex."

"I know." Alex picked a hammer up from the workbench. "I just wish I could fix this."

"I don't think you can. Hopefully, some time to sort things out over the summer will help. With Arthur staying here for June that gives her some time away from everyone."

"Maybe."

Alex picked up the piece of iron with the tongs and pushed it back into the furnace. A wave of heat rolled off the blazing hot coals, and Bran knew that Alex was done talking for now. He shook his head and stepped further away from the anvil to give Alex more room. He glanced over at Aiden and Nicki who were arguing over Aiden's hammering technique and chuckled as he headed for the workshop door.

Stepping outside, Bran sucked in a deep breath of fresh air. While the May weather wasn't cool by most standards, compared to the inside of the workshop where both furnaces were running, it felt like stepping into an icebox. Bran lifted his water bottle and took several greedy gulps of the liquid. It had warmed up from being in the workshop but still eased his dry throat. He leaned against the side of the building and looked over towards Arthur who was sitting in the grass. Merlin was seated in front of him, guiding the newest magic user through meditation.

Bran tilted his head in consideration as he observed Arthur. He hadn't known the other college student well this year; he'd met him through Alex of course, but never had much interest in him until the announcement that he was the Iron Soul. Football wasn't his sport, and while he enjoyed cheering on the occasional game, he wasn't the sort to worry much about individual players. When he'd first met Arthur along with Lance and Jenny, he'd been amused by the contrast between those three friends of Alex and himself, Nicki, and Aiden as the second trio of Alex's friends. He'd even been a little envious of Alex's ability to move between such different groups even if she'd been uncomfortable at first.

Still, Arthur seemed like a nice enough guy even if maybe a little too perfect at times. Bran was waiting for the inevitable reveal of a fatal flaw. It was obvious that Alex liked him as more than a friend, always had been. She tended to get excited when talking about him, even if she didn't notice it herself and blushed a lot when he came up. He'd always been torn between amusement and worry about the situation, not wanting to see his friend and fellow mage hurt. But over the last three weeks, Arthur had been almost desperately trying to get Alex to talk to him, so Bran was pretty sure that Arthur had feelings for Alex too. Maybe that was why he hadn't noticed his girlfriend since sophomore year of high school cheating on him. If he was distracted by having feelings for another person, then it would explain a bit more about his behavior towards the whole thing.

The fact of the matter was that Bran had never seen Arthur hesitate about the whole mess. He'd quickly accepted Merlin's explanation in the car, even asking him if he was alright after his vision. It was a major change from Alex who'd been very afraid to accept magic and that was just based on her role as a mage. Arthur, on the other hand, had been informed that he was critical to protecting the Iron Realm and had barely blinked. It had been followed by him forgiving Lance and Jenny and throwing himself into learning magic. He was eager to please Morgana and Merlin but had yet to show the kind of magical strength described by Alex when he vaporized the Sídhe on Beltane. Taking another sip of water, Bran pondered the oddity that was the new Iron Soul and kept watching even as he heard the crashing of hammers against metal from inside the workshop.

Arthur moved out of his meditative position, pulling Bran out of his thoughts a few minutes later, and turned so he could open his backpack. Leaning forward, Bran grinned as he caught sight of what Arthur was pulling out of his backpack. It was the triskelion sign that Alex had forged and given to him. Arthur held it gently in his hands and said something that Bran couldn't hear to Merlin who chuckled and nodded.

Merlin climbed to his feet and moved away from Arthur, giving him a lot of room. Taking another sip of his water, Bran decided that it wasn't time to go back into the forge just yet. At first, nothing happened, Arthur simply sat in the grass with closed eyes breathing slowly. Morgana came out of the house, and Merlin turned and started speaking with her in a low voice. When Arthur opened an eye, the two of them moved further away to continue their discussion.

Arthur focused on the triskelion sign in his hands for several more moments before sighing dramatically. He glanced towards Morgana and Merlin before reaching into his bag once again. Bran frowned as Arthur did something he couldn't see around the bag and then closed his eyes once more. Bran straightened up, easing more of his weight on his legs than on the wall and leaning on his cane.

Then the triskelion began to glow softly, a strange mix of gray and red with sparks of white jumping along the metal. Bran took a small step forward, walking towards the patio to get a better look at what was happening. Arthur's fingers released the triskelion, and it slowly began to move into the air, magic swirling around it. He heard Morgana gasp and glanced in the direction of the professors quickly. Both their faces were bright with relief and excitement.

The thin iron bands forming the shape suddenly twisted, glowing as it moved. Unrolling, the three spirals straightened out forming a small triangle with long prongs off each corner. Then the metal rippled and shimmered before curling back into position with a strange scratching sound. A loud laugh of triumph escaped Arthur and Bran smiled at the sudden display. He'd been getting a little worried about Arthur being ready in time. The iron triskelion stopped glowing and fell out of the air, hitting the ground in front of Arthur with a loud thunk. Arthur kept laughing for another minute before he gently reached out and picked up the triskelion and brought it back to his lap.

"Wonderful, Arthur!" Morgana cheered, walking across the grass to him. "Well done!"

"Thanks," Arthur replied, glancing down at the triskelion with a smile. "I'm really glad that worked."

"You did great," Morgana told him. "Connecting with your magic can take time, I know we've put a lot of pressure on you, and the deadline for June has made things difficult."

"I get it," Arthur assured her quickly with a beaming smile. "But I think it's going to be okay."

Morgana smiled at Arthur, a warm, comfortable smile. Bran had the strong urge to turn away, suddenly feeling like he was spying.

"I'm a bit tired now," Arthur said breaking the moment just before a yawn escaped him. "Classes plus magic and weight training... it gets to be a bit much."

"Understandable," Merlin said from behind Morgana. "Well, I can't argue with your progress today, so you're welcome to go home unless you want a turn at the forge."

Arthur shook his head quickly. "I don't want to get in each other's way."

"I thought that you and Alex were alright?" Morgana asked with a frown, her eyes darkening slightly.

"We are," Arthur countered quickly. "It's just... well, things are still a bit weird."

Morgana and Merlin glanced at each other with strange expressions, but then Merlin nodded and gestured for Morgana to follow him. She lingered for a moment, watching Arthur as he fiddled nervously before she turned and followed Merlin inside. As they left, Arthur visibly sighed in relief, and Bran fought the urge to chuckle, knowing how overwhelming Merlin and Morgana together could be. Arthur reached into his bag again, pulled out some tissues, and started fiddling with his hands. Curious, Bran started walking across the yard.

There was blood on the piece of iron and Arthur's hand, Bran realized with a start. Arthur was wiping off the blood from the piece of iron with a tissue which he shoved into his pocket. Morgana and Merlin were talking to each other with quiet, but excited voices near the back door of the house. Glancing towards them, Bran made his way over to Arthur.

"Are you okay?" Bran asked with a frown, gesturing towards the blood.

"What?" Arthur asked before looking down at his hand which still had some traces of blood on it. "Oh yeah, I'm fine." Arthur blushed slightly and looked embarrassed. "I uh... actually, I did that on purpose."

"On purpose?" Bran asked with a frown.

"Yeah, Merlin was telling me that the first Iron Soul used his blood when creating the original Iron Gates. The iron in his blood was charged by his magic at all times and could help boost the power of what he was doing." Arthur shrugged and ran a hand through his hair, a habit that Bran was beginning to recognize. "I haven't been able to affect iron yet despite the fact it's supposed to be one of my major powers so I thought that maybe a boost would help me connect." Arthur looked down with an air of unease. "My magic is still giving me trouble; Morgana tells me that it's odd I haven't had a Connection with anyone but Alex."

"We've been wondering about that," Bran said carefully as he studied the young man. "Well, the blood seemed to work; you were able to move the iron."

"Yeah, I'm just worried about trying to create a new gate. Arto had been using magic for years. I'm going to have five weeks."

"Merlin said that we'll be able to help you," Bran reminded him. "Share our magic. As long as you're directing the iron, it should be fine." He gestured at the piece of iron that Arthur was holding. "And you've got that now."

"Yeah," Arthur replied, relaxing his shoulders, and smiling. "I guess I do."

"Just be careful about how much blood you use. After all you and Alex are still giving blood together, right?"

"That's right." Arthur looked towards the workshop and sighed loudly. "It's pretty much the only thing she does with me anymore. And of course, Jenny and Lance won't talk to me."

"The last few months, hell the entire year, has been hard on Alex," Bran pointed out gently, watching Arthur's face carefully. "She's just trying to get through this week."

"Finals," Arthur muttered. "I thought I was ready for them too."

"Well, that was before you were splitting your time between studying, classes, and magic lessons. It sucks up your time really fast." Bran paused and frowned slightly. "Are you staying on the football team next year?"

"That's still the plan, but I'm a bit worried about things going wrong when I'm gone. We have to travel a lot."

"We'll work it out," Bran said. "If Morgana and Merlin haven't brought it up yet then they probably don't think it's a problem. Or they may think it's a good idea for you to get away from this insanity occasionally."

"Yeah maybe." Arthur pushed himself off the ground and swung his backpack over his shoulder. "I'm a bit nervous about you guys heading off for the summer. I'm not sure how I'll cope with it just being them and me."

"Nicki and Aiden will only be across town. School may not be in session, but you'll probably see them a lot. And it's not like Alex and I are more than a few hours away. She's in Spokane, and I'm in Eugene."

"Are you looking forward to seeing your family?" Arthur asked conversationally.

"It's just mom and me, but yeah it will be nice to see her, and my aunt will probably make an appearance this summer," Bran answered with a shrug. "Dad died a few years back and no siblings," he offered. "How about you?"

"Just my mother for me as well," Arthur told him with a small smile. "Dad died a little before I was born, so I never knew him. No siblings for me either." Arthur shook his head and glanced over towards Merlin and Morgana. "She's not thrilled with me not coming home until July, but thankfully she didn't argue."

"So, are you going to tell her about all this?"

"About magic and me being the reincarnation of the apparent, uh what's the word, prototype or inspiration for the King Arthur legend? Hell no." Arthur shook his head, his jaw tightening. "Mom's pretty straight forward and analytical. I'm pretty sure she'd think I was crazy and if I showed her magic, she'd worry that she was crazy."

Chuckling, Bran nodded in agreement. "None of us have plans to tell our families either," he admitted. "My mom barely accepted me leaving Eugene for college. I don't think she could cope with the danger of being a mage."

Arthur nodded in sympathy and tightened his grip on his bag. He looked past Bran over his shoulder just before Bran heard Aiden's voice shouting for him to get back inside and help.

"Sounds like you're in trouble," Arthur observed with a short laugh.

"Only a little. Uh, if I don't see you before I go then have a good June and I'll be back for the summer solstice."

"Yeah, thanks" Arthur agreed with an uneasy nod. "Good luck for finals week."

"You too," Bran replied politely before turning around and heading back to the workshop. At the doorway, he stopped and glanced back towards Arthur in time to see him vanishing through the wrought iron gate. Sighing, Bran shook his head and stepped back into the workshop, hitting a wall of heat as he entered.

35

A New Iron Gate

Nicki pulled her car into the small parking lot by the hiking trail and stopped sharply making Alex sway in the passenger seat. Taking a deep breath, Alex looked around the parking lot that she hadn't been in since Morgana escorted her away on Beltane.

"You okay?" Nicki asked.

"I'll be fine." Alex made no move to leave the car.

"It's weird for me too," Nicki told her with a smile. "And I've been in Ravenslake all summer helping out where I could. I can't imagine what it's like coming back after a month away from the insanity."

"It's kind of a relief." Alex shook her head as a small chuckle escaped her. "As crazy as that sounds. It's not like I could tell my parents or brothers about magic. I thought about it, but..."

"It's dangerous," Nicki finished with a nod. "I understand. It's been hard for me not to tell Gran. She's been the only family I've had for so many years that secrets feel awful. But like you say it's dangerous and I don't want to scare her."

"My mother's a doctor: she'd be horrified at some of the injuries I've gotten," Alex reminded Nicki with a sad laugh. "And Dad's a journalist, I think he'd keep the secret, but you just don't know how they'll react."

"Yeah," Nicki agreed weakly with a sigh. "I hope your time at home was at least good."

"It has been so far. I'm lifeguarding at one of the local pools and helping teach a swim lesson in the mornings. My younger brother must have enjoyed being the only child at home because he wasn't too happy with Matt and me coming back."

Nicki laughed before it dissolved into a sigh as Aiden's blue truck pulled up next to them. "Well, here's the boys." Nicki reached for the door handle. "Ready or not, it's iron gate or bust time now."

Nodding, Alex unbuckled her seatbelt and climbed out of the car, shutting the door behind her. "Hey guys," she greeted with a widening smile. Walking around the car, Alex moved closer to Bran as he climbed out the passenger side. He held out one of his arms, using his cane with the other, to hug Alex.

"Good to see you," Bran said warmly. "Sorry meeting up yesterday didn't work out."

"Oh, it was fine," Alex said. "I just turned up the tunes and then crashed with Nicki."

"Don't I get a hug?" Aiden moved around the car and held out his arms expectantly while Nicki hugged Bran. Rolling her eyes, Alex walked over and hugged Aiden in greeting. "So, you've been staying out of trouble?"

"Yeah," Alex answered with a smile. "It's actually a lot easier when there aren't Sídhe around."

"Part of me envies you living somewhere else," Aiden admitted.

"Have there been more attacks?" Alex asked with a frown, turning to look at Nicki.

"We didn't want you to worry," Nicki told her quickly. "And nothing too bad. Just a few Hounds here and there. Merlin and Morgana have done a good job limiting the tunnel's stability. The last attack was... two weeks ago maybe."

"You should have told us," Bran chided them.

"Look you guys needed time with your families," Aiden replied calmly. "Nicki and I have our families here; we get their support whenever we need it. You two don't have that."

"And we didn't want you guys to try and come up with excuses to come back early," Nicki continued. "Bad enough that you had to 'come and visit' us as it is."

"Speaking of which, we are going out for pizza after this is done like normal college kids," Aiden said quickly. "Proper Italian pizza, of course, none of that mass produced crap."

"Careful Aiden your Italian is showing," Nicki teased with a grin.

"Better that than my Irish temper."

Alex leaned back against Nicki's car, her shoulders relaxing as the familiar sibling like banter of Nicki and Aiden washed over her. Closing her eyes, Alex took a deep breath. The mix of evergreens and deciduous sent a pleasant scent into the air, and the breeze over the hillside provided a soothing sound. Then the others fell silent, and she heard wheels on gravel. Alex opened her eyes and straightened up as Merlin's SUV pulled into the parking lot, coming alongside Aiden's truck. Morgana was visible in the passenger seat with Arthur in the back seat.

Arthur climbed out of the back; his eyes fixed on Alex and he smiled widely. Alex's insides squirmed, and her heart beat faster than normal, but Alex gave him her best friendly smile even as her mouth went dry. She made no move to hug him, but she did see Arthur's shoulders relax at her smile which she took as a good sign. Despite the warm summer day, Arthur was wearing an open long sleeved flannel shirt over a Ravenslake t-shirt.

"Welcome back to Ravenslake," Arthur told Alex. Then he turned his attention to Bran and nodded in greeting.

"No place like it," Bran replied dryly.

"At least that's what we're trying to make sure of." Arthur watched Morgana and Merlin climb out of the SUV. "We don't need more than one town besieged by invaders from other worlds."

"Good to see you, Alex, Bran," Merlin greeted as he pulled a duffle bag out of the back and set it on the ground with a metallic thunk. "How are your families?"

"Mines good," Alex replied, eying the bag of iron with worry.

"Mom's fine."

Then Morgana pulled out several backpacks, and Alex felt a surge of relief. Morgana gestured them all forward and handed out the backpacks, giving Alex a forest green one that already had two water bottles stored in small side pouches.

"I put some snacks and an emergency pack in each backpack." Morgana handed Bran's backpack to him. "We aren't expecting trouble, but the current tunnel is a bit of a hike up into the hills, and I don't want anyone getting hurt."

"We'll split up the iron," Merlin said. He opened the duffle bag and pulled out a few of the short iron rods, placing them into his backpack. "But let us know if your bag is too heavy. We don't want anyone getting hurt."

Bran's ended up being the lightest as no one wanted to risk unbalancing him and despite looking displeased Bran didn't argue. Alex had to adjust the straps on her bag a few times before the strange load was comfortable. Arthur ended up with the heaviest load of them all, being the tall and strong football player. Then they were off up the trail with Merlin leading the way, Arthur behind him followed by Aiden, Nicki, Alex, Bran, and Morgana.

It was strangely quiet on the trail as they made the climb. With it being a beautiful sunny summer Saturday Alex would have expected more hikers to be out and about. But then again as they climbed the hill Alex could feel a tingling over her skin and the horrible silence created by the aversion of animals to the area started wearing her down. Maybe non-mages didn't understand what they felt in the area, but maybe it was enough to repel them. Everyone was quiet during the hike up with only Aiden speaking to the others occasionally in a low voice. Stepping off the main hiking trail, they began to follow a smaller, but well-worn game trail that was wider than normal.

The further they got in the forest, the more evidence of large creatures moving through the underbrush Alex could see. Bushes were trampled, and branches were snapped and hanging limply. Alex figured that the Sídhe Riders had to blast their way through much of the forest to get anywhere while mounted. Then, finally, the game trail widened onto a small flattened area on the side of the hill. It was a lot like the area where the last tunnel had been with no vegetation growing close to the dark hole in the side of the hill. The ground had been beaten down, and Alex thought she could still make out a few imprints of hoofs.

"Alright," Merlin said making Alex, and most of the others jump in alarm at the sound of his voice. "Let's get ready. Keep your packs near you just in case and your daggers ready."

There were nods all around, and Alex slowly shrugged off the heavy backpack and lowered it to the ground. Her eyes stayed glued to the tunnel nervously. Finely fitted together stones created an archway around the tunnel making it stand out sharply from the surrounding reddish-brown rock of the hillside. Staring into the darkness, Alex swallowed thickly. Her fingers twitched remembering the smooth feel of the stones and their strange chill. For a moment Alex thought she could hear the Sídhe talking far away, their voices echoing down the tunnel.

"Alex, you okay?" Arthur's warm voice asked softly from right behind her. His breath tickled the back of her neck under her ponytail.

"Yeah," Alex replied in a shaky voice. She managed to swallow before adding, "Just some bad memories."

"I've heard," Arthur whispered. "I can't believe you were taken down there and got out. Saving those kids was really brave."

Alex blushed, certain that she was bright red which did not work with her complexion. Managing a quick nod, Alex tried to think of something to say, but thankfully Merlin called Arthur over towards him. A few moments later, Merlin clapped his hands to get everyone's attention.

"We are in luck today, the sun is shining, and the Sídhe are at a disadvantage. Morgana and I have done everything we can to ensure that today is successful, but without Cathanáil to help direct Arthur's power we need the help of all of you." Merlin glanced at Arthur with a proud little smile. "Arthur has requested that all you use your blood to help enhance the magical connection. The iron in your blood is infused with your magic and will hopefully smooth the transition of the magic."

Alex shared a worried glance with Nicki, but they all lined up as Merlin instructed. Alex stood next to Arthur with Aiden on her right, Nicki beside him, and Bran next to her. Merlin and Morgana gently took the iron rods out of everyone's bags and set them out flat on the ground a few feet in front of Arthur who was standing straight in front of the tunnel entrance.

"I'd suggest you cut a small incision on your arms." Morgana stood and brushed off her hands. "You don't need a lot of blood for this," she said.

Glancing at the others, Alex saw Arthur kneeling by his bag and Morgana making a small cut on her arm and letting some of the blood run down to her hand. She saw Nicki grimace in the corner of her eye as she made a long cut on her arm as Akex pulled out her iron dagger, wishing that she had a way to sanitize it. Alex flinched but drew her dagger over her left arm making a long, but shallow cut. Blood instantly began to seep from the wound, and Alex brought her right hand up to collect some of the blood. Smearing it over both of her hands, Alex curled her nose at the sticky feeling and the sight of her blood. She glanced over at Aiden and Nicki, noting their bloody hands as Nicki muttered the word eew under her breath several times. Then a bloody hand was held out to her and Alex looked up at Arthur.

He was pale, his blue eyes dark and focused on the tunnel. She saw him swallow thickly and relaxed slightly at the knowledge that he was as nervous as them. Reaching out with her left hand, Alex took his offered right hand and did her best to ignore the slick feeling on their skin. Her arm stung, but Alex knew it would clot soon. Shaking her head, Alex forced away the thoughts of how ridiculous her life was that she had to bloodlet herself. Aiden took her right hand and squeezed gently to reassure them both.

Breathing slowly, Alex heard Merlin instructing Arthur in a low voice next to them and closed her eyes. She could already feel the tug in her gut and the warmth spreading in her chest as her magic began to gather. Behind her eyelids, Alex could see flashes of light but kept focusing on the growing feeling of her magic. There was a warmth that spread in her chest, curling around her heart and Alex could almost see little sparks of magic zinging around in her mind's eye. She felt Arthur's thumb brush the back of her hand and relaxed.

Her left arm tingled. Alex shivered as foreign magic brushed over her skin. It was familiar and similar to her own, but different enough that her magic flared up. Alex visualized the new magic as a swirl of sparks of different colors and reached for it. She had to send it to Arthur, combining all their magic so he could use it. Every remark and every word of Morgana's lecture coursed through her mind, and Alex's shoulders relaxed. Her magic rose up and surrounded the new magic gently like an orb of water around an ornament to form a snow globe. Alex chuckled at the mental description and pushed on her magic, willing it towards Arthur. But then the colors began to fade, slowly turning the dark silver color of Alex's magic.

Arthur's grip on her hand tightened, almost painfully, but Alex kept focusing on the swirling magic around the iron bars. Her limbs shook, breathing was becoming harder and harder as her magic was pulled forward sharply. The tingling in her arms was becoming overwhelming as dark gray sparks danced down her limbs. Her right hand was glowing a kaleidoscope mixture of red, blue, and yellow as the magic of the others flowed towards Arthur. Risking a glance in the other direction, Alex saw Arthur's left hand was glowing with a mixture of green and white sparks, magic circling his and Merlin's joined hands. Her eyes dropped to her left hand, glowing a solid dark gray and traveling up Arthur's arm. She had transformed and taken over the magic of the others. Alex wanted to laugh, tell Morgana right away, but her lips couldn't move properly. Everything was fixated on the magic, and Alex was finding it harder and harder to breathe as she observed what was happening around her.

The iron rods gleamed in the sunlight pouring into the small clearing and sparkled with magic. Alex gasped as the rods floated in front of them, no part of them touching the ground any longer. They struck each other gently as they shifted in the swirl of magic, almost sounding like a wind chime. Alex exhaled and smiled cautiously as she saw magic of different colors dancing over the metal.

"Focus, Arthur," Merlin's voice instructed. "You're almost there."

Arthur squeezed her hand again, and Alex tightened her grip, feeling her magic flowing out of her. Dark spots appeared at the edge of her vision, but Alex eased her hold on her magic. It was like a dam breaking. Alex almost fell to her knees as a strange sensation in her chest left her gasping for air. Her heart was on fire, and bright sparks appeared in her vision. The blood on her hands felt hot, and she heard Aiden hiss next to her, the sound nearly lost to the strange hum in her ears.

The iron rods glowed a bright gray color tinted with gold and suddenly one of them flew out of the mass of magic before them. There was a metallic clang followed by the sound of rocks being struck in the tunnel. Then another rod sailed into the dark tunnel followed by another and another. From her place next to Arthur, Alex could see the rods twisting together, fusing in bursts of magic that sent sparks falling onto the rock floor of the tunnel, the light of the magic illuminating the darkness.

Each of the rods followed the first in driving into the rock and merging with the others in a swirl and flash of magic. Metal crashed against metal, echoing the sound of a hammer in a blacksmith shop and rock crumbled. They wove around each other, forming a grid of iron over the tunnel entrance a few feet in. From deep within the tunnel, Alex could make out musical voices and the snarls of Hounds, but none came forward. There was a pained howl followed by a high-pitched scream of anger just as the last of the iron rods surged into the tunnel and fitted itself into place, diagonally crossing over the center point and curling against another curving piece to form the triskelion.

Her vision blacked out and Alex fell to her knees as Arthur suddenly released her hand. Around her, Alex vaguely heard the others gasping for air and felt Aiden release her hand. As her vision cleared, Alex let her fingers curl into the dirt, barely breaking through the packed down top layer. Underneath her hands, she could feel a soft, comforting pulse of energy from the ground. It traveled through her, calming her breathing and relaxing her muscles.

"God let's not do that again," Nicki groaned nearby. Alex turned her head slightly to see Nicki lying on her back, her long red hair sprawled around her in the dirt. She was panting with one arm thrown over her eyes.

Aiden wasn't in much better shape; he was sitting in the dirt and leaning back on his hands with a pained expression. Bran was on his back, his leg stretched out and groaning softly. Sucking in another deep breath, Alex forced herself up slowly and carefully stood. She glanced towards Morgana and Merlin who were on their knees next to Arthur, checking him over. Stumbling around the others, Alex made it over to Bran just as Nicki was getting up. Together they helped the exhausted Bran to his feet. Nicki retrieved a water bottle and one by one they rinsed off their hands and checked their wounded arms.

"Mages," Merlin called in an exhausted, but pleased voice, "Take a look."

Bran, leaning heavily on his cane, moved towards the tunnel first. He leaned against the outer edge and gasped softly when the rock began to crumble just from his weight. Alex's eyes widened, and she moved forward to the tunnel archway. Kicking at one of the lower rocks, she laughed as it fell apart at the impact.

"Infused with Sídhe magic," Morgana explained quietly. "This area will begin to return to normal. The tunnel will remain for a time, but it will eventually be covered over and buried."

"I am the grass; I cover all," Alex whispered suddenly thinking of the line, but she couldn't remember where from.

"I am the grass," Morgana continued with a sad laugh. "Let me work. Carl Sandburg." Morgana stepped past Alex and peered into the tunnel. "A sadly accurate statement on the ability and willingness of humanity to remember." Morgana turned and shared a look with Merlin before she strode back to join him.

Frowning at Morgana's words, Alex leaned around the edge of the tunnel and studied the gate. The magical glow had faded, but the criss-crossed grid of iron still seemed to shimmer in the darkness. Carefully, Alex stepped past the threshold of the tunnel, holding one hand out towards the gate. She heard the others inhale sharply behind her, but didn't stop. Then her hand touched the metal: it was warm under her palm and felt impossibly smooth. She could see beyond the gate, a pair of glowing violet eyes, but they came no closer. Grinning, Alex stuck out her tongue as a burst of energy surged through her before turning on her heel and leaving the tunnel.

"We're all very tired," Morgana observed as everyone collected their bags. "I fear that without Cathanáil this will be quite the task."

"I have faith that Cathanáil will be back with the Iron Soul soon," Merlin said calmly, swinging on his pack with a grin. "And this is an important victory for us, Morgana, smile."

Morgana gave Merlin another one of her irritated looks, but her lips did begin to twitch into a smile. Aiden huffed as he pulled on his backpack and glanced around.

"So, is that it?" Aiden asked Merlin. "Are we done?"

"Yes," Merlin sighed, shaking his head. "We're done."

Aiden gave a whoop of happiness and started down the path with Nicki right behind him. Merlin shook his head even as he smiled and followed. Morgana glanced over at Alex and Bran as Alex helped Bran pull on his backpack and nodded. Arthur was lingering by the trail, swaying on his feet slightly and very pale, but standing. He said something in a low voice to Morgana which made her smile and nod again before she followed Merlin onto the trail. Bran glanced between Alex and Arthur and with a soft chuckle, headed after them.

"Good job," Alex said, gesturing behind her to the tunnel.

"Thanks," Arthur replied with a growing smile. "I'm a bit surprised it worked."

He swayed on his feet making Alex jump forward. She caught his arm and steered him towards the trail. "Come on, you need rest," Alex told him. She pulled a water bottle out of the side pocket on his backpack and shoved it into his hand. "And water."

Nodding, Arthur gulped down the water and started following the others down the trail. The lingering exhaustion made the trip very slow with both Bran and Nicki losing their footing and nearly falling on the downhill hike. Thankfully, Arthur caught Bran and Aiden caught Nicki before either was hurt. Bringing up the rear, Alex gratefully inhaled the thick smell of the forest. The soft chirping of a bird overhead made her grin like a fool. Then thankfully the parking lot came into view, the hood of Merlin's SUV gleaming in the sun.

"Hallelujah!" Nicki called to the sky. "Air conditioning!"

"Good," Bran groaned in front of Alex and Arthur. "I can't take much more of this."

Merlin waited at the bottom of the trail, collecting the packs. Morgana vanished for a few moments before returning with more water bottles that she shoved into Nicki, Aiden, and Bran's hands. Alex sighed in relief, the bag on her shoulders feeling heavier than before despite the iron being gone. She moved to join the others, but Arthur caught her arm and stopped her.

Turning to look at him, Alex felt a stab of guilt seeing how nervous he looked. He adjusted his bag and cleared his throat awkwardly. Alex shifted nervously on her feet, glancing over to see the others dispersing to their vehicles.

"I know that things have been a bit weird between us," Arthur said carefully. "And I take some of the blame for that. Jenny was your friend, and all of this put you in a bad situation."

"That wasn't your fault, or hers or Lance's," Alex replied quickly as she turned back to him. "And as for it being hard... well, I made certain choices to keep everyone safe, so I did it to myself."

Arthur stared at Alex for a moment with a strange look on his face before he smiled and laughed softly. "You are really something else, Alex."

"What do you mean?"

"From what Aiden and Nicki told me over the last month you've gone through hell this last year to fight the Sídhe and keep me safe and yet you're just shrugging it off."

"I'm not shrugging it off," Alex protested, feeling herself blushing at the compliment. "I just... I did what I felt I had to do."

Arthur stared at her, his blue eyes oddly calculating as he watched her face. What he was searching for Alex didn't know, but she forced a small smile and told herself to calm down. Then suddenly warm lips were pressed against hers. A large hand came up and cupped her jaw gently. Alex's mind reeled for a moment before sputtering to a stop just before Arthur pulled away.

"When you come back for school can we go on a proper date?" Arthur asked.

"What?" Alex asked her mind still dazed.

Arthur's smile widened at her expression. "I like you, Alex, and I'd like us to date when school starts up again."

"Oh," Alex breathed, stunned for a moment before a brilliant smile took over her face. "I'd really like that."

"Yeah?"

"Yeah," she answered firmly.

"Come on, guys!" Aiden's voice called from the parking lot. "Pizza, remember? I don't know about you guys, but I'm famished after that!"

Arthur grinned at Alex and held out his cleaned hand to her. With a wide smile of her own, Alex took his hand and let him guide her down the trail to the parking lot. Maybe next year would bring new enemies and more Sídhe, and maybe their war against the Sídhe was just beginning, but at least they were in this together.